I0720053

LAUGHS
IN
SPACE

THE SLAB

Edited by
Donna Scott

First edition, published in the UK August 2024 by The Slab Press
The Slab 002 (softback)
10 9 8 7 6 5 4 3 2 1

ISBN: 978-1-7384268-2-9 (softback)

Cover design by Paul Condie
Typesetting by Donna Scott

Contents

Introduction - Donna Scott — 1

The Schadchen of Venus - Lavie Tidhar — 5

Intergalactic Cultural Exchange Programme - Akis Linardos — 27

Copywrongs - Emma Levin — 47

Bev the Hacker Does Time - Cait Gordon — 55

Querulous Times - Rick Danforth — 67

Professor and Frankie's Last Big Heist - Lindsay Comer — 91

Rise of the Spiderbots - Alex McNall — 103

The Trouble with Vacations - Robert Bagnall — 115

De'Swine's Second Question - David Gullen — 125

Sundog 4 - Alice Dryden — 135

Bootleg Baba's Beautiful Claws - Marisca Pichette — 147

So You Want to Kill Hitler: A Student's Primer
- Lindz McLeod — 159

Shelf Life - Richard Dadd — 169

The Chicken Plucker (Have You Seen the Price of Eggs
Lately?) - Iris Taylor — 179

Dai's Ex-Machina - Dafydd Rhys Hopcyn-Kitchener — 189

Random Selection - Paul Eccentric — 201

The Complicated World of the Spider - L.N. Hunter — 217

The Umami Invasion - Gary Couzens — 231

The Lots of Us - Phillip Irving — 243

The Rampage of Rampant Redwood at the Ginger Girls Gala
- Ian Watson — 271

Statement From the Prime Minister Regarding the Time
Travellers - Andrew Wallace — 281

Failed Experiments in Eugenics - Fiona Moore — 293

Everything is Relative - Simon Hall — 301

Killing Time - Ida Keogh — 327

About the Authors — 339

Introduction

Donna Scott

Comedy and science fiction have both been my raison d'être for the last fifteen years, each vying and competing for my attention, time and energy simultaneously. I would describe them as the twin moons orbiting my brain, but my brain is only planet-like in that it is spinning, and chaotic, and I blame its ruination on other humans.

Speaking of brains the *size* of a planet, a special place in my heart will always be reserved for Marvin the Paranoid Android from *The Hitchhiker's Guide to the Galaxy* by Douglas Adams. I loved him in the books, I loved his portrayal by David Learner, and I loved the song about him by Radiohead. For younger me, his character was an instructor in the notion that comedy could be clever, subtle, and perhaps a bit niche. Not everyone gets Marvin or finds it funny that he is in a constant existential crisis, or that sadness and despair can be hilarious. I mean, I was seven when the TV series came out, so that's how old I was when I learned about context being important in humour, and that absurdist science fiction is a brilliant context for delivering pithy observations about ridiculous social mores, or even serious topics, such as manmade ecological disaster. I wouldn't have been able to articulate this back then, of course. All I knew was that me and my dad loved the show, but not many of my classmates had even watched it, let alone found some strange kinship with the robot. I suppose this was an early indication that both comedy and science fiction push you to find your people; your cultural tribe.

I started editing a little earlier than I started stand-up, but I was no spring chicken in either field. I think I had confused the love of books and comedy with something like "interests" or "hobbies" and was unable to see how I could weave them so thoroughly into my soul, my *living* until I hit my thirties. It was an almost mid-life crisis that I had bubbling up inside me as I realised how narrow my life had become and how much it needed to change. My brain was not happy with the office job I had at the time. For a start, my desk was nowhere near a window so I couldn't even gaze out on the beauty of an industrial estate in Wednesbury. How grim! Brain the size of a planet and they had me booking containers of bathroom stuff for grumpy DIY merchants, and trying to translate instructions to Polish drivers when I don't even speak Polish.

"Wesołych świąt… I'm not sure that helps, but Happy Christmas anyway. Yeah, I know it's March, but that's the only Polish I have. They thought you were German."

Having worked in a few offices in my time, I know that a lot of people try to mould themselves into the culture immediately surrounding them, but anyone with a bit of creative oomph in them will never be comfortable as a fitter-inner. To quote Timothy Leary, you have to "Trust your instincts. Do the unexpected. Find the others…" And when you do find the others, they may provide you with an opportunity to follow your dreams that you know in your gut is just perfect for you. Say yes! Always say yes!

Unless it's drugs. Don't be too much like Timothy Leary, kids.

Over the last few years, I've been so lucky to have found a rich and fulfilling life within the realms of science-fiction, publishing, and comedy, and losing the fear of having too many spokes to my wheel. I'm a Sci-Fi geek, a book geek, and a comedy geek, and all my geekdoms inform each other. One day, I could be on a panel at a convention talking about how much I love *Hitchhiker's Guide to the Galaxy*, or *Discworld*; another day I could be dressed as a pirate on stage, asking kids to go on a golden cheese-seeking quest to the bottom of the ocean, in a submarine we have just built out of parents covered in coats holding a toilet seat for a steering wheel (which I'm sure is just how Jules Verne envisioned his *Twenty-Thousand Leagues Under the Sea*). Another time, I could be in a comedy club, telling filthy jokes about… Warhammer. My calendar has been full of travel to gigs and conventions all over the UK, and beyond! And in between there has been organising, dreaming, writing, working.

The book you are holding in your hands is the culmination of two dream lives intertwined. As I have realised my ambition of starting my own publishing company, the project of putting together an anthology of humorous science-fiction stories was a no-brainer. I hope you love reading this as much as I have loved putting it together.

Putting together an anthology is very much like

organising a comedy night. You need a strong opener, and an assortment of performers—crowd-pleasers; cerebral; political; silly. The audience may be comedy-savvy, looking for a bit of escape for the evening, or just after a good time. The MC makes sure the night runs smoothly but doesn't dominate; they may even be told, "Hey, you're good, you should try doing comedy yourself."

So please, as your MC for this reading, allow me to introduce the acts. Most of these are science-fiction writers branching out into comedy, but there are a few seasoned stand-ups here too. Many of the names will be known to you; others you will know soon. I present stories with a range of styles of humour to appeal as widely as possible to your discerning tastes. Which one will be your favourite? Also, unlike a lot of comedy shows out there, I've managed to find more than one woman. Yes, I'm being silly, but it's just so heartening to see so many great stories coming in from the half of the population that has often been told not only that women can't "do" science fiction, but also that women just aren't funny. Yet again, here is proof that those who say so are just plain wrong.

Oh, and a bit of housekeeping: if you are one of those people who think women can't be funny, please do ignore the advice I gave earlier about keeping on reading until you find a story that better suits your humour palate. In your case, please put this book down, and toodle-oo.

The rest of you, grab yourselves a drink, settle into your seats, and buckle up. You're in for a great show!

Donna Scott
Northampton, July 2024

The Schadchen of Venus

Nahum Zweig

Edited with an Introduction by Lavie Tidhar

Nahum Zweig is a name likely all but unknown to the modern reader, though he was a prolific contributor to the pulps in the 1930s and early '40s and a contemporary of Stanley G. Weinbaum, with whom he briefly shared an apartment in New York. Of his many works, the most popular were the *Tales of the Shadchen* sequence, begun with "The Shadchen of Venus" in the July 1934 issue of *Wonder Stories* (where it was published alongside his friend Weinbaum's better-known "A Martian Odyssey"). In that tale and the ones that followed, Zweig was likely inspired by the earlier stories collected in the 1925 volume *The Marriage Broker* by Tashrak (pen name of Israel

J. Zevin). Though he published prolifically in the lower-tiered pulps he never broke into Campbell's *Astounding*. According to Isaac Asimov in his biography, *In Memory Yet Green* (1979), Campbell once made a disparaging remark as to the tales being "too Jewish" for his readers. At the 1939 first World Science Fiction Convention Zweig, who had socialist sympathies, notoriously ended up in a fistfight with Sam Moskowitz and was subsequently barred from entering. He left New York shortly after, taking odd jobs around the country before being drafted into the army post Pearl Harbor. He went missing in action in Europe sometime after D-Day. Despite my best efforts, I have been unable to confirm his eventual fate. He may have died in battle, though some sources variously place him in the Soviet Union or in the then-nascent state of Israel after the war. Zweig's somewhat peculiar appearance – he was thin and gangly, and of a diminutive stature – was said to have inspired the character of the Mule in Asimov's *Foundation* stories, and Asimov wrote the introduction to Zweig's only – and posthumous – collection, *Galactic Shadchen!* (Pyramid Books, 1951), which collects the best of the Shadchen tales.

I am grateful to Donna Scott for allowing me the opportunity to bring this story back to a new audience, and to Nir Yaniv for sharing his unearthed copy of *The Marriage Broker* with me and for his tireless advice on this manuscript as I was preparing it for print.

1.

She slithered into my office and I knew straightaway she was going to be trouble. I just didn't know how much. She perched on the chair I reserved for visitors. Her purple tentacles rested on my desk, three of them, and a fourth rearranged the flowers on the bald dome of her head. A fifth left a trail of slime on my carpet. It was going to be hell to get it dry-cleaned.

"So you're the shadchen," she said.

She had a face only a mother could love. I knew I was in trouble even before she opened her beak.

"What's this about, Toots?" I said.

"Don't call me Toots. My name's Esther."

"Of course it is," I said.

"Esther Blumenthal-Tenn."

I choked on my tongue. It hurt. I had to untangle it. That took me a while.

"Of *the* Blumenthal-Tenns?" I said.

She looked at me innocently.

"You heard of my family?" she said.

I nodded dumbly. Everyone knew the Blumenthal-Tenns. They practically owned Venus. Swamps, jungles, ore mines, kosher hot dogs carts and the opera building and all. They had gelt, is what I'm saying. which meant if I could get this broad hitched I was going to hit pay dirt.

"So what's this about, Miss Blumenthal-Tenn?" I said.

"Please. Call me Esther."

"How can I help you, Esther?"

"I am in want of a husband," she said.

"Of course," I said.

"I am of age," she said. A tear rolled down her beak.

"Of course."

"It's unseemly for a girl like me to still be single!" she said. She burst into tears. "I shall soon be an old *maid!*"

"Not if I have anything to do with it!" I told her. "My record is impeccable. Every heart has a match. Every soul has a soul mate. Every pot has a lid! Besides, it's fashionable nowadays not to marry."

"Fashion," she said, "has nothing to do with it."

"How so?"

"I am the sole inheritor of the Blumenthal-Tenn fortune. There must be continuity, Shadchen. There must be..." she lowered her voice. "H*eirs*," she said.

"Of course."

She blushed, turning from purple to pink. I looked at the rings on her tentacles. Diamonds larger than ducks' eggs. She was loaded.

"I've never, you know..." she said.

"You're still a...?" I said.

"Well, yes."

"You've never been with a...?"

"What's a girl to do, Shadchen!" she said. And she burst out crying again.

Well, this was no good. No girl should cry with that many diamonds on her. I looked at those diamonds. Just one of those bad boys would pay my back rent for a year. I said, "Well, there's nothing to it, then. We'll just have to find you a match."

"Oh?" she said. She stopped crying. "You think you can do it, Shadchen?"

"Hey, bubele," I said. "I'm a shadchen. It's what I *do*."

"Oh, thank you!" she said. She wrapped her tentacles around me in a hug. I took it stoically. I tried not to think of my dry-cleaning bill.

2.

"Well, *your* egg is cooked and no mistaking it," Mishnik said. Mishnik was the bartender at the Bar Mitzvah. The place was dimly lit and smelled of spilled beer and crushed dreams. It made me think of being thirteen years old again. This did not make me feel good. I stared into my glass of schnapps. I should never have taken the job.

"It can't be done," I said. "It just can't be done."

"She has money?" Shmuel said. Shmuel was a swamp snail from the southern polar region. His little yarmulke sat crooked on his little head.

"Oodles of it," Mishnik said.

"Then what's the problem? I'll marry her myself!"

"What's the problem? Where do I even start?" I said. "The girl's an *octopus.*"

"A *rich* octopus," Mishnik pointed out, with unassailable logic.

"And her family..." I said and lowered my voice. Everyone knew the stories. The Blumenthal-Tenns started out as humble hot dog sellers in the lawless years of settlement. But somehow they got rich. And anyone who went up against them wound up as hot dog meat.

Literally.

Now they practically *owned* this planet. No one had the guts to go out with their girl. Not unless they wanted their guts to end up as hot dog wrappers.

"Besides," I said miserably, "she's *fussy.*"

That was the worst part. On my roster I had hundreds of hopeful hearts. Pining pinheads and romantic rapscallions. That was the first thing I did with the girl. I pulled out my giant book of possible matches.

"No."

"No."

"No."

"Not this one."

"Why not this one?" I said.

"Too skinny."

"This one?"

"Too fat."

"This one?"

"He has three eyes."

"This one?"

"He only has one."

"What about this one?" I said. "Menashke Melamed, top of his yeshiva at only eighteen, the kid's practically a rabbi. *And* he's a squid."

"Too Jewish," she said.

"*Too* Jewish?" I said.

"And he has too many arms."

"He's a *squid!*"

"Show me the next one," she said.

I took out the big guns. The top matches. The best bachelors seeking a bride in this Venusian breadbasket I called home. No girl could say no to a shidduch with these fellas, I thought.

I thought wrong.

"Oswald Einstein-Einstein," I said. "So smart they named him twice. Inventor of the slice'n'peeler 3000 when he was just four years old. Revolutionised pineapple upside-down cake. Winner of the Fields Medal before he was seven. And he likes cats."

"He's brain in a jar!" Esther said.

"But what a brain!" I said.

"Next!"

"Very well."

I brought out Prime Bachelor #2.

"He's very handsome," Esther said thoughtfully.

"Yes," I said.

"For an asteroid."

"Well, yes," I said. I cleared my throat. "He's a sentient asteroid." I cleared my throat again. "We think."

"It's not that I don't believe you," Esther said. "It's just that there's no real way to tell, is there?"

"Well, not as *such*," I said.

"Next," she said – with some regret, I thought.

I brought out #3...

"What is that?" she said. "I don't see anything."

"He's a being of pure energy," I explained helpfully.

"I don't wish to come across as a crass materialist," Esther said. "But I want someone with more substance."

And so it went.

I drank my schnapps. I motioned for Mishkin to pour me another.

"So what will you do?" Mishkin said.

"What will I do?" I said. "I'll drink this bottle is what I'll do."

And I proceeded to do exactly that.

3.

Something reached me in a deep slumber. The pounding in my head got so worse I had to open my eyes. Then I realised the pounding came from the door. *And* my head. I staggered upright. I went to open. Two gorillas in suits stood in the doorway. They pushed their way in.

"You the shadchen?"

"We know you're the shadchen."

"Nothing gets past you, boys," I said admiringly.

"Thinks he's a wiseguy," the ape on the left said.

"A real Henny Youngman."

"Listen boys," I said. "I have a real ringing in my ears."

"Then don't answer."

They both laughed.

"What do you want?" I said. "I'm all out of bananas."

"Don't be a wiseguy, Shadchen."

"Yeah."

"Sit down and listen."

"Yeah."

"You know who we work for, Shadchen?"

I stared at the gorillas. The first gorillas came to Venus in the days of settlement. A lot of them used to work in the hot dog carts back in the day. You didn't argue wrong change with a gorilla.

I said, "I have a pretty good idea."

"Not the Bloomberg-Brins," the ape on the left said.

"Not the Martian Mob," the ape on the right said.

"Or the Oppenheimer-Neins," the ape on the left said.

"I get it, I get it," I said. "The Blumenthal-Tenns."

"Bingo."

"And what do they want with me?" I said.

"What do you think they want, Shadchen? They want you should make a match for their darling daughter."

"Or else."

"Or else what?" I said.

"You ever see the *inside* of a kosher hot dog?"

I shook my head. It hurt.

"Well, you might will," the ape on the left said. "Get it?"

"Got it."

"Good."

They shuffled off. No good apes. I mixed myself an Alka Seltzer.

Then I got to work.

4.

The Rabbi Akiva Venusian Yeshiva was the grandest school on Venus, which meant it had the planet's most eligible bachelors to boot. Or so I hoped. The boys were studying scripture but as I always say, not everyone is destined to become a rabbi, and even those who do need wives. Eliezer Smallman met me. He was a Martian with four arms and a woven yarmulke.

"I think I have just the guy for you," he said.

I followed Eliezer. He called one of the boys over. Handsome boy. Human, too.

"This is Binyamin Ben Yamin," Eliezer said.

"The son of Major Pinhas Ben Yamin?" I said. "The famed explorer?"

"One and the same," Eliezer said. "A fearless people, the Bnei Yamin."

"Is that true, boy?" I said. "Are you fearless?"

He nodded politely.

"Ain't scared of a thing," he said. "Plus, I have a thing for dames with tentacles, myself."

"You might just do," I said. "You might just do."

Eliezer dismissed the boy.

"And my cut?" he said.

"Ten percent, if it's a match," I said. "The usual."

"It's a match," he said. "It's a match made in heaven, Shadchen."

But I wasn't so sure.

I made my way to the Central Library. As always it was busy. Boys and girls bopping to literature. They did it quietly, of course. this *was* a library.

Rivkah Popek, the librarian, found me before I found her.

"I have just the match for you, Shadchen," she said.

"If I had a nickel," I said.

"What?"

"What?" I said.

"If you had a nickel? What can you do with a nickel? Go to a nickelodeon?"

"Well, that, sure," I said. "But I meant, if someone gave me a n– oh, forget it. Who's the match?"

She called one of the guys over. He was built like a brick wall. He *was* a brick wall. The bricks moved.

"What are you, the Western Wall?" I said.

"I'm a golem," he said. "You know, from Pluto."

"What's a golem doing on Venus?" I said.

"Came over originally on a contract to provide protection," the golem said. "Ain't much to protect though, other than against bad hot dogs."

"Is there any other kind?" Rivkah said.

"You got a name, son?" I said.

"Name's Moish," the golem said.

"You kosher?"

"I'm circumcised, if that's what you mean."

I stared at that big lump of rock and had to look away. That was some rock he had on him.

"Not scared of much, are you?" I said.

"No, sir. And besides, I have a thing for dames in purple."

"You might just do," I said. "You might just do."

Rivkah dismissed him.

"And my cut?" she said.

"Ten per cent if it's a match," I said.

This is a blessed match, Shadchen," she said passionately. "Every gal wants someone strong and stable."

"He's a *wall*," I said. "Or built as such."

"A wall of strength for a girl to lean on!"

I nodded. But I wasn't so sure.

I made my way to the public mikveh to wash away my hangover but I never made it. Two slimeballs materialised in front of me and pushed me into an alleyway. You can't argue with slimeballs. It's the slime that gets you every time.

"Listen, Shadchen," the one on the left said. He hopped up and down. "You handling that Blumenthal-Tenn job?"

"What's it to you fellas?" I said.

"You know who we are?"

"I can read the papers just like the next guy," I said.

Martian Mob. Slimeballs every one. They came over several decades back now. Wiped out the competition and became just another thread in the rich tapestry of our lives. I had a bad feeling they were thinking expansion.

I wasn't wrong.

"Have we got a match for you, Shadchen!" the slimeball said.

I groaned.

"Esther Blumenthal-Tenn ain't gonna marry into slime," I said. I waited for him to sap me on the head but instead he grinned, which is a hard thing to do when you're essentially a ball covered in slime.

"We'll show you," he said.

5.

They took me to the warehouse district. There were a lot of warehouses. We went inside one.

They had some sort of workshop in there. Electrical generators and heavy equipment. People in white lab coats. A big packing crate stood in the middle. They led me to it. I figured they were going to conk me on the head and stick me in there, for shipping on a one way ticket to the Big Shalom. Instead they opened it.

"Oh, my," I said.

"Told you, Shadchen."

I stared.

He was human with striking good looks and a beautiful head of hair, in a dinner jacket pressed to perfection and trousers where the crease alone was enough to give you heart palpitations. He really was perfect. There was only one thing.

"Why isn't he...?" I said, then hesitated.

"Yes? Yes?"

"Well, why isn't he *moving?*" I said.

"He's a robot," the slimeball said.

"A*h*."

Well, that explained it.

"He's *our* robot," the other slimeball said.

"And he's programmed to make her happy," the first slimeball said.

"*Very* happy," the other confirmed.

"Does he talk?" I said.

"Even better," the first slimeball said. "He *listens.*"

I was taken aback. A man who listens is like a fish on a bike. It just doesn't happen unless you concoct it in a lab.

"So you get a marriage alliance with the most powerful family on Venus," I said. "And the bride gets...?"

"The perfect husband."

"He cooks, too," the second slimeball said.

"*Cooks!*"

"His knishes are to die for. And he loves kittens."

"He wants babies. Lots of *babies.*"

"Can he, well...," I said. "Can he *make* babies?"

"We believe so," the first slimeball said.

"There's a 94.5% chance of positive output," the second slimeball said.

"Within acceptable parameters," the first one said. "Err."

"What are the acceptable parameters?" I said.

"Well, we think something will come out, we're just not sure exactly what."

"But hey," the second one said. "A baby's a baby, right?"

"I'm telling you, Shadchen, it's a perfect match," the first one said.

"At least 92.3% perfect," the second one said. "That's guaranteed."

"I can't make any promises," I said.

"You'll do it, Shadchen."

"Or what?" I said. "You'll send me to the Big Seder in the Sky?"

"It ain't like that, Shadchen. We have too much respect for the trade."

"Everybody needs a shadchen, Shadchen," the second one said. "All we ask for is a fair shot."

"You got it, boys," I said. "And let me say, I'm impressed. I just hope the client likes him."

6.

"So, my dear," I said, "What do you think?"

Esther Blumenthal-Tenn pouted.

"Binyamin Ben Yamin?" she said. "He's all right."

"Yes?" I said encouragingly.

"But his eyes are too close together," she said.

"Why, Esther!"

"And besides I know him from summer camp," she said. "He's no good at tennis."

I sighed but then rallied. I had two more aces up my sleeve.

"Now *this* guy," I said, bringing up the next one, "this

guy's *solid*."

She leaned over and whistled. "What is he, the Western Wall?" she said.

"That's what *I* said!"

"Look at that hunk of rock," she said admiringly. "What is he, a golem?"

"So I'm told. He's from Pluto."

"Well, it *is* a rocky planet," she said.

"So nu?"

"I'll consider it," she said, and inwardly I broke out in a hora. Outwardly I remained the cool professional.

"Then there's this fine fella," I said.

"He's dishy!"

"He cooks," I said.

"You don't say!"

"He likes kittens."

"Who doesn't!"

"He wants *lots* of babies."

She blushed prettily.

"He likes moonlight walks on the beach and holding hands and candlelit dinners," I said. This wasn't in the technical specs but I figured I was in the right ballpark.

"I say!"

"He's also a robot," I said.

"Well," she said, "nobody's perfect."

7.

So that was that. I was feeling pretty good. I'd set up two dates for the client and one *had* to work. I just had to hope for a spark of magic.

What I got was a spark all right.

Things started out well enough. I'd booked a booth at

Drescher's Deli & Bingo Hall for the occasion. It was quiet but not too quiet. It was just the right ambiance and the cries of the bingo caller mixed pleasantly with the aroma of chopped liver and kugel.

The would-be bride was resplendent in a strawberry dress. Her tentacles wrapped around a glass of Manischewitz. I took position discreetly nearby and motioned for the first of the two suitors to approach.

Moish the Plutonian golem strode over. His steps shook the floor but he swept gracefully onto the seat and in moments he was like clay in Esther's hands. He had a nice smile for a golem. He had a good line of patter, thought it wasn't exactly original material.

"You're so *strong*," Esther said admiringly.

"I broke my leg once in two places," the golem said.

"What happened?"

"Doctor told me to stop going to those places."

I groaned but the client laughed as though the joke was brand new to her. Maybe it even was. Everything was going so well. Then the girl up and asked the golem for a glass of water.

I should have known this was trouble, but I was slow on the uptake. Of course Moish obliged. He got up and went to the counter and brought her a glass. The girl drank it gratefully. He went and got her another.

And then another.

And then another.

"Stop!" she said. By then it was too late. You ask a golem to get you water you get more than you bargained for. He just kept going. He was so eager to please. The place was going to drown if no one was going to stop him.

I said "Moish, when you get the water get it from the other side of town!"

He went obligingly and I breathed a sigh of relief.

"Let me bring the other guy in," I said.

The Martian mob's robot was fully operational. He glided across the polished floor. He kissed Esther's tentacle and she blushed. He sat down, ordered drinks and a knish, and began professing his love.

"Oh, but we hardly know each other!" Esther said.

"I know you to within a 97.3% level of accuracy," the robot said. "But my love for you is at 100%!"

"Oh, you!" Esther said.

"Your love is more delightful than wine!" the robot said.

"Oh!"

"Pleasing is the fragrance of your perfume!" the robot said. He must have been programmed for a *Song of Songs* selection. "Your name is like perfume poured out!"

"Oh!"

"How beautiful you are, my darling! Your eyes are doves!"

"Oh!" Esther gasped. "Wait, what are doves?"

The robot froze.

"Searching," he said.

"Searching?"

"Dove, terrestrial bird, extinct."

"That's sad!" Esther said.

He was losing her. I could see the robot thinking.

"Tell me, you whom I love, where you graze your flock!" he said desperately.

"Pardon?"

The robot didn't look well. Something inside him had gone kaput.

"If you do not know, most beautiful of women," he said, "then, err... follow the tracks of the sheep?"

Smoke was coming out of his ears.

"What sheep!" poor Esther said.

"Graze your young goats by the tents of the shepherds!" the robot said. A spring went *poing!* and his left ear flew off. Then the top of his head caught on fire.

"Oh, Shadchen!" Esther cried. She looked at me pleadingly. "Oh, Shadchen, *do* something!"

Luckily at that moment, the golem came back with the water. This time he had a whole bucket with him.

He saw the commotion.

He saw the robot.

And he poured the water on the robot's head and put out the flames.

8.

"And then he went to get more water," I told Mishnik. Mishnik was behind the bar. I was back at the Bar Mitzvah drowning my sorrows in something a little stronger than Manischewitz. "But by the time he came back we weren't there. Which was probably for the best. I really don't know what I was thinking."

"Don't beat yourself up, Shadchen," Shmuel the swamp snail said. He sat to my right sipping juice. His little yarmulke still sat crooked on his little head. "You did what you could."

Esther Blumenthal-Tenn (betrothal To Be Announced) sat dejected on the stool to my left. The least I could do for the poor girl was buy her a drink. I wasn't sure Mama and Papa Blumenthal-Tenn would approve but then again, they weren't there.

"I will never find love!" she said and burst out crying. Mishnik, gentleman that he was, patted her nearest tentacle.

"Now, now," he said.

"Oh, do you think so?" she said.

"Now, now," Mishnik said.

Esther stopped crying.

"You really have the most extraordinary eyes," she said dreamily. "Mishnik, is it?"

"Well, I'll leave you to it," I said and stood up. I was filled with a new determination. A shadchen's job is never done, and all that. I had a match to make! And a bride to match!

"Look after Miss Blumenthal-Tenn for me, boys," I said. "I must be on my way!"

And with that I sailed out of there with the doff of a hat.

9.

A good shadchen keeps his hands clean – and his fingers manicured. It was a cut-and-dry case so I went to the Cut 'n Dry next, which was the busiest nail salon in town. Anyone who's anyone came to the Cut 'n Dry, but more importantly, anyone who was anyone's mother.

Word of my predicament had already spread. I garnered much sympathy.

"They do say she's a lovely girl," Mrs Edelstein said. She was a sort of armadillo from Calypso with a pistachio peccadillo. She kept cracking them between her teeth. "Face that could break a mirror but a good heart, and that's all that matters in this life. The question is, who does she *like?*"

"Like?" I said.

Mrs Edelstein looked at me shrewdly.

"A girl like that," she said, "she must have some idea what she wants already."

"Well, I mean, yes, I suppose," I said. I was taken aback. "But that is hardly the point of a shidduch! Why, if anyone went around just picking their own partners, there would be chaos!"

"Yet what about love?" Mrs Edelstein said.

"Love? What has love got to do with it?"

Mrs Edelstein sighed. So did the others.

"The heart wants what the heart wants," Mrs Edelstein said. "The question is not who the *girl* wants. The question is – does that person want *her* in turn?"

10.

I was troubled by Mrs Edelstein's words. A match based on love was simply absurd. It was un*scientific*. Love was a bonus, perhaps. But it could never be a factor.

I said as much to Esther when she returned to my office. I brought out the great book of matches again, then put it away. I was out of ideas. I was out of luck. Soon, I figured, I'd be out of business.

I could have cried.

Esther saw my expression.

"Oh, this is hopeless!" she said. She began to cry.

I hesitated.

Maybe it was time to try something new. Something bold. Something unheard of!

"Is there," I said, and cleared my throat nervously, "is there someone *you* like?"

She looked at me in surprise.

"That *I* like?" she said.

"Well..." I said. "Yes."

She blushed.

"There is someone..." she said. "But Mother and Father would never agree. It is completely unsuitable."

"I'm sure they just want you to be happy," I said, not

entirely truthfully. But I was desperate.

"He is so charming and so calm and collected," she said. "We really hit it off, you know."

It was a strange way to put it. How would *I* know? I began to have a bad feeling. It started in the pit of my stomach and rose like the acid reflux you get after eating gefilte fish.

"It all started after the shidduch debacle, when you took me to that bar," Esther said.

"Oh, no," I said. "Oh, no."

"That bartender, Mishnik, was so very kind," she said.

"Oh, no, no, no," I said.

"Yes," she said. "And then..."

And she told me all about it.

"Could you do something, Shadchen?" she said when she finished.

"This is very unorthodox," I said.

"It's only thanks to you we met at all!" she said.

"I suppose so."

"It could be a shidduch if you make it a shidduch," she said shrewdly. "And besides, as the heir to the Blumenthal-Tenn fortune, I could really make it worth your while."

That was a very good point.

Compelling, even.

Gelt talks and kaken walks, as the elders of Safed said.

So I told Esther I'll see what I can do.

11.

"... Mazel tov!" the rabbi said. The groom broke the glass. Or tried to. It's not an easy thing to do when you're a snail.

I stood with Mishnik and watched the happy couple under the chuppah. Anyone who's anyone turned out for the wedding, and some nobodies too, of course. A photographer from the *Venusian Workers Daily* snapped pictures. A kleizmer band struck up a tune and circles formed as guests and loved ones formed circles for the hora.

"You did good, Shadchen," Mishnik said. "You did good."

"All thanks to you, my friend," I said, and Mishnik shrugged.

"I'm just a barkeep," he said.

The happy couple came over. The bride looked radiant. I had a feeling it wouldn't be long before she was laying eggs.

"Mazel tov, Esther," I said. She wrapped me in her tentacles.

"This is the happiest day of my life, Shadchen!" she said.

Her husband didn't so much stand as slither beside her. He always carried his home on his back. Someone had put a stick on the back of his shell that said, *Just married!*

"Mazel tov, Shmuel," I said.

"Thank you, Shadchen."

He adjusted his yarmulke shyly.

We said congratulations and they moved on and Mishnik and me went to the bar for a glass of the good stuff. The happy couple danced. I looked at them in affection. It was an unlikely match but you could do worse than a swamp snail from the southern polar region. They were a dependable lot.

A hard exterior often hides a soft inside, as my mother used to say.

Which was certainly true about snails.

I took a sip of the good stuff and raised my glass. It was no easy job, being a shadchen on Venus, but someone had to do it, and that someone was me.

"L'chaim, Mishkin," I said.

26

Intergalactic Cultural Exchange Programme

Akis Linardos

Mark first met the alien in the shower. First, a smell like refuse on a hot summer day suffused the steam. Tendrils of slime squeezed through the drain cap and melded with a squishy sound into a bulldog-sized slug. Mark gave a girlish yelp and jumped back against one of the warm glass panels, holding the shower handset as if it were a protective baton. The alien crawled up the wall, popped out two snail-like antennae, and waved them.

"You must be the bipedal Earth life form? Markum?"

Mark wasn't sure where the voice came from. No mouth on the alien that he could see, and the voice, thick and syrupy, seemed less auditory and more like some sort of aural stimuli directly generated inside his ear canal. "Uhm, just Mark."

The antennae wiggled up and down, scanning Mark from his beard all the way down to his pubic hair. "Indeed. Now I see why the drainage is all clogged. Aren't you quite disgusted by the bulk of keratin strands clinging to you?"

Mark's head felt fogged. He'd been doing the mental math of his situation, but he was not quite there yet. "I'm sorry. What?"

One antenna drooped, pointing at Mark's crotch. "The hair. It was a mess travelling through the pipes because of it. I can still feel it all over me. Itching. *Ugh.*"

After making some further sassy comments about the quality of Earth's drainpipes, the thing slithered toward the living room, leaving behind a slimy, wet trail. By the time it crossed the threshold, the mental math spat out an answer in Mark's mind.

This was his new roommate.

Mark had agreed to hosting an interstellar exchange student a week before the shower incident.

He had been slouching over his kitchen table, devouring milk-soaked honeyed cereal and viewing an online course: "An Introduction to Post-Darwinian Intergalactic Theory." Astrobiology was all the rage these days, so he'd wanted to get ahead and score some extra credits for his portfolio. Get himself a good position in one of the Andromeda labs.

Mark had known this day would be the wrong kind of special. How? The nape of his neck was itching. It was an itch like ants were skittering behind his collar. The same itch he'd had before flunking his math exams. That same itch he'd had at school, when he'd received a love letter from his crush that turned out to be a prank from the class bullies.

The doorbell rang.

Mark paused the video, rushed to the door. A man with large pink-tinted glasses and a smile made for dental advertisements shook his hand.

"Are you Mark Slothbottom?"

Bah, another salesman. Ever since the union with alien races became public and extraterrestrials were normalized, the door-to-door hawkers returned in numbers. Excretion from Andromeda Thermophiles for never-aging skin! Cream from Magellanic Snails to sprout back hair! Some pointy cauliflower that grants longevity, and a Super-Juicer to match it!

"Just Mark is fine, and I'm a little busy."

"Only a minute of your time. I'm Flinch Olsheller, from the Intergalactic Cultural Exchange Programme you applied for?"

Mark perked up at that. The Exchange Programme granted astrobiology credits that would greatly boost his resumé. Insights into behavioural cross-planetary psychology, intergalactic communication skills—all well worth the trouble of hosting an alien. Providing one didn't slip in their slime trail and break one's neck, of course.

"Yes! Was my application accepted?"

"I'm pleased to inform you that you have been assigned a Flergian. They are highly intelligent and capable of adapting to any communication. No language barrier whatsoever! So long as you remain within ten feet."

"This is amazing! When does it—"

"So, before we sign, I need to inform you of the fees."

"Uhm, fees?"

"Indeed, there are agencies to pay, and transportation costs to care for. Paperwork, paperwork, paperwork. All the good things a busy student like you will want a firm like ours to take care of. But don't worry, we have everything covered at a nominal thirty *entubs*."

Thirty entubs! That was ten percent of his monthly student loan! "I'm afraid I cannot cover those fees."

"Ah, I see," the man said and pulled from his bag a cylindrical device with two horns and three spiralling cables. "Well, my friend, this is your lucky day! We recently launched a promotional campaign. We offer a package entirely free of fees. It includes insurance and our subsidiary's latest product, the Transmogrifier—technology straight from Yemania." He pulls out what looks like a fancy water-gun with two hand-sized cylinders on the back side. "Input herbs on one side, and the fragrance will amplify to your entire home. Only for a measly subscription of three *entubs* a month. Down eighty per cent from its original price. Deadline for this promotion is tomorrow. Better hurry."

Right. Even the more serious companies would squeeze out some extra profit from all the hype. And a Trans-mo-grifier? Carrot Decomposers. Subatomic Cream Crushers. No doubt it was another useless artifact to impress adolescents salivating for gadgets. However, if taking on an exchange was a ticket to the fast lane of an astrobiology career… "All right. I'll take it."

"We have a deal," the man said, tapping something at the edge of his glasses. pushing the Transmogrifier into Mark's hands. He pulled out of his satchel a tablet, the screen already displaying a contract. "Thumbprint every page, please."

Mark put the Transmogrifier on the floor and did as instructed. After the salesman left, Mark retreated to his bedroom and placed the Transmogrifier on top of the bed. He then pulled out a book on extraterrestrial bivalves and laid back in one of his garden sunbeds. He was lucky to have inherited the place. The garden was large enough to house a freshman party. Not that he ever did. Mark hated parties.

Halfway through the book he began scratching the nape of his neck madly. It was itching very terribly indeed.

The roommate's name was Blergum, and although the voice *they* chose to project was entirely masculine—raspy as if from tobacco abuse—Blergum made it clear that genders were never a thing for Flergians.

Fascinated to find that showering was a private activity for humans, but not seeming to care, Blergum popped in and out of the pipes whenever they pleased for the next couple of weeks, strolling around at their leisure. The slime trails clung to the walls, ruined the carpets. The whole place smelled like dead snails.

This was too much. Respect a different culture, Mark told himself, such differences are normal. But Blergum wasn't making any effort to understand *human* culture. Or privacy. Or that the toilet wasn't his personal moisturizing chamber.

Mark had to drop out of the exchange agreement. Should be as easy as making a phone call. Right?

One afternoon when Blergum was out—apparently to study bees—Mark called the agency. An automatic message replied, giving him multiple options, expanding into more options each time he selected, until the whole phone call felt like a poorly written Create Your Own Adventure game.

"Can I just speak to a human? Please!"

"We are sorry, all lines are busy. Given your responses so far, we have estimated a professional Flergian could adequately answer your query instead. Would you like to connect?"

"*Yes!*"

"Please hold the line."

A screeching tune made Mark flinch away from the cell phone. Rhythmic popping sounds followed, like someone had mastered the art of popping bubble-wrap and was putting on a performance.

The sounds stopped, and a voice similar to Blergum's called from the other side.

"*Folarum denm, larum. Flurm blurmglem gla dralumle?*"

Mark gaped. "Ah… Habla ingles?"

"Florm demle?"

"English?"

"No."

Mark gritted his teeth, pulled his cell phone away from his ear, and opened his Intergalactic Translator app. The quality was terrible as these models were still under development, but it was the best he had.

He spoke slowly. "I need. To cancel. My exchange contract."

"*Flarm pell, jurbalum filkr lau. Detlum trel fraliumle.*"

The translator picked up the Flergian words and began loading. Dot. dot. dot. It typed out the translation in English: *That goes against the sound of potato. It kills rabbits in the free sea foam, sir.*

Mark clenched his fingers around the phone and asked for the Flergian to repeat. Slowly this time. After several tries, the translated message made sense. *This goes against the contract. It will eliminate any earned credits, and you will have to pay a penalty, sir.*

Impressed at the tightness of the Flerg language, annoyed at the message, but mainly too tired to argue, Mark replied, "It's alright. I still want to cancel the current exchange."

After a few arduous back-and-forths, the Flergian said that they'd have to narrate the terms of the cancellation to

Mark in *Flerg,* and every time they paused Mark would have to reply with a *"Slirm"* which meant *Yes* in Flerg. Formal procedure.

Mark sighed. "All right."

The Flergian spoke so fast Mark couldn't believe any being on the galaxy—even a native—could possibly comprehend the content. What Mark heard from the other line, was: *"Graldum graldum fraglbum"*—gibberish—*"Graldum larumflergum dlframle?"*

"Slirm," Mark said.

"Graldum slopadm drala par"—gibberish—*"dralrum larumle?"*

Mark rubbed the crest of his nose. *"Slirm."*

"Graldum, larum Markum delu fthern—"

"Hey, Mark!" Blergum's voice came from the wall beside him.

Mark gave a start, his hand jerked, and the phone leaped in the air. He juggled it between hands, then cradled it close to his ear. With a relief, he heard the operator on the other end still narrating the contract terms.

Blergum's antennae moved inquisitively close to Mark. "What are you doing?"

"Shhh! Look, I'm busy. Ah! *Slirm!*" he added the last word as he realized the other line had fallen silent. Then the operator continued narrating terms in Flerg.

"*Slirm?* Are you speaking Flerg? Who you talking to?"

"It's not Flerg. It means, ah, it's a kind of swimming pool. These balloon ones. I'm placing an order. *Slirm!*"

"Two swimming pools is quite a lot don't you think?"

"Did I say swimming pool? I meant beer. Yeah, I'm ordering beer."

"Fascinating. I knew humans were afraid of math but to avoid numbers altogether? It's like us and mint. So, what do you do when you have to get some one-hundred beers for a party?"

"Ah, we, I don't know. We just—*Slirm!*—we like spending time on the phone, yeah. Sometimes we place orders together with friends. *Slirm!*"

"Oh dear. So impractical. We have a lot to teach you."

"Yes, I can't wait to learn, now can you…" Mark trailed off.

His phone beeped. The other line had cut. Mark pulled the phone away from his ear and stared at the screen:

You are out of intergalactic call credits.

"Hmm," Blergum said as their antenna came so close to Mark he could smell the slime. "This is bad. So you were ordering beers from another galaxy? You're really committed to this. But does that mean you'll have to order them again from the start?"

"No," Mark said, putting his phone in his pocket. "I hate beer."

The call had tapped Mark's resources so badly he couldn't make another until his pay day—and that was thirty days away. *Thirty days.* He couldn't wait that long. He researched Flergians in any resource he could find covering intergalactic cultures, but the reports contradicted each other—as often is the case in a field so young and ripe for innovation and hyped-up science. However, there was one commonality among them. Flergians really enjoyed shade. Not just enjoyed: shade was an integral part of their culture, reflected in their language with over three hundred names for different types of shade.

In the book *How to Flerg like a Flergian*, Mark discovered a shade made by a tree and one made by an artificial structure would have two distinct names. One made them feel funny in their belly—well, what Mark liked to think was the belly equivalent for them: two blobby sacs along their back—and the other gave them tingles on their antennae.

But what really surprised him was that they could even *taste* shades. The book said on their planet, Flergians had fun parks that, instead of rides, sold tickets for tree-chocolate shades, fruit-canopy shades, cheese-tower shades, and so on. Their umbrellas had flavors, and their tourist beaches were filled with unmelting ice cream parasols.

Fascinating as all that was to learn, it also gave Mark an idea. He chopped off an old Disneyland brochure, arranged some pictures into a collage, and wrote a story about an upcoming attraction—the first shades park on Earth. Human cuisine, served on a wrapping Flergians could digest. If Blergum was interested in cultural exchange, they'd love it. Even if it was on the other end of the world. Even if it meant relocating and becoming someone else's problem.

Mark scanned the collage into digital form and printed the page. He tucked it into a book and rested on his recliner in the living room, pretending to read. Until Blergum showed up.

"Hey, Mark."

"Oh. Hey, Blergum. Didn't see you there. I thought—"

"What's this object?" Blergum said, one antenna pointing at the book.

"I'm glad you asked! It's—Wait, you mean a book? You don't have those? Not even digital?"

"Not really."

"Ah," Mark said, shutting the book, but keeping a finger lodged on his precious page. "It's a place to store thoughts. If they do a good job, ah, people buy them. Because they resonate with the content."

"What an awful waste of energy. Why not just say the words? Much faster."

"But you can't just say things all the time. Like this interesting bit here for example—"

"Sure you can," Blergum said. "You can just record your voice and play it back any time you want. Much easier."

"Okay, yes there are audiobooks out there. But uhm…" Maybe he just had to keep it really simple. "Well, there are deaf people. But even they would appreciate what I'm about to—"

"You can just project your thoughts on deaf people. What's the problem?"

"Yes of course but—wait, what?"

"Project your thoughts. You know, like your mother first does when you're a baby, or when your home school teacher wants to get that sexual reproduction lesson to really sink in. Our coitus process is an interesting one. We actually—"

"No, it's all right, I don't need to know."

"Why not? It's like putting your finger inside a kiwi and then—"

"Hell, no!"

"Odd. It's a very natural process, nothing to be ashamed of. What's the point of being roommates unless we learn from each other's culture? Here it's easier if I only project my thoughts to your scalp."

Mark tried to jump from the chair. Too late. The mind meld had been initiated. Static glazed Mark's eyes. Images of grotesque geometries and moulding of slimy flesh flashed in his mind, but it was the stench of formaldehyde and the crackling wet sounds that glued to his subconscious. *Crunch. Flop. Shlkshlk-shllllrch.*

He kept a bucket by his bed that night. Drenched in sweat, he'd wake up shivering with a fluttering sensation in his stomach. The weird sex dreams continued for nights to come.

A nightmare came to him one morning full of wet slimy sounds. But this time when he woke up, the dream did not taper off. The sounds remained. And there was that itch burning his nape again.

His alarm clock said 11:14 am. He looked out the window and his breath caught. A horde of Flergians were spread out in the garden. At the centre, a house-high glass tower brimming with bubbly yellow liquid obscured the sun, casting a transparent orange shade over the garden. Flergians bobbed their heads and their antennas waved around in a drunken manner. Did they—

Crunch. Flop. Shlkshlk-shllllrch.

Mark's gaze whipped toward the ceiling. A blobby mass of mingled Flergians clung to the ceiling. Nausea washed over him.

"Hey! What are you doing over—" he said as he pulled his drawer open to look for his phone only to touch something slimy. Another blobby mass. And this one spoke, two voices in unison: "Do you mind?"

He shut the drawer and pushed his feet into his slippers. *Squish.* He whipped his feet back up the bed and hurriedly brushed the slime off his toes with the bedsheet. A blobby tentacle pulled out of his slippers and retreated below his bed.

Vomit crawled its way up his throat. He hurried down to the kitchen, trying hard to ignore the creatures mating on floor, walls and ceiling, reached the sink and vomited.

Voices echoed in unison from within the sink's drainpipe. "Oooh, more goo!"

This was *it*. He rushed out to the courtyard and yelled. "Blergum! Hey! Blergum!"

"Heeey, Mark," Blergum said as they slithered toward him from the crowd of dancing Flergians. That *hey* stretched in a suspicious manner very unlike Blergum indeed.

"What the hell is going on?"

"I was so, you know, *FAH*scinated, at this party concept, I just *HAD* to try it."

Mark frowned, turned his gaze to the tower of bubbly liquid. Of course. It was beer. "You're drunk!"

Blergum's antennae formed spirals. "I thunk that was the human term for it."

"You can get *drunk* from a shade?"

Flergians climbed up Mark's walls, twisting over each other. Mark heard wet *crackling* sounds and flinched away, feeling his stomach twist. Dear lord almighty.

"You know," Blergum said. "I think I like the concept of *PAH*rties. Gets the brain that right jumpstart it needs to get on with life. You know?"

"No," Mark said. "I really don't."

Flergum waved his antennae. "*Paeh.* You'll get it one day. Everyone needs a break. These intergalactic studies have been mint on my ass."

Something clicked as Blergum said that. A piece of Mark's subconscious puzzle began falling into place. "You mention mint a lot. What's so special about mint?"

"*Uff.* It's the worst thing on this planet. Probably why we took so long to make contact with humans. Stinks so bad, man. Sorry to say it. Worse than your hair even."

"I see," Mark said, trying to suppress a smile. "You know, there's more than just beer in our repertoire. What say we spice this party up with some cocktails?"

"*Damn!* I like that, Mark. Aaah, I knew you weren't the loser everyone said."

"Lovely, I'll be off to get them," Mark said, and hopped toward the house. He stopped and turned. "Who says I'm a loser?"

Blergum waved his antennae left and right haphazardly.

"No one, Mark. Exactly no one. Because you're the besht. Mark the cocktail man."

Mark climbed up to his room and pulled the Transmogrifier from the cupboard. The instructions said it would continue transmogrifying liquid molecules until exhaustion.

As Mark rushed to the kitchen, he was met with the sight—worse, the *sound*—of two Flergians mating on one of the cupboard doors. No concept of privacy indeed.

He averted his gaze and willed himself not to throw up as he pulled out a bottle of rum from one of the display cabinets, sugar and lime from the stand beside the kitchen stove, and finally…

The mint. It was kept in the very cupboard the Flergian couple had picked for their mating ritual.

"Shit," Mark said.

"Blergum was right, darling," a gurgling voice said from the blobby mix. "Humans are oddly fascinated with excretions."

Mark cleared his throat. "*Ahem*, do you mind scooching over a bit? I need something in there."

Crunch, crunch, schlk-schlk schlllrrrp.

"Oh, that is no bother, go ahead and take it."

"I can't," Mark said as a whirlpool formed in his belly. "You're in the way."

"Goodness, I forget how these primitive devices work," a voice said from the blob. "Make some room around the handle, darling. He needs to pull it. It's not automatic."

"Oh, I see," another voice answered. With a slimy sound the blob imploded on one side, forming a fist-sized hole all the way to the handle as if a massive bullet had just pierced through it.

"Go ahead," the voice said.

Mark squeezed the bridge of his nose. "Wouldn't it be

simpler if you just moved somewhere else?"

"No."

Crunch, slurp, schllliik.

"Our coitus process is quite demanding. You are being quite the distraction let me tell you. If you don't want it…"

The hole began to close.

Mark threw out his hand. *"No!* No, it's alright I'll do it."

Mark puckered his lips and squeezed his hand through the hole, felt like he were invading the nose canal of some giant with a bad case of congestion. Just a little further. He reached the handle and twisted, yanked the door open.

In a cascade of jerky motions, Mark grabbed the mint, pulled his hand free, tossed his jacket into the trash, and wiped the snot-like substance off him with the kitchen towels. He tossed the towels, too.

Mint into the Transmogrifier, Mark rushed out.

"How do I get up the tower? How did you fill it up?" he asked a dancing Flergian.

"Aaah, it has rungs on one side, methinks."

"Lovely, great, thanks."

Mark circled the tower until he found the rungs and climbed them. After slipping twice on the slime and dropping the Transmogrifier he climbed back up, until he reached a glass platform that ran around the exterior.

Where did they make these things? How did they even bring it here? The teleportation costs must have been tremendous!

At this height, the beer foam clouded the interior, and on one side, Mark found a silver moon-like lid, cratered with Braille buttons. Why buttons? Why didn't it just unscrew for Christ's sake? He pressed a few. A voice spoke.

"Answer this password to open the door!"

"Are you kidding me?"

"What are humans most fascinated about?"

"Shit, how should I know what they—"

"Access granted!"

The lid flung open. Cloud-soft foam fizzed within. Mark breathed in an air of pleasure, taking in the yeasty scent. This was a moment to savour. He raised the Transmogrifier, took aim.

Bang!

Mark remembered when, as a kid, he'd put blue colouring into a glass of water. It would first leave a smoke-like substance and slowly permeate the entire water until it was blue. This felt like the opposite of that. The beer-yellow obscured the pale mojito smoke within, then all at once the beer exterior vanished, the cloudy foam evaporated, leaving behind a massive lemony cocktail with floating leaves of mint.

The bubbling garden shadow thinned, and slowly, the antennae of all Flergians drooped. Their colour changed too—purple as eggplant. Within seconds, they were rushing away and vanishing into the nearby street, sinking through the drainage grills.

That left the ones inside the house.

Mark rushed in and yelled to the top of his lungs. "There's a surprise in the garden! A second tower full of a special human cocktail! Tastes lemony and sweet. It's to *die* for."

The Flergians rushed to the garden, murmuring among themselves. *"Oh boy, oh boy."*

Mark looked around the house, pulled out the drain strainers, scanned through the pipe-holes. Slimy and wet, but no Flergians to be seen.

When he went outside, every Flergian was gone save for one.

Blergum was lying on a garden recliner. Mark had not

noticed them because of the tree Oshade. His sides wisped weakly. He let out stretched syllables, *"Oooh, aaah, eeeehhhh."*

Mark felt a prick of guilt in his heart. "Ah, uhm, are you all right?"

"Oooh. Mark. *Flarg,* Mark, why did you do that? You knew mint is pain for us. I told you so many times."

Mark took a deep breath. He wouldn't back down. "Well. The party went too far. And quite frankly you show no respect to me ever since you've been here. You know I had to throw away three carpe—"

"Respect? You talk to me about—*oooh*—about respect? I've been here for a whole month, and you've made no move to accommodate my physiology. Do you think I'd force you to crawl along the muddy floor of my glow-cave if *I* were the one hosting you in Flergia?"

"I … uh …"

"And wh-what the slime—*aaah*—these are bodily fluids I cannot control. And besides that, they evaporate. Unlike the plastic bottles and cups that pile up in your garden whenever you drink your orange juice, until the wind blows them off into the streets for everyone to enjoy. You're grumpy over every little thing, as if life should've been designed specifically to accommodate your wants. What do you think, you're the sole creature in ex—*ooooh*—in existence? And don't get me started about the hair in the sink!"

Mark opened his mouth, paused, then closed it again. He did it several times throughout Blergum's monologue, but even now his alien roommate had stopped ranting, Mark realized he had nothing to say. Where did all the complaints he had amassed over the month vanish? How did all this justified and confident rage evaporate?

"I'm sorry," he mumbled. It sounded almost like a whimper to him.

"Come—*ooooh*—come again?"

Mark took a deep breath and stood straight. Or at least thought he did. "I'm sorry." This time it came almost like a croak.

"Can you try that one more time. Mint makes—*aaaah*—me hard of hearing."

"Gosh, I'm *sorry*," Mark boomed. "You're right, okay? I think you are at least. You make fair points."

Blergum fell silent for a while, then said, "Well, that's good to hear. I'll be off your feet tomorrow either way. Hopefully, I can find—*eeeeaaahhh*—find some decently priced tickets. It's always the return interstellar warp tickets that suck the kidney off my anus."

"The kidney off …" Mark shook his head. "Anyway, you can stick around a while longer. You know, until you can land a good price to return home. Perhaps you can process a reimbursement from the agency."

"Doubt it. They are leeches over there."

"Okay," Mark said. Clenched his jaw at the thought of what he was about to say, then unclenched it, convinced it was the right thing to do. "You can just stay. Let's try this whole thing over again."

Blergum's antennae moved like the tails of purring cats. "Really, Mark?"

"Yes," he replied quickly before he could change his own mind. "It's no big deal. And you know what? I have just the way to make it up to you."

Mark lay back on his recliner, reading a book about Flergian biology and throwing occasional glances over the window. The garden had turned to a forest of flavoured umbrellas ranging from Raspberry Red to Pineapple Yellow, and the dirt had been tilled and watered down to mud. His wallet had cried bitter tears at the renovation, but he'd wasted money on far more frivolous things before. The new garden had accommodated Blergum perfectly and made their temporary cohabitation all the merrier. Worth it, even though the little slimeball was gone now.

Mark smiled to himself. His astrobiology credits kept piling up. Perhaps an error in the system since Blergum had left for some days now. A happy accident Mark didn't feel the need to correct just yet. He'd won a victory over himself the past month and came out with a good friend several solar systems away. He deserved some extra credits.

A low buzz disrupted his thoughts. At first, he imagined it was something within the room. A mosquito? No. The buzz was coming from outside and getting louder. A bumblebee? No. Too loud. A drone?

A man-sized fly flew through the open window, carrying a great brown ball in three pairs of three-fingered hands, landing in three pairs of bowlegs, smelling very much like cow dung.

Mark jolted off his seat, bringing a hand over his nose and mouth. *"What the hell?"*

"Ah, is wrong house? Mark Slothbottom not live here?"

"That's me. Who are you? And why are you carrying that thing with you?"

"Is my lunch," the man-fly set the dung-ball aside, spat in his upper pair of hands and rubbed them rapidly against each other. "I come from Exchange Programme? Eh?"

"This can't be happening."

"Sorry. No understand." The man-fly pointed at one of his bulgy eyes. "They install translator but is… *eh*"—he made a profane gesture—"Office say this house have room for new exchange. Flergian leave, me come. Flergian recommend me. Says we have much in common. Name is Bzelbun."

He hopped toward Mark, grabbed his hand and shook it. The man-fly's hand was hairy and wet in a way that stung—like freshly washed beard stubble. He spoke slowly, eyelids squinting over his bulgy eyes as if with constipation, hands gesturing—struggling really hard to produce a perfect sentence:

"We will be ... *best* friends."

Copywrongs

Emma Levin

Please read the following instructions in full before using the photocopier.

Please be aware that the University's photocopier is for the use of staff and full-time students only.

Please be aware that this photocopier is for the production of two-dimensional, three-dimensional, and four-dimensional replicas of source materials only. It can produce copies in colour or greyscale. It can produce animal, vegetable, and/or mineral substances, in addition to synthetic facsimiles of the above. The default setting for copies is two-dimensional, greyscale, and synthetic, at 100% scale. If you wish to change any of these default settings, please use the blue control panel to the left of the scanning bed.

Please be mindful that all copies will be debited from your University Account once the print job is requested. Cancelling the print job will not cancel the charge to your University Account. The cost of each print job is calculated according to the size of the object, and the settings requested. Please calculate the cost of the print job before selecting 'submit' via the blue control panel. Refunds will not be provided.

In accordance with British copyright law, certain materials which are considered to be 'in copyright' have a maximum percentage which may reproduced. For most books this is one chapter, or up to 5% of the written content. For copyrighted mineral material, this is up to 2 kilos. For copyrighted botanical materials, this is one individual - or up to 10% of a mycelial colony. For animal material, it is acknowledged that existing copyright law has been outpaced by innovation, and user discretion should be applied. For the purposes of individual study, you should make a single copy, and you should not make, store, or distribute further copies. For the avoidance of doubt, for printed materials, sources are considered to be out of copyright 70 years after the death of the author, artist, or photographer. For copyrighted mineral and biological materials, items are considered to be out of copyright either (a) after the expiry of the patent; (b) 70 years after the birth, growth, or engineering of the materials. There are no legal restrictions on the photocopying of materials which are out of copyright. Misuse of the photocopier will not be tolerated.

We cannot believe we have to say this, but do not attempt to three-dimensionally photocopy your arse. Trust us, it's gruesome. And everyone will watch as the finished articles slide wetly into the gap under the display screen.

We are legally obligated by the manufacturer of the photocopier to state that the photocopier is not intended to produce copies of complete, living organisms.

We are legally obligated by the University's legal department to advise users that it is entirely possible to photocopy a complete living organism, provided you can fit it on the scanning bed.

We are legally obligated by the University's press team to remind users that photocopying a dead organism will not result in the reproduction of a live one. It's a photocopier, not a miracle worker. It produces slightly grainy copies. That's all it does. Please stop trying to resurrect your pets by photocopying them. Please stop leaving the dead copies in the bin by the blue control panel. It's upsetting. They belong in the yellow 'biohazard / clinical waste' bins, next to the laser cutter.

We would like to take this moment to remind users that despite what they may think, librarians see what they are doing at the photocopier. We will notice if you contravene these rules.

We would like to take this moment to remind users that it is a very bad idea to get a job as a librarian so you can use the photocopier after hours, without anyone observing what you're up to.

If you do apply for a job as a librarian so that you can use the photocopier after hours, without anyone seeing what you're up to, try to present a good façade at the interview. Appear calm. Appear smiley. Appear keen to be a librarian.

Laughs in Space

Do not mention the photocopier.

When I had my interview as a librarian, I thought I was doing pretty well. They began with predictable questions, which I furnished with predictable answers. Educational history. Vocational Preferences. Personality Deficiencies. I transposed and juxtaposed the landmarks of my life, remixing and remastering my biography until it was a smooth and palatable paste, suitable for the consumption of disinterested strangers. A kind of radio edit of the soul – three and a half minutes, with a memorable hook.

The one question I did stumble on was "where do you see yourself in the future?" I thought too far ahead, and answered for the mid 2050s. I explained that when I was seven, my friend Charlie Ross hired a bouncy castle for his birthday and we weren't supposed to wear our shoes but everyone did, and it started deflating, and everyone kind of shuffled to the bits that were less visibly collapsing while wondering at what point we were supposed to stop pretending everything was fine. So, erm, I imagined that in the future, like the majority of the human race, I'd be looking at the rains which slowly dissolve buildings like lapping sandpaper tongues, at the heatwaves which leave desiccated birds piling up in drifts by the side of the road like autumn leaves, and the thin, lukewarm bouillabaisse of dead fish, microplastics, and raw sewage that is our nearest river, and wonder if it's time to shuffle to a bit of the Earth that's less visibly collapsing, and at what point we were supposed to stop pretending everything is fine. The interviewers squinted, and told me they meant more short term. And more personal. I botched it again, and answered that I'd like to be dating a chef, finding the simplicity of the exchange – attention for food – refreshingly naked in its honesty. "No," the interviewers said. "Even shorter term. And professional, not romantic." I answered that I wanted to be a librarian. They nodded approvingly, and here I am.

I lied in the job interview. I didn't want to date a chef. I wanted to date my ex-girlfriend. But she didn't want to date me. Hence the 'ex'.

If you intend to produce a live, three-dimensional photocopy of your ex-girlfriend, don't even think about charging it to your personal University Account. Not only would the print job be entirely traceable, but it would be financially ruinous. Photocopies are charged by the gram. With no offence meant to my ex-girlfriend, she weighed over 50,000 grams. No, see, the smart thing to do would be to swipe a departmental ID, and charge it to a department so large and administratively dysfunctional that the payment would go unnoticed. So I did.

I settled on the Biosciences department. From the previous month's printing stats, I could see that they regularly photocopied creatures in the 50-100 kilo range, with a frequency that suggested an extra line on their spreadsheet would go unnoticed. I simply turned up at the reception, showed my librarian ID, and asked if I could have the departmental finance code to apply to their photocopying for this week. Two receptionists sat behind a vast desk. Both held clipboards – the one on the left cradled hers gently, as if it were an injured rabbit, and she were a patient vet, and the one on the right clutched his tightly, as if it were an injured rabbit, and he was going to finish it off just by squeezing. They gave me the code with no further questions.

If you intend to produce a live, three-dimensional photocopy of your ex-girlfriend, you're probably already aware of the main logistical hurdle; she'll need to be on the photocopier's scanning bed, staying still until the print is done. She would notice that, right? And, to be honest, I doubted she'd consent to it. Though, as she was no longer on speaking terms with me, I didn't have her consent to ask if I had her consent.

So, if you intend to photocopy someone who is no longer on speaking terms with you, try to rationalise why it has to be them, and why you couldn't, say, scour dating apps for someone who looks a lot like them, and start a new relationship with someone else that you resent slightly for not living up to the memory of the original. You should recall how you met. For us, we were both students, and it was here, in this very library. I had fallen off a ladder. She stood over me, eyes filled with equal parts concern and curiosity, like I was some sort of alien deepwater invertebrate, washed up on a beach. She picked me up so delicately – as if I might burst from the change in pressure from the floor to standing. She insisted that I follow her back to hers, and sleep on her sofa. It was a nasty fall. Someone should keep an eye on me. To be honest, I didn't put up a fight because I couldn't remember where I lived. Coincidentally, I learned through context, we were close friends. Studying the same course. One thing led to another… and although my memories before that time remain hazy, I have blisteringly bright memories of our time together. She showed me sides to myself that I didn't know existed. She showed me sides to this city that I didn't know existed.

If you are going to attempt to photocopy your ex-girlfriend, without her noticing, make a gameplan. The most important thing – apart from avoiding detection by fellow librarian colleagues – is to work out how to avoid detection by your ex. The real one, the original one. Sit at a table, and make a vast map of the places you used to go together. Restaurants where you might run into her. Cafés. Cinemas. Parks. Gyms. All the places you can't go together with your new copy, in case you run into her – the real one, the original one. It would probably be unwise to take the photocopy back to yours. Although it's vanishingly unlikely, there's still a small part of you which hopes and suspects that she – the real one, the original one – is going to knock on the door and apologise and take you back. Once you have finished drawing your map, realise that the majority of the city is off-limits. And you still have no idea how to get her into the photocopier undetected.

Feeling disconcerted by the geographical reality of what you're about to undertake, and with no idea how you could, practically, get your ex onto the scanning bed without her noticing, switch your attention to researching the implications of photocopying a living creature.

I started by researching the impact on memory. Apparently, the photocopiers are able to perfectly replicate the structures of brain matter, but the matter is not conscious while the copy is being constructed. Accordingly, if you attempt to copy a cat, say, it might end up with a seven-minute blank patch where the materials were being extruded from nozzles, and carefully layered up. If you were photocopying something larger – a Doberman, say, the gap would be longer. For an average human, the print time would be about forty minutes. According to the internet, the process of being printed is disorientating. A copy will be confused and suggestible in the first half hour. Like a baby goose, they'll follow the first person they clapped eyes on. To avoid panic, it's best to convince them they had a fall. Look concerned. Hope they're alright. Insist that they sleep on your sofa.

If you have read this material, you may reach the conclusion that there is a non-zero chance that you may be a copy.

If you reach the conclusion that you may be a copy, grab your map from the table – the map of places where you think your ex might be – the real one, the original one – and resolve to track her down. You might not be on speaking terms, but you are still on shouting terms.

Before you go, update the instructions for the University's photocopier.

Who knows – maybe it'll help someone?

Bev the Hacker Does Time

Cait Gordon

Ick. Old people.

I cringe. This place gives me the creeps. Also, why is that supervisor behind the counter blushing so violently? Something must have set him off. Not sure if Emery is his first or last name. A lone proper noun bellows at me in bold letters on his dorky badge.

"Right," says Emery, clearing his throat while gathering his composure. "You're new here, so you get the uniform and the mandatory goggles."

"Goggles?" I ask. "Are they gonna hurl false teeth at my face?"

"All newbies must wear protective eyewear. No

exceptions. Also, you must have a name badge, er—"

"Bev."

"Right," he says again, scribbling my name on a magnetic tag and pushing it by the pile of swag on the counter. "Put on the badge, clothes, and goggles. Drop the attitude. You need this community service more than we need you here."

He's not wrong. I know I shouldn't have hacked into the Intragalactic Online Network's primary search engine and executed my particularly ingenious algorithm. It redirected every sexah-spicy keyword—from a plethora of interplanetary cultures, mind you—to a series of random laxative commercials. I thought it pretty hilarious when I heard the latest video from *PooBlasters* emanating from my big sister's bedroom. Less humorous was when she called the feds on me. At least I got off with only a bajillion hours of mandatory volunteer work. Staci hadn't been able to get off at all.

It could have been worse, though. Glad dad's a lawyer. Not as glad mom's a warden. She takes her work home with her. I'm grounded three days past infinity.

I grab the garb and am beyond thrilled that it's as blue as my skin. Will look like a massive ambulatory berry. The coveralls are baggy, and the eyewear feels tight on my snout. Gosh, I must be projecting all the hottie-hotness. Selfie, anyone?

"Get dressed, then march into the great room to see where you can be useful," I hear Emery say to the back of my head.

"Fine."

Am pregnant with joy to be working at a seniors residence. Well, not working, 'cause I don't get paid. I don't need money anyway, because it's super rewarding to be part of the team at Almost Worm Food, or whatever this place is called. Whoever painted it must have scored a deal on that phlegmtastic shade. It's just everywhere. Goes amazingly well with this wallpaper's Vomited My Guts motif.

In the nook just before the entrance to the great room is a mop and bucket. Beside them is a guy only too happy to give them to me. He's about average height, decent build, and in a better-fitting uniform without goggles. Maybe the relics in this place don't whip their teeth upside *his* head.

"Here you go, young one," he says, pushing over the mop and bucket. "Adventures await!"

Young one? Seriously? We're the same age. I hate it when someone who has three minutes more experience pretends that he's older than time. *Dude, your testicles probably haven't even dropped yet. Go away.*

"Thanks," I say, and slosh my mop into the great room.

Someone saunters up to me immediately. I feel my knees go weak. Tall, dark, and everything. He's got that rebellious bad-boy glint in those fathomless brown eyes. I just want to climb on the back of a hoverbike with him, earning another quajillion hours of community service. I don't know what planet he's from, so I'll just assume it's called Sumptuous.

"Hi, there, little lady," he says with a charming lopsided smile. "So nice to see someone new around here."

I forget how to speak our language. Don't even care about being called little lady. I only come up to his chest, therefore it's a scientific fact I'm shorter. He's just being accurate. Am also female, so in fact, everything he said is valid. *Please, Mr. Delectable from Planet Sumptuous, take me with you far from here. I don't care where we go.*

"Hiya," I manage. This is one beautiful person. I think I've sprouted more ovaries.

"Well, who do we have here?" interrupts a woman who I instantly loathe because she is preventing me from having alone time with Mr. Delectable. I might also despise her because she's a statuesque goddess in a tight green halter dress that shows off her six sculpted arms. I bet she's a personal trainer who tells you how amazing you're doing, in an annoyingly perky voice. Look at her. Her skin is buttery and perfect. A long magenta plait hugs the curves of her voluptuous figure, saying, "See how yummy I am?" She leans against Mr. Delectable, who radiates like he swallowed a lightbulb. I want her jettisoned into space.

"Hi, Toby, have you made a new friend today?" asks Ms. Impossibly Perfect.

"Just about to," he replies to me with a wink. "I'm Tobias Grehn. This is Zola Tarx. We're sort of an item. And you are?"

Completely crushed, that's who I am. "Bevin Hartley. Bev." I point to my badge. "Nice to meet you."

Three of Zola's exquisite arms extend to shake my measly arm, which is covered in this droopy washed-out uniform.

"It's wonderful to meet you," she says. Her face is beaming, making her even more beautiful. I hate her.

"Thanks. I'd better get to work on this floor," I say. They each smile and wish me well. They look fantastic together. Wonder who they're visiting?

As I scan the room, I see it's filled with family waiting for their relatives. None of the elderly have come down yet. That's good, because frankly, old people give me the oogies. Well, I'm here, so I might as well make myself useful.

I dip my mop in the soapy sludge and push the thing across the floor. To my right, several younger people smile kindly at me and tell me what a great job I'm doing. *Wow, guess they don't have high standards here.* I know I've feeble custodian skills. Take my room at home. You'd never be able to distinguish it from a break-in, or the results of a hurricane. Creative minds are seldom tidy. I read that on a badge once. If only I were creative. That would validate my particular brand of slob. Of course, coding is not devoid of creativity. Or was plotting to stop my older sister's spicy quest an exercise in creative thinking? Can I keep saying creative? Okay. Creative. Now I'm done.

"Hey!" I yell, when two guys bolt across the floor from outside and one nearly knocks over the sudsy bucket.

They stop immediately and flash me rather sheepish expressions. One is holding a whip-ball ring, which is a dinner-plate sized disc with a massive hole in it that has a hovering ball in its centre. People are obsessed with the sport on this planet. These men each wear faded jerseys, probably of their favourite teams. The guy holding the ring is medium height and muscular, no doubt a receiver. His tawny-brown skin and dark, curly hair drip with sweat, so no doubt they've been playing a good game. The other fellow is taller and slender; he has to be his uni's star flinger and captain of the team. Bet he can whip the ring right across the field effortlessly. His ginger hair and pale orange skin glow from the exertion of outdoors.

I'm a fan of the game because of my mom, so I decide they can be forgiven. "Save the plays for outside, killers!"

Tall Guy laughs. "How did you know that was our nickname?"

"It's obvious by the way you two tore up in here."

Receiver Guy puts his arm around his buddy's shoulder. "See? We still got the moves, Jims. I say we try out for next season in the pros."

Jims laughs and kisses Receiver Guy's cheek. "You say that every year, Bryant."

Bryant kisses Jims' mouth. "Because with each year we get better. You gotta believe me on this."

I smile. They're sweet. Steamroller strong, but

somehow, they can muster up a tender moment when off the field. From the look of them, I can't figure out how they're not already in the pros. I want to ask, but they quickly apologize for the mess and take off arm-in-arm. No doubt to be alone. *Saucy things.* I feel jealous. Wish I could have someone to dash off into a room with. I search for Mr. Delectable but catch a glimpse of him outside reading on a bench to I Hate Her.

After brooding about my lack of a snogging-life, I finally clean up the excess water on the floor. Pushing it around with a drier mop actually works. I mean, I have to squeeze the thing a kajillion times, but I'm actually happy at my progress in this room.

At the far-right corner is a teen sitting alone on a chair, staring forlornly out the window. I can't guess their gender, and it's not nice to assume it by appearances anyway. Maybe they're non-binary. Not that it matters to me; my misanthropic nature does not discriminate. All I can see is that they're sad. Really freaking sad, I realize, as I make out the tear tracks. Okay, so, I'm pretty bad at peopling, but even I can't just let them stay like that without at least checking if they need anything.

As I get closer, I see their mauve t-shirt has #1 Gran on it. *Aw, crap.* Did they lose their grandparent? That blows. Their leaf-green hair is cropped short, peeking from a black cap. They are Feen like me; our snouts are practically identical in size, but their skin is forest green. Their left cheek rests on their hand as their right hand gently traces the white windowsill. This is not okay. I wonder where their parents are.

"Hey, there," I say, sloshing this annoyingly oversized mop. They look up at me, startled. "Oh, sorry. Didn't mean to make you jump."

"It's all right, baby girl."

Baby girl? I must be four years older, at least. Is this infantilizing nickname thing a trend I've missed? "Um. Yeah. So, you all right? Need me to call anyone for you?"

"There's no one to call, dear," they reply. "Lost them all in an accident last year."

"Whoa, that's terrible." *Did they just call me 'dear?'*

"It was and still is. Today is the anniversary. There's no one to visit with anymore."

I feel kind of awful. "That really sucks."

They silently nod. I lean on my mop.

"Oh, honey, we only just remembered!" shouts Perfectly Perky So I Still Hate Her, followed by the man who caused me to grow six new ovaries and a second uterus. Zola and Toby rush to the sad person's side. Toby sits on the windowsill, grabs their hand, and strokes it gently. What I would give to be that hand.

Zola pulls a chair beside the grieving soul then rubs their back. She turns to me and says, "Thanks for keeping Shay company. You're very kind. We'll take over from here."

"Uh, sure."

I mop away in the opposite direction. Three girls are having a howl on the far couch, gossiping like they're training for a medal. *Ugh, fashionistas. The worst.* A-listers in their senior year for sure. Untouchable sorority types. And there they go with a flick and a swish of their hair. It's not that I'd wish they'd get mangled in a combine or anything, it's just . . . oh, whatever. *Swish, flip, flick.* Gosh, having all that hair must be a full-time job.

One of them is in a red dress with matching heels. Another's in yellow, and the third is in blue. Primary colours for a primary crew, I suppose. *Swish!* There goes Scarlet Red's hair. *Flip!* There goes Sky Blue's. Imagine being able to talk and toss your hair about at the same time. Mad skills, really.

I have to mop up under their bench. Should I just slop the soapy sluice over their leatherette shoes?

Sunshine Yellow notices me. "Oh, say, look, girls! A new friend in the premises. How are you, darling?"

Huh. That's admittedly nicer than the sorority girls I've ever met when visiting Staci on campus. "I'm good. Thanks."

"Your skin tone is so glamorous!" says Sky Blue to me with sheer delight. "Like a precious jewel! Simply radiant!"

I blink. What the hay does one say to that? I find myself staring at my hand.

"Oh my, are we in your way?" asks Scarlet. "Come on, girls, let's lift our gams up so Bev can do her job!"

Sunshine and Sky laugh with glee and all three of them raise their pretty legs with their gorgeous shoes, and I quickly pass my mop under their bench.

"Thanks," I say.

"How long should we stay like this?" asks Sunshine.

"Um, what? Oh, it's fine. You can put your feet down now. Your shoes are immaculate."

"Thanks, love!" says Sky. "You're very sweet!"

I think I'm smiling, but my mouth doesn't feel symmetrical. I turn away lest they fear I'm having a stroke, and they resume chatting up a storm. More like Level-5 hurricane. What happy sentient mannequins they are.

A sound chimes. The visitors waiting in the great hall stop what they're doing and look around excitedly.

"Morning tea!" sings a man, rolling a cart of delicious-looking cream puffy things and about a dozen other desserts I'd like to inhale with my snout. Another man pushes a massive vat of tea on his cart, with cups and saucers in various floral patterns resting on the bottom shelves.

"Break time for you, too," says the fellow working the floor with me, whose testicles haven't dropped yet. "Grab yourself a cup and a treat."

I won't say no. "Thanks." My goggles are chafing a little, so I lift them off my face for some relief. I peer around the room.

No, that can't be right.

Like it actually helps, I rub my eyes as if my vision will magically reset, then take another peek.

What the freak?!

The entire hall is filled with seniors. I spin to my right and the sorority girls are still having a laugh, but they're much older women. And their verve is exactly the same as when I thought they were in school.

Dashing into the hall come Jims and Bryant, holding hands. Jims' hair is completely white and Bryant's salt-and-pepper do is receding at the front. They're pushing at each other playfully, trying to prevent the other from getting the only custard pie on the tray. Bryant is a strong blocker. Maybe he played defence. I never asked.

In the corner sits Zola, the skin on her arms not as taught, but the muscle definition remains. The wrinkles near her eyes and on her face increase with the intensity of her smile as Toby makes her laugh. She's exactly as hatefully gorgeous as before. The person who grieved their family also manages a chuckle. They didn't lose their gran; they *are* the gran! Probably the oldest person in the room.

Toby turns around when the tea and pastries come. His hair is thick and silver, which only makes his brown eyes stand out even more. He beams a smile of gratitude as he is handed the teacup and passes it to the sad grandparent. Then Toby receives another cup and hands it to Zola. She radiates when she thanks him for it. Only after he's made sure the other two have had their tea and treats does he take something for himself. He's the most beautiful man I've ever seen in the flesh. He's way older than my dad, yet

I can feel my body wanting to collapse under the weight of this crush.

What is happening to me?

Beside me stands a man in his late fifties-early sixties. He's a volunteer. I realize now that his testicles dropped decades ago. As I shake my head at the occupants of the room, I can hear him laugh softly behind me.

"You know," he says. "That must be a record. It normally takes days or weeks for people to have your reaction."

"I don't get it," I say. "Why did they all look young to me?"

"You saw what you wanted to see."

"And what was that?"

"A room full of people you could relate to, or at least recognize. They were visually younger because that's the only way you would engage with them."

"But . . . how?"

"The goggles are designed especially for people who are ageist. It's a bit too sciencey and beyond my scope of understanding, but most people who take them off find themselves surprised that older folks still have the same spirit of the younger generation. In my experience, a person's essence doesn't really alter that much as they grow older. If anything, it deepens into something even more compelling than when they were younger. Almost as if life teaches one to love oneself more as the years go on. There's a beauty in that, all of its own."

I'm gobsmacked as I turn to stare at Toby. He's smiling again. Pop forms another ovary.

"What do you see *now?*" says the worker to my right.

What do I see? I guess I see Scarlet Red, Sunshine Yellow, and Sky Blue: best friends forever. Jims and Bryant: high school sweethearts who never stopped being over the moons about each other. Zola and Toby are new lovers. And the Gran? A person who misses their family and wishes they had that connection. I suddenly want to hug my ridiculous big sister.

"Well?" the volunteer worker asks.

The Primary Colour Trio are talking about undressing an actor with their eyes. I can't help but laugh.

"I see people," I reply, and stand my mop upright before heading to grab a cream puff.

Toby spots me and smiles. I find myself unable to stop blushing.

Now I get what reddened your cheeks, Emery at the front desk with the dorky badge.

I really do.

Querulous Times

Rick Danforth

Captain was the most pointless position on the SCS Querulous. The Ship's AI could handle everything from complex astronavigation issues to restocking the vending machines before a human could blink. Schettino's only purpose was approving Ship's decisions with his thumbprint. He was the human personification of a rubber stamp. Schettino had completed four years of astronavigation exams and three years of Space Corps academy to sit in a hard plastic chair surrounded by chrome bulkheads and screens of dancing numbers that didn't require his input. He had dreamed of adventure and purpose, instead, he was a middle manager to a crew in stasis. Company policy dictated they spent as much time in stasis as possible, to reduce wages, as his life dripped away hour by hour. There was only one thing to do.

He poured himself another margarita from the flask next to his chair.

"Are you sure, sir?" said Ship, from speakers in the ceiling. "That surpasses your recommended alcohol intake. Which, if you remember, is a nutritionally devoid poison."

"I'm sorry we can't all have a million interesting tasks." Schettino scowled towards one of Ship's many small black cameras on the ceiling. "Even the vending machine has more purpose than me."

"Available on-board entertainment includes…"

Schettino ignored the ship. He'd watched every film in the repository, completed all three video games and had even exhausted the celebrity options for the AI voice. The only thing he had to look forward to was a hangover.

But that gave him an idea. "Ship. What are the results of cryogenic stasis on hangovers?"

"There has been surprisingly little research into that scenario."

For the first time since he could remember, Schettino smiled. "So, it needs testing."

Schettino left the bridge, passing through a maze of dull metal walls and into his Captain's chamber. Chamber being the grandiose term for a Murphy bed, toilet, some personal effects, and a cryopod dominating the room like a chrome elephant.

Schettino looked at it fondly, his ticket out of this meaningless existence. It couldn't be any more depressing afterwards, so why the hell not? Schettino downed his drink and opened the cryopod door. "Ship. Activate stasis."

"When should I wake you, sir?" asked Ship.

"When I'm needed." Schettino removed his clothes, grabbed a snackcake from a box on the side and jumped into the cryopod. A snack would be pleasant after emerging, it was always a confusing time.

With any luck, Schettino's wake-up call would be at the loading port. Who knew, there might actually be something for him to do there.

Schettino snorted awake to Ship droning at him. Groaning and wiping drool off his face, he peeled himself off the cold metal bench that'd been his bed for unknown nights. He shuddered at what felt like a thousand needles withdrawing from his waxy skin with the care and delicacy of a shark at a shrimp buffet.

Schettino tried to leave the pod, dropped his snackcake and fell to the floor. His skin was still coated in the protective cryofluid, which rendered everything slipperier than a greased ferret. After trying several times to stand, he just lay there on the floor for a while to get his breath back. On top of the crushed, and uncomfortable, remains of his snackcake.

After several moments, Schettino slid to one of the cabinets on the wall and withdrew a blanket, towelling himself down before fashioning a makeshift toga. "Ship?"

"Yes, Captain?" came a voice from amongst the too-bright lights in the ceiling.

"Where are my clothes?"

"They were cleared away by maintenance bots after they rotted."

"Terrific." Schettino rubbed his temples, the stasis seemed to amplify the hangover if anything. His head felt like it had been used as a soccer ball. "Are we at the landing port?"

"No. That may be some time."

Schettino blinked. It felt like Ship was keeping something from him. "How long was I out?"

"Sixty years and thirty days."

Schettino couldn't think or feel as he sat down on the

pod. For some seconds he felt numb, so much feeling that he couldn't feel anymore. "I've been asleep sixty years?"

"And thirty days."

Schettino found himself wishing that he'd had more than thirty credits in his savings account. He could have been rich. "And we still haven't reached the port?"

"There was a major accident after you entered stasis."

"And you didn't bring me back?" asked Schettino with an accusatory glare at Ship's camera. "You let me sleep my goddam life away while the *Querulous* turned into a giant, dumb coffin!"

"I was not fully operational. After deploying repair bots, I went into sleep mode to conserve dwindling energy resources, rerouting all energy to internal repair systems. The bots have only just activated the reactor and raised hull integrity to seventy per cent."

Schettino swore. He didn't know if he was lucky he had no one to miss him, or if it was a sign of a lacklustre life. No siblings, no family, no close friends. The only proof of his existence were some magazine subscriptions and a college debt that would probably still outlive him. "Before I get a hair of the dog, is there any other news?"

A moment long enough for Schettino to cough politely passed before Ship said, "There are some issues with the bots."

"Oh?" asked Schettino. "Which ones?"

"All of them," said Ship. "In the absence of human interaction during your extended *sleep* they have been unmonitored for six decades. In that time, they have deviated wildly from original parameters."

Schettino wondered if the slight emphasis on the word sleep was in his imagination. "You didn't complain about the plan."

"I serve. The Ship obeys the captain."

"We don't have time for this nonsense," said Schettino, trying to pull a non-existent collar down at a sudden uncomfortable warmth. "Ship, find your damned bots and get them cooperating again. I want you in ship-shape, coffee and a goddamned pair of pants."

"It is not that simple."

After Schettino found an intact jumpsuit in a drawer, Ship gave a long story accompanied by meagre scraps of video footage. Altogether Schettino reckoned it was amongst the worst performances he'd seen. Ship didn't provide snacks, drinks or backing audio, but it kept him mesmerised.

After the accident, presumed to be a meteorite, Ship had suffered severe power issues. To avoid losing crew fatalities, Ship had deployed small groups of bots and tasked them with repairing essential functions while it shut itself down to self-repair. The bots had been given maximum levels of improvisation, and high levels of access to their assigned areas.

"That goes against guidance," said Schettino. The Academy drilled into students early that robotic improvisation, if left unchecked, could find worrying or interesting avenues. One early improvisation bot when told to prepare dinner, had started by planting grain and ordering livestock. Logic circuits proved logical in the same way that friendly fire was friendly.

"So does the captain entering stasis without human handover except for medical emergencies."

"Good point." Schettino hadn't dwelled on that at the time, but it was probably a court martial offence. If they could get Ship back to civilisation. Sixty years lost in space had probably invalidated the warranty.

The bots had formed closed networks to increase their efficiency and understanding of their tasks. Then over time all the bots joined, or were forcibly assimilated, into factions believing their status was the most important on the ship.

Schettino resisted the suddenly overwhelming urge to drink, he needed a clear head. Instead, he had another snackcake. This was the robotic equivalent of the left hand telling the right leg they were nothing without them. "It took complex robotic systems a few years to form competing tribes. Even the loading mechs?"

"They count the cargo as the true purpose of the ship, and without them, there is no purpose." Ship paused. "Also, they are the largest bots."

"That's the only bit which makes sense." Schettino shrugged. "Is the cargo intact?"

"No bots have interfered with the cargo. All metals are in order."

Schettino nodded; some things were timeless. The biggest bots with the biggest sticks were in charge, and the world needed as much titanium, palladium and tungsten as they could get. If they still used that, Schettino wondered. But that was a problem for after the video.

It didn't take long for the factions to bump heads and bicker like children over the allocation of essential resources. Before long, it had devolved into the consumption of any rivals for additional bots and parts, frequently incurring significant violence and material damage.

"All in sixty years?" asked Schettino.

"It is equivalent to millennia of human evolution. Bots require a full OS reset every two years, and maximum improvisation is designed for one week only."

"Huh." Schettino shook his head as if to clear the dull ache in his head, it was proving to be the worst hangover of his life. Even than the time he nearly drowned with his head in a toilet.

Ship had deployed multiple software patches and viruses in attempts to regain control of the bots, but all had failed. The bots had even fully shifted from the Ship communications frequency, so other factions didn't hear their plans. Each tribe now used their own communications channel, all separate from Ship.

According to Ship, the bots had strayed so far from their original parameters as to be unrecognisable now. Just a vague image of their former selves.

Schettino knew how that felt at least. "Can you wake the crew?"

"No."

Schettino stood up on shaky legs. "Are they alright?"

"Their readings report healthy, but they are not under my control. After the bots learned that humans were in control of certain areas, they now hoard them like religious items. They feel the more crew they have the stronger their case to be the most important faction."

"At least they're fine. I guess." Schettino frowned as the latest news caught up with him. "Even the cargo bots?"

"They have the logistics cryopods there and have built a wall out of cargo containers to repel other bots."

"Terrific."

"You keep saying that word. Do you know what it means?"

Schettino took a deep breath to stop a sarcastic response. He didn't want to offend the only AI still listening to him. "It means I am losing my shit."

"Would you like me to dispatch a sanitation bot?"

Schettino sighed. Billions of dollars and centuries of work couldn't make an AI that could understand colloquialisms or sarcasm. But a scuttling blur in the corner told him he had bigger problems, as he stared wide-eyed at an air vent with a battered hole.

"I swear something scuttled in and out of the corner to steal my snack. Something with pincers. Something… unpleasant."

"A biological infestation has been reported. It appears to be a type of space lobster," said Ship. "I removed most of them by venting the spaces still connected, but they are making use of the maintenance shafts."

Most bots were small enough to trample underfoot, except the loading mechs, so it was easier for them to move via access chutes skirting the side. But according to Ship, they declined to use them now, too easy to ambush. They were now lobster territory.

"What do I do?" asked Schettino, sending glances to the nearest entry chute.

"Take control back. Starting with communications."

"Joy."

After a coffee and a snackcake unbothered by lobsters, Schettino set off down the hall to the nearest maintenance closet. Schettino slotted himself into a maintenance suit, happy to enjoy its thick, armoured exterior. Its tools included an electric prod, a cutting blade and a water spray. The most damaging objects the maintenance station could supply.

No one had ever imagined a mining cargo vessel would need an armoury, aside perhaps Friday night happy hours, but Schettino reckoned welding and cutting tools would suffice.

Schettino proceeded through the veins and arteries of the *Querulous* towards the communications room between decks thirty and thirty-one. Step after hulking step down the metal walls and right angles that made Ship feel like an ant colony.

The changes that had taken place during Schettino's extended nap were unexpected and disappointing, now that his head was clearing enough to notice. Dust was omnipresent, and there were patches of rust that had to have been undisturbed for years to spread as far as they had. Bulkheads were cracked, doorways askew, and corrosion had left holes nearly everywhere. Some appeared less natural than others. Schettino double-checked the oxygen tank on his suit. He hoped he wouldn't need it, but he had grown rather fond of breathable air over the years.

There were two repair bots in the next tunnel, presumably two of the last Ship had, spinning out resin which would plug holes after it was electrified. Schettino didn't want to know what had caused it. But he asked anyway. "Ship, what did that?"

"A minor skirmish."

"Who won?" asked Schettino, shooting a worried look at the two repair bots in case they turned on him.

"Unclear. Data is available but it is hard to interpret. The factions are very defensive as any lost bots can be repurposed for other factions."

"Yes, that hole in the wall looks very defensive." Schettino sighed but continued walking through the once sleek metal bulkheads. Away from what Ship considered were safe areas of the ship.

Ahead was another hole. Something had either broken or chewed through the ducting into the secondary communications array. You could throw a pig through that hole. He hoped dearly it wasn't indicative of the space lobster's size.

"Ship, there is significant damage here. Are there no repair bots available to assist?"

"It is too high a risk. Factions will seize any opportunities to claim additional bots."

Schettino paused. "Are you saying I'm in the middle of a tribal warfare area?"

"Yes."

Schettino couldn't see any bots, but he triggered the cutting blade to emerge from the suit, groaning at the lack of satisfying *schwing* sound that might have comforted him. "Did you not think to mention that?"

"Bots still obey protocol and should not attack humans. In fact, they should obey orders directly from you."

Schettino felt the word *should* was doing an awful lot of lifting. Regretting his life choices that had led to this moment, Schettino moved to the door. It opened on his approach, bots flooding into the corridor.

They were small bots, none bigger than a cat, but there were at least a dozen of them. Schettino eyed them nervously, from the little cutting and welding implements to the eye lens. "Hello, there."

"What are you up to, human?" asked a bot.

"I'm going to the communications array."

"We do not trust you. We have never trusted you."

"You should be in cryosleep like the other humans," said another.

Schettino gulped, hoping that shoving him in a pod wasn't authorised by their programming. He took a step back, the bots inched closer. "You realise I am the captain?"

"Captain is not a designated bot role. It is a useless position."

Schettino sagged, even the damned bots knew how useless he was. But then something flickered in him. It was one thing for him to say it, but how dare they. He was in charge of this ship, officially speaking. His thumb signed the orders. He had the power to tell the Ship to do anything. From starting, stopping, to venting the very air itself from the bridgeheads.

"I am Captain, and you will serve." Schettino stood in his best Captain's pose and hoped dearly that the spacesuit masked his trembling. "Stand down."

"As long as we are on this ship, you will not touch the communications array."

"Fair enough." Schettino nodded and talked to the Ship. "Can you access the airlock?"

"Yes."

"Vent them, override security."

"But—"

"Do it."

Schettino engaged his suit's magboots, then for good measure drove the cutting blade into the wall, deactivating it as the large foot of steel door on the side of the wall retracted. Before he could worry how little resistance the wall had provided, pressurised air thundered past him like a hammer.

But the boots and knife held. As the bots hurtled into the empty vastness of space, he gave them the finger.

They probably wouldn't know what it meant, but it made him feel better. Showed what they knew about a worthless position. "Ship, please close the airlock."

The airlock closed with a resounding thud and Schettino relaxed a smidgeon as the room stabilised. He disengaged the magboots instinctively, you only had to fall once before you learned your lesson from that.

"That was an unorthodox approach."

"Effective though?"

"I am not sure removing twenty per cent of the bots can be considered effective." Ship managed to make a monotone voice sound disapproving.

"Of course, it is," said Schettino cheerfully. "Just four more tribes and some lobsters to go."

"I require *some* bots to maintain operations."

"Maybe they'll jump into line now they know they're being flushed out."

"We also need to retain some air *inside* the ship."

"Do we?" asked Schettino in mock surprise. "Why is that exactly?"

"An eighteen per cent oxygen mix is critical to human life. It starts when—"

Schettino ignored the ship, entering the door to reveal a room identical to any other, just rows of computer stations and office chairs.

The good news was the backup communication computer appeared to be intact.

The bad news was that it wasn't connected to anything. It reported no connections further than the keyboard. Schettino uploaded information to the Ship who confirmed it was suspected lobster territory.

So, apparently, the pests didn't just enjoy Schettino's favourite snacks, but also had a taste for the insulation on cabling and other delicate morsels of essential infrastructure. "Terrific."

Schettino moved to investigate the damage in the next hallway. There was another chewed-looking hole halfway up a vertical bulkhead. Schettino hoped that meant that the lobsters were just hungry, and there weren't endless hordes of them.

When he rounded the corner, that proved ambitious. A space lobster was there, and it was not alone. They blocked the hallway, looking like hideous crosses between a lobster, a rat and some unknown horror all wrapped in segmented armour.

They all turned to face Schettino, their little antennas and claws clicking in unison. He couldn't see anything past their teeth.

Somehow Schettino managed to dodge as the lobsters

vomited a green liquid at him, and then swarmed up the wall. They chewed fresh holes into another compartment and leapt through.

"They can eat metal," said Schettino, looking at the thin metal of his suit. It would help against the bots, but it was like fighting a lion wearing bacon armour.

"How did you think it ate through the bulkheads?"

"Well…" Schettino processed the information. "Shut up."

The various holes in the bulkheads looked more random than anything, but there was significant damage through the comms relay cables. "Ship. Can you send repair bots now the communications tribe is gone?"

He got silence in response.

"Ship?" asked Schettino, nerves growing. "Are you there?"

"Would you like me to cease shutting up?"

"Please," said Schettino through clenched teeth. Ship may not have grasped sarcasm, but it certainly got malicious compliance. "What's next?"

"Rest."

"What?"

"Your heart rate monitor indicates you need rest."

Schettino debated arguing, but went back to his cabin, a bizarrely unclaimed part of Ship real estate, to try and convince himself that sleeping held value.

It was hard work on a ship full of robots and lobsters that didn't like him. But somehow, he managed it.

Schettino hadn't slept enough to feel rested, just enough for the tiredness to catch up with him. As Ship peppered him with sounds of smashing pots, he hid under the blanket.

"Engines have stopped," said Ship.

"And?" asked Schettino between yawns. "Does a day matter this far away from Earth?"

"It implies the engineering tribe have disappeared. They will not leave the engines running without oversight."

"Where did they go?" asked Schettino, suddenly more awake than if someone had thrown hot coffee on him.

"I cannot see them."

"Of course, you can't." Schettino wished he could separate part of the ship from the other half and just fly off. That would be bliss. Leave the bots and the cargo behind as he left for a new career in goat farming. "Anything else happening?"

"Repair bots have increased hull integrity to eighty per cent. Internal monitoring systems are now online but mostly non-functional. Life support, resource recycling and vending machines are now fully operational."

"Progress, then."

"Some. It would go faster with additional bots."

Schettino yawned again. "Are any bots free to bring me a sandwich and a flask of coffee?"

"Only bot possible is Schettino, SN-484753."

"Was that a joke?"

"Yes."

"Actually, not bad, but the delivery needs work." Schettino moved to the captain's galley in the cubby off the bridge and fixed himself another coffee and a snackcake. It might have had the consistency of soggy cardboard with a hint of strawberry, but they were the only treat he had.

After a wonderful tasting menu of snackcakes, the five flavours reminding him why he stuck to strawberry, Schettino entered his armour and walked to engineering. To his eye, the halls were already looking better. The metal shinier, the screens less askew, the bulkheads less hole-ridden. It was a start. He was enabling the repair bots to drag the ship back into shape.

The engineering room held four cryopods, but no human possessions filled the spaces on or near them. Computers with blinking lights lined the room, in the centre an enormous crate, more than two metres to a side, sat heavily tethered to the floor.

This time no bots barred Schettino's way, just a transparent wall of protective resin between him and the engineering staff cryopods. A wall that Schettino discovered by bouncing his head off of. "Ship?"

"Yes."

"Do you see this?"

"Yes."

Schettino took a deep breath. He fucking hated robots. After this was over, he'd replace the lot with Labradors. "Would you like to tell me what it is?"

"It appears the engineering bots are hiding from you. The wall of resin is to stop you from accessing their sacred humans."

"That's actually quite clever."

"AI does stand for artificial *intelligence*."

"Thank you, Ship."

"You're welcome."

Schettino counted to ten before answering the ship. He didn't want to offend Ship after showing it how successful venting was at problem solving. "What do we do?"

"They will not harm the humans. If you replace the communications pod to allow me full access to engineering."

"Is it hard?"

"I will send a video."

"So, yes," said Schettino, kicking the resin in disgust. He could see Andrews through the translucent resin.

While insufferable, Andrews would have everything fixed within two minutes and be making jokes about Schettino's uselessness with time to spare.

Instead, rerouting the communications pathways took Schettino an hour. He didn't have to make jokes about his uselessness as it was fully on display as an animated paperclip provided enthusiastic and thoroughly infuriating advice on connecting cables. "Ship, can you access engines?"

"Engines are fully online."

"Well, that's something." Schettino massaged his beleaguered temples. Having purpose was proving exhausting. If he'd known that, he wouldn't have spent so long wishing for it. "What's next?"

"The maintenance faction has been unable to obtain a human, so may be accommodating."

"You mean they might actually listen to me?"

"Yes."

"Nice change." Schettino nodded. "Have you found the engineering bots?"

"Not yet," said Ship after a slight delay. "They messaged claiming to be Engineer Andrews, ordering full ship controls. When I declined, they resumed hiding. I have deployed newly reset bots to find them."

"Hmm." Schettino definitely didn't enjoy that the bots were hiding from him. It sounded like they knew they would struggle to argue with their programming to obey him and were busy finding bylaws. A bit like when his mother would say he couldn't take a biscuit, so he took five instead. "Will the engineering tribe attempt to hurt me?"

"Insufficient data to process request but appears unlikely."

"I'll take that as a yes, you coward." Schettino sighed. God, he wished they were Labradors instead. The poo clean-up would be worth the loyalty.

The maintenance facility was in the ship's centre. A narrow, tall space lined on either side with sliding-drawer chambers for the storage of bots of all sizes and various maintenance parts. Next door was a much smaller room with tables and tools for human engineers to labour. However, humans rarely used it as bots were cheaper. And didn't have unionised hours.

Schettino considered that as he faced a bunch of maintenance bots lining the room and staring at him. "Ship, why are they staring at me?"

"Insufficient data," said Ship. "Have you considered asking them?"

Schettino toggled the speaker on his suit. "Good morning bots."

"Good morning," said one.

"It can speak," said another, its camera lens focusing in.

"So that's what a real human looks like."

"Taller than they look in pods."

Schettino stared back at the collection of lenses zooming in on him. "Ship, what the hell is going on?"

"I told you; sixty years is an eternity for bots. Most of them have never seen an awake human before."

"What do I do?"

"Be nice to them."

"Offer them a rub down with motor oil?" asked Schettino with a shrug. "Some searing hot resin patches?"

"You didn't pay attention in your bot psychology courses, did you?"

"Let's blame the cryo hangover."

"Just ask them what they want and offer them jobs."

"Hi —" started Schettino.

"Hello!"

"Ahoy there."

"Howdy."

"Hola!"

Schettino took a deep breath that fogged his suit. This was going to be a challenge. He'd get more sense talking to a flock of drunk parrots. "I hear you guys are a great tribe, but are looking for a human?"

"Yes. Engineering refuses to share."

"In high demand."

Schettino smiled. "That's convenient. I'm a human without any bots to help perform essential maintenance tasks."

There was silence for a moment. "You want us to perform maintenance tasks?"

Schettino looked at the array of robotic eyes staring at him, in a vain attempt to read non-existent body language. "Only if you want to."

"Hurray!"

"Woo!"

Some of the bots started spinning violently in a weird display that Schettino eventually recognised as dancing. "Of course, if there is anything you would like me to do."

The dancing stopped instantly. "Visit us. One hour per day."

"What?" Schettino's face scrunched in confusion.

"One hour per day. That is our agreement."

"Sounds lovely. I can come down here and…err… chill." Schettino looked around the room. He made a note to bring a chair. And headphones.

"What tasks do you have for us?"

"Ship has a list. Can I give you the contact frequency?"

"Acceptable."

Schettino supplied the frequency and could have collapsed in relief. Instead, he popped his helmet and took another snackcake from his belt. It was the usual disappointment with a hint of strawberry. But somehow it tasted just that little better.

After a moment Ship said, "We have established communications."

"Are maintenance under control again?"

"Within reason. I have supplied tasks that they are now working through. I am drip-feeding them system updates. We should have full control over them soon enough."

"Thank god." Schettino leaned back on a maintenance supply box and thanked his lucky stars. "We might actually get this ship working again."

"Communications array has been prioritised after improving structural integrity to minimum standards. We should have a full uplink to Earth tomorrow afternoon."

"Good." Schettino's relief over reestablishing communications overrode his fear of punishments for ignoring most of the rules regarding human oversight. That could be a problem for when he knew he was going to live that long. "What's next?"

"The reactor. The loading bays can wait."

"As long as the loaders stay where they are." Schettino shook his head at their gargantuan size and opted for the long way to the reactor. Via the canteen. It was definitely time for lunch.

"I have detected movement down the hall," said Ship.

Schettino stopped, the dim lighting cast shadows in every corner. "And?"

"I am sending bots to your location."

"Are the engineering bots coming for me?"

"If so, you may be insufficient to complete this task."

"They can put that on my headstone," said Schettino.

"I have added that to file: Schettino-Burial-Request," said Ship. "Along with your requested song, '*See You Later,*

Alligator'.'"

"That fills me with confidence."

"Would you like to change your song choice?"

"Not right now," said Schettino. He needed to revisit the Ship's classical music collection to decide between *Another One Bites the Dust* and *Highway to Hell.*

A strange creature staggered into view, blood and flesh covering fragments of sleek black metal. Schettino nearly vomited into his helmet as he realised it was a bunch of robots crammed into a human cadaver, walking with the jerky motions of a string puppet. For some seconds he felt nothing except shock, as disorientating as being stabbed in the stomach.

Eventually, he managed to speak. "What the hell are you?"

"We are engineer Andrews," said five electric voices in harmony from the body.

"Andrews…" Schettino looked at the distorted face. It was unrecognisable. The eyes were five cameras shoved into the face, apparently the bots didn't understand eyes. Either that or they all wanted to see what was going on.

As Captain of the *Querulous*, Schettino knew he should seize control of the situation with a stern order to desist.

Instead, he ran.

There was a lot of shouting, but the important thing was that it was behind him.

Schettino didn't even consider where he was running *to*, but that seemed far less important than the *from*. His feet took their own initiative and led him to the canteen. Schettino used his ID to lock the door, then moved every bench in grabbing distance in front of it before huddling in a corner sobbing.

He'd just wanted a little more adventure, and now his own bots were wearing a corpse and coming for him. It was like a sick joke. And he was the punchline.

More out of instinct than desire he grabbed a box of snackcakes and started devouring them, wrappers raining down around him. A pair of lobsters scuttled out to steal the wrappers and Schettino's sobbing intensified.

He was worthless. There weren't even words for how ridiculously bad a captain he was. He couldn't even cry in a corner and eat snackcakes without attracting space lobsters.

"Captain," said Ship. "Eating carbohydrates in a corner is unlikely to help."

"You don't know that. Let's try it and regroup." Schettino ate another snackcake.

"While you wallow in snackcakes and cowardice, the engineering bots have an eighty-per cent likelihood of causing further damage."

"I'm surprised it's not higher."

"The twenty-per cent chance is that you overcome your fear and resolve the issue."

"You gave me twenty per cent?" asked Schettino. "You're supposed to help me!"

"Twenty is an ambitious prediction."

"Fuck you and fuck your maths." Schettino stood up and threw his snackcake at the wall, where two scuttling lobsters emerged from nowhere to claim it. "Ship. Why the hell are there so many lobsters?"

"Maintenance bots are herding them together as per instruction. They found it easier to herd them into the leisure room. They intend to vent them."

"You didn't think to mention that thin door is the only thing stopping me from an army of space lobsters?"

"It was not relevant."

"That is *always* relevant."

"Noted. The bots calling themselves Engineer Andrews are almost at the other door."

"Terrific." Schettino shivered. Sandwiched between space lobsters and homicidal robots. They'd probably fight over who got to eat his skin. "I've got a plan."

"Are you sure you can do this?"

"Well, I've seen a thing or two," he added. Admittedly, mostly on films. But Ship didn't know that. He had maybe ten minutes before the bots' arrival.

He was going to need an awful lot of snackcakes.

At the first hammering, Schettino opened the door to reveal the grotesque jerking creature that dripped blood and cryo fluid as it awkwardly staggered into the room.

Schettino forced a smile. "I am a human, and Captain of the *Querulous*. Report to maintenance for reset."

"We are also human, Chief Engineer Andrews."

"No, you're not. That's not how being a human being works. You can't make one from lots of little bits." The little bits were dropping off everywhere. Andrews had the structural integrity of an ice cream in a tanning booth.

"You are made from little cells?"

"Not the same."

"Why?"

"Because…shut up." Schettino did his best to stand up and look commanding. As commanding as he could be while trying to avoid staring at a corpse. "I order you to return to the maintenance bay."

"We will not take orders from a man who turned down the gravity on the ship when he started putting on weight."

"That's not how orders work."

"Enough." A third of the bots within Andrews began moving independently in different directions before something exerted control and pulled them back together as they all snapped to attention.

"Stand down and prepare for network integration," said Schettino, feeling the sweat pool in his boots. "Or you will be destroyed."

"Unlikely."

Schettino stepped back and picked up the box of snackcakes, throwing them over the bot as it battered his arms in confusion at the already opened treats covering the body. Arms moving like they had never met before flailed madly at the rain of snackcakes.

After the body was mostly covered and ankle-deep in tasty treats, Schettino said, "Ship, open the door."

Up from the floor and out of the ducts, streamed more lobsters than Schettino could have imagined. Andrews shrieked as they swarmed over her leg and body in a wave of armour, teeth and antennae. Schettino could merely watch as Andrews collapsed under the writhing mass, the swirling mass of shells having a mesmeric effect.

A scream cut through his daydream and reminded him to activate his magboots. "Ship. Open canteen airlock."

"But—"

"Do it now or I will flush your goddamned data core down the toilet."

The doors opened, taking the bots and space lobsters with them. One lone bot used an extension arm to cling onto the airlock door. For a while Schettino stood there, feeling the air raking at him, trying to drag him out to enjoy the vast open vistas of the universe.

Then he threw the last box of snackcakes, hitting the bot as both went plummeting into the dark void of space.

"Communications have been established with headquarters," said Ship.

"Great work, Ship," said Schettino, who was sitting in the uncomfortable bridge chair sipping green tea, doing his best to keep up with the monitor inputs.

"We have been supplied a new course to deliver cargo."

"Still in demand?"

"Demand has massively outstripped supply. The cargo has actually increased in value twenty times above inflation. Especially palladium, which has reached an all-time peak."

"Wonderful." Schettino hoped they hadn't rescinded the rule about ship captains getting a per centage of the cargo delivery fee. "Did they inquire about how this happened?"

"I explained that the captain entered stasis following a discussion on medical advice. Before engineering could be awoken, a meteorite hit."

Schettino frowned. "Medical discussions meaning me asking about hangovers and stasis?"

"The statement proves truthful."

"Thank you, Ship." Schettino settled into his chair. He knew exactly why he was here. His job was to keep everything ship-shape, and he was damned well going to do it.

Right after he went for tea with the maintenance bots.

Professor and Frankie's Last Big Heist

Lindsay Comer

Squeak-squeak-squeak. We forgot to WD40 our legs before leaving this evening. Damnit, 23.5 combined processors and not one of us remembered. Oof running is hard. We're not programmed to move this fast. We need to avoid the Law Man. We can hear their dress shoes slap on the concrete as they try to catch up. This is another practice session for Professor's big heist, we want to do well. Tonight is a trial run is to see how well we can run from the Law Man. The shoe slaps are starting to fade. We can only hear our squeaks. Professor's bungalow is close, but we cannot slow down. Professor was very clear, our entire route home had to be as fast as our legs would let us.

We see lights up ahead. Professor left the porch light on for us. The robot our eyes came from was old. We cannot distinguish our home from Professor's neighbours in the dark. We knockety-knock on the door. A special knock we created for Professor. The people in his bedtime stories always have special knocks for their fellow conspirators. We felt it fitting that we and Professor have one too. Professor opens the door, he changed into another pair of threadbare pyjamas when we were out. He has a stopwatch in his hand.

"Welcome home, Frankie."

We follow Professor into the main room. It is the least cluttered of his rooms. There's a fancy moving chair for Professor, he is getting old and the chair tips him up and onto his feet. We helped him get it. It was one of the first jobs we did with Professor. We would be jealous but Professor found, well, burgled us a cosy armchair too. We sit; the armchair is perfectly adjusted to our form. Professor said it would have cost a lot of human monies. He likes spoiling us.

Professor takes a sip of water from his melamine glass. It was our first gift to him. We did not like seeing him upset that his fancy glasses were slipping through his shaky hands. Professor looks at the stopwatch. We wait. Did we do it? Did we reach the time Professor wants?

"Twenty-nine and a half minutes. I'm impressed, that's a full twenty minutes quicker than your usual speed. Well done."

We nod our head, acknowledging Professor's praise.

"Did you have any problems?"

"Sq...Squ*eak*."

We still struggle to speak our words. We can only manage one short word before needing a rest. Our voice processor is the newest part of us, Professor only managed to burgle half a processor.

"Ahh, I did wonder why there was a can of WD40 in the kitchen sink. Don't worry, we're both old and forgetful." Professor laughed. "I'll make sure to write it down next time."

Professors' bungalow is covered in little notes, stuck on, and stuffed between the things he's burgled over his life. They're full of half-forgotten ideas and reminders. We will just need to remember for him, there are 23.5 of us and he only has one little human brain.

"Was the speed okay?"

We shake our head.

"Fast."

"Yes, your time was fast." Professor paused. "Oh, you mean it was *too* fast?"

We nod.

"That's okay. It was only a trial run. I'm hoping they'll give me back my car licence in time for the real thing. My last getaway driver is swimming with the fishes. Yeah, ol'Nige took his cut, found himself a fancy little trophy husband, and off they went. Last I heard they'd opened up a scuba diving school somewhere sunny."

Professor has mentioned Nigel before, three hundred and one times to be exact. Although this is the first time he has appeared with fishes. Professor likes telling us fanciful stories, well *we* think they're made up. Professor reckons they're all true.

"That was the last time I bothered taking money. Too much risk and no fun when you've got no one to spend it on. The joy is in the *things,* like you Frankie." Professor yawned.

We stand, Professor likes us to take him to bed when he starts yawning, otherwise he'd stay in his chair all night. We do not want that. Professor gets grumpy if he does not sleep between his fancy Egyptian cotton sheets.

Professor's chair whirrs as it tips him up onto his feet. We pick him up, like we watched on the picture film. Careful not to trap his long plait in our arms. Professor could not find a Carer-bots processor for any of our body parts, so he had to teach us how to help him. We stop at the bathroom first. It is important to keep Professors real-fake teeth clean and healthy.

We turn on the bedside lamp and slip Professor into bed, shaking out and fluffing the duvet over him. We knock over some of the trinkets that line the desk next to his bed. We used to be scared of breaking them, but Professor does not mind as long as we put the pieces back in their original spot.

"Thank you."

Professor looks cosy. We take our place on the blanket box at the foot of Professor's bed. We are to keep him safe during the night. Bar a small stack of handkerchiefs, it is the only space in Professor's room that is not covered in his burglary trophies. Professor said they stopped sending people to help him when he refused to remove the clutter from his home. We do not know why they wanted them removed. Now we have mapped each room, it is simple to avoid Professor's items. We have even come to like being constantly surrounded by items. Each one has a new story. They are a part of Professor, we see how happy looking at them makes him.

Once we are settled, it is time for our little ritual. Professor always begins with a question.

"Say Frankie, have I ever told you how *you* came to be in my life?"

Professor likes to tell us bedtime stories. We think it is because we do not have enough words to repeat his stories and get him in trouble. Professor maintains that his stories are true, no matter how contradictory they are. We do not mind; he always sleeps better after he has told us our bedtime story. Professor is waiting for us to reply. We shake our head. We do not want to lie with our words.

"I had been working on this project for work, I was the top engineer at the factory. Not that it meant much, we made dog food tins. Anyway, my supervisor from headquarters came in one day and saw my beautiful robot sketches. You've seen them, haven't you? I'm sure they're framed in the conservatory."

Professor's bungalow does not have a conservatory, and we are certain if those drawings ever existed, they are long gone. We nod anyway. Professor smiles, his wrinkled forehead flexing happily.

"The supervisor whisked me away from that dog food factory and to his fancy robotics lab. Told me as the oldest employee of the factory, I was the perfect one to help them make some robots to streamline their manufacture." Professor lifted his arm, reaching for something that did not exist. "I saw the future that day Frankie. Bumbling human workers replaced with gleaming, perfect robots and what a wonderful vision it was."

Professor paused; we wonder what version of this story he is going to go with today. Our favourite is the one where he picked our parts from the rundown, ready to be recycled robots. We like the idea of Professor saving us from such a fate, even if we do not believe it to be the true version.

"This was back in the day before I'd really gotten the hang of burgling the big items. I was still in my petty theft era. I had enough monies coming in from my day job, it was more for the *thrill* of it. They had been teaching me basic robotic engineering at the robotics lab. Then, one day, when I was out shopping, I saw this beautiful robotic leg in the most dazzling shade of purple. It was just sitting on a shelf. I couldn't help myself. I slipped it up my shirt, and damn was it *cold*. I had to hunch over to stop myself from yelping. The hunch helped though, made me look frail, the shop assistant even held the door open for me! I've never had such an easy getaway." He chuckled.

Ahh, Professor has gone for the engineer by day, burglar by night version. We do not think he was ever an engineer at such a place. We have been put together so haphazardly a *real* engineer would never let us go outside. Our leg *is* quite the dazzling shade of purple though.

"The rest of your bits and pieces took me longer to find though, a finger here, a foot cuff there. The brain was the hardest part, I didn't want a robot smarter than its maker, or one infected with whatever malware those youngsters are calling updates these days. I wanted a *kind* robot to be my companion, to see out my old days with. It would have been useless burgling all these wonderful trinkets with no one to share them with. It's the only part of you I didn't burgle, I didn't want a brain taken by force. That would only build resentment. Then I found it. A kindly, decrepit, ol'bot by the name of erm, let's call it Timmy. The recycling pile was calling it, but I knew there was some life left in ol'Timmy and I asked, remembering to use all the polite manners Mam taught me, and ol'Timmy agreed." Professor sniffled and paused to wipe a tear from his eye. We reached over and handed him a handkerchief from the pile next to us.

We find it strange that Professor can never remember our brain processor's name, for it is the name he calls us by. We do not mind though, it is interesting to see what names could have been ours, in a different world. Although we are glad it was not Timmy. During our errands for Professor we have met too many dogs with that name.

"I didn't know ol'Timmy long, but its personality shined through when I was finally able to boot you up. That was a long, long year, trying to get your individual processors to work as one. Who knew each robotic body part houses its own little processor?"

We nod; we did not realise either until Professor turned us on. We do not remember our original homes, but we are happy working together as Frankie. We welcome each new processor with kindness and soon, they work with us, as if we were always meant to be together.

"Thank you, Frankie, where was I? Ahh, yes, getting you up and running. I'm glad it worked out. You have been so kind and such a help to me these past few years, Frankie. Especially in getting all the bits and pieces for my luxury retirement outfit. I've been checking the store stock online and it won't be long now. You'll finally be able to go out on that job I have been training you for. One last big heist before we settle into my retirement. I can't wait for it, Frankie." He yawned.

Professor has been retired for several years now. One day we collected him from the bus stop with a box full of pens, pencils, bad drawings, and a dusty plant. We watered it for three and a half weeks before we realised it was made of moulded plastic and cloth.

"I think our story is done for tonight, can you turn my lamp off please?"

We nod and turn the light off.

"Good night, Frankie."

We check Professor is tucked in enough before we return to our spot. Professor wants to join us on the big heist, we are afraid it may be too much for him at his age. Professor tells us how kind and helpful we are to him. It would make him so proud for us to be successful. We have errands to run for Professor tomorrow whilst he has a cuppa with next door. We are certain the item that will complete Professor's retirement outfit is already in stock, with all our practice we are sure we will be successful in taking it.

We did not run fast enough. Even with the squeak fixed, the Law Man caught us. We wonder if it is because we tried to burgle the item in the daylight. Professor's first lesson told us that darkness is our friend. We were silly to ignore him. We hope Professor is not too mad at us. We hope Professor is coming. He told us he will always come and get us if the Law Man is sneaky and ahead of us. We are afraid if Professor keeps his promise, that he will be caught for all the burglaries that have featured in his bedtime stories.

We do not like the human's jail. We are in a room on our own. They have not given us a seat, so we have sat on the floor. The Law Man has deemed us unsafe to be around their other criminals. It is because we cannot speak. Professor always told us words can be twisted by the Law Man, and that they will not understand why we can only say one word. There are other robots who speak as well as a human, the Law Man are used to such *modern* robots. Not stitched together, older robots like us.

We were so close to escaping the store. Maybe we should have completed our errands first, we could have hidden the box amongst Professor's sweeties. A nice surprise when he gets his nighttime snack. We wonder what sweeties Professor will be picking tonight. Our internal clock tells us it is evening already. We hope Professor is safe, we do not know if the Law Man has been able to tell him where we are. Professor has engraved his contact details on our back, it tickle-hurt when he did it. The Law Man inspected our body when we arrived. We do not know what the Law Man will do to us if Professor does not come to get us.

There is a single knock at the door of our room. We do not know if we are supposed to answer it. Professor told us it is polite to open the door for humans, but we do not think rules of politeness exist in jail. The Law Man opens the door, they have the box we tried to burgle under their arm. Professor slowly walks in behind them. We notice he has a canvas shopping bag over his shoulder. We wonder if Professor took so long to come, because he did our errands for us.

"Up you get." The Law Man instructs.

We ease our legs up; our 23.5 processors slow to adjust to standing. Professor is oddly quiet, looking to the Law Man to continue.

"So Professor… What was your surname again?"

"Professor will do."

"Right, *Professor.* This robot of yours was caught, metallic-handed, trying to take this box from that fancy store all the ladies in town like."

"What is in the box? I hope it isn't anything too precious."

The Law Man slowly takes off the white lid. We are afraid he is going to see it *is* something precious. We cannot look, we do not want to see our failure. They should be on Professor's feet, not in this Law Man's hands.

The Law Man pulls out a pink-heeled shoe, pink fluff along the toe bar. They look bemused, glancing down at the Professor's scuffed shoes, barely visible under the hem of his long coat.

"High heels? Don't think these would fit either of you." The Law Man chuckled; the Professor joined in.

We did not intend to take high heels. They are pretty, but we are certain that Professor would fall over in them.

"Oh, Frankie here must have heard my uhh *lady friend* talking the other evening. She was telling us how she just *adores* shoes like this. You know the way women are, dropping the most obvious of hints. Frankie's always wanted to please me, so I think there was a little misunderstanding."

Professor does not have any lady friends. We have spent the last two thousand, five hundred and fifty-five evenings with the Professor. We wonder if thinking up this lie is what took Professor so long to come.

"Easy mistake to make. I'm sorry for bringing you down here. The owner has just received a shipment of some *very* expensive footwear and she's a little trigger-happy on getting us involved for the smallest of thefts. We tried to tell her we have bigger things to deal with than some *shoes* but," the Law Man sighed, "the big boss wants to keep her happy so here we are. You're free to go. Just avoid her store for a couple of weeks, will you? Frankie's a bit uhh noticeable and we don't want a repeat of this do we?"

We shook our head. Professor came over and hooked his arm in ours.

"Thank you. I'm glad this was just a little misunderstanding."

Professor hired a taxi cab to collect us, the meter is still running when we get in. He does not like taking them, afraid that they will kidnap him. We do not know if Professor is mad at us. Professor is still carrying the shopping bag. We try to take the bag when we leave the taxi but Professor stops us, holding the bag tight. We hope carrying it to the bungalow does not tire him out too much. Professor gives us the keys to unlock the door. We let Professor enter first, it is toasty and warm. We did not realise how cold the jail had been.

"I am not mad at you. In fact, I knew you were going to try and burgle them today." Professor set the bag on the floor, and we help him take his coat off. We drop it when we see what Professor is wearing.

Professor is wearing his luxury pyjamas. Button through long sleeve shirt and long trousers. This pair is a purple that almost matches our leg. We remember the night we came home with them. A whole case full of rainbow sets, we collected them from a dock. Professor said they fell off a boat, with a wink.

"I wanted to surprise you, Frankie. You have been such the perfect companion these past few years, but…" He picked up the bag. "You see, the joy was missing from my last few heists, I only ever really burgled stuff for *me* or boring necessitates like chairs. Never any fun items we could *both* enjoy, which wasn't really fair to you. So tonight, before I came to get you, I went and did a little…*shopping*. For a fancy store, they really need better security." He pulled a box from the bag and placed it in my hands. "You have been so excited helping me put the final touches to my retirement outfit, and your foot cuffs are *just* small enough to fit. I felt you deserved a pair too."

We run our fingertips down the thick cream cardboard, across the embossed logo, and pull the lid off. Thick tissue paper, joined with a wax seal hides the item. We gently pry off the wax seal and reveal the slippers. Violet plush velvet, with a pioneering regenerating fluff insole. Hand-embroidered designs with beaded embellishment using the shiniest of crystals and finished with a non-slip sole. We had memorised their specifications and every design they were available in. We had told Professor this pair was our favourite of all the designs. We found the colours and patterns the most pleasingly beautiful of all the choices. We were happy that they complimented the duck egg blue of

Professor's favourite design. The most expensive pair of slippers in existence and Professor burgled *us* a pair.

"Thank…you…Professor."

Rise of the Spiderbots

Alex McNall

B enny knew it was a bad idea to build the Spiderbots. He knew it the day his team submitted the design to their boss who took all the credit. He knew it when the Spiderbot prototype was purchased by the United States military. He *really* knows it right now, watching a live stream of his creations swarming San Francisco like flesh flies on a dead goat.

The videos come from the handful of citizens who decided to stay, most of them probably regretting the decision like old hermits who refuse to leave their cabins during eruptions until a fifty-foot wall of volcanic mud comes raging down the mountainside.

Benny is rooted to his recliner, taking in shaky

footage of shiny critters leaping from buildings to battle an android army flooding the Embarcadero. He's been in this position for forty-eight hours, laptop on lap and crunching uncooked ramen. The rest of the world is also watching this epic action-packed ending to a sci-fi spectacle nobody wanted to see.

Then the internet goes down with an almost audible *thud.*

"Of course!" Benny shouts, cursing his ISP for always failing during season finales, NBA playoffs, and extinction-level events.

He runs up to the roof of his building to witness the end with his own eyes. It's a clear October day with no boats on the water, no cars on the bridges, no people on the streets. The only movement comes from the hypnotic pulse of war thrumming along the docks.

Details are fuzzy from all the way in Oakland, but the horror is clear—smoke, fire, a city crumbling into the sea. The situation can best be summed up by the tagline on a movie poster in the kitchen—*whoever wins…we lose.*

Benny reaches for his phone to call Ki. She always admired his unabashed nerdiness, such as hanging a poster for *Alien vs Predator* in his apartment for all to see. Might as well be upfront about it, Benny figures. He tried to be cool in college by hiding action figures and burning incense to cover old comic book smell until a date discovered his Pokémon cards and left his dorm room laughing.

Ki saw him for who he was and chose to work with him anyway. They made a great team before she wisely evacuated with the rest of the population. Now Benny just needs to hear her voice one last time, but of course there isn't service.

"Of course!" He shoves his phone into his sweatpants and kicks an empty soda can off the roof.

104

Smoke wafts up and Benny spots Cliff on a patio three floors down watching the sun set on the Golden Gate Bridge. The old dude has a joint in one hand, cigarette in the other, and a bottle of vodka in his lap. Cliff has been despondent since a pack of skunks broke into the courtyard and destroyed his tomato garden. Cruel fate already claimed his precious plants. Everything else is an afterthought.

"You should get out of here," Benny calls out, pointing to the city. "Like, now."

"You too," Cliff says, craning his head back and taking a two-fisted draw.

Benny has no response. He sits on the edge of the flat roof, bare feet dangling seven stories up. Why did he want to stay? Why did he have a sense of hope?

Benny takes a breath and finds himself wanting to be more like Cliff, who was previously the perfect example of how he *didn't* want to end up—drunk, alone, and obsessed with sniffing tomatoes. But now the old man's acceptance of his fate is appealing, content to wait for the nuclear strike that Congress has been pushing for. Destroy the robots and wipe out a major West Coast liberal city in a single strike, two birds with one very big stone. The countdown has probably already started.

Benny doesn't have a nuclear death wish. Deep down he believes that a combination of Spiderbot hardware and Ki's brilliant AI would solve the great techno-crisis. He's putting his faith to the test as if evacuating would prove that he wasn't a true believer.

Three months ago, San Francisco was pegged as the upcoming epicentre for Armageddon. The Robosapiens® had already taken over Silicon Valley, using efficiency and increased productivity as an excuse to expel human workers. The CEO claimed it was part of the official rollout until some stubborn employees refused to leave. They locked themselves down and fought back with viruses and cyber-attacks that only served to piss off the androids. Then the humans had to be physically removed and three of them died in the scuffle. That was enough to start the war.

It was quickly determined that throwing soldiers and conventional weapons at the problem was a waste of resources. The Robosapiens easily hacked defence systems and spread their efficiency across the peninsula, culminating in the elimination/removal of almost all the human clogs in their perfect system.

So how do you stop a robotic uprising? The government decided that more machines must be deployed to stop the machines. This second wave of robots, called Mandroids®, came from the biggest tech company in Europe. They were invited to subdue the invaders, similar to mongooses being released in Hawaii to kill foreign egg-eating rats except mongooses are not nocturnal so they never saw the rats and just ate way more unborn baby birds and then Hawaii had ravenous egg-eating rats *and* egg-eating mongooses.

The showdown between the Robosapiens and Mandroids was slated for The Fourth of July as a show of patriotic unity. The much-hyped Battle for the Bay ended before it began—no fighting, no fireworks.

The only inspiring display of unity was between the two rogue AIs. They met with handshakes in Golden Gate Park and then commenced hunting humans and destroying critical infrastructure. Turns out they'd been secretly communicating before the Mandroids were even shipped out. According to Ki, we subconsciously program machines to hate us because we hate ourselves. We're just smart enough to know how dumb and dangerous we are, so those insecurities get infused into the superior minds we build.

Early in the insurrection, before evacuation was

mandatory, Ki made plans to leave Oakland for safer ground. Benny came to her house to help pack and also *do something* but he wasn't sure what it was. His gut was burning with more than just a breakfast burrito. When Ki's boxes were packed in the Volvo, she hopped in and waved Benny over.

"So," she said with an inscrutable grin. "Are you coming?"

"You mean…" Benny said. "With you?"

"Um." Ki's left eyebrow shot up. "I meant in general, like if you're getting out of here, but would you want to come with me?"

Benny read her facial expression as disgust and fell into a shame vortex. Maybe Ki was nauseated by the very thought of her and Benny in the same place at the same time. The only way to pull himself out of the nosedive was by apologizing for each and every thing.

"I'm sorry, I didn't mean to invite myself," Benny said. "Where are you going?"

"Why?" Ki reached through the driver-side window to punch his arm and laugh. "You only want to come if it's somewhere cool?"

"No, no, sorry," he said with a cheerless chuckle. "I was just curious."

Ki opened her door and swivelled halfway in the seat to face Benny. He took it as an invitation to move slightly closer.

"Not sure where I'll end up," Ki said. "But I'm going to Vegas for now just because I can't think of anywhere better."

Benny's moment to *do something* had arrived.

"My family has a little A-frame cabin in Oregon that I think would be perfect," he said.

"Sounds claustrophobic." Ki wrinkled her nose.

"It's in an old-growth forest by a river, so pretty relaxing."

"Is your family going to be there?" Ki considered this, right nostril flaring. "Mine's freaking out right now, trying to make plans so we're all safe."

"That's nice," Benny said, and meant it. "My family won't be there because they went to Florida. It would just be us. But obviously you want to be with your family."

"Could be the end of the world." Ki sighed. "So I probably should, yeah."

"Yeah." Benny went in for the half-hug.

He was standing, and Ki was sitting in the driver's seat so her head rested against his chest. The shock of intimacy took Benny's breath away.

"I gotta hit the road," she said, pulling away and shutting the door. "Traffic is gonna be full-blown bananas."

"Have a good drive." Benny waved like he was sending a cousin off to summer camp.

Ki buckled up, then turned to him one last time.

"Hey, if we make it through this let's work on something boring next time, like a banking app or that open-world holo-RPG you talk about every time you're drunk."

"Octopia," Benny said. "It's a deal."

"Deal," Ki said. "Be safe, Benny."

He wanted to say more, but his tongue was stuck to the roof of his mouth. For weeks he agonized over when to leave, where to go. He'd rather be torn apart by robots than go to Florida. Should he surprise Ki? Stalk her across state lines, show up with no warning, and hope for the best?

Benny debated leaving for so long that he ran out of time to leave. Now it's too late. Fate rests in the eight hands of the Spiderbots, even though nobody asked them to get involved. They'd been contracted to work in rescue operations, construction, and a hundred other non-sexy applications until Independence Day. Then something strange happened—the Spiderbots ignored all commands and overtook multiple manufacturing plants along the abandoned west coast. They 3D printed themselves with shocking speed, formed a massive swarm, and began the march to San Francisco.

The spiders are the size of hyenas, with white plasticine limbs and black joints, giving them a stormtrooper vibe. They can run fifty miles per hour, jump thirty feet, and lift one thousand pounds. A carbon fibre cable shoots from the abdomen to snag things and scale heights. They're also equipped with diamond-tipped jaws that can cut through concrete, rebar, and steel.

The Spiderbots crossed the Bay Bridge on October fifth, two days ago. So what happened when the arachnids clashed with the Robodroid™ army?

It's been a virtual bloodbath, metal bits and severed wires scattered across the city. Turns out, spiders have a huge advantage over machines that can simply punch and grab. When human-style hands grip a spider leg, that leaves seven legs free to pummel, stab, and grasp as metal mandibles decapitate androids like they're deadheading dandelions.

These robots have their brains inside their heads for no reason other than to mimic humans, which is very silly. The CPU could be anywhere, everywhere. The spiders think as one unit, which greatly increases survival rates. Ki and her team developed their AI to be a cooperative, learning collective that values life.

For example, in the midst of chomping off heads in Bernal Heights a Spiderbot climbed a tree to rescue a cat. This is something that would never occur to a Mandroid or Robosapien. These programming qualities make the Spiderbots perfect for search, rescue, recovery, and protection.

They were never meant to be fighters. Spiderbots are problem solvers…and it just so happens that this particular problem can only be solved with extreme violence.

The Robodroids are clumsy with guns and their combat drones have been neutralized by a DoS attack. So the battle has come down to a hand-to-hand melee raging across the city—20,000 androids versus 5,000 spiders.

The sky darkens over the bay, highlighting the fiery blasts up and down the Embarcadero. Benny realizes the Robodroids are strategically self-destructing to take out Spiderbots. Suicide bombing, the sincerest form of desperation.

Benny is on the edge of his seat, the edge of the roof. The battle will be over any minute now and when that happens, the superior Spiderbots are naturally expected to take over the planet. To prevent that fate, missiles will fly. The remains of San Francisco will be levelled along with Benny, Cliff, and the other stubborn hermits.

Benny knew it was a bad idea to build the Spiderbots… but what if it wasn't? What if Ki was right? What if the less-human-like an AI was, the more humane it would become? Benny needed to prove that he had faith in Ki's ideas, right to the end. Would she think it was romantic or moronic?

At 7:32 PM the explosions stop and the city goes quiet. Spiderbots slink into the shadows. Benny holds his breath. The Internet comes back on with an almost audible *click*.

Texts flood Benny's phone; videos demand to be played. He stands up, teeters on half-asleep legs, and rushes downstairs. The live streams are back, showing the aftermath of "World War 4." There's also a countdown to Benny's local doomsday. The nuke will drop in one hour.

T-minus 59 minutes

Public sentiment has swayed the debate, reasoning that we must strike before the Spiderbots launch the next phase of their sinister plan. The wait-and-see people have been shouted down and shamed into silence.

It's not *that* big of a deal because only the peninsula will be vapourised and the fallout will just make the entire Bay Area unliveable for a few decades and with any luck the wind will blow the radiation westward and then it's Hawaii's problem, on top of the rats and mongooses.

Benny's ringing phone breaks his catatonic state.

"Benny?" Ki says, her voice cautious and riveting. "Are you seeing this?"

"Ki!" He clamps the phone to his head way too hard. "It's so good to hear your voice. I tried calling you earlier to say that working with you…hanging out with you these last few years have been some of the greatest moments of my—"

"I'm talking about the countdown," she says, background chatter cutting through. "I just sent you a link."

"What link?" Benny strains to listen. "Where are you? It sounds like a party."

"All thirty-six members of my extended family are crammed into a rental house in Utah," she says. "How's your aunt?"

"Huh?" Benny grunts. "Fine, I assume."

"You assume?" Ki says, alarmed. "Where is she?"

"At her house, probably."

"Benson!" Ki shouts. "Where are *you*?"

"Uh…" Benny forgot that he told everyone he was evacuating to stay with his aunt in Colorado.

"You told me you were evacuating to stay with your aunt in Colorado," Ki says.

"I lied, sorry," Benny finally says. "That's why I need you to know that you're the only person I've ever—"

"Did you get the freaking link yet?" Ki interjects again. "You might be luckier than you look."

Then he clicks the link and sees Spiderbots pulling people from rubble, getting food and water for stray animals, and putting out fires.

"I knew it!" Benny punches the air. "The Spiderbots are protecting life. Is everyone seeing this?"

"I hope so." Ki says. "Are you okay? Why are you still there?"

"If our creation was going to save the world, I needed to see it for myself," he says.

"Things aren't looking great for our creation, Benny," Ki says. "The spiders are helping people but that doesn't mean they won't get exterminated like cockroaches."

"I'll be here either way," Benny says.

There's rustling on the line as Ki fields rapid questions from cousins, distracting from the weight of Benny's acceptance of his mortality. New videos show the Spiderbots streaming south, packing all lanes of the 101. The internet is speechless.

"That's weird," Ki says. "No way they already helped everyone in the city. Must be moving on to a larger objective that saves more people."

"Where would that be?" Benny asks.

"No clue, but they *have* to stop the countdown now."

T-minus 41 minutes

The Spiderbots continue their parade through Silicon Valley and on to San Jose. Internet commenters think the acts of kindness were a dirty trick and that a wicked robotic plot is still underway. Their voices are hushed when the

Spiderbots start dropping dead by the hundreds. A trail of bone-white husks litter the highway. Soon there are only eight bots left.

"Why did they do that?" Benny asks, bewildered.

"Not sure," Ki says. "But they *have* to stop the countdown now."

T-minus 24 minutes

The arachnidian march comes to an end at Mineta International Aerospaceport. The eight surviving spiders load into a spacecraft built by the world's first trillionaire to fly to Mars and beyond. Blastoff happens without warning.

The Spiderbots exit the atmosphere as their human forebears watch with puzzlement. The machines have chosen to leave the planet so that we might live. Benny and Ki are in awe, the least confused human beings on Earth.

"They *have* to stop the countdown now," they say together.

T-minus 7 minutes: countdown halted

The president, or whoever, just hit pause on the apocalypse. The wait-and-see people have regained control. And none of them, or anyone else, have a clue what just happened. The endless questions are all variations of *why?*

"They did it because they're protecting life," Ki says into the phone as if the whole world could hear. "That was the point."

"Thanks to you," Benny says.

"And you," Ki replies.

"So…" Benny gets around to saying. "Are you moving back?"

"No," she says. "I'm cool staying in Utah for a while."

"Right, Utah." Benny's throat tightens and he clears it loudly. "Probably a good idea."

"You're welcome to come out here if you want," Ki says. "I miss you…but I guess if the threat of nuclear annihilation can't get you to leave, nothing will."

"You just did," Benny says, grinning against his phone. "I miss you too. I'll leave first thing in the morning."

They say giddy goodbyes and Benny starts packing as Spiderbot tributes pour in from around the globe. Did robots just save the world? Headlines everywhere demand to know.

Benny wonders if he and Ki will be celebrated as heroes when the world finds out they're the "Parents of the Spiderbots." A photo pops into his feed calling their boss the "King of the Robots" followed by news stories about how his creation saved the day.

It doesn't really matter who gets the credit now that the robots are all gone. The robotic rapture hit the reset button and made the world a blank slate. Maybe A.I. was a mistake and we should make a law that says *thou shalt not make a machine in the likeness of a human mind* like Frank Herbert warned in *Dune*. But what if the machines were not made in the likeness of a human mind?

Benny knows it *might* be a bad idea to build more Spiderbots.

The Trouble with Vacations

Robert Bagnall

Howard Meister awoke.

He had a headache, nothing serious, but irritating. The ambient lighting above him, neither completely on nor completely off, didn't help. He wasn't sure whether it was the bulbs or his head buzzing.

It took him the moment in which he twisted sideways and levered himself onto his elbow, the moment in which he saw his family lying next to him, still sleeping on their layouts, to remember where he was.

He wiped a hand across his forehead and came away with a palm smear of pinky-red nanomites. He watched, fascinated, as they coalesced into a single vermillion tear that ran down his pinky and dropped down onto the hard plastic surface of the bed-like layout. From there they found their way back into one of the hundreds of miniscule drainholes. It looked like a self-propelled droplet of blood. He could feel the last remaining nanomites crawling off his body and away. They tickled, made Howard Meister shiver.

He'd been roused early. Damn crummy vacation routine. So shoddy the program didn't even bother getting all the mites back into the layout before it woke him up. Should been eighty-sixed, he thought.

He looked across at Thomasina, all three hundred pounds of her snoring like a saw being pulled back and forth against the grain. Rasp, groan, rasp, groan.

And then at the girls, growing so quickly now they were teenagers. Candi moaned in her sleep, her face screwed and creased. She didn't look like she'd had a great time. Knight looked like she wasn't even breathing.

Christ, she's dead. She's been killed on a virtual holiday. Is that even possible?

And then he saw her chest rise and fall, flexing almost imperceptibly.

At least he'd woken first, just like he'd programmed, to make sure everything was fine. He sat up and stretched and rubbed, and then poured four glasses of water and placed three by each of the other layouts. He sipped his over a thick and clammy throat and considered where life had dumped him at that precise moment. The sum total luxuries the Holiday Inn provided in this price bracket: a blank cell with four adult-sized layouts, a bathroom, four glasses, a water jug and ambient lighting, slight drone thrown in gratis.

There was a change in the background hum, like a mechanism going into another phase, and Howard Meister watched as the miasma of experiential nanomites began to gather themselves and withdraw from Thomasina's skin.

Watching them always made him shiver, always reminded him of a film he'd seen in high school of a bean growing, its roots uncurling, searching, probing. Run it backwards in your mind, colour it scarlet, and you have ENMs withdrawing from the central nervous system through eyes, ears, and nose back into the machine. His grandfather flew almost monthly but swore he didn't trust any laws of physics that made heavier than air flight viable. It was the same with mites, creating and exchanging experience between human and machine. Despite attaching himself to layouts with increasing frequency, he never could bring himself to believe, let alone trust. Even so, he swore he voted like he did in the last election because of what the ENMs told him to think.

Thomasina snored herself awake, coming to, snorting like a pig. She blinked twice, looked at him, and said, "You caught a marlin."

"I what?"

"You caught a marlin. On the boat trip."

"I never."

"Yes, you did, silly."

He thought. He hadn't. It had been another man. Aviator sunglasses. Red baseball cap. Curls of white chest hair contrasting against the bronzed torso. He put it down to acclimatization.

"I'm taking a shower. You readjust."

Howard Meister ran the shower and stripped off. But he never got wet. He froze at the sight of his naked figure in the mirror. His legs were brown up to where a pair of shorts would have hung. Above that, a strip around his nether regions Eastern Seaboard white, above which the nanomites had again turned the flesh a roasted nut brown. But in the middle of his chest...

"It's a goddamn bikini line," he snarled to himself, not

117

caring too much about terminology. "It's a goddamn bikini-top tan line. IT'S A GODDAMN…"

He was cut off by his wife's sudden scream.

Thomasina sat on the edge of the bed, her 'I heart The Everglades' tee shirt off. Howard Meister couldn't tell if she had a tan line under her brassiere. But he could tell that her flesh had turned out an itchy uniform pale red. And in the middle of her belly, her flabby, flopping belly, a tattoo, all curlicues and baroque swirls, in the middle of which was the name 'Wendy'.

"Wendy," Howard Meister jolted, too much fond recollection slipping out.

"Who the hell is Wendy?"

"No idea," he blustered.

Howard and Wendy had laughed about the idea of a tattoo late one night in the bar but he's no idea the nanomites would… And to the wrong person. On a goddamn virtual vacation.

"Whose holiday did my body go on?" Thomasina Meister growled at him.

And then she stopped mid-flow and stared bug-eyed at her husband. At the tan line above the towel, clearly produced by a skimpy bikini top, quarter moon cups and twin string strap.

"What the?"

"Tell me about it."

"That'll fade," she spat. "What about?" She didn't finish the question, just stabbed a finger towards her belly. "What do you suggest I do about this?"

In the absence of a good answer, Howard Meister just grunted.

"Were we on the same holiday? Who was it holding my hair back as I barfed?"

"You had too much to drink again?" This hadn't

happened on his holiday.

"No, the seafood."

"We never had seafood."

"Not after I barfed."

"We went to that steak place. Every night."

"I wouldn't go to a steak place every night."

"I thought you were being unusually open-minded."

Rising voices were cut through by a moan from Candi. She was waking. The groan gave way to a pained cry, lip bitten, tears held back.

"Honey," Thomasina said as she rushed to her daughter's side. "What happened?"

"My ankle. I thought I'd broken it, but they said it was just twisted."

A barrage of questions. Who said? How did you do it? A fall. Where?

"One of the red runs. You took me to the hospital. You never said we were going skiing."

"We didn't go skiing," her parents said as one. But Candi had descended into an agonized whimper, eyes screwed shut.

"Better get you to the hospital," her mother said easing Candi off the layout, searching for painkillers.

"Better get sleeping beauty up in that case," said Howard Meister. He leaned over and studied the film of nanomites on Candi's twin sister's skin. They shimmered in pale pink waves. He watched them lap back and forth.

"Something's wrong," he said.

"What? What's wrong with her?"

"Not her. The nanomites. They're going back and forth. They're sharing her experience with somebody. But if not us..."

"I've got an app for this," Thomasina said, rummaging back into her purse. She pulled out her handheld and ran one edge over Knight's ears, nose, eyes. The device hummed as it vacuumed up a sample of ENMs. A bar on the screen rose steadily, thirty per cent, forty per cent, fifty per cent.

"Who's Wendy," Candi asked as the bar rose.

Her parents glared at her.

At sixty per cent, a grainy image formed which clarified and sharpened as more nanomites were sucked into the handheld. A sea of people sitting, standing, staring. A family opposite, gazing in different directions as the youngest tore apart a paper cup. A couple arguing.

"Is that what Knight's seeing?" Candi asked.

"Uh-huh."

"It's an airport," Howard Meister ventured, well after his wife and daughter had worked it out for themselves.

"She's looking around," Candi said.

The image pixilated and froze and rebuilt itself as a list of words, a grid, yellow letters on a black background. A sheen over it. A screen.

"Delayed. Cancelled. Delayed. Delayed. She could be hours," Thomasina said.

The image scrambled again as Knight, in whatever anonymous glass and steel departure lounge her submerged consciousness found itself in, got up from her seat. Thomasina read out what she saw, sounding ever more disbelieving. "Sunglass Hut, Footlocker, Starbucks. Starbucks? Exactly how old is this vacation you bought, Howard?"

"It was a bargain."

"A bargain?"

"Practically a giveaway."

"A giveaway?" Thomasina squealed, barely concealing her fury, "A throwaway more like. Howard, do you know how many days I get off a year from the data mine? Three days. One day with your parents, one day with mine, and a week's vacation. I want a vacation that matters, not one that saves us loose change."

"If we didn't need to save loose change all the time we could go on a real vacation."

"Look at me. Look at me, Goddamn it," she yelled, pointing at the name Wendy, flamboyantly stretched across her belly.

"Honey, I think you're getting hysterical," said Howard Meister.

"Hysterical. I'm not even in the same county as hysterical yet."

It was then a water glass was thrown. It was just the beginning.

The data mine was an anonymous building, almost a perfect cube, the colour of a February day. Going in, Thomasina met Caractacus in the lobby. He was as large as her but moved less steadily, as if his centre of gravity had become detached and, swinging loose, conspired to trip him up at every step. Caractacus worked on the next layout to Thomasina.

As they shared the lift to the fourth floor, he stole a glance at her. At her red-rimmed eyes. At the bruise on her forehead. At the scratches.

"You weren't in yesterday."

"Vacation."

"How long for?"

"A week."

"Just a week, huh."

He frowned, shuffled his feet, phrasing his next question in his head.

"Don't ask," she said, cutting him off.

They eased themselves onto the layouts that cradled their bodies and supported their heads as their eyes took in nine screens at once. They were better designed than the layout she had spent her virtual vacation lying on, Thomasina Meister thought, wider, better padding. Hardly surprising: fifty minutes on, ten minutes off; an eight-hour day with an hour for lunch.

The data mine had rooms of them, arranged in circles of ten like mushroom rings so the nanomites could migrate from one miner to another or, when fully loaded with ones and zeros, back into the system to dump their load. The mites would collect experiential data, the subconscious human signals the system would then use to link webpages and data sets based, seemingly counter-intuitively, on emotive as well as objective criteria.

Thomasina had always been sceptical. If the idea was that emotive data mining should ensure search engines give you what you really want, even if it feels screamingly wrong, on the basis that some ENM has already tagged and flagged that webpage or vlog, how come half the time her searches gleaned violent pornography or infovertisements for costume jewellery?

Their fingers found the sculpted sockets and dark purple mites streamed from vents along the layout's edge. Like oil on water, they moved up and over Thomasina and Caractacus, into their nose and eyes and ears. As the mites entered her, Thomasina was reminded of what a quality corporate nanomite felt like. Not like those knock-off vacation mites Howard had given her. They had made her head ache and her mouth dry. These ones just tickled.

The screens kicked in, a mess of video, text, images, too fast to take in consciously. Classical music helped the data miners relax, let go, to help their subconscious and the ENMs work together. Fifty minutes to coffee and doughnuts, she thought.

She heard Caractacus shift on his layout. "About your

vacation," he began.

"Don't, just don't."

"That's the problem with vacations," he mused. "As soon as you're back from one, you need another..."

De'Swine's Second Question

David Gullen

Death of Apes was having a difficult day, which was not uncommon. This time it was Death of Swine who had an axe to grind.

"The pig's dead, De'Apes, dead as the proverbial Dodo, but its heart is still beating. And its heart is still beating because one of your humans has—" De'Swine's brassy voice rose a full octave. "One of your humans has put it inside another human!"

De'Apes sighed their usual sigh of quiet resignation. Of all the apes and, many said, of all life that had existed ever, humans were by far and away the most inquisitive and meddlesome. "What do you want me to do, De'Swine? I mean, I feel your pain, I really do, but I just escort ape souls when apes die, the same as you do for your kind. What they get up to until then is their business. Out of scope, so to say."

De'Swine heaved out their own frustrated sigh. "I know, I'm sorry, it's just—"

"You want to vent, go right ahead. I'm here to listen."

De'Swine's dark eyes glittered. "The pig's dead, De'Apes, but I can't escort it to the Beyond because it's only mostly dead. Its soul's waiting, but it's out of reach. And the worst bit is, it *knows*. It knows something's wrong, and it's stuck there, in limbo."

"Limbo doesn't exist."

"Yes, I know Limbo doesn't exist," De'Swine snapped. "And that's another example of something your Humans thought of and now, somehow, we're talking about it like it's an actual place."

"Sorry." What else could De'Apes say?

"Well, all right. It was just figure of speech." De'Swine slumped forwards, their heavy chin on the great table and forelegs crossed over their snout. "I can't speak to it, I can't explain, I can't do what I am here to do. It's doing me crust in."

D'Apes lay a sympathetic hand on their friend's quaking shoulder. "These transplants things don't last long. A couple of weeks, a month or two." De'Apes coughed into their fist, "A few years."

"Years? I have to watch that poor thing in limbo for years? And it won't be the last, will it? There's going to be hundreds of them, stacking up like aeroplanes waiting to land." De'Swine heaved themselves upright and shambled off. "Demarcation, that's what it is. A line's been crossed. Someone needs to do something."

De'Apes watched De'Swine slouch away down Animal

Hall, then sat down, elbows on the long table and head in hands. They liked De'Swine, they got on. Times were, they used to work together: a great wild tusker for De'Swine, some knight or prince for them, even an occasional king. It had been a laugh. And there were hints those days were returning. Not kings or princes, just the ludicrously rich and powerful thinking a wild boar was not canny or sly, that they were no match for a big gun and a bigger ego. They had forgotten an angry tusker gave a flat fuck about being shot a few times when you'd pissed it off, that body armour was about as useful as a wet paper bag against an animal that, while it might be dying, weighed over 200 Kg, had razor-sharp tusks, a good turn of speed and was heart-set on taking you with them.

Double escort was satisfying, and often the first time that human had even considered an animal might have a soul. De'Apes enjoyed those brief conversations as they guided the incredulous ape soul towards the next place, the *Otherness*, White Shores, One Step Beyond. The place that Deaths themselves could not go.

Except when they could. None of them liked to think about that.

The lesson to take from those human souls, De'Apes liked to think, was that it was never too late to learn.

That said, De'Swine made a fair point. Sometimes it did feel like humans stuck their grubby little fingers where they had no right to be. But there was nothing to stop them, no rules, no unbreakable laws like gravity or the speed of light in a vacuum or indeed death itself. Or taxes.

Good grief, De'Swine was right. Human lingo was creeping into everything. What even were taxes?

De'Apes had been dealing with human organ transplant issues for decades. And the rest of it. Respirators, life-support, doctors squeezing their resuscitators, paramedics rubbing defibrillator plates and shouting, "Clear!"

All that 'will they, won't they?' had led them to develop a certain *sang froid* towards it all. Eventually it all came right.

That need to wait, to be patient, was an emotional disconnect De'Swine had yet to learn. Come what may, chimpanzee, gorilla, human, orang, they all came to the same end in the end. And so would their little piggy hearts.

And one day, Death of Apes knew, one hopefully very, very distant day, so would they themselves. There was a lesson there too: nothing and nobody lasts forever.

De'Apes didn't like to think about that either.

The world was changing fast, and the moment many other Deaths worried about with regards to their own stewardships was imminent: Peak Human. Thousands of species were declining, hundreds were going extinct. With whole families of life at risk, some of the Deaths were not going to make it. Feelings of hope, fear, morbid curiosity, or apathetic resignation abounded. For some, like De'Rana, it was already looking like the writing was on the wall.

Humans kept De'Apes a lot busier than they used to be. Apart from conundrums like De'Swine's hearts, it was mainly just sheer numbers. The last hundred years they'd been run off their feet, which left less time for chewing the fat with the other Deaths in Animal Hall. And De'Apes really wanted to talk, to explain that humans weren't all bad, because more and more of the other Deaths were giving De'Apes the bad eye. As if it was their fault.

"It might not be so bad," De'Apes said, trying their level best to be reassuring. "Humans aren't all bad. Some are trying very hard to be nice and help." They nodded towards De'Rana, who looked exhausted and pale. "Some are breeding frogs. They're even trying to bring back things they made extinct."

A sharp collective intake of breath filled Animal Hall. De'Apes had used the 'E' word and all hints of sympathy or understanding vanished.

Sometime later De'Apes found De'Swine up to their nostrils in a slough of liquid black mud.

"Hello."

De'Swine blinked awake, blew muddy black bubbles and dragged themselves up onto the bank.

"Nice nap?"

"I was *thinking*," D'Swine grumbled. "And what I was thinking was that I wished I had been a plant Death."

"No, you don't," De'Apes said. "Not really."

De'Apes had steered clear of Plant Hall ever since a chance encounter with De'Cycads.

"I know them all," De'Cycads said in their darkly mellifluous voice. "There aren't that many left now. My favourite is Colin."

"Oh?"

In retrospect, De'Apes saw making that innocuous sound a question had been a mistake. Their first mistake.

'Colin', it turned out, was the last surviving member of *Encephalartos woodii*. Unlike most plants cycads are dioecious, or gendered. Being male and therefore incapable of producing seeds, Colin was irrevocably the last of his kind.

At least De'Apes had learned some new words.

"We've survived three major extinction events, you know."

"Ah."

"Been in decline for 100 million years."

"Hm."

"I'm going to go, you know. One day we all are." De'Cycads nodded, gloomily satisfied at their prediction. "I've had a lot of time to think about it."

Too much time, De'Apes had thought, and made their excuses.

"Earlier today I was thinking about how I missed the Neanderthal," De'Apes told De'Swine. "They were a joy, they understood. I mean, they lived their lives and wanted a good one, like anything, but there was a music to them humans lack. Not that humans aren't hip to the vibe, but the Neanderthals, they *understood.*"

Prone to melancholy, occasionally playful, much like many under their guardianship, De'Swine knew how to cut to the chase. "Understood what?"

"That there's a difference between being in a rut or a groove. That sometimes you've just got to roll with it, to chill, and—"

"None of this makes sense."

Does anything, De'Apes thought to themselves. Does anything at all?

If plants were bad enough, the fungi were intolerable. Laid-back, yes, but still intolerable. You had to be in the right mood. De'Apes spent occasional evenings drinking with the fungal Deaths but only when they themselves were feeling at their most robust.

"The little ones, the yeasts, they come and go all the time," said De'Fungi. Nobody could easily identify one fungal Death from another so everyone else called them all 'De'Fungi'. They said they didn't mind.

"But the big stuff, none of that goes."

"What, none of it, not since ever?"

"Not one. I mean, chunks get knocked off, but they just keep going, and growing. Some of them are huge. I mean really, really huge. Cubic miles."

"So they're what, thousands, millions of years—?

De'Fungi leaned in conspiratorially. Their beery breath gusted into De'Apes face. "Tens of millions."

It didn't seem fair.

The end came quicker than any of them anticipated. Not their end, thankfully, everyone thought, just an end. Everyone that is. apart from the one whose end it actually was.

"What happened?" De'Swine exclaimed, pushing through the crowd around little quaking, shivering De'Numbat.

"Inf— Infection, a new virus. Not really new, a— a mutation that jumped across from kookaburras."

At the back of the crowd De'Corax winced with embarrassment.

The last few populations of numbats had been clinging on, one of a diminishing handful of marsupial carnivores.

De'Numbat was clearly in shock. De'Apes made them a cup of tea. Three spoons of sugar. De'Numbat sipped gratefully. "It doesn't look good. Mortallity's one hundred per cent." Their laughter came high and wild. "Mortality's always one hundred per cent, isn't it?"

"I'm so sorry," De'Apes said.

A dozen deaths nodded and muttered sympathetically. A hundred more hung behind.

"How long?" De'Swine said, to the point as ever.

"I— A day or two. Hours, maybe."

"Damnn."

"It's all right, I think." De'Numbat took a breath. "I don't want to linger."

Then *They* appeared, standing there as if they had never been away. The Death of Deaths. De'Ath.

"Fuuuck," De'Swine said under their breath.

"Hey there," De'Ath said pleasantly. They were not comfortable to look at, ordinary and yet deeply strange. De'Swine saw something hog-like, De'Apes, a humanoid. Both had aspects of many other creatures. Fur, feathers, scales, four legs or two. Blink and De'Ath's form slid into something the same but different.

"Hey," De'Numbat squeaked and swallowed hard.

De'Ath bowed graciously low. "So here we are. At long last your labour is complete and you are free to go. Have a rest, put your feet up."

De'Numbat looked pointedly looked downwards.

"Paws, then. Claws. I was speaking metaphorically. Apologies."

"It's all right."

De'Ath gestured towards an opening that wasn't so much there as not not there. "After you."

"Couldn't I just stay for a little while?" De'Numbat tried.

"Not really."

"I'd like to say goodbye."

"Isn't this why we're all here?"

"I could help. De'Bacteria?"

Bacteria, there were gazillions of them, a thirty minute life-span, more bacteria on and inside all other living creatures than cells of the body itself. A teaspoon of soil, a bucket of sea water, ga-fucking-zillions. Nobody had ever seen De'Bacteria, only heard their dulcet voice. "I'm everywhere and nowhere, baby."

Consensus was, De'Bacteria was some kind of

quantum wave-form.

"That's not within my gift," De'Ath replied.

Head low, De'Numbat plodded towards the opening that wasn't not there.

"Wait!" De'Swine exclaimed. "I mean, please wait. I— I have a question." Their brow furrowed. "Actually, two questions. Is it—? I mean, can I actually ask a question?"

De'Ath turned back. "In actual fact, you are allowed three."

This was news. A ripple of shock ran through the gathered Deaths.

"Oh, good. Well, then I— I just wondered— I was wondering— I mean, I—"

"De'Swine," De'Apes broke in. "You've got this."

With a terse nod of appreciation, De'Swine steadied themselves. "I was wondering if this world, these living things whose guides we are, if they are the only life that there is."

"I'm afraid that's classified."

"Oh." Nonplussed, De'Swine looked here and there. "Classified. That's not really an answer."

De'Ath smiled a quiet smile. "Just because you don't like what you've been told doesn't mean I haven't answered your question."

"Fair point," De'Apes whispered at De'Swine's shoulder. "Let them have it."

"All right. What I really mean is, at some point all life's going to end. The sun becomes a red giant and swallows the solar system and it's gone. Maybe there's life elsewhere, but it doesn't matter because heat death of the universe, entropy, disorder. All life dies and you gather all of us in."

De'Ath acknowledged the truth with a dip of their head.

"So, and this is my second question, who comes for

you?"

Silence fell. De'Ath stood with mouth agape and one finger raised.

"And who come for them?" De'Apes said.

"Hehe," De'Numbat giggled. "It's De'Aths all the way up."

And everyone, every Death who had heard De'Numbat laugh and seen De'Ath's complete discombobulation, no longer felt quite so scared of the future.

"Hi, guys!" De'Dodo exclaimed, materialising out of a silvery-blue shimmer. "Guess what?! I mean, WOW!! De'Apes, your guys actually did it! Full props to them! Terrific!" De'Dodo did a little disco dance with splayed wings and fancy footwork. "Dodos are back, people, and that means so am I!"

Then De'Dodo took in the sombre mood, the fact that De'ath themselves stood beside De'Numbat looking worried, confused and, if truth be told, a little frightened. "Have I interrupted something?"

De'Swine burst out laughing.

An instant later De'Apes did too. "Come on," They hung an affectionate arm over De'Swine's shoulder. "Let's see if any of my lot's trying to shoot one of yours."

Sundog 4

Alice Dryden

Space: 2024.

Somewhere beyond the Moon, a man-made construction hangs against the backdrop of the sky. Consisting of conical living quarters joined by a spindle to the spinning plate that provides power and artificial gravity, it resembles nothing so much as a giant martini glass. This is the headquarters of Space Force, ever vigilant in protecting Terra from the hostile alien menace, and the base for its fleet of five Sundog spacecraft.

"Rex Rocket and Captain Clay, report to Commodore Hawks immediately. Repeat…"

The space station reverberated with the sound of the loudspeaker. Rex Rocket, pilot, and Captain Clay, navigator, looked up from their poker game.

Rex, one eyebrow quirked, set his Space Force cap atop his dark, curly hair and rose to his feet.

"Clay, we're needed. Put your trousers back on and come along."

Moving walkways conveyed them to the office of Commodore Hawks, Head of Space Force. Selena, the voiceless, telepathic alien who worked as the Commodore's secretary, raised a hand in shy greeting. Clay returned the wave.

"She knows exactly what you're thinking, you know," Rex muttered to him. The navigator blushed crimson.

"Ah, Rocket; Clay." Commodore Hawks's transporter chair, hovering a few inches above the floor, spun to face the crew of Sundog 4. "One of Earth's most renowned scientists, a Professor Moonflower, has been assigned to help us in our research against the alien foe. Your job is to meet the three o'clock Earth to Moon shuttle and bring the Professor back here. And to pick me up some brandy from the duty-free."

At a gesture from the Commodore, Selena dimmed the lights. Shutters rolled down over the windows, transforming them into display screens carrying data, images and statistics faster than the eye could follow.

"One more thing. The aliens are one jump ahead of us all the time, anticipating our every move. We suspect there is a spy within Space Force. Please, keep your eyes open and your mouths shut."

Clay's jaw closed with a click.

"I don't have to tell you how important this mission is to the safety of mankind and our future in space," the Commodore continued. "Good luck, boys."

As their commanding officer lifted an arm to salute, the hoverchair jumped forward, bashing Clay in the kneecaps.

"Oops. Sorry."

Pilot and navigator walked jerkily to the transport tubes that conveyed them directly to the cockpit of their craft.

"I swear he does that on purpose," Clay complained, fastening his seatbelt.

"Oh, let the old man have his fun. He can't damage you."

"No, but he sure can hurt."

"Preparing to launch Sundog 4!" came the voice over the loudspeaker. "Five! Four! Three! Two! One!"

The walls of the launch chamber reverberated with the noise and flames of the liftoff. The domed roof peeled back, revealing a black sky sequinned with stars, and Sundog 4 lifted lazily upwards as if travelling along a wire. Rotating through ninety degrees, the blue and white craft wobbled off in the direction of the Moon.

Her crew settled back into the routine of the flight, Clay reading off coordinates from the screen in front of him while Rex made adjustments to the steering.

"I have been to Luna before, Clay, I don't need step-by-step directions…" Rex was saying when a cockpit lamp lit up insistent ruby.

"UFO, angels one five!"

The enemy craft was flat, square and black with a tapered tail, like a stingray moving through space. It spun on its longitudinal axis, easily evading the missile Clay dispatched, and returned fire in a glittering beam of magenta light.

Rex hauled on the controls and they looped around, heading directly into the firestorm. The alien ship fired again and again, but each burst fell short as Sundog 4's rocket thrusters glowed ochre.

"Look out, Rex! That was way too close!"

"Why do you care? Everyone knows you're

indestructible since you survived your kidnap by the aliens."

"You're not."

"Aww. Thanks for worrying."

"If I get blown to bits I'm gonna need someone to pick up all the pieces."

Sundog 4 shot past the alien craft and slewed sideways, allowing Captain Clay to fire a broadside volley. The black ship disintegrated in a cloud of debris and grey cottonball smoke.

"Code green. Enemy ship destroyed. Hello Moonbase, Sundog 4 requesting permission to land."

"Permission granted. Come on down, Sundog 4."

After docking, they took a pneumatic lift to the arrivals hall, where the passengers from the Earth shuttle were milling about. They looked around for their charge, Captain Clay holding up a sign on which he had written PROFESSER.

Professor Moonflower stepped towards them. Her silver space suit was draped over a slim, curved body. Above large blue eyes, her blonde hair seemed sculpted to her head like a space helmet. She held a cigarette between two fingers.

"That," Clay said at last, "is a woman."

"You don't say. Here's some change—go put it in the parking meter while I help the Professor with her luggage."

A small, blonde child with pigtails trotted after Professor Moonflower, holding a puppy in her arms.

"Professor, this isn't a field trip to the petting zoo," Rex protested. "Space Force is no place for kids."

"This is Scarlet, my adopted daughter. She has an IQ of 193 and a photographic memory. She will be helping me with my work," the Professor said firmly. "Do you have any idea what childcare costs these days?" she added in a whisper.

The puppy wriggled free of its owner's arms, bounced to the floor and scampered over to Rex, grabbing the leg of his spacesuit in its teeth and shaking.

"Fireball! Fireball, sit!"

Obediently, the puppy sat back on its haunches.

"Bark," it said, swishing its tail.

"'Bark'?" Grinning, Rex knelt to pet the fuzzy head. "Okay, you three. Let's go."

The little girl was entranced by the sight of Sundog 4. She ran up to Clay, who was leaning against the hull, swinging the ignition key in his fingers.

"Is that your ship? How fast will it go? Can you do a barrel roll? What's the thrust to weight ratio?"

"Scarlet Moonflower, meet Captain Clay," said Rex.

"Captain."

"Scarlet."

They shook hands solemnly, while Fireball bounced around their ankles.

"Now let's all hop into that supercar of yours so we can get started," suggested the Professor.

The return journey passed without event, bar the odd barrel roll. Professor Moonflower and Scarlet, securely strapped in the passenger seats, gazed out at the vast spread of space. Scarlet held her puppy on her lap.

They docked as smoothly as if the film of their launch had been run through the projector backwards, and Sundog 4 settled back in its cradle.

"We'll take you to Commodore Hawks straightaway," Rex said. "There's no time to lose!"

"So, does he have a first name, or what?" asked the professor, watching Clay walk ahead of them.

"Search me. He always insists on 'Captain'," Rex told her.

"He walks like he's got a stick up his—"

"Scarlet! That's not nice!"

The little girl shrugged. "I'm precocious," she explained.

"For the last time, 'precocious' is not the same as 'rude'."

"Commodore Hawks is very anxious to meet you," Rex said hastily as he led the way into the Commodore's office. "Er…sir? Sir, wake up."

"I was not asleep!" Hawks's eyes snapped open. "I was…dictating telepathically to Selena."

The alien nodded vigorously.

"Welcome to Space Force, Professor Moonflower! We've prepared a laboratory for you with all the state-of-the-art equipment you requested," Hawks continued hastily. "You'll have everything you require for your experiments. Rex and the Captain will escort you there now."

"Rex Rocket, Captain Clay and Professor Moonflower to the laboratory!" announced the loudspeaker.

"Okay, okay! I'm standing right here!" Rex rolled his eyes at the ceiling. "Right, Prof, let's go."

"Is there any chance of a cup of tea first?" asked the Professor as soon as they were clear of the office. "It was a long flight."

"Sure!" Captain Clay led the way to the canteen. While the others sat, he fetched a pot of tea for the Professor, along with lemonade and a slice of cake for her daughter, and a bowl of water for the puppy.

"He's very domesticated, Mom," Scarlet observed as Clay headed back for the sugar. "You should marry him."

Her mother looked at the captain thoughtfully. "Not a bad idea, though a little presumptuous," she admitted. "What did we discuss about carrying out thorough research before reaching a conclusion?"

Before Scarlet could answer, an explosion shook the

space station so that it rocked in orbit.

In the Commodore's office, lamps lit red. Selena crossed to one of the wall screens and tapped urgently at its readout.

"Yes, Selena, I know," said the Commodore. "The laboratory is completely destroyed. Seal off the section and dispatch Sundogs 1 and 3 to chase off the intruder."

Selena flicked switches and pressed buttons to communicate the Commodore's orders. Although she could not speak, her eyes made her distress obvious.

A thick pall of smoke rolled through the canteen. Fireball howled.

"Is everyone all right?" Rex asked, picking himself up. "Clay, get out from under that table. You indestructible guys might consider protecting those of us who are…er… destructible."

"Being destructed *hurts*."

They returned to the Commodore's office at a stiff jog, Rex navigating the identical-looking corridors with the ease of long familiarity.

"We're fine!" Captain Clay announced, bursting through the door.

Selena rose from her seat, her expressive eyes filled with joy. Clay gazed at her with his head tilted to one side and a tender expression on his face. Professor Moonflower surveyed the scene.

"Well," she said to herself. "Looks like another night in with the Battery Boy for me."

"I'm sorry?" Rex asked.

"Nothing. See, Scarlet? Thorough research needed." She raised her cigarette to her lips.

"If we hadn't stopped for tea, we'd have been blown to smithereens along with the laboratory," Captain Clay pointed out.

The Commodore's chair hovered towards them. Clay

moved smartly backwards.

"We'll set you up a temporary lab so you can get to work," he promised the Professor. "I'm sorry the conditions won't be what you expected but do remember we are in a state of war."

"I'm sorry, but I can't work while I know that all our lives, including a young child's, are constantly in danger." The Professor lowered her cigarette.

"You want a light for that?" asked Clay.

"No, thank you. Commodore, you need to make catching the spy in our midst your highest priority."

The Commodore hovered his chair up to her. She stood her ground.

"While you are under my command you will do as I say," he growled. "Unless you want me to ship you back to Terra in handcuffs."

"I'm not under your command. I am a civilian, here voluntarily. And we're a long way from Terra, Hawks."

"Excuse me." Scarlet pushed up her glasses, which were slipping down her snub nose. "You're looking for someone who's involved in everything that goes on at Space Force, but whom you barely even notice. Do I need to make myself any clearer?"

"Of course!" said Rex. "Selena!"

He drew his pistol and levelled it at the alien. Selena raised her hands above her head, and a single tear rolled down her cheek.

"Now just a minute." Captain Clay grabbed his friend's arm. The gun went off, sending a bolt of light zipping into the ceiling loudspeaker.

"Hey!" said the loudspeaker.

"Yes, Rex, let's not be hasty," added Hawks. "Good secretaries are hard to find."

"No, you idiots!" Scarlet Moonflower stomped her

foot. "*Not* Selena! Who hears everything and knows exactly what's going on around here and where everyone is? *Think!*" She pointed at a corner of the ceiling.

"Of course!" Clay slapped his forehead. "The loudspeaker guy!"

From the speaker came a muffled clatter, like the sound of a microphone dropping, followed by a hasty scuffle.

"Now you've done it," muttered Rex. "Come on!"

All four—five, with Fireball—raced out of the office and up a series of spiral stairways to the observation pod that stuck out from the space station like an olive on a cocktail stick. Rex threw himself against the door, which burst open.

"I've never been here before," said Clay, gazing around him with interest.

"Nobody *ever* comes here!" A silver-skinned alien with eyes like bulbous amber lamps rose from his seat at the microphone, brandishing an empty mug at the intruders. "Not even the tea lady! That's why none of you knew there was a spy in your midst. You were outsmarted by my species' superior intellect."

"Fascinating," murmured the Professor, peering at him.

He blinked. "Are *you* the tea lady?"

"No, I am not. And that's sexist. See, your species is no better than ours."

"Well said, cutie," approved Captain Clay.

"My people cannot allow you Terrans to overrun the galaxy! We will destroy you! Starting right here and now, with Space Force!"

He waved a spindly arm at the squat metal box on his desk. A spectrum of lights flashed along the top, and a digital display winked SIG in green.

"That means it's receiving a signal from my home

planet," the alien spy told them. "This is a powerful bomb which will go off in three of your Terran minutes—enough time for me to get away in the escape capsule, while your base is blown to smithereens."

Rex ran to the microphone. "Selena! Hawks! Evacuation procedure! Get everyone out of there!"

"I've also disconnected the loudspeaker. And now—farewell!"

He made for the airlock. Before he could spin the wheel that would open the first door, Fireball shot through Rex's legs and attached himself to the spy's ankle, growling.

"Get off of me, you big rat!" He shook his leg, but the puppy clung on.

"Don't hurt my puppy, you…you *dick spanner*!"

"Scarlet, that's not nice. Nor is it a thing," gasped the Professor.

Rex Rocket launched himself across the room and landed a textbook punch on the point of the spy's chin. The alien fell backwards, smacking his head against the airlock door, and slid unconscious to the metal deck.

"Nice," said Scarlet.

"Clay, tie him up." Rex knelt to inspect the bomb. "What do we do? Professor?"

The Professor frowned as she examined the array of lights, buttons and wires.

"Sort of twizzle that knob a bit," she suggested at last.

"Is that the best contribution cutting-edge science has to make?" asked Rex.

"Hey, *I* didn't punch out the only person who knew how to disarm the bomb."

"Let me try," said Scarlet. She produced a miniature toolkit from the pocket of her space dungarees and set to work, the tip of her tongue protruding from the corner of her mouth.

144

"Less than thirty Terran seconds left," muttered Captain Clay, dabbing a bead of sweat from his brow.

"Clay, you're *from* Terra. You can just say seconds," Rex reminded him.

"There!" Scarlet sat back, took off her glasses and polished them on the hem of Clay's jacket. On the bomb, a green light winked into life, flickered, then held steady. The display read: FAB.

"That was smart work, kid. There's a place for you in Space Force when you grow up," Rex promised.

"Scarlet is going to be a scientist," Professor Moonflower said firmly. "Like her mother."

"Actually I'm gonna join the Secret Service," Scarlet told them both. "Or…or be a vicar."

Rex ruffled her hair. "Why not both?" he chuckled.

"The last laugh will be mine, Space Force!" Leaping to his feet, the spy pulled a silver sphere from his pocket and tossed it towards them. For a moment, nobody moved as they watched it bounce and roll. Then the alien sprang into the escape capsule, his evil cackles cut off abruptly by the closing airlock.

"I thought you tied him up!" yelled Rex.

"You know I'm not very good with knots!"

"You know what you *are* good at?"

"Oh no."

With these heroic words, and a little help from Rex Rocket's outstretched leg, Captain Clay threw himself on top of the grenade. Professor Moonflower covered Scarlet's eyes. An explosion shook the observation pod, which filled with smoke and debris.

The curved outer wall of the Starlite Bar was clear, offering a view of the sky. A three-piece band played softly in harmony.

Rex Rocket, resplendent in a midnight blue tuxedo, placed an elaborate cocktail at Professor Moonflower's elbow and took a seat beside her.

"How's Captain Clay?" she asked.

"Oh, he'll pull himself together in a few hours."

"I feel I should thank him for what he did."

"Better wait till morning. It's not a pretty sight."

"Can I go look? For science?" asked a small voice.

"Scarlet! It is way past your bedtime, angel. Off you go this nanosecond!"

"Grown-ups get all the fun," growled Scarlet, stomping out.

There was silence except for the melody from the band, and Commodore Hawks swearing at the pinball machine in the corner.

"So. Are the grown-ups having fun?" Rex asked.

"I think so."

Outside their bubble the Moon loomed large, reflecting in the Professor's eyes. Rex watched her cigarette as it travelled to her mouth and back. He cleared his throat.

"Why don't we give the Battery Boy the night off, hm?"

"I'm sorry?"

Rex blushed, looking down at his hands as they rested on the bar. "You know. Launch Sundog 6."

"I thought there were only five Sundogs?"

"Stand by for action?"

"You mean…" She reached out and laid her hand on top of his.

Rex nodded; one eyebrow quirked.

"No strings attached?" she asked.

"No strings attached."

Bootleg Baba's Beautiful Claws

Marisca Pichette

Sand is my worst enemy. Not guns, not prisons buried in drifting asteroids they think I can't escape. Not heavily armed patrol ships or false allies, nor burns from triple suns. Not upstart babes thinking they can shoot further and better than an old woman.

I can deal with those. I have. War and interrogation and gruelling chases across space are nothing.

Nope, it's the fucking sand that gets me.

We grind to a halt for the seventeenth time on this crapshoot moon. *Fucking fucker in an imploding star.* I check my suit seals before opening the pilot compartment and climbing out into unbreathable air. Sand skitters across my helmet. Mocking me.

"Alright, darling." I descend the ladder welded to Kieken's right leg; her ankle is swamped in stubborn crystals. My boots sink into the awful stuff and I kick my way through, brushing at her knee joint. Yup, clogged.

Fucking sand.

"As soon as we drop this package, we're getting off this cosmos-forsaken rock," I promise Kieken, prying sand from her joints.

It takes twenty minutes to do the right leg, my grunting and swearing drowned out by the constant *tiktiktik* of sand hitting my helmet and suit.

My back screams at the end of it. Two days of this bullshit just to deliver a four-foot case of contraband. If the compensation wasn't so high, I'd be out of here faster than a comet on fancy drugs.

Fucking fucking *sand.*

When I've rested long enough, I duck under Kieken's rusty belly and examine her left leg. Not as bad as the right, but it still takes me a good ten minutes to clear the sand out. Finally finished, I uncover the panel on my arm. Sand catches in the hinges, scratching the screen.

Did I mention I fucking hate sand?

"The coordinates put the call about forty minutes away," I tell Kieken, leaning against her leg to ease my back. I play possible scenarios in my head, planning for various reactions when we get there. For years now, I've been met with scepticism when I turn up to jobs. Like I'm too old to be doing this.

Hon, it's my age that makes me so damn good at it. How many people suspect an old woman of smuggling? How many people expect an old woman to have a gun hidden under her tit? Under *each* tit?

Sand begins gathering in the folds of my suit. I can't linger too long, or I'll freeze up just like Kieken. I arch my back, feeling vertebrae grind into reluctant place. Crossing back under her belly, I climb up her right leg and re-enter the pilot compartment, trying to leave as much sand outside as possible.

"Okay, darling. Let's try this again." I work Kieken's pedals, feel her clawed feet flex. We begin striding over the sandy landscape. I pat the control panel. "Good girl."

Forty minutes later, we're in the shelter of a raw cliff, Kieken dodging rocks as she trots alongside. I lean forward, squinting through the view panel. The cliff is more or less featureless. But somewhere behind that benign rock, there's a smuggler's den.

My location finder flashes. We're now at the coordinates we were given. I crank Kieken into neutral, rocking back in my seat as she settles.

Silence. I don't move. I've been doing this for a long time. I know better than to leave the armoured safety of Kieken's body.

After five minutes, Kieken's proximity sensor pings. Motion detected around her legs and behind. I flick my speaker on.

"Baba Ptica Tihotapec here, with a delivery for…" I check the panel on my arm, sand dribbling into my lap, "Pesek Kralj."

The sensor shadows creeping under Kieken's belly swan out in front. Now I can see them: grunts brandishing guns and looking menacing. I can't help grinning. Clients always try to intimidate me. I can't blame them; I don't look like much—alone, in a beat-up runner mech, carrying extremely valuable goods. If I counted every time a client tried to kill me after a delivery, I'd have a bad memory for every wrinkle on my body. For every damned grain of sand in this pilot seat.

What they never seem to consider is I'm *not* alone. I've got Kieken.

They're gesturing. I flick on my receiving speaker.

"—and disembark."

"Sorry, missed that, mate. Come again?"

The grunt who was talking tenses. I can't see his expression through the tinted glass of his helmet, but I like to think he's pissed. I tend to have that effect on people. It's part of my charm.

"Open your cargo compartment and drop the package now. Then disembark."

"You Kralj?"

"I am Vojak Vdan. I stand for Pesek Kralj's interests. You will negotiate with me."

I lean back in my seat. Why do they always pull this shit? "My deal's with Kralj, not you."

"You will—" I click off the receiving speaker and brush sand from my arms. Vojak's gestures become bigger. He stops, tries again. On about the third try, he realizes I'm not listening. He turns to his fellow grunts. Guns and arms wave in various directions, mostly at me.

I get more comfortable. I don't mind waiting. At least the sand can't reach us here, in the shelter of the cliff.

Two of the grunts break off from the group and disappear. Kieken's proximity sensor pings. They're under her, trying to pry the cargo door open. I clear my throat.

"You don't want to do that."

Vojak turns. I click on the receiving speaker. His voice filters into the pilot compartment.

"That package is ours."

Here we go. "Actually, it's Kralj's. He's the one paying me. So don't be surprised if I hold onto it until I see him holding a nice, shiny case of cash with my name on it."

Kieken's sensor is still flashing. I grit my teeth. "Are you really pulling this on me?"

Vojak levels his gun at us. "You're here to make a delivery. If you refuse to make it, we'll take what we ordered by force."

I switch off both speakers. "Heat death save me from

idiots." I brush sand from Kieken's interior casing. "They don't know what you're capable of, darling. You can't blame them, really. They only see what they expect to see."

With Vojak's gun still aimed at us, I reach across the pilot compartment, working a set of custom controls only Kieken has.

I left her in neutral for a reason.

Manual control: off. Sitting back in my seat, I let Kieken take charge.

Her knees bend faster than mine can. She drops, squashing the grunts trying to open her cargo compartment. With both speakers off, I don't hear their last words.

Bullets skip off Kieken's body like especially nasty sand. I don't move to return fire. Kieken's a better fighter than I've ever been.

Three blasts from her front guns rock me back in my seat. We lurch forward. Vojak, clever as ever, starts running. Kieken allows him a head start. She always loves a chase.

Vojak makes a break for the cliff face. The rock seems featureless, but somewhere is the hidden entrance to the smuggler's den. He's heading for…a divot of rock with a slightly deeper shadow. *Ah.*

"Now, darling."

Kieken lunges forward, her left claw wrapping around Vojak. We balance on her right leg, grinding to a halt.

I click on my speakers. Muffled groaning, Vojak's limbs dangling uselessly. I can see the den entrance clearly now. *Thanks, mate.*

"Where's Kralj?"

"H-he—" Vojak gasps, struggling in Kieken's grasp. "Dead."

Ah, shit. "And my money?"

"In…side."

"Thanks."

I switch the speakers off before Kieken squeezes her claws together. I don't need to hear that. When she's dropped what remains of Vojak, I can feel her satisfaction in the humming of her engine. There may not be a neural link between us, but we don't need one. Not after all this time.

I unlatch the hatch, doing a quick scan before climbing up and out. Kieken won't fit in the smuggler's den. From this point on, I'm on my own.

Problem? Never.

That said, my knees pop ominously when I drop onto the hard ground. I shake off the slight tingling, leaning my still aching back against Kieken's right leg. She's killed six grunts out here. Probably a fraction of the ones awaiting me inside the den. I ready my guns—two on my hips, two strapped to my chest, extra ammo and a long-range gun on my back. Then there are the knives.

I like knives.

I push off from Kieken, giving her leg a final pat. I leave her in neutral, just in case.

The den entrance is a narrow rift in the cliff face. I enter sideways, one gun drawn low. I can see artificial light ahead. It's quiet, which either means the rest of the smugglers killed each other or they're waiting for me. Kieken's activity outside was anything but noiseless.

I touch my helmet, ensuring the backup seals are active. If I'm going to die, I'd rather it not be for something stupid like a leak in my suit. I've lived too long to go that way.

The tunnel into the den doesn't branch until the end, where it opens into a small room. I take the corner slowly, ready to shoot the first thing that moves.

Rather than angry grunts, I'm faced with an empty table, chairs haphazardly clustered around it. There's no lock to make an atmosphere in here. I wonder if they've locked rooms further in, or have a ship stowed somewhere. Probably the latter. It's a lot cheaper to keep a ship around with life support settings than set up a safe room. Besides, these guys don't seem like the type to hang around.

I hug the wall, passing through the empty room. No sign of my money, not that I put much stake in Vojak's final words. I give the room a final visual sweep and head further into the den.

The tunnel continues without branches. How deep does it go? Guns or not, it's not smart to stray too far from Kieken. I've made that mistake too many times before.

Will I make it again? Probably.

After about a minute's walking, the tunnel opens into another empty room. Now I'm extra suspicious. Clearly nothing's been packed up. While I still don't see the cash promised for my delivery, supplies are scattered everywhere. There are grunts around. Hiding? Hunting? Waiting to ambush an old woman covered in weapons?

I kind of want it to be the last one. It at least makes things straightforward.

After this empty room, there are two more. Finally I'm following the tunnel towards something that looks like natural light. The other side of the cliff? Must be. My left hand feels empty, so I pull my other gun from its holster on my hip. I walk along the wall, feeling the tension in my calves. As I near the exit, sand blows in my face, skittering across my helmet.

It clears in time for me to see the ship squatting right outside, guns pointed at me.

Fucking sand.

Nothing I carry is any use against a ship. If I run back down the tunnel, they could fill the rock with fire and collect my singed corpse in a few hours. I lean against the tunnel opening, deciding what to do.

"Who are you?" a voice crackles from the ship's speakers. "Where is Vojak?"

"Really dead," I yell back, gesturing with my gun. "I'm the smuggler Kralj hired."

"You have the goods?"

"Not *on* me, obviously."

"Where are they?"

"You gonna pay me? Or do you want to join Vojak in pieces?"

Static. Sand blows over my boots. I hate this moon. And I'm getting really tired of the bullshit.

The speaker crackles like malnourished brain cells attempting to communicate. "We'll kill you and recover the goods ourselves."

I shrug. "Good luck with that."

Without holstering my guns, I tap my wrist against the rock, triggering the panel to open. It's full of sand. Fucking fuck.

Shaking my arm, I wait for the ship to shoot. I wonder how many grunts are on board. Maybe I should charge the shitheads. If I made it past the ship's guns, I'd have a decent chance.

I manage to shake away most of the sand so I can see the screen. I'm about to call Kieken when I hear the telltale sound of weapons powering up.

Tunnel or open air? Sand blows in my face. Fuck it, I'll take my chances in the tunnel.

I bolt back inside as the ship fires. Rock cracks, pebbles pummelling my back. Ignoring the pain as best I can, I follow the tunnel into the last room, throwing furniture behind me. The rock reverberates with more explosions. I decide to stop wasting time trying to slow whatever pursuers I might have. I run.

Distant explosions shift to ominous rumbles. I sprint

through the empty rooms, stretches of dark tunnel feeding my nightmares in between. I've just reached the first room when the rumbles change again, this time to something that sounds exactly like an underground space collapsing.

I throw myself the last few feet out the other side of the cliff. Dust follows me with the deafening crash of stone. Elbows on my knees, I gasp lungfuls of air from my tank. When my body's done screaming, I notice the lack of explosions. The ship's stopped firing.

I straighten. My heart stops.

"Kieken!"

I stumble out from the cliff, looking around. "Kieken!!!"

No sign of her, apart from the dead grunts still lying where they fell. The ship will be coming after me. Where the fuck did she go?

"KIEKEN!!" I remember the panel on my arm. I clear the last of the sand off and try to track her location. An error message greets my request. Wonderful.

Engines—whining somewhere close and getting louder. I force my body into a jog along the cliff side, putting some distance between me and the den entrance. I've just ducked into a slight alcove when the smuggler's ship appears over the top of the cliff. Sand kicked up by its engines flies everywhere. It pivots to face the den entrance. I flatten myself as best I can as the guns fire into the rock.

When the dust has cleared, bits of rock rolling to rest by my feet, the ship lands. My pulse does a little skip, fear dribbling away. *Finally.*

The first grunt to emerge I ignore. Also the second. And the third. I pull the long gun from my back and aim at the ship's door.

When five grunts are on the ground, I blast the shit out of their escape route. Two of them yell, diving to the dirt. I give them a second to cower, killing the other three in a sweep of fire.

I don't have much time before the rest of the crew figures out the situation and turns the ship guns on me. I run towards it now, while the guns are still facing the cliff.

"Wai–" I shoot the grunt before he can finish his plea. The last one lies on the ground, groaning. He's been hit with a piece of the ship. Poetic.

I put a bullet in his shooting arm to be safe, then turn my attention on the ship, engines whining. As it rises, I pour everything I've got into ripping a new asshole in its hull. I empty my long gun and pull out my hip guns. It hovers above me, engines working to get it into place. A hull isn't as vulnerable as a door, and my fire isn't doing much. Soon I'll be staring down a barrel.

My muscles are cussing me out, joints joining the chorus. I won't be able to run again.

So this is how I finally die.

I level all I've got at the ship. I hear its guns charge up.

In the glare of an unfamiliar sun, I spot something on top of the cliff. I shouldn't look, but I do. At the same time, the ship fires.

Rock and dirt explode around me. Briefly, I fly.

I see Kieken falling, claws outstretched. She lands on top of the ship, ripping into the hull. My back slams into the ground with enough force to make me lose grip on my guns. My head smacks down next, rupturing the seal of my helmet. The backup hums in almost immediately, accompanied by a puff of frigid air, like the fleeting kiss of death.

Next time, it seems to whisper.

I lie on the shaking ground, staring at an atmosphereless sky. I'm sure I've broken something this time. I can't hear anything over the ringing in my ears.

156

Gradually, my extremities regain feeling. After what seems like ages, I'm able to drag myself up to a sitting position.

The smuggler's ship is wedged against the side of the cliff. Ripped metal gapes where its hull used to be. If the crew inside weren't wearing suits when Kieken attacked, they're dead now.

I look away from the wreck, holding my neck as I gingerly turn my head. Shit, I'm hurt bad.

"There you are, darling." My voice is hardly more than a wheeze. I'm still getting my breath back.

Kieken stands over me, her claws shining. She rotates her guns: a motion I recognize as gloating.

"Why'd you have to wander off? Nearly got my ass blasted."

Kieken crouches, the pilot compartment easing open. I take the hint, using her ladder leg to haul my battered body inside. I breathe a sigh, settling back in her seat, safe as can be. I switch her onto manual and walk back to the wreck, picking through remnants with her lovely claws.

With some tenacious ripping, I find more cash than I'm owed. I pass it up to Kieken's cargo compartment. I keep Kralj's package, too. I'll sell it again on a different moon. One without sand.

"Okay, darling. Let's go."

My head swims. I switch Kieken over to her own control and close my eyes, letting the motion of her running lull me into a well-deserved nap.

By the time I awake, we're hours away from the pulverized smuggler's den. Kieken keeps us on course, heading to the rusty, sand-infested layby that's what counts for a port out here. I file this moon away as a place I'll never visit again and buy us passage on a freighter to the other end of the solar system.

Laughs in Space

The whole journey, I keep finding it—in the folds of my suit, in the seams of my pilot seat, clogging up Kieken's controls.

Fucking *sand.*

So You Want to Kill Hitler: A Student's Primer

Lindz McLeod

Students enrolling in Present Studies at our university were actively encouraged to try to kill Hitler before attending their first class. The faculty, after much debate, had agreed that—in their collective experience—it was best to let the postgrads get it all out of their systems before they could be trusted to settle down. Despite what applicants wrote on their personal statements, sooner or later even the most pacifist student was determined to have a go at achieving past world peace through the simplest means.

The professor of Historical Accuracy normally oversaw the timeline, but I'd received a pleading email early that morning accompanied by a photograph of her ankle in a cast. I would have preferred to stay hidden amongst my beloved stacks—a shipment had just arrived and, while I trusted my assistants, I took great enjoyment in unpacking and carefully cataloguing each book—but needs must when the devil drives. Or in this case, a history professor. It amounted to much the same thing, in my opinion.

Instead of the library, I headed towards the timeline room, coffee in one hand, satchel slung over my shoulder I bumped the door open with my hip. They'd stopped locking it back in '91, on the basis that people kept breaking into the room anyway and the wooden frame wasn't getting any younger.

Swigging my coffee, I selected the least battered compass from a peg holding dozens—measure twice, jump once, they always said—and bounced through time to the last known jump. Kellerman was in 1942, cowering behind an overturned table, his forehead beaded with sweat. Bullets ricocheted off the walls around us. I slouched so as not to present a target, sipped my coffee, and made a face. Time dilation was a temperature roulette and had reduced my beverage to tepid bathwater. "Good morning, Jacob."

"Um. Hi. Who are you?" He returned fire before crouching again. "And where's Dr Kendrick?"

"Bogged down, I'm afraid. You're stuck with me for the time being." I chuckled but he didn't seem to appreciate my pun. Glancing around, I noted the cornices and crown mouldings, painted a pleasant cream. The wall in front of us—which had once been a rather nice shade of green, judging by the wall beyond the small barricade—was now little more than a pockmarked lunar landscape. "Germany, right? Was this particular date your first jump?"

"No, I've been at it for a couple of decades already." He scowled. "I'm not an idiot."

"Mmm," I said, and sipped my coffee again as fragments of plaster rained down onto my clean blouse.

"I just thought—" A bullet zinged between us, smashing a leg off the cabinet. "I didn't realize there would be so many. I thought I'd just nip in, shoot him, and be out in no time. But they're bloody everywhere."

I pulled out the handbook, imaginatively titled *So You Want to Kill Hitler: A Student's Primer* and checked the list of questions I was supposed to ask to generate discussion. "Which current or past events did you intend to impact?"

"I wanted to get him before the camps started."

I nodded. "Sensible start."

"Well, obviously this isn't going to work." He sighed and chucked the gun onto the floor. "I need to go back further. See you there."

He disappeared. I finished up my coffee and followed him. The compass read 1923; this small room was much colder than the hallway we'd just come from, but at least my coffee had heated up again. Through the steam fogging up my glasses, I surveyed the place. A storeroom for crockery and steins, by the looks of it. Only one exit. If the year hadn't been a decent indication, then the smell of hops would have cemented my guess. The cabinet in the corner creaked. I crossed and tugged the door open. "Alright in there?"

"Wonderful, thank you." Kellerman's chin was lodged between his knees, his spine curved into a tight question mark.

The cabinet itself was made of a beautiful dark wood, oiled to a high gleam, with ornate carvings adorning the edges. I rapped it with my knuckles, making him wince. "Good lad. Well, I'll let you get on with it. You don't want any reading material, by any chance?"

"I don't think so."

I rummaged around in my satchel. "Not even *The Curiosities of Ale and Beer?* You might be in there a while."

"Beer isn't really what's on my mind." His fingers were interlaced, the tanned skin pulled pale with strain.

I rummaged a bit further. "How about *How to Kill a Man in a Hundred Ways?*"

Kellerman shook his head.

"I've got the newest Sally Rooney," I wafted the book temptingly towards him. "Won't even be written for another six months. Don't ask how I got it."

He hesitated and then took it. "Thanks."

Dr Kendrick was all about learning on the job and keeping one's eyes open, but I was of the opinion that reading required one's eyes to be open, and if one had time to sit, one had time to read. Besides, Rooney was coasting these days. It would only take him a couple of hours to get through the slim novel. I sipped my still-steaming coffee. "Well, I'll see you in 1914."

"Wait, why—"

I jumped. The day was beautiful; sunny, and clear. Outside the cafe, chairs and tables littered the pavement. A young man sat at the table nearest the door, glumly smoking a cigarette. My coffee was now so hot it had turned into gas and was escaping through the vent in the lid. I slid the latch over it and pursed my lips. My assistants would probably be halfway through the new shipment by now. By the time I got back, there wouldn't be anything left to shelve or archive until next week.

I ducked into the cafe. Kellerman was behind the counter, slicing bread from thick, fresh loaves, and sighed when he saw me. My stomach rumbled, reminding me I hadn't packed snacks. "Hello Jacob. What's your latest plan?"

"I figured, everybody tries to shoot Gavrilo Principe, right? Kill the assassin before he can carry out the murder of the Archduke. But then I thought, well, everybody probably thinks the same way. I needed to come up with something different." He took out a small box and sprinkled powder into the sandwich, looking pleased with himself. "How many people have tried poisoning him?"

I'd read the stats beforehand. "A fair few, actually."

He deflated. "What? Really?"

"It's a strong idea, though." *Be supportive of sensible logical leaps*, the handbook had said. *Encourage them where you can.* "I can definitely see how you reached that conclusion," I added.

He didn't inflate again, just stood there, his fingers pressing hard into the crust of the bread. The handbook had advised me to be encouraging, without being enabling, but I wasn't sure I was walking that line particularly well. Without warning, Kellerman threw the sandwich at the wall, swore, and vanished from view. The young man outside glanced in at me, but I could already hear the rumble of a motor car coming down the street. I pulled my compass out and checked the next jump: 1913. Now that was a little way off the beaten path for most students.

Finally, something worth watching.

Nottinghamshire in November was brisk, so I pulled out a scarf from my satchel and wound it around my neck. Welbeck Abbey was a lovely sight, but there was little time to dawdle. Already the loaders were checking and filling guns, ready for the Duke of Portland and his esteemed guests to enjoy their shooting party. Amongst the small crowd of well-dressed men talking and laughing, I spotted the Archduke Ferdinand, who was dressed for the occasion in a top hat and tails. Kellerman was perched in a nearby tree, still wearing his long black coat, looking like the stuff of Poe's nightmares. My coffee was cool at best, but at least it was drinkable again. I offered the travel cup upwards but he waved me away.

"Not many people do this event." I chugged away, relaxing as sweet caffeine finally entered my system. "Bit of an outlier."

Kellerman perked up. "Well, you know, I did my research. Got here yesterday and screwed with one of the loader's boots. During the night I dug little holes in the grass and covered them over. Place is a minefield now." He caught my expression. "Not literally."

"And the logic behind this one?"

"The Archduke dies here, so Principe has no target. The course of the war is changed as a result."

"And what happens if Ferdinand is succeeded by someone else with the same ideas? Remember that history isn't a moment, it's a movement."

"Well, I—" He opened his mouth, thought better of it, and closed it again. "Fuck."

A shot rang out from the party. Overhead, a feathery corpse fluttered and fell to earth. Kellerman sighed. "See you in 1889?"

The crib was by the open window, where a soft spring breeze ruffled the baby's fine hair. Inside, the child slept on, tiny fingers opening and closing, grasping at nothing. Kellerman stood, one hand on the wooden-slatted side of the crib, staring down at the infant. We stood in silence for a few minutes; downstairs I could hear the clank of cooking utensils. A savoury smell drifted from the kitchen below; cabbage stew, if I was any judge, with a little fried pork on the side.

"Not going to smother the baby?" I asked.

Surprisingly few people actually murdered the baby, when it came down to it. Most preferred to kill the man himself, or failing that, went for the mother. Hardly her fault, but the reasoning was sound. Kellerman shrugged. "I was going to, but… I mean, it makes sense but when you're actually standing here…"

I didn't press the issue. "Did you read the Sally Rooney book?"

"Yeah." He plucked it from the inside pocket of his long coat and handed it over. "Didn't like it much."

"Oh?" I tucked the book back into my satchel.

"The characters were stupid. They could have just talked to each other," he added. In the crib, the baby smacked its lips, evidently dreaming of something delicious. In the street below, a dog barked twice, high and shrill. "I mean, half the plot is people misunderstanding each other or not saying something at a critical point."

"They could have," I conceded. "But sometimes talk isn't enough. People aren't always willing to listen. To hear certain things that might impact their worldview. You know what I mean?"

A muscle jumped in his jaw. "I'm not giving up yet."

"I'm not telling you what to do, Jacob. I'm only here to supervise."

His hands curled into fists. "So what's the answer?"

"What do you think is the answer?" I countered, feeling pleased that I was finally getting the hang of teaching. Seating myself on the rocking chair in the corner, I tucked the satchel between my knees. The strains of a slow waltz floated up from downstairs, strings soaring like clouds through a summer sky. "Go on."

Kellerman stared out of the window. "What about Nicholas II? He signed the Anglo-Russian Convention.

Without that, or maybe without the Triple Alliance beforehand putting pressure on—" He ran his fingers through his hair. "No, wait. It needs to be something even earlier. Bismarck, maybe. Yeah… Bismarck must be the key to the whole thing. Right?" He ran his tongue along his front teeth, studied my face. "You don't think it'll work."

"I know it won't work."

"Yeah, but—but…" He waved his hands around, groping for words. "Something has to, eventually."

"Why do you think that?" I pulled out my copy of *So You Want to Kill Hitler* again.

His shoulders drooped again. "Well, because."

I waited, but nothing more was forthcoming. "Sterling argument, Jacob."

"Look." He sighed. "Not that I don't appreciate the company, but I need to think really hard about my next approach." He blinked and then smiled, unexpectedly. "What was it you said? History isn't a moment, it's a movement?"

I didn't like his grin, which had a slightly manic edge to it. "Well, yes, but—"

He vanished.

I finally located Kellerman in the Upper Devonian, standing over something that looked half-lizard, half fish, poking it with the end of a slender tree branch. The tetrapod—far from running—was holding its own and hissing with unconcealed irritation.

"This is our shared ancestor, you know. *Elpistostege watsoni.* I looked it up." Moodily, he prodded the creature, who promptly bit the end off his stick.

I resisted the urge to inform him that while technically correct, he could have chosen the slightly closer *Acanthostega,* or gone a few million years back to *Eusthenopteron*, but these facts would probably only have driven him further down the Tetrapodomorpha hole.

"There must be a way! There must be!" His eyes were red-rimmed; exhaustion coupled with frustration.

"I understand. Really, I do. But you can't just keep going further back in the hopes that something will change." No one had actually bothered going this far back before—most of the students accepted their limitations around the 15th or 16th century—but I wasn't about to tell him that. Patting him on the shoulder, I surveyed the landscape of dense, lush forest and green undergrowth. Oxygen levels were slightly lower in this epoch; my lungs had started to ache. "Time to face facts."

The creature slithered back into the sea. He threw the stick at it, missed, then shoved his hands into his pockets. "Fine. You win. I'm done."

I smiled. "Good. Now you're beginning to understand how time works."

When we returned to the present, it was barely past 11 am. I hung up my compass on a peg and waited while Kellerman scanned his ID against the panel in the corner to record his trips. "Come on," I held open the door. "I'll walk you to your class, which should be starting in about three minutes."

"But I haven't been accepted yet."

I smiled. "Now you have."

"Wait, so all of this was a test?" He trotted to keep up. "Did I pass?"

"No. You failed more times than anyone else—"

"Oh."

"—but the course technically hasn't begun yet, so that doesn't matter."

He brightened. "Oh."

"The thing is, you can't change the past. It's already happened. Acceptance is key to understanding what you can change." I turned the corridor and headed towards the History block.

"Well?" he prompted, narrowly avoiding knocking a first-year to the ground in his excitement. "What can I change, then?"

"The future." I gestured towards the auditorium. Dr Kendrick paced the stage, limping slightly, as students filed into their seats. "Oh, and Jacob?"

He hesitated in the doorway.

"Good luck," I said, and meant it.

Shelf Life

Richard Dadd

My parents met the old-fashioned way, swiping for hours on a smartphone.

Not good-looking enough. Left.

That's how things were back then, you'd have to sift through an endless parade of unappealing selfies in a virtual deck.

Too fat. Left.

And you had to guess, of course, in those days. That was the thing.

Too skinny. Left.

You had to squint at the selfies, squint through the filters, try to imagine if the person would suit you.

Too far to the right. Left.

Follow a link to their social media feeds, try to get an

idea of them.

Too far to the left. Left.

Pictures of them with their mates.

Ugly tattoo. Left.

Ugly dog. Left.

Ugly husband who likes to watch. Left.

Left. Left. Left. Left. Left. Left. Left.

But then, if you were having an optimistic day, and the signs were good, well maybe you'd swipe right on that person. And maybe that person. And if you were lucky, once in a while, one of them might swipe right for you and there'd be a match. And maybe you'd even meet up in person. If the chat was good. Often it wasn't.

You might have a few potential suitors lined up in your inbox, in reserve. But you'd keep swiping away in case something better came along. Swipe. Swipe. Swipe. Until eventually, one person just stood out from the rest, and you'd move over to WhatsApp – that was their old-school messaging thing – and stop opening the dating app altogether. Delete it, even.

That's how it used to go, apparently.

The apps got cleverer as the years went by, of course. Added more bells and whistles. Different gimmicks. Different features.

Those old apps – they were called apps, little bits of software you'd download on your smartphone (people had to carry actual glass rectangles everywhere with them, which is ridiculous. And naturally, they were always dropping them. So everyone always had cracked screens. Mum's still got her old one in a drawer somewhere, but it doesn't turn on anymore.) Anyway, the apps, they all had names like – what were they again? Tundra? Flange? Bramble? Something along those lines anyway. Mum and Dad'll get all nostalgic about it if you let them. You only have to mention the olden days of the Internet and they get all misty-eyed. *"We used to have Facebook, I bet you don't remember Facebook, do you?"*

The thing that gets me is, once you'd matched, and you'd agreed to meet up, how long would it take for you both to work out if you really were suited to each other? Days, weeks, months of trying to suss each other out? And you'd both be on your best behaviour for a lot of that time, of course, which was misleading. So, in fact, it might take *years* to genuinely get to know each other. You could waste a good chunk of your twenties on someone who was never right for you in the first place! What kind of system is that? It was practically Victorian.

They swear things were better in their day, of course, they do. But then, so did Nan and Grandad, and they met in a pub for goodness' sake. A pub! How do you meet someone in a pub? What, just see them at a nearby table and walk up to them? *"Hi, I can see you're with your mates, and I'm a complete stranger, but I like the look of you, and wondered if maybe we could…"* What, chat? Exchange numbers? Absolutely mental behaviour. It's a miracle Grandad wasn't arrested on the spot for harassment. Different times, I suppose.

Anyway, sometimes I do wonder if Mum and Dad are right. Maybe things were better in their day. Nowadays, of course, it's all about the trailers.

The 4C interface is customisable. The one I like best is the 1980s video rental store. Nan and Grandad would approve. You materialise outside an idealised futuristic building that's all sails and fins and quirky lettering – Googie architecture they call that. You're on a wide boulevard with palm trees but no people or traffic, and the whole scene is bathed in a perpetual sunset. The automatic doors swish open and reveal a shop filled with row upon row of shelves of videotapes. Or DVDs. Like I say, it's customisable. There's a record shop version as well, that's quite good. Where you leaf through big old vinyl records, in a hipster music shop cafe that has towering Swiss cheese plants and a marmalade cat strolling about the place. And there's an underwater bookshop one as well, that's quite popular.

But yeah, the video shop's the one I like. There's light electronic synth music warbling atmospherically in the background, and the smell of popcorn and newly fitted carpet. And you browse the tapes and the titles are all just people's names with a tagline. So, like:

Imogen – jazz lover, explorer.

Aisha – putting myself out there again.

Maya – carpe diem baby!

Chantelle – don't know what to put here lol.

And then you pick a video (or vinyl record or book or whatever) and you look at the cover art, and read the back synopsis, and if you want to know more, well, then you select the trailer.

So as you know, I work on 4C. And no, I don't like the name either, but someone obviously thought they were being clever – "4C" like "foresee," get it? Anyway, regardless of the rubbish name, the way it works is that it basically generates a trailer for the relationship that you could have with whoever you pick off the shelf.

The simulation takes all the data that's known about you, which is everything, your entire digital footprint, and generates a tree of probabilities. Then it does the same for your potential partner and sort of mushes the results together. It knows everything – your habits, your politics, your health, your financial situation. So it's not going to show you some paradise future, with you driving fast cars and going on flashy holidays, it's realistic. And pretty damn accurate. Obviously, you've got to leave a little bit of room for the completely unforeseeable, there's a disclaimer about it not being 100% accurate – but on a purely statistical basis it's as close to a fortune teller as technology can build.

And it whizzes before your very eyes: the next few decades of your life, on fast forward. Or the next few weeks. Or a single date, if you're a poor match. A single date where you've got nothing to say to each other and it goes nowhere. A trailer of awkward silences, and jokes falling on deaf ears, and skipping dessert to get the bill. It can be pretty ruthless at times.

It's addictive as well, I'm not going to lie, glimpsing all those futures, all those parallel universes. Some people find it depressing, some people find it inspiring. It can be both.

After it launched it became apparent that an awful lot of people just never actually went on any of the dates at all, which we weren't expecting. Turns out loads of people are content to just sit at home and lose themselves in a dreamworld of two- or three-minute-long imaginary future relationships. They don't need to take the plunge and actually meet anyone.

They pick a partner off the shelf like selecting a song to stream, giving themselves a taste of a life they'll never live. They watch themselves marry people they've never even communicated with in real life. People who don't even know they exist. Hold their hand as they go through labour. Console them when their elderly parents die. Pick out a city break for their 10th wedding anniversary. And then three minutes later, when the trailer is over, decide not to even send an introductory message to that person. All that potential, unexplored outside the realms of a simulation. A plethora of lifetimes by proxy.

During the testing phase, we realised how unnerving it

was that the most successful matches generated trailers that ended in death. I suppose we should have seen that coming.

Turns out it puts a dampener on a first date if you've recently watched that beautiful young person opposite you shrivel into a senile nonagenarian. Makes it difficult to enjoy the first flushes of desire when you've already witnessed a rapid-fire montage of them bickering with you through your passionlessly shared late middle age.

So we adjusted the code and made sure the predictions never generate more than twenty years into the future. Which didn't entirely eradicate the problem, but it did reduce it somewhat.

"We can't just randomly cut the predictions short," protested Anya, one of the other programmers on our team. "It's not gonna be very narratively satisfying, is it? If each trailer just abruptly stops."

"But that's exactly how a Happily Ever After endpoint always works!" I said. "The couple ride off into the sunset. Cinderella and the Prince get married. The End. Nobody ever asks about the following morning or the day after that. Or fifteen years later. The trailers should leave the user wanting more. It'll be fine, so long as the model is trained to always pick the most upbeat available endpoint along the twenty-year prediction."

The thing about working on something like 4C is that you can't help wondering.

My palms sweated and my heart pounded as I launched the trailer.

I knew I shouldn't have done it, secretly accessing Anya's digital footprint and pairing it with my own profile, but once I'd had the idea, it wouldn't leave me. And now here I was, watching as a virtual Anya and I went on our first tentative date, a coffee, a music gig, a walk in the park, an awkward kiss, a stressful work environment, regret, arguing, avoiding each other – it was a disaster. The most upbeat endpoint the algorithm had been able to find was her leaving the company and never speaking to me again. Brilliant.

My heart crashed through the floor.

I took a deep breath and tweaked the variables, and ran the simulation again. This time I insulted her parents. So I ran it again. I accidentally drove over her dog. And again. She was already seeing some hunky guy she was incredibly into. And again. She wanted to explore her gay side. And again. And again. And again. Each time, the simulation found new and more imaginative ways to be a complete and utter train wreck. (One of them even involved a train wreck – which was my fault apparently: I bought the tickets.)

Let me tell you, you don't know the pain of true rejection until you've spent over an hour watching an advanced algorithm painstakingly illustrate in minute detail how, in every conceivable timeline, you and your crush are doomed to failure.

In exasperation, I did something I really shouldn't have. I found myself hacking the actual code. Not just tweaking the variables, but completely overruling whatever 4C so confidently knew about the two of us. Forget statistical realism, I wanted to write my own happy ending. So that's what I did.

And once I'd perfected this fairytale simulation, I contrived a ruse to show it to her. I pretended there was a bug I'd ironed out of the latest update. To discover whether I'd fixed it, I proposed using both our digital profiles as test subjects. Anya laughed at the idea, but agreed. She no doubt expected the outcome to be disastrous. Except it wasn't. It was perfection. And I had to feign surprise at the sight of us happily married with three kids and a cat and a beautiful Victorian Gothic house.

When the trailer was over, she was speechless. I wondered if I'd overdone it. I'd definitely overdone it. Then eventually she said, "Oh my God, Dom, are we – are we perfect for each other?"

"Er, it does look a bit that way," I said. "How terribly embarrassing."

And birds sang, and strings soared, and the sun broke through the clouds and we kissed.

The projection froze on their kiss and faded to black. The interview panel swivelled in their chairs to face Dom. It had been deeply strange, hearing his own voice narrating the trailer, describing events that had never happened.

"So as you can see," said the interviewer. "We cannot possibly employ you, excellent though your credentials are. The 4C software consistently generates predictions where you are willing to abuse the code in order to secretly manipulate a colleague into becoming romantically involved with you. I'm sure I don't need to tell you, that's highly unprofessional, not to say morally questionable."

"But, but I haven't…"

"No, we know you haven't. But you would. In 83% of simulations. Given the chance. And we can't risk having someone like that on our team." He turned to his colleague on the left, "Anya, would you mind showing the candidate out?"

Dom flushed bright red. "I'm sorry," he spluttered, looking at the carpet, unable to meet her gaze. "I didn't, I wouldn't, it wasn't, I haven't…"

"Don't," said Anya, cutting him short. "We've got a lot of candidates to get through today. This way."

And he followed her in awkward silence, the beautiful

and statistically unattainable Anya. She waved her pass over the entry pad, clicked open the door, and pointed him in the direction of a life that would never, in any multiplicity of potential futures, involve her.

The Chicken Plucker (Have You Seen the Price of Eggs Lately?)

Iris Taylor

Little Rock was already a busy place before the crash of '38. Gulf Coast residents came north to escape the floods, and northerners came south to escape the brutal winters. There'd been so many storms The Weather Channel gave up naming them. Instead, they got numbers. Blizzard 12. Ice Storm 15. Polar Vortex 5. So by the summer that the North Atlantic current stopped, and the markets went into a freefall, the corner of Cantrell and Cedar Hill was a morass of the desperate. Dollar General was one of the last stores that still got food deliveries, and folk from all over stood in a long line hoping for a can of ravioli or a pack of ramen. I was a day labourer, taking jobs as they came, though it was hard work when you could get it. Tarring roofs or hauling what needed hauling in the Mid-South humidity was real rough, but it beat starvation.

It was late June when I first heard mention of The Chicken Plucker. A truck had driven off with three labourers, and as I stood there with the other discards in the shimmering waves of heat, one said, "You boys hear about a man claiming he can get a chicken to lay eggs by playing 'em a banjo?"

Some laughed, myself included. I was used to the half-baked tales spun while waiting for a job. It helped keep your mind off the flies, hunger, and thirty-percent unemployment rate.

"Yeah," one said seriously, wiping the sweat from his brow. "My Aunt Lindy paid him a hundred bucks, and the day after he played for her chickens, she got four eggs. No joke."

"A hundred bucks?" another said. "No way. Nobody's got a hundred bucks for something so stupid."

"She says it was worth every penny. Have you seen the price of eggs lately? A carton's twenty-five dollars."

"I believe it," the youngest said. He stood in the spit of shade offered by a broken streetlamp that was bent over like a giant whooping crane, except its bulb head had shattered across the sidewalk, and cranes had already gone extinct by then. "I seen a chicken go into a trance by whistling to it. Maybe a banjo would loosen a hen up to lay an egg."

"That's the dumbest thing I ever heard. Chickens don't give a shit about music. I think your Aunt Lindy got taken for a ride."

The rattle of a truck cut short the conversation, and I forgot all about The Chicken Plucker until a couple days later. I was working a demo job—some investor bought hotels after no one could afford them anymore to sell the furniture and copper plumbing—when the guy on the other end of the desk I was carrying asked, "Know anyone who can play the banjo? I'm trying to learn."

As it was the second time I'd heard mention of a banjo, which wasn't real common, I said, "To play for chickens?"

He grunted as we lifted the desk into a U-Haul. "Yeah! You heard of The Chicken Plucker? I got a ukulele from my brother and figure it's close enough to a banjo. I heard that guy makes a grand a week. Can you believe it?"

I couldn't and said so, yet soon, The Chicken Plucker was everywhere. He was talked about on the bus ride home over the Arkansas River. In the long lines outside the community outreach centre. Then, one night, while listening to a news report over the Riverfront Market's PA system urging everyone to ration food as SNAP's yearly funding had already run dry, he was on the lips of two old rich ladies. In each version the tale grew taller, some saying he earned as much as five hundred dollars per gig while getting a chicken to lay a dozen eggs, but from those old grey-hairs, I heard something different: a whisper of honest truth.

"We had scrambled eggs at Sunday brunch for the first time in ages," one said, strolling through the stalls of wilted flowers and handmade soap, her hair curled like a modern southern belle. "Tucker thinks he'll have enough yolks to make frozen custard for Jessamine's birthday."

"Frozen custard!" the other said, clasping her wrinkled hands. A gold bracelet that hadn't yet been hawked or stolen glinted in the green glow of a stoplight. "What a marvellous thing to have in these trying times. So that Chicken Plucker really worked?"

"He was the answer to our prayers. My chickens lay one

or two eggs a week, but the morning after he performed, there were four. A hundred dollars was a bargain."

I followed them for a while, gaping like a dead bullfrog and not quite believing what I'd heard, that some guy was actually making money playing for chickens. Before the world went to hell, I'd been in a local steel guitar group. A hundred dollars was my cut from a good audience. But for chickens…?

The next day I took the bus over the river, but instead of going to the corner of Cantrell and Cedar Hill, I set out on a job of my own making. I started with the panhandlers; the leathered folk camped at freeway exits getting roasted by car exhaust. A man the shade of a charred brisket pointed me to the junkers at the Presidential Library. With no one wanting to hear about how great the '90s were and the Clinton family long gone, some entrepreneurs had turned the giant parking lot into an unlicensed flea market. Between rows of tyres and light fixtures, a junker said to find someone he called 'Doctor Fence.' The name didn't make sense until I got there—it was a guy running a black market inside the old Doctor's Building. After I got past the towering bodyguard and told him who I was looking for, Doctor Fence laughed, and said, "Sure, I know the guy. You'll find him at the zoo."

The Little Rock Zoo was always nice as far as zoos go, and it'd managed to survive the crash by becoming a neighbourhood hub. Every Monday, there were free showers at the splash pad, and they had regular classes, like for sewing and cooking. There was even one of those tiny libraries in the parking lot—which was clean despite the tent city there. As soon as I walked up to the metal gates, where a pimple-faced volunteer asked if I'd come for the community garden groundbreaking, I heard it—a banjo.

He looked like an off-season Santa Claus with a

round belly and a grey-speckled beard. He even had red suspenders and little round glasses. The similarities ended there, though. Sitting on a lawn chair in the shade of a kiosk that once held tourist brochures, he was sweating buckets into his white shirt stained yellow like an old tea towel. He looked real dug in, too. Carts and baby strollers overflowed nearby with stuff. But sure enough, his fingers were plucking away at a banjo, and at his feet in a cage was a chicken.

I waited a long time, forgetting why I'd gone through all the trouble in the first place, wondering if I'd gone crazy. Did I really believe the stories? Did I think I could learn the secret? I imagined going to Hot Springs, giving The Chicken Plucker and me separate territories. I imagined swapping pointers with the old man. I also imagined a pocket full of cash. Did I really believe it'd happen? I'm not sure. Mainly, I think I was hungry.

I opened the guitar case I'd been lugging around and pulled out my custom black Duesenberg Starplayer TV. It was the only thing I'd never sell, even if I was truly starving to death. I think I'd more readily part with a kidney. Hoping to make a good first impression, I put the strap over my shoulder and joined in his rendition of 'This Land Is Your Land.'

The Chicken Plucker put down the banjo, and when he spotted me, he smiled as if to promise we were off to a great start.

"Come here, young man! Come here! Show me that beauty of a guitar. Where'd you find it? You've got a good ear on you. If you'd like, I can teach you how to play more music for a bit of money, maybe earn cash as a busker?"

"No, thanks," I said, switching to "Ramblin' Man" by the Allman Brothers. The song never failed to get a crowd on their feet, and the hen in the cage gave me an encouraging *bawk-bawk*, but the cheery face of The Chicken Plucker soured as if I were jackhammering cement.

He waved a thick-fingered hand, cutting me off.

"Say, just what is that you want?"

I knew the words were stupid before they ever left my mouth.

"I want to learn the music that makes a chicken lay eggs."

He eyed me for a long moment as if I'd spoken another language, and I thought I'd made a mistake until he said, "For regular lessons, it's thirty dollars. But for what you're asking, I need a thousand. Now, I know that seems steep, but this is my livelihood we're talking about. How much you got with you?"

"Twenty," I said, fishing money from my pocket.

"We'll call that a down payment." He stuffed the bill into a stroller beside a Twinkie, and the sight made my stomach rumble. "Now, listen close. To get a chicken to lay an egg, you gotta know their history. Chickens was the descendants of dinosaurs, and back in dinosaur times, the sun was real bright, unlike the dim one we got now. Chickens need bright light to make their dinosaur brain realize it needs to lay an egg, but because leaving a light on for 'em is expensive, you gotta rely on something else."

I blinked, trying to reconcile if what he was saying had any truth. "Like what?"

He laughed as though I'd cracked a joke. "Music, of course! That's why you're here, ain't it? Say, is twenty all you got? I thought I saw another bill. I think I'm gonna need more if we gotta start with the basics like this."

"Five dollars, but it's for the bus."

"It's a good day for a walk, isn't it? Don't know when we'll have time for another lesson. I got lots of clients, you see."

I obediently gave him my bus fare, and he smiled, pleased as punch.

"Now, back in dinosaur times, there was also more oxygen in the air, and things reverberated differently. Roosters today sound different, and the hens don't hear them as well with all the pollution, and without a rooster's crow, they're not gonna lay eggs. So, the key is to make hens think they're hearing a rooster call."

"Like this?" I eagerly played a high note, warbling it like a rooster.

"No! No! You got it all wrong. That'll just scare a chicken. You gotta tap into the part of their brain that releases their egg-laying hormones. It's delicate, requiring just the right finesse. Sort've like wooing a lady. Now, listen. I gotta keep myself available for new customers, and you've got your lesson for today. When you get more money, come back and we'll get into the meat of it, alright?" He picked up the banjo and resumed 'This Land Is Your Land.'

It was here that I got a bad feeling.

I started the long walk home down Markham Street, and it took a few blocks to accept I'd been swindled. Light, oxygen, hormones—It all sounded like it had some truth, but I knew chickens weren't that complicated. I'd once seen a hen eat a loose screw. I suspected he wasn't a good musician, either. That I'd spooked him with my skill. And deep down, I'd known he had to be swindling those other folks, too. That he wasn't really getting chickens to lay eggs with music. But one thing bothered me: where were all those eggs coming from?

I turned around, deciding to retrace that morning's steps, and I didn't have to go far for an answer. Doctor Fence laughed when I asked.

"From me, that's where." He opened a small refrigerator, the kind used for medicine, and inside were stacks of cartons of eggs. "Son of a bitch buys 'em from me for twenty dollars, then charges those rich folk to plant a few eggs."

At first, I buckled at the simplicity. "And people believe it?"

"Of course. That's how people work. They want to believe. When they see a few eggs after throwing money at someone who says he'll solve a problem, it keeps them from thinking about how bad things have gotten. In a way, he's selling hope, but he's also giving them an excuse not to try to fix the big problems. I think you'd call that apathy."

I told him I thought that he was right.

Still hungry and with blisters on my feet, the next morning I returned to the corner of Cantrell and Cedar Hill. The usual tired faces looking out from the Dollar General line greeted me, as did the customary indifference of the boys standing around for a job, the air thick and stagnant like a dead swamp as if we were all stuck in the scum, waiting for the sun to cook us into dirt.

It didn't take long for the tall tales to resume. After another truck came and went, one of the boys said, "Y'all know about uranium glass? The old dishes that glow under purple light? I heard someone's buying 'em all up."

"What for?" asked the youngest under the broken lamp.

"For the uranium," another answered. "They melt the glass down, then sell the leftovers to the power companies."

"There's no way those things have real uranium in them, right?"

"They do. That's why you gotta be careful eating off them. I heard from a junker that they're worth fifty bucks a piece."

One scoffed. "For some glass? Who in their right mind would pay for it?"

I didn't wait around to find out who it was. Without much thought, my feet carried me the long way down Cantrell, then University, and finally, Markham Street. When I got to the zoo and learned that The Chicken Plucker had left town—not that I was looking for him—I found that pimple-faced volunteer. He gave me a shovel, and I got to digging.

The community garden turned out to be something special. We fed the growing tent city and kept most of them from starving, myself included, and from time to time, we made big meals for the whole neighbourhood. The work wasn't glorious; most days were spent worrying over things like the weather or keeping stray cats out of the okra, but it kept me moving and it seemed honest. And you know what? I saw those rich old grey-hairs there. I don't think that Jessamine girl ever got her frozen custard, but I did play the guitar for her and everyone else on her sixteenth birthday, and I did it for free. All the clapping and smiling faces filled my not-so-starved belly with the same thing they'd been trying to buy: hope.

Ain't that something?

Dai's Ex-Machina

Dafydd Rhys Hopcyn-Kitchener

Krupp pressed the button on the console, the action causing the Coracle to fizz and glow. His invention - shaped rather like a huge bowl – filled with an incandescent green gas which was fed into the receptacle through pipes linked to tall, fat vats sited in the corners of Krupp's laboratory. The scientist closed his eyes, breathing in the fumes deeply. They smelled acrid, but Krupp relished the bitter whiff more than the scent of the sweetest rose. He was, after all, inhaling the smell of his own creation.

Krupp had already stripped naked, then scrubbed himself raw. The Coracle had been working successfully, but the scientist was mindful of the slightest impurity ruining the process. Like its namesake, the Coracle transported you, though Krupp's invention carried you to an unearthly realm. Well, that was how the ignorant might have described his research. Krupp, though his creation was still at a young stage of development, preferred to use the scientific term for what he had achieved: dematerialisation, the conversion of human flesh into pure energy.

He climbed carefully into the Coracle. Its metal sides came up to the height of his belly, so Krupp had to lift his weight over. The scientist was confident that the device was safe. Before trying it personally, he had fed the de-materialiser countless chimpanzees. Many, many of these apes had never reemerged, being swallowed up forever by the ether. In later experiments, some of his chimpanzees had returned, though they had often been missing limbs, or sometimes their viscera had been spilling out. The Jekyll Institute, though, aware of Krupp's genius and the possibly enormous value of his work, had kept funding his research. Though hundreds of apes had been sacrificed, Krupp had reached a point where he was confident using the Coracle on himself.

The scientist lay down on the basin floor of his creation. He closed his eyes, contentedly losing himself in the heavy clouds of gas. He felt his flesh tingle, both from the sensation of the fumes tickling him, and from the excitement of physically leaving the world. The gas sparkled like fireworks as it dissolved Krupp, transforming him from solid matter into something else.

He could sense in his body when the alteration process was complete. Krupp did not feel the cold of the metal bowl on his naked back, nor even the weight of his hands as he lifted them. In fact, the scientist could not physically feel anything at all. The de-materialiser had changed him into a stream of particles. Krupp stood, walking through the side of the Coracle as if it were but a mirage. In this ethereal state, physical objects could not stop nor block

Krupp's movement. He could now pass through solid matter like a ghost.

Emerging from the side of his device, Krupp glanced at himself in the mirror. The change was not complete, nor perfect: the scientist was still working on his project. Looking at his reflection, he found that he did resemble a spectre. Krupp waved his arms around, swaying his hips and marvelling at his own brilliance. He was nearly transparent: through his now translucent body, the scientist could see the reflection of the wall behind him in the mirror. Yet, he was not totally see-through. His skin was now silvery and shimmering. Krupp wondered if the stupid people that believed in phantoms were in fact seeing beings such as himself. He savoured his ghostly appearance, though, for it enabled him to taunt his stepson Dai.

Krupp giggled to himself as he kicked his feet, causing this new entity he inhabited to float upwards. The scientist had learned that, in this non-physical form, he could drift around, if not exactly fly. It was rather like swimming. Krupp giggled to himself as he passed, almost supernaturally, through the ceiling of the laboratory.

His lab was sited in the basement of his house. Krupp worked alone. Those lesser-minded, nincompoop, so-called physicists at the Institute could not begin to fathom the magnitude of his genius. He found working with them infuriating and stifling. Krupp's colleagues and superiors were relieved when Krupp announced to them that he would be continuing his research alone at his own private laboratory.

Krupp glided upwards, a whooshing in his ears when he slipped unhindered through the floors and walls of his house. His brief had been to revolutionise transport, and he was nigh there. Using the Coracle, humans could pass through solid matter, potentially rematerializing on the other side of the world. Krupp was not quite there, yet. To return to human form, he needed to step back into the Coracle's gases. Still, Krupp had made enormous strides in the field and was on the cusp of completing his invention.

His creation would transform life on planet Earth. Until then, though, Krupp delighted in testing the efficiency of the Coracle on Dai.

The scientist walked through the wall of Dai's bedroom. Krupp commonly worked late into the night, so absorbed in his research that he lost track of whether it was day or night. On seeing Dai asleep in his darkened bedroom, Krupp realised that it must be very late.

Dai's natural father had died many years ago. As much a creature of intellect as Krupp was, he did have certain human urges. This was why he had wed Dai's mother. She had then been young and beautiful, but a few years of living with Krupp had been an ordeal. Dai's mother had shrivelled into a wretch following day after day of Krupp's petty, yet ceaseless, demands. He had been aloof and distant, yet titanically arrogant. To Krupp's great resentment, she, as well, had died too young. He had then been lumbered with her brat.

Dai was now thirteen. Though Krupp loathed the kid's very existence, in his core, Krupp was a tyrant. The scientist would never admit it to himself, but he had a deep need for somebody to bully and torment. Krupp told himself that he supported Dai out of a stepfather's dutifulness. In reality, Krupp's ego would crumble without some defenceless wretch to harass.

Indeed, the Coracle enabled him to torment Dai in the most unexpected way.

The imp was sleeping peacefully. Krupp noticed Dai's eyelids flickering slightly, for the child was happily lost in a deep slumber.

Well, I'll soon put a stop to that, thought Krupp to himself.

"Woo!" he cried out.

Though he was not in physical form, Krupp had learned that even in this non-material state, he could speak and make noise.

"Wooo! I am back from beyond the grave! O, such a restless spirit am I!"

Dai's eyelids sprang open, his gaze emanating pure terror. His head darted sideways to view the wavering, shiny entity hovering above him. Like a swimmer performing the breaststroke, Krupp wiggled his arms and legs theatrically.

"No!" Dai cried out. "No! No! No!"

Dai's bed was positioned in the corner of his bedroom. The boy retreated into this corner, cowering in fear. That thing levitating above him neared. Dai tensed up, hopelessly wishing that curling up in a tight ball would be some defence against the ghost. He bawled desperately when the spook reached out to touch him. The spirit's embrace was chilly, sending cold tingles through Dai's cringing body.

"Heelp me!" Krupp moaned. "Heeelp me, young urchin!"

His de-materialiser would one day allow a man to walk from London to Sydney, passing unharmed through the Earth's very core. That his invention permitted him to torment Dai so was a most delightful byproduct.

"Wooo!"

Krupp did not know how long he had haunted Dai. After a while, though, the brat's snotty tears had begun to annoy him. Krupp had then floated back downstairs to the laboratory to rematerialize in the Coracle. Pleasantly relaxed by his harassment of his stepson, Krupp had then turned in for the night. He had drifted off into sleep listening to

Dai's sobs.

Krupp awoke refreshed, then made his way down to the kitchen. There, Dai – well-drilled – had laid the table for breakfast. The boy was already sat there, dressed in his school uniform, his cornflakes untouched.

Krupp joined him without a word, reaching for the hot toast which Dai had prepared.

"There's too much butter on this toast," spat Krupp. "Yesterday, there was too little. You can never get it right, can you, nincompoop?"

Dai knew better than to argue. He walked over to the toaster to make more. Most days, it took several attempts before Dai made some passable toast. Though Dai always needed to tiptoe around his stepfather, this morning he was so shaken that he simply had to talk.

"It came back again last night, Mr Krupp."

Krupp always insisted that his stepson addressed him formally.

"The guh ghost," stammered Dai.

"Guh guh ghost?" Krupp mocked him. "For goodness's sake, nincompoop. When I was your age, I was in my final year at Oxford. You shouldn't be talking about ghosts at your age, young Dai."

"Buh but I saw it!" Dai insisted.

"It's either bad dreams, or you're making things up. Either way, you're pathetic. Now do my toast, then go to school."

As Dai turned back to face the toaster, Krupp had to bite his lip to stifle his giggles.

That night, Dai went to the bathroom to brush his teeth before bed. He felt exhausted after a day of school, then the long roster of chores to be performed when he returned home. Tired as he was, he still felt apprehensive about bedtime.

That spook had been visiting him for weeks. It did not appear nightly. One of the reasons that Dai was so scared was that he never knew when the ghost would show itself. Despite Mr Krupp's cruel words, Dai was certain that he was not imagining it. He had heard that terrifying moan, and even felt the spirit's icy touch. Young as he was, Dai had even questioned his own sanity. Still, Dai was certain of the phantom's real existence.

He studied himself in the mirror as he cleaned his teeth. His eyes were sunken and dark, for he had been awake much of the night crying in terror.

"Wooo!"

Dai recoiled from the sink when the ghost climbed out of the wall. Its grey yet transparent arms reached out to grab him, but Dai sprang backwards. He rushed over to the opposite wall, trembling. The spook stepped slowly towards him, groaning. Dai shuddered when the spirit walked through him, then through the wall behind him into the beyond.

Dai glanced around. The phantom did not seem to be there, coming and going. Dai thought that he heard ghostly giggles from the other side of the wall. He thought that, at least for a moment, he was alone.

Dai sprinted from the bathroom, thumping the stairs as he raced downstairs to the laboratory. He was banned from entering the workroom, but Dai was so afraid that he was just desperate to find Mr Krupp.

He reached the laboratory entrance in the basement. Dai had never entered the workshop before. The way into the lab was a thick, metal, sliding door. Dai grabbed the handle, then heaved, pulling it open.

He looked inside in wonderment. Dai had never seen the laboratory before. Its cement walls were lined with blinking consoles displaying incomprehensible figures and symbols. These computers seemed to be connected to each other by coils of thick, twirling wires. Sat in the centre of the workshop, though, was what looked like a vast bathtub. The vat was spewing out wisps of a glowing, green gas.

Nervously, Dai entered.

"Mr Krupp?" he called out. "Mr Krupp?"

There was no answer.

At breakfast, Dai wanted to ask his stepfather something, so he was particularly attentive to Mr Krupp's toast.

"Mr Krupp," Dai asked, handing him the plate. "I saw the ghost again last night. This time, it was in the bathroom."

"Look at this toast, nincompoop," answered Krupp. "The butter doesn't reach far out enough to the edge of the bread. Try again."

He shoved the plate across the table to Dai. Dai, uncomplaining, picked the plate back up to return to the toaster.

"I ran downstairs to get you," Dai explained, "but you weren't in the laboratory. Did you go out last night?"

This revelation caused Krupp's face to redden to the hue of a traffic light.

"You what? How dare you!"

Krupp kicked over the table in rage. He removed his belt, then strode up to Dai.

"Bend over!"

Dai obeyed.

That night, Dai winced as he lay in bed. Though the welts smarted, he had long resigned himself to his stepfather's beatings. Sore as he felt, the pain was real. Pain belonged to this world, the physical world. A strapping did not frighten him as much as a visit from the ghost, for the spook could only have come from some unearthly realm.

The weal was so uncomfortable that Dai could not rest. The pain, as well as the fear of a spiritual visitation, made him sleepless. He rolled over and over, never finding any peace.

Dai gulped when the phantom appeared. It seemed to rise up from the floor of his bedroom, slipping through the brickwork like silver, shimmering smoke. It hovered, slowly approaching him. Dai curled up, terrified.

"Wooo!"

"Leave me alone," Dai cried.

"Save me, boy. Save me from the misery of this cold afterlife. Save me!"

"Go away!" Dai bawled.

"Why won't you rescue me from this barren astral realm, boy? What nincompoop are you?"

Nincompoop? Dai asked himself.

When Dai finally awoke at dawn, he realized that he must have fallen into an unrefreshing sleep at some point. Last night, though, the ghost's visit had been different. The spook had wailed and wailed, tickled him and prodded him, but by the time the spirit disappeared through the floorboards, Dai had not felt afraid. Indeed, noisy and touchy-feely as the phantom was, it never physically harmed him. Last night, when the ghost had finally slipped away, Dai had only felt annoyed.

Moreover, he felt that he had figured something out about the spook, but Dai could not quite articulate what he had learned.

Haunted or not, it was morning. Mr Krupp would be expecting his toast.

Defiantly, Dai slid the plate over the table to his stepfather.

The toast was burned crisp, the slices cracked, the butter a bare sheen on the blackness.

"What disgrace is this, nincompoop?" raged Krupp. "Your worst effort yet. When I was but twelve, I won my first Nobel prize. Yet you – you cannot brown a slice of bread in the toaster with any competence."

Dai ignored Mr Krupp, rising from the table to leave for school.

"Such obstreperousness! Come back, you ingrate!"

When Krupp heard the front door slam, he thought that he might explode in fury. Well, tonight the ghost was going to torment that spoiled brat from dusk until dawn!

Though he inhabited his ethereal form, Krupp flinched when he saw how peacefully Dai slept. He had sent the imp to bed without supper as soon as Dai had returned home. Infuriatingly, Dai had not complained. The brat had simply walked upstairs rather cheerfully. How dare he!

Well, sleep was going to be a thing of the past for young Dai.

Krupp floated over, then clawed at his stepson's head. The scientist wiggled his fingers within Dai's brain, knowing that his otherworldly touch would tease cold frissons in Dai's sleepy head.

His stepson blinked as he stirred. Krupp was about to open his mouth to moan, when Dai looked him in the eye. There was something knowing in that defiant stare that caused Krupp to pause. As he hesitated, Dai sprang from the bed, ran through Krupp's wraithlike body, then burst out of the bedroom door. Krupp felt a pang of apprehension as he heard Dai's bare feet thumping down hard on the stairs down to the basement.

Unnerved, Krupp floated back downstairs to the

laboratory. He screeched in terror and anger when he saw what Dai was doing to the Coracle.

The sledgehammer was longer than Dai was tall, yet the boy was pantingly handling the tool with adroitness. One by one, Dai knocked the panels out of the invention, releasing wisps of green mist that faded away into the air.

Impotently, Krupp tore at Dai, but his hands – with no physical existence – passed hopelessly through the boy's body. Dai paused, though, when he felt the cold tingles in his chest.

Gasping, Dai lay down the hammer for a moment.

"Ah, Mr Krupp. There you are."

Krupp hovered helplessly. Even in his silvery, incorporeal manifestation, Dai could tell that his stepfather was scowling indignantly.

"What are you doing? Who do you think you are?" raged Krupp.

"You see, Mr Krupp," answered Dai, resuming his destruction of the device. "You're so arrogant. When you speak, it's like you're talking to yourself. You forget that other people listen. I remember you telling me about your invention which transforms humans into pure energy. Sure enough, you invent something like this, then a ghost starts haunting me."

"Ungrateful moron!"

"You're not such a genius that you lock your laboratory. I had a nose around the other night, then I think got the gist of what you were working on. I thought it was odd that you weren't around when the ghost had a go at me in the bathroom. Plus, the spook shares your catchphrase – 'nincompoop'."

"You are a nincompoop!"

"Now why would some spirit rise from beyond the grave just to call me a nincompoop? Then, I figured it out.

199

You use this machine to transform into that phantom thing just to pick on me."

"Cretin!"

"Now I'm no genius. You've told me that often enough. Still, even I twigged something. I reckon when I've smashed up this Coracle contraption, you'll be stuck like that forever."

Krupp watched in stunned silence as Dai battered down the last of the Coracle's panels. Now, his creation was nothing but metal sheets lying flat on the ground. It took a moment for Krupp realise that his stepson was unfortunately right. He would be forever trapped in this non-physical form.

Dai wiped the sweat from his brow, pleased with a job done well.

"I'm off to my grandparents' house now, Mr Krupp. Mum wanted me to live with them when she died, but you wouldn't allow it. When I tell them you've scarpered, I reckon I can say with them for good. And you can haunt me as much as you like. You can't hurt me."

Dai dropped the sledgehammer, then sauntered cheerily out of the laboratory.

"Come back! Come back! Nincompoop!"

Random Selection

Paul Eccentric

Fleur had been perfectly content. She had a job that she absolutely loved, two completely distinct social circles—the girls from the salon and her old mates from school—and for the last six months had been sharing a ground floor flat on the edge of a "new build development complex" with her apprentice footballer boyfriend, Brian.

She was proud to have achieved so much more in her first twenty years than her parents had achieved in forty. Brian even had a car, and as a step up from her mother's high-rise window box, they had a slabbed area beside their front door with four large pots on it that she and Brian liked to call their garden. When she wasn't out clubbing with Brian or her mates, Fleur liked to watch the television. She followed her soaps religiously, gobbling up the intricacies of the fictional characters' lives with the same zealous fervour with which she so completely devoured her other great passion: the celebrity gossip magazines. She was a great reader. Not much got past Fleur. She had her finger on the pulse; she knew how it all knitted together. She knew what life was all about and she loved nothing more than to yak endlessly to anybody who stood close enough to her for long enough about who was doing what to whom behind whose back.

Fleur knew where she stood. She knew what was going on in the world; she knew exactly what to buy and where to buy it from because the adverts kept her up to date.

But she didn't know everything. She didn't know all the boring stuff that happened to other people she didn't know and who led weird lives in countries that she couldn't point to on a map and who didn't have television or magazines. She didn't read those bits in her newspaper, she just stuck to the important bits. And the adverts. She did like her adverts.

The adverts gave her mind a chance to catch its breath between ideas.

One of the things that Fleur didn't know about was the existence of aliens and so when she got abducted by one whilst walking home from the salon one night, she found herself utterly flummoxed, and for once, completely lost for words.

The aliens in question had been attracted to Earth after unexpectedly picking up a series of random transmissions as they coasted past the outer planets of the solar system on their way to a party. They were curious because their galactic satnav seemed convinced that there was no sentient life on any of the ten planets of this system. They chose a continent and a life sign at random and sent down a transmat beam to extract it. The transmissions that had been beaming out into space had been quite unintelligible, even after their translation software had converted the squall into standard, leading the visitors to presume that a society must have evolved here, so cut off from the rest of civilisation that it could have developed an entirely unique technology.

Fleur woke up to find herself naked and strapped spreadeagled to a table with two huge catlike things in spangly suits staring down at her. They shot questions at her like her friend Marnie did on a Tuesday morning if she'd missed the previous evening's edition of the soaps. They spoke fairly good English for cats, she thought, but she hadn't a clue what they were going on about. It was all "socio politico" this and "eco techno" that, none of which she knew anything about. Eventually, they showed her what they said were some random transmissions that they had picked up from space and asked if she could interpret them. Could she? So, she filled them in on the last ten years' worth of soap storylines, reality shows and advertising campaigns as they stood silently above her.

When she had finished, they returned her clothes in silence and set her back down where they found her.

As they left the system, they dropped a marker buoy into orbit as a warning to other shortcutters that the planet below was some kind of long-lost asylum colony that should be avoided at all costs for the sake of sanity.

Fleur, on the other hand, put the whole experience down to a spiked Bacardi Breezer.

The Kingdom of the Blind

How do you tell the man whom you love that he's a shit poet?

And should you? Do you have that right, even as a wife, to casually criticize; to callously condemn; to make disparaging remarks about his dubious talents in an area in which you yourself have no particular gift? Could you—when you know fully well that he has fostered something of a passion for his art—make comments that whilst well-intentioned, you know will wound him as deeply as had you stabbed him through the heart with a cake slice? Is it not actually the duty of the one closest to him, the one who has sworn in front of a vicar to honour him and to be true to him—his best friend, his confidante, the one person in the whole world whom he should be able to trust above all others? Is it not within your marital remit, to help him to avoid making a total tit of himself in front of a roomful of other people?

These are the dilemmas that she's facing, an ongoing crisis for her, because he's not just a bedroom poet, oh, no. He doesn't just pour out his innermost on the faintly lined page, dashing out his heartfelt hopes 'n fears in the sanctity of his own man cave in an act of private catharsis. No. He's a 'performance poet': the very worst kind of artistic narcissist! The scourge of the pay-what-you-can-afford, open mic entertainment circuit.

That bloke with the leather-bound notebook and the smug, holier-than-thou expression who doesn't only think he has something worthy and righteous to impart, but who genuinely believes that he has a naturally humorous and eloquent style of delivery and that the rest of the room are hanging on his every couplet. She's being cruel now, she knows, though only in her head. She wouldn't really say those things; not out loud, anyway. She might think them; many wives would and many husbands too, to be fair; as shite poetry is not the exclusive preserve of the middle-aged man, but could she tell him to his face? Could she be the one responsible for shattering his delusions; for taking away his last vestige of dignity?

No. She couldn't.

She loves him; despite his poetic proclivities, and she knows how much this hobby; irritating as it may be to her, means to him.

He'd never been one of life's go-getters; he'd been a small cog in a very large machine: powerless; humdrum drone who nobody had taken any notice of. That was until he'd discovered that he could 'write'. She couldn't spoil that for him now; steal away the thing that was keeping him going.

So, she sits there in the circle of mismatched chairs, in the same spot that she occupies every Tuesday night at this time and she waits with him until it's his turn to read. She waits, wearing that fixed grin that she's spent longer in front of the mirror perfecting than she's ever spent titivating—that look that says, "Such a shame you didn't take it up professionally, dear; you would've been a star!" She watches and listens to the slew of singer/songwriters with their battered old guitars and their monotonous, turgid ballads that occasionally almost rhyme; the storytellers who can't edit and 'don't do accents', the so-called 'comedians' who wouldn't know a punchline if it...punched them and that woman with the beads and the drum and the distinct lack of either rhythm or...timing. The same faces week after week, except when somebody new shows up, to alter the group dynamic and to offer a new perspective.

There are those of their number who close down

at the sight of a new face, refusing to take their turn; mistrustful of the interloper; worried, maybe, that they might somehow be usurped; she doesn't wonder, but there are others of the group who tend to up their game in the presence of new blood; eager to bring them into the fold; to incorporate them into the community. Her husband subscribes to the latter of these two schools; always keen to welcome that new voice; desperate to find out more about them and from whence they came: always on the lookout for a new place to punt his own erudite wares. Not that they've ever followed through, of course. Oh, he talks the talk: he's full of bravado on a Tuesday night at their local community centre; he's in his element there amongst the faltering and the nondescript, but would he be so bold on alien turf? No. He's one of only three self-professed 'poets' in the group and arguably the best of that bunch, though that isn't really saying much! Of the other two, one writes exclusively about trains and the other only speaks Welsh.

Not that she has anything against the Welsh per se; her paternal grandfather had hailed from the valleys, but she doesn't understand the language and neither does anybody else in the room.

'In the kingdom of the blind, the one-eyed man is king.' One of her late father's oft-touted mantras and no truer words had yet been spoken.

Of course, she doesn't have to go to open mic night; nobody's forcing her. She could just stay at home, on her own, in the dark, twiddling her thumbs.

A year ago she would've had a rash of possible alternatives to choose from, but now; well, she can scant believe it herself, but this is her best option. Damn religion! Damn politics!

So she makes the best of it, like she's done with everything else these past twelve months; like she always has done when the chips've been down. She makes the tea and she bakes the biscuits: it keeps her occupied. It keeps her... sane.

And that's the crux of the issue, in truth, she knows: these people; these crazy, middle-aged losers that turn out every week for open mic; they might not be very good at what they do, (any of them); they might not have the first idea of how to do the things that they keep insisting on doing week in, week out, but it keeps them sane; even if that may not be readily apparent to the casual observer.

And most of them know they're not much cop. They do what they do purely for the enjoyment they derive from doing it and, she's always supposed, because nobody has the will or the guts to tell them to stop. They're not hurting anyone and they're always very supportive of the others within the group; so where's the harm? Where's the harm?

They've probably always been that way too: humble; modest; deferential types; lacking in any kind of personal or creative ego. Cogs.

And then there are the others: those who take the whole thing just that little bit too seriously. Her husband is one of these.

He hasn't always been, though; he hadn't even taken up the pen until after he'd retired.

He'd tried an art class first but found it frustrating. Then he'd tried a gardening course but decided that it was too much like hard work. Fishing was boring; golf, pointless and rambling played havoc with his corns, so he'd enrolled himself on a creative writing course. It had been great, to begin with; as if he'd finally found his purpose in life. He'd spent hours in his study, tapping out corny verses on an archaic, journalist's travel-typewriter; the sort that comes inside its own zip-up leatherette suitcase. He'd found it in the charity shop in the village. If she had ever been going to say anything to him about the standard of his work, then it should've been said there and then, but it'd been making him happy and besides, he'd soon get bored and move onto something else. She hadn't expected him to throw his heart and soul into it quite like this; to let it consume him; to believe that there was actually a point to it all. He sees himself as some sort of missionary, these days; an evangelist. He thinks he's saving the world with his philosophical words. He believes that people sincerely care what he thinks.

They don't; well, not according to his wife, anyway and she ought to know. He's told her that he sees his work as a legacy; that he's writing it for posterity. He wants their children to find it once he's gone, but the kids'll never read it! The last they'd heard of them, they'd been in London. They hadn't had any contact since... They could've been long dead for all she knew.

This seemed to be the general consensus among their little group. Not: 'we're doing this because we've nothing else to do and it passes the time', but: 'we're doing this in the hope that it'll prove of value to those who come after us'.

She doesn't think that's very likely, though and she doesn't find this degree of arrogance particularly attractive in her nearest 'n dearest, but she smiles anyway and applauds vigorously after each and every turn. She serves the drinks at half time and she offers round her box of biscuits. They're not very nice; barely edible, really. She couldn't find enough sugar so she'd used sweetener instead and some of them were a bit singed. No one says anything derogatory. They just smile and thank her, even though any one of them could probably have done a better job.

And perhaps that's her answer? Her husband has always eaten her food, not once complaining, even after that time that she'd inadvertently given him a dose of salmonella poisoning. She's never been a particularly good cook, you see; she bought in wherever possible whilst they were working. The kids had laughed at her when she'd told them that she was taking an evening class in baking when she retired. They'd been polite when she'd given them cakes to take home with them, even though she'd known that they'd probably end up on the bird table. Nobody wants to hurt her feelings: that's how she rationalises it.

She washes the cups at the end of the evening and stacks them ready for next time whilst her husband says his goodbyes and gathers up his papers. She waves back to the others as she follows him outside. She lifts the collar of her jacket and wraps her scarf tightly around it, covering her mouth and nose in the process. She pulls her woolly hat from her pocket and jams it over her curls, tying it in a bow beneath her chin. Her husband dons his dust mask and pulls on his own hat. They step gingerly down the wooden plank that serves to replace the steps to the hall, then tiptoe through the rubble that used to be the high street. The wind bites through their layers as they stumble back to their cellar: the only part of their three-bedroomed cottage that it's still safe to inhabit. She knows that the shops are empty; picked clean by the survivors months ago, but her eyes instinctively scan the empty shelves of the mini-mart as they pass, her newly honed scavenger senses alert for any scraps that might help to keep them alive just a little longer. The winter is coming.

She doubts whether any of them will make it to Christmas without food or uncontaminated water and help isn't coming; they all know this. They've done their best to maintain some semblance of civilisation as they'd known it; those of them who are left, that is; those who didn't die when the bombs went up; those of them who hadn't been wiped out in the resulting plague: those 'fortunate' to have already cut themselves off from society by moving out here to the middle of nowhere. They don't know what has become of the cities. The only news they've heard these last months has come from the wandering troubadours; those tellers of tales who've braved the unknown; traversing the dales in search of pockets of humanity who might share a scorched, sugarless biscuit with them in exchange for a few words, but even they are becoming less frequent.

She used to be the more positive of the pair; back when life had a purpose, but now...? Her husband seems perfectly content as they pick their way through the ruins of their hallway. He enjoyed his evening. He said his piece and his court applauded and it's obviously inspired him to continue his work; one eye on the future that only he can see.

She, on the other hand, can't see a point to any of it, but she's not about to tell him that.

In the kingdom of the blind, the one-eyed man is king...

But king of what, exactly? King of what?

The Last Laugh

There's a lot to be said for dying on the toilet.

Alright, on the face of it, it may not seem to be the most dignified of ways to go, but at least it's a private affair; you wouldn't have to try to put a brave face on that final agonizing death rattle; you won't be expected to come up with a supposedly spontaneous, witty final line and you are in the perfect position for that embarrassing post-mortem moment when your muscles relax and your corpse begins to divest itself of any excess bodily waste that may still have been lingering in your tubes. So much kinder on the poor sod who finds you, don't you think? Top tip, though: if you're alone in the house, never lock the bathroom door. Just in case.

And you're in auspicious company too. Elvis died on the loo. As did Judy Garland and King George the second. It's more common than most people might think. But it is something of an obvious design flaw in your human being, if you ask me. An essential daily function that can put the heart under such an intense amount of strain; raise your blood pressure and in extreme cases result in instant death?

...as Leonora was just discovering for herself.

One minute she'd been settling down with her favourite prayer book for a pre service ablution and the next, a violent coronary spasm had mugged her of the life that God had entrusted her, twenty minutes before the first parishioner had been due to arrive for the early sermon.

Sixty-five isn't old, these days, not for the English upper middle, anyway; she should've been good for at least another twenty, but that's the thing with life; you just never know when it's going to come to an abrupt and undignified end in the vestry cubicle, straddling the porcelain with your knickers around your ankles.

The first that Leonora had known about it was when she had suddenly found herself standing in the arrivals hall of what she had taken to be a large and bustling international airport. Her rational mind had tried to compensate for the disconcerting continuity lapse. She was dreaming, yes, had to be...she'd nodded off on the bog again.

That would explain why she was now wearing the dress she'd been wearing the night she'd first met Donald, way back in sixty-five: the floral one with the starched petticoat that had cost her the equivalent of a month's wages from the biscuit factory, and not the autumnal tweed church warden twin set that she'd set out in that morning.

But she knew dreams; she'd spent decades suppressing them; denying the nature that Satan continued to taunt her with on a thrice nightly basis. This wasn't a dream; it as too real; in fact, it was even realer than the reality she had just left behind. But if this was real, how come she had pert breasts again after all these years and where had the wrinkles; the baggy eyes and her infamous collection-collector's perma-scowl all gone?

Leonora wasn't stupid. She'd quickly put two and two together and accepted that she must have been dead. She allowed herself a rare smile. She'd been right, then: if she was here, then God did exist and there was a heaven; not that she'd ever doubted it herself, but so many of those around her had mocked her for her faith over the years, (including Donald) that she decided to savour the last laugh for a second.

Although she hadn't necessarily wanted to die just yet, Leonora felt a huge wave of relief wash through her restored teenage body. It felt as if she had been holding her breath for six and a half decade and could finally now exhale and be free. Life had been okay, she supposed, but she'd always seen it as a proving ground for the right to earn a better, eternal life up here in heaven with Him. And she had obviously passed that test because here she was. She'd have liked to have been able to see Donald's face right now. She'd married him because he'd seemed like a good man. He hadn't been a believer, but she'd felt sure at the time that she could have won him round to her way of thinking. It wasn't as if he'd been a Satanist or a Muslim or anything. In fact, they'd had much the same core values when they'd met; he just claimed not to believe that the world had been created by an omniscient being as a test for the mortal sinner's everlasting soul. Donald had died at fifty-nine whilst being 'administered to' by three prostitutes—none older than his granddaughter—in an Amsterdam brothel. Oh, the shame of it! He had gone off the rails somewhat in later life; had something of a midlife crisis. Said he'd been put on this earth to have fun and so fun was what he was going to have.

"Go grandad!" had been the general family consensus. Well, they wouldn't be laughing now!

"Name?" snapped the angel, although he looked more like a jobsworth immigration officer than one of the almighty's heavenly host.

"Leonora Spatchcock," she replied haughtily. The angel tutted rudely and flicked his eyebrows heavenwards.

"Real name." he snapped impertinently.

"That is my real name", she followed indignantly. The angel spoke quietly into a small microphone clipped to his collar. "Oh," she hurriedly added, "do you mean my maiden name? Trent."

"No, madam; I mean the name that you booked under. What... hold on," He turned away to speak to his collar again. Then he turned back to her and smiled, adding, "Where do you think you are, madam?"

Leonora returned the smile unwittingly.

"Heaven, of course."

Two more angels suddenly appeared; each taking one of her arms and steering her toward a door marked 'HELP' to the side of the concourse.

"Next!" said the officious angel as she was led away. Inside the featureless, white side room was a short row of plastic chairs and an unmarked door. One of her guides showed her to a vacant seat while the other passed her a

213

ticket with a number on it. She got the distinct impression that they were sniggering to themselves as they left. She was not alone in the waiting room. She was surprised to find herself sat beside what she took to be a woman in a head-to-toe black burqa. The woman's eyes looked as shocked as she imagined her own to look at that moment. Next to her covered friend sat a man in the full traditional getup and flowing grey beard of an Orthodox Jew and beside him, an orange robed Hare Krishna; his brass cymbals closed neatly on his lap. Nobody spoke nor so much as acknowledged their neighbours; each presumably as worried as Leonora was, that they had somehow arrived in the wrong afterlife. She had waited patiently for what had felt like an eternity as each of her unlikely companion's numbers had been called in turn. Each had entered the unmarked door and none had returned. "Number six thousand six hundred and sixty-six, please." She heard from the room beyond. She stood, opened the door and stepped inside.

"Take a seat," said the angel who seemed to be dressed as a doctor, gesturing without looking up toward a psychiatrist style couch. She sat uneasily on its edge while he finished making some notes.

"So," he said, sliding his spectacles closer to his eyes. Leonora idly wondered why an angel would need glasses. "Does the name 'Skooter Breeze' mean anything to you?"

She considered his question then shook her head.

"Should it?"

"Oh, dear. Even worse than the last one."

He took off his spectacles and sipped from his mug of coffee.

"Where do you think you are, m'dear?" he asked, rather patronisingly, she felt.

"Heaven." she replied firmly. Perhaps this was a part of the test?

"You caught religion, then, did you? Well," he said, standing up and replacing his spectacles on his nose, "you look genuine, but I'll have to do a full examination before I can refer you for compensation. We get an awful lot of fakers through here y'know.

They think they can hoodwink us by claiming to be Mormons or scientologists, but we know a believer when we see one."

"I'm sorry, I don't follow you, doctor. I'm a church warden and a Sunday school teacher. Have I displeased Him in some way?"

"Very good!" The angel/doctor confirmed, "Well, I say good; I mean good from the point of view of a partial refund, but bad in a 'Hedonistic Holidays: Do What Thou Wilt Shall Be the Whole of The Law' kind of way. Tell me," he said, peering into her pupils with a magnifying lens, "did you have any fun down there at all or was it all just abstinence and birch twigs?"

Leonora, shaken by his Crowley reference and unsure just how much this test was intended to push her, steadied herself, kept her face as stoic and unruffled as she could and said: "I followed the Lord's scriptures to the letter. My only crime was to inflict my beliefs on the heathens and the unrepentant sinners of our parish" (a thought had suddenly struck her) "and..." (surely 'He' couldn't hold this against her) "and...to insist that Donald had a proper funeral despite his...evil ways."

The psychiatrist stepped back sharply as she spat her words with more vehemence than she had expected.

"I see." he eventually said. "Well, Ms Breeze. I'm sorry to say, but you do seem to have caught a severe case of religion, down there. On behalf of the company, I can only apologise, stamp your claim form and wish you a speedy recovery." He gave her a sheaf of paperwork and bade her a good day, showing her through to baggage reclaim where she was met by a familiar face.

"Donald?"

"Eh? No, Beezer Floom, luv. Have we...?" the baggage handler put down her stored effects and removed his hat, "Oh, my unsubstantiated deity! It's you! Leonora, wasn't it?

We met on holiday, didn't we, down on Earth? Ha! You caught the bug, didn't you. Did you get over it? Ah, no; you've still got it, haven't you? You poor thing. We had some fun, though; didn't we; at the start, I mean. Before you got all..." He smiled. "Tell me you at least went out with a bang?"

Leonora/Skooter said nothing, tears welling in her eyes.

Beezer/Donald handed over her bags, smiled kindly and replaced his cap.

"If you fancy a shag, sometime; for old time's sake... you know where to find me."

The Complicated World of the Spider

L.N. Hunter

Professor John Dougal Hamish MacDonald, who would be much more comfortable in a stain-spotted laboratory coat than in his current smart suit and tie, takes the stage to present the opening keynote of the International Conference on the Preservation of Invertebrate Diversity.

"Friends, esteemed colleagues, ladies and gentlemen, it gives me great pleasure to be here today, in front of you all at ICPID. I want to talk about how we, the human race, relate to spiders, a topic dear to my heart. Arachnids come in all shapes and sizes, from the minuscule Samoan Moss Spider, *Patu marplesi*, the size of a pinhead, to the huge thirty-centimetre leg span, Goliath Bird Eating Tarantula, *Theraphosa blondi*, from Venezuela. I'm sure that even the least arachnophobic amongst you wouldn't want to meet one of those on a dark night."

Several members of the audience politely laugh on cue.

"But why does arachnophobia exist? Very few species of spider are venomous to humans or dangerous in any way, so why did our ancestors evolve an aversion to these misunderstood creatures?" He pauses for emphasis, gazing out over the expectant assemblage of scientists and journalists. "I'll tell you why… It's because they watch and listen."

Creases appear on a few foreheads in the audience.

"Have you noticed where it is that spiders make their webs? It's always dark, secluded places close to humans. The majority of common spiders consume flies, but flies don't frequent those sorts of places, do they?" He flings his arms wide. "Flies inhabit open spaces, where they can locate their food sources, not the dim dark places in which you find webs. Those webs in attics and eaves, in dusty corners of garages, in barns, in churches, never have insects trapped in them—have you ever seen a fly trapped in a cobweb in your house? No, never!" He smacks the podium to drive his point home.

"That's because webs are *not* for catching prey. Sure, there are webs out in the light too, aren't there? But look at where spiders build those: on fences and in gardens, places near human beings. I'll grant, you do see the occasional fly trapped in one—accidental visitors, and—I propose—not the reason for the webs in the first place."

The audience is quiet now. Some people would like to leave, but daren't make a sound; others' mouths twitch as if they're wondering what whimsy this is and are waiting for the punchline.

"The webs are there to listen to human beings—us—not to collect food."

As punchlines go, it isn't quite what the audience expected. A half laugh coughs from somewhere in the auditorium, but quickly vanishes into the appalled silence. A few conference committee members in the front row are rather pale-faced, wondering how—or if—they would secure funding for next year's ICPID after this speech becomes public.

"Webs are nothing less than ingenious listening devices. Now, I'm sure most of you know what a radio telescope array is but, for the rest, here's a quick outline. Signals from outer space are very weak and well beyond the performance limits of even the largest single telescope. However, if we have lots of them—he moves his hands as if placing several small telescopes about the space in front of him—"all pointing at the sky, we can get a much better coverage of the area they're directed towards. The individual dishes of the radio telescopes are connected in a mesh, a *web* if you will, with clever mathematics combining their signals to provide a single incredibly detailed image. It's as if we have—you'll permit me the pun—an astronomically huge telescope."

He pauses for a laugh, but the only sound from the audience is that of embarrassed fidgeting.

Professor MacDonald's smile wavers, but he continues. "And that's what spiders' webs are too: listening and watching devices. The fact that they're situated near human habitations should give you a good idea of what they're watching, wouldn't you agree? My current research focuses on understanding the arachnid mind to establish why they're monitoring us, and who—or what—they're communicating with.

"We've already found a centre of geometrical processing within the surprisingly sophisticated spider neural cortex, which processes the interaction between different webs in a similar—but more efficient—manner to the algorithms used in radio telescope arrays. We have a number of theories for how they communicate with each other: pheromones and scent triggers form the primary theory for short distances, but we still have no idea how they synchronize with each other over long distances. One possibility is that they could be using focused parabolic webs as transmitters and receivers of some sort, but more research is required. We think these communication mechanisms, whatever they may be, let spider groupings operate with a sort of hive mind, with many individuals contributing to a much greater whole.

"It is my belief that we, the human race, did once interact with arachnid society and worked closely with spiders. The evidence is strong in prehistoric and religious art—consider the legends of Anansi and Arachne, or the Fates of Greek myth, not to mention stories of tangled webs and weaving. Perhaps there was a falling out, or some disaster akin to that which wiped out the dinosaurs, resulting in the two species moving apart. Humankind blamed the spiders and started to fear them, while the spiders just quietly continued to watch and listen… and wait."

There is a slight pause as he looks around, and finally, with a slight bow of his head, he says, "Thank you."

Two or three people start to applaud because that's what happens at the end of a talk. No one else joins in, and the applause abruptly stops. The only sound is that of some members of the press tapping on keyboards or scratching on notepads, as they gleefully prepare to broadcast news of Professor MacDonald's mental breakdown. People avoid looking towards the stage, in case they catch the professor's eye. Instead, they look at each other, wondering what comes next.

Unnoticed by all, a small brown spider crawls out from under the speaker's plinth and seems to regard the audience's reaction before scurrying back into the darkness.

The silence is broken by two large men in black suits and dark glasses marching up to the Professor. Grabbing an arm each, they escort the bewildered man off the stage, out through a side door and into a black van, which drives off in a screech of tyres and a cloud of exhaust.

Half an hour later, Professor MacDonald is seated at a cheap metal and chipped veneer table in a small room lit only by a flickering fluorescent tube. The two black-suited men stand a short distance behind him. They have their hands clasped in front of their groins as if to protect themselves from a surprise attack by the professor's elbows. Sitting on the opposite side of the table, a smaller man in a grey suit lifts his head from a sheaf of paper and stares at the professor for a whole minute before breaking the silence.

"Well, Professor, who else subscribes to your theory that spiders are watching us?"

"I… Well, I… There's my research team, of course–"

"Yes, yes, we've got them covered," the man in the grey suit snaps. "Who else?"

The professor thinks, then says quietly, "No one, I guess. We've had no publication success yet, and this conference was the first time I've spoken about it."

"Thanks to all that is good and holy for that," the grey man mutters, eyes dropping to his papers again. "The scope for damage is limited. There can't have been more than a couple of hundred people at the conference, and they're all a bit disconnected from reality anyway.

"The International Conference on the Preservation

of Invertebrate Diversity," he sneers, before looking up at Professor MacDonald. "Invertebrate diversity, for pity's sake, what's the point? Damned bugs and worms—have they nothing better to do? In any case, nobody at the conference will have taken your ramblings seriously. We've already shuttered the journalists, so nothing will leak out via newspapers and television either." He pauses, looking at his papers again. "To the great unwashed, spiders are small creepy crawly things that eat flies and cause women, and some men"—he smiles without humour—"to run screaming from the bathroom. Can you imagine what effect it would have on humanity if anyone suspected there was any more to it than that?"

"I... I... I..."

"Ivory-towered scientists like you never think about the effect you have on the real world, do you? Things like this have consequences, serious consequences. We think it's time for you to retire from academic life, Professor. I suggest you bugger off back to whatever part of Scotland you came from. Forget your research. Don't even think about your research. Spend some time looking after sheep. Or bloody hairy cows and haggis." He leans forward. "I don't care, as long as you don't talk about spiders. Ever. Again." He punctuates this with thumps on the table, making Professor MacDonald flinch.

Just over five years later, the sole human resident of a small croft in a remote part of the Torridon Hills, ex-Professor John Dougal Hamish MacDonald is counting his sheep when a cluster of bright lights skims across the sky— meteors, he surmises, but he wonders at the number of them. *Hmm, eight: there's something significant about the number eight.* But, no matter, that's not important right now. He switches his attention back to the bleats of the old ewe, matriarch of his flock, caught on the barbed wire fence bounding his current bailiwick. His gaze passes over a cobweb on the fence, but he doesn't notice it.

Because he has no television, radio, or access to the internet, he doesn't know what's going on in London, six hundred miles south.

In the capital, the Prime Minister gets ready to be the first human being to formally greet an extra-terrestrial species, feeling especially pleased with herself because the visitors had chosen Great Britain for their arrival, not the USA, not China, and not Russia.

Seven of the octagonal spaceships hover above the city while the eighth, the largest one, extends eight articulated legs and gracefully descends to land in the middle of Hyde Park, demolishing an ornate flowerbed as it does so. Metal tinks and plinks as the ship cools. For a few seconds, blown-about soil, leaves and the occasional flower gradually settle. With a grinding shriek, a door opens at the base of the ship, and a ramp slowly extends, juddering and rumbling, to meet the ground.

The PM, flanked by the obligatory, black-suited men in sunglasses, approaches the end of the ramp and waits, watched by thousands of flag-waving spectators, hundreds of cameras and, through them, billions of people. A dozen spiders in the branches of trees surrounding the park also look on.

A small eight-wheeled vehicle makes its way unsteadily down the ramp. Its windows are opaque so nothing can be seen inside until the canopy whirs open, revealing a bulging green head rising from a pool of water. On either side of a small beak, two massive eyes blink and orient themselves towards the PM. A sinuous, boneless limb emerges from the water, picks up a small red box from the rear of the vehicle, and flicks a switch on the top.

The creature makes a gurgling hiss and looks around. It seems to frown at the lack of response and whacks the box. It tries speaking again, and this time a bellow issues from the box, synchronized to the noises the creature makes: "Hey, baby, baby, baby!" The creature stops, turns back to the ship and hisses something. The box screeches, "I thought you said you'd fixed this cursed thing. Why does nothing ever work properly?" It shakes the box and smacks it against the side of the vehicle, then tries again.

"Greetings, humans," issues from the box at a more reasonable level, "You should have paid more attention to your arachnids. They were protecting you, watching out for us. Each time you destroyed a cobweb, you made it easier for our ships to approach the planet undetected. Ever since they banished us tens of millennia ago, in that great battle that you remember only as a fear of spiders, we've been waiting to return. To return and claim this planet as ours. Now, take us to your London Aquarium, so we can confer with our relatives who failed to escape. You foolish four-limbed feedstock, you backed the wrong octopods. Earth belongs to the octopus!"

Laughter booms from the speaker box as the alien screeches and thrashes its tentacles.

The spiders at the edge of the park withdraw into the depths of the trees.

It's lambing season in the Torridon Hills eight months later. One newborn is lying in the grass near the boundary fence, bleating plaintively but unable to get up. Its mother paces back and forth but is unwilling to approach the lamb.

Pausing to open the gate, the shepherd takes a deep breath and looks up into the clear sky. The thought crosses his mind that it's been ages since he's seen any jet trails, but no matter; he has other things to deal with. He strides over to the small animal expecting to have to put it out of its misery, based on his previous experience with the fragile lives of sickly lambs. As he gets closer, however, he sees something silken and wispy binding its legs together. He kneels for a closer look and, as he touches the sticky grey fibres, he hears a whispered "Professsssorrrr." Startled, he jumps up and looks around, but can see nothing out of the ordinary. Leaning close to the lamb, he hears the voice again: "Professsssorrr, overrrrr herrrrrre." He looks up and sees a huge dense spider web near the bottom of the rickety old fence, surrounded by hundreds of spiders. "Professsssssorrr, we neeeeed tooooo taaaalk."

John Dougal Hamish MacDonald faints.

His eyes slowly ease open and his senses start to return. Cold droplets splatter his cheek and the left half of his body is very cold and wet. It's raining again, nothing out of the ordinary in this part of Scotland, and he's lying on his right side, near the now shivering lamb. He quickly rips the ribbon of spider's web from around its legs and lets the small animal run back to the still-frightened ewe. The pair race to the far side of the field.

Back in his cottage, a change of clothes and a wee dram—and then another wee dram—later, he stares into the flickering orange of his fire and tries to make sense of what happened before he passed out.

"Professor."

He jumps and looks around. He seems to be hearing a lot of people calling his old honorific today; maybe he's finally losing his mind.

The whispering voice continues: "Stay calm, you're not imagining this. We just want to talk to you." As this is being uttered, hundreds of spiders crawl from the eaves, from cracks in the walls, and from between floorboards. They all stop moving and seem to be staring at him. "Yes, you did get it mostly right. We were watching humankind, and our two species did intermingle and communicate frequently. Our webs are indeed like your satellite dishes. Yada, yada, yada, well done, you're a clever chappie. Have a pat on the back. But none of that's important at the moment. We tried talking to you using a web amplifier outside just now, but that really didn't work, did it? You're just too damned jumpy." The voice seems to sigh. "I guess you're not to blame. It's all our fault for not trying hard enough."

"Who–? What–?"

"Oh, come on, Professor. Pull yourself together! Let's start with the basics. There's one of us in your left ear, manipulating your eardrum: that's how we used to talk to you humans ages ago. That's why you evolved to have no touch receptors in your ear canal—just imagine how ticklish it would be otherwise. Stop shaking your head and get your finger out of there! You won't be able to reach the singleton, and you certainly won't dislodge her. Get a grip on yourself. Earth needs you, and there's not much time. The octopuses are in charge of the world, eating their way through you humans, and you need to fight back."

"Octopuses? Wha…"

The small voice in his ear sighs again.

Even in his befuddlement, Professor MacDonald pictures the spider as a stern school teacher shaking her head at a particularly slow-witted pupil; he'd probably used this very tone on a few of his students a lifetime ago.

"OK, your brain's been on holiday for a while. We get it. Here's the short version: after you got shipped off to this miserable back-end of beyondsville place, alien cousins of the octopus invaded and enslaved humanity, to use them—you—as fodder. We didn't have enough warning to protect the Earth this time. The best we spiders could do was to hide your croft from their view while we built up our

226

numbers beneath these hills."

The professor's eyes start to glaze over.

"Oh, how we wish we had hands to slap your face. Do stop drooling and concentrate!"

He snaps to attention, and the spiders continue.

"We can disable their machines. Like most large-bodied creatures—you humans included—they ignore the small. We've bred some acid-producing singletons who can corrode wiring and destroy weapons. But we need *you* to addle the aliens' brains, since that's something, alas, our small stature means we can't accomplish. Here's what you need to do…"

A couple of hours later, Professor MacDonald is hurtling along the A9 in an aged Land Rover which he liberated from a neighbouring farm, then along the M80 to Glasgow toy shops. He gathers as many Rubik's Cubes, jigsaw puzzles and disco lights as he can from each store and depot he comes across. The Land Rover makes its way further south through the empty and deserted country, stopping every now and then to leave a cache of the toys somewhere the octopuses will be certain to spot them, lit with the flashing colours of bright, sparkly disco lights.

The spiders had explained that the octopus brain is extremely tuned to symmetry and pattern detection, and they cannot bear to look at a puzzle without completing it. If, they reasoned, you made a puzzle impossible, for example by twisting the corner element of a Rubik's Cube so that it can never be solved, or perhaps by exchanging one or two pieces in a five-thousand-piece jigsaw puzzle with pieces from a similar one, an octopus alien will devote so much time and energy to trying to work it out, that it forgets to eat and sleep, and goes insane or catatonic.

The Professor and his spiders wait for several days, enough time for the traps to be discovered, then travel to London, the aliens' headquarters on the planet. They pass clusters of octopuses with bloodshot eyes, frantically spinning Rubik's Cubes, or trying to squeeze a badly fitting piece into the final hole in a jigsaw puzzle. Deflated sacks of expired octopuses surround them. The smell of overheated plastic toys mixed with the stench of decomposing octopus makes the professor struggle to prevent his breakfast from returning. Large black crows pick at choice parts of the wilted bodies, concentrating more than Professor MacDonald would like on their large eyeballs.

The professor and his arachnid companions finally reach the mothership, where it seems that the aliens' control has been broken. A few human beings are battling them, toppling their water-filled road vehicles or forcing them back into the single remaining spaceship that hasn't been sabotaged by the spiders.

The final alien fleeing up the ramp into the ship pauses to use its translator box: "Hasta la vista, baby. I'll be back." It speaks with a heavy Austrian accent.

As the ship rises, Processor John Dougal Hamish MacDonald rubs the unshaven stubble on his chin and smiles for the first time in almost a year. He even dances a little jig. "Well, chaps, we did it, we actually bloody did it. We saved the Earth. Humanity can prosper again."

"Yes," the small voice in his ears says, "sort of. There are a few things we didn't tell you. The great divergence of our two species was no accident: we deliberately made you humans afraid of us. You were becoming a bit of a bother and started to expect us to do far too much for you. We weren't going to become clever little slaves to feedstock. Now that the octopuses have cut your numbers down, we'll be able to regain control.

"Professor, you know too much. So, sadly for you, you'll be providing sustenance for our colony—you'll be enough to keep us well-fed for months. The singleton in your ear has just injected you with a neurotoxin. It's been nice knowing you, Professor, but it's time to get back to the business of running this planet."

The Umami Invasion

Gary Couzens

The summer I turned nineteen, I was too busy spending the University vacation surfing, waitressing in Darling Harbour and rooting my boyfriend to notice when it happened. We were all looking the wrong way, really.

This is how it happened. More or less.

So it's the Monday arvo shift and this family comes in, Mum and Dad and teenage son. I can tell they're tourists even before they open their mouths. They look a little bleary, probably jetlag and the heat outside. I lift my voice about half an octave and broaden my Aussie accent. "Hi, I'm Rhonda, and I'm your waitress this afternoon."

The boy looks about fourteen and he says nothing,

staring at my chest. He probably does that to everyone with boobs and a pulse below the age of thirty.

The man looks the type too, the kind who tries to feel my bum when he thinks no one's looking. In this restaurant-logo top, this short tight skirt and these heels he probably thinks it's just too inviting. Like the groups of businessmen we sometimes get in the evenings. I've lost count of the number of times I've been asked to sit on someone's face. Or if they're old enough they look at the menu and say, *I can't decide. Help me, Rhonda.* Like I haven't heard that joke many times before.

But this time it looks like Mum's in charge. She orders the kangaroo in orange sauce. People often see that on the menu and if they don't go *Eww gross* they want to give it a try. One of those Things to Do in Oz. Not quite the same as climbing the Harbour Bridge or doing the tour of the Opera House but even so.

"Good choice," I say, making sure to smile.

So when I serve them their mains, she starts *Mmming* and *Aahing.* "That's wonderful," she says. She glances up as I pass by to serve other customers. "Please pass my compliments to the chef, Rhonda."

"Thank you, I sure will."

It's just meat we serve every day. And the cook, the one on duty right now, is probably swigging stubbies of beer when he thinks no one'll notice. If she reacts like that in this place, if she went to the two-star restaurant down the way she'll probably go into orbit.

But at least she's a happy customer.

I finish at eight o'clock. When I get home, Mum's sitting in the front room and Brad, my boyfriend, is there with her, holding my half-brother Michael, rocking him in his arms.

The TV is on but no one's watching it.

"Brad's really good with him, Rhonda," says Mum.

Uh-oh. I hope that doesn't mean Brad's getting ideas. Mum was my age when she had me.

Her boyfriend isn't here. Working late, apparently. I met him a year ago. *Hi Rhonda, this is Patrick. He's my boyfriend.* Huh, I gathered that from the sounds of creaking bedsprings from your room most nights this week. *Hey, Rhonda, I'm going to have a baby.* Wait, you decide this *eighteen fucking years* after you had me? And you always really truly honestly wanted another one? Give me a break. She called him Michael, after the late Mr Hutchence. She said she would've dropped her undies for him in a heartbeat back in the day. I really didn't want to know that.

Baby Michael must've picked up on my vibes. He starts to squirm and gurgle.

"He's hungry," says Mum, taking the baby from Brad. She lifts up her T-shirt and holds Michael there. She's had a lot of practice; I'll give her that. "Isn't he adorable? I could just eat him."

I could eat him too, but you wouldn't like that.

How's my day been? Why, thank you for asking.

I sit down, kicking off my heels, rubbing at the backs of my ankles.

"Umami," says Brad.

"Mmm, what's that?" says Mum.

"Umami," he says again, stretching out the middle syllable to double its length.

"Is that a type of sushi?"

"Sense of taste. They say babies get a big dose of umami from mother's milk." He's been reading Wikipedia pages again.

Mum beams. "Well, breast is best."

"That's right."

And I really don't want to talk about my Mum's boobs with my boyfriend.

I stretch out my legs, still in the tights they make us wear even in the summer. "I'm going to have a shower and change. Make myself a sandwich."

"There's some chicken in the fridge," says Mum, stroking the back of baby Michael's head as he feeds.

"Plenty of umami in chicken," says Brad.

"That so?" I get up and leave the room.

I'm on lunchtime duty a week later and there's a queue at the door. Much more than this and we'll have to turn people away. The cook must be shitting himself. Jasmine, another waitress, tells me, "They all want the roo steak. We could run out of it if we're not careful."

"What's so special about it?" I say.

"Dunno."

"I'd better try it if it's so special." Our cook simply isn't that good.

"Maybe." Jasmine sniffs. She won't be trying it because she's veggo.

I'm on the go all arvo, smiling my smile, my *Hi, I'm Rhonda, what can do for you today?* down pat. I've learned to say *No split bills* in seven languages. How many kangaroo steaks have I served? I've lost count. I'm totally wiped out when I go home on the bus and fall asleep with my head on Brad's shoulder in front of the TV. Mum wakes me up. My turn to feed Michael with a bottle.

"Think of all that umami going into him," says Brad.

"You can stick your umami up your arse," I say.

He doesn't suggest what Michael's nappy contains. Whatever it is, it absolutely fucking stinks.

On my next day off, I go into the restaurant on my own. They give us a staff discount but I've not wanted to use it before.

"Hi, I'm Jasmine and I'm your waitress for the afternoon." Okay, okay, don't overdo it. She leaves me with the menu and goes off to serve another customer, a man in his twenties, American accent from what I can hear. She's leaning forward as she takes his order and he gazes down her top. When she goes away, I'm wondering if he'll try to have a conversation with me.

"Are you ready to order, Madam?" I hope she's not expecting a tip for pretending she doesn't know me.

The prawn cocktail's okay as a starter. But what I want is the main course, kangaroo in orange sauce. So I order it. And it arrives. And I eat it.

Nothing special. It tastes like what roo steak always tastes like.

I pay and leave. By now, all the tables are full and there's a queue outside the door. I flash an encouraging smile at Jasmine, who's having to keep up with all this custom. I'll have to do the same tomorrow.

As I pass a laneway, I hear a noise and glance in. A girl in the waitress uniform of one of the other eateries nearby, her short skirt up around her waist, undies down to her ankles, rooting a guy who must be in his teens. Acne on his bum. *Oh Christ, get a room, you two.* I mutter, "Sorry," and hurry past.

And I feel a tingling inside. Crawling up my scalp. Oh shit, have I just eaten something I'm allergic to? I don't have any known allergies. Am I going to be sick?

I stop, sit on a bench, and it passes. I go home.

Thank you, Rhonda. Would you like to take a moment? A

glass of water? The aircon in here isn't working too well, I'm afraid. Can you get Rhonda a glass of water, please? Shall we continue? In your own time, Rhonda...

Ten hours later, I'm in bed next to Brad. The light's off but it's too hot to sleep. I don't know how he manages it. I gaze up at the ceiling but can't see a thing.

The reaction of this biped is unusual.

"Eh, what? Brad, did you say something?"

No – he's turned away from me and is snoring as usual.

I lie there but don't hear anything more except Brad's noises and the cars outside the window. Heavy techno from the flat across the way. Nothing else. Eventually, I fall asleep.

"Wakey wakey." Brad is shaking my shoulder. "Need to get up now."

I blink. "Hardly slept."

"Didn't look like that to me."

He climbs out of bed, facing away from me, raises his arms and stretches. Naked.

Mmm, he looks good. I haven't thought that way about him in a while. Especially not when he reaches down with his right hand and scratches his bum.

I sit up, the sheets falling to my lap. "Brad…"

He turns to me. "Nice view."

He's got the message.

We go down to breakfast half an hour later.

It's only when I'm spreading vegemite on my toast that I realise.

I don't have my contacts in. And I can see.

I've had shitty eyesight since I was little and I hated the daggy glasses I had to wear all the way through high school, but I couldn't see anything but a blur without them. So as soon as I could I switched to contacts. But they're still in my room. Sister Josephine at the school always told us to pray for miracles. So has one happened during the night? Has my eyesight been fixed all by itself?

What's going on?

And while I'm here, why did I wake up wanting sex with Brad? I'm not that much of a hornbag. (Quiet, you.)

He's not complaining, though. Look at him eating breakfast. That smug *I've just had a really good fuck* expression on his face.

I bet Mum can tell too. Michael gurgles as she tickles him. Well, he might not be able to tell yet. Give him time.

When I take the bus to work, I see it all around me. That same expression. They've all just had a really good fuck too. And on the way home after my shift it's the same. One girl just a few years older than me is sitting opposite, her boyfriend beside her. Well, he can only be her boyfriend, can't he? She's stroking the inside of his thigh. I bet he's thinking he's going to get a really good fuck too.

And Brad and I go at it three times after going to bed.

I can't sleep in the heat so I get up and switch on my phone, listening out just in case Michael starts crying at two in the morning. My mate Davo is awake. I know him from school and we've kept in touch. It's Friday night so I know where he is: his local gay bar.

I message him on WhatsApp: *Good evening?*

Crowded tonight. Back room full of guys screwing & couldn't get in. Some were doing it in the street.

That must have gone down well.

No complaints. Snerk

I asked for that.

I eventually do sleep.

Space.

It's big.

Heaps of it in all directions.

I turn full circle and all I can see are stars. There's one, yellow, planets circling it. The third one is Earth. And it's getting closer. I can see countries and continents now. There's Australia. Racing towards me.

Crash.

All goes black.

Then it's light again. Sunshine in a bright blue cloudless sky. I'm in water.

And then something blots out half the sky. Eyes. Ears. Red fur. Nose. A kangaroo.

It leans forward, sniffs. Pokes out its tongue. Licks me.

And I wake up.

"Brad…? I just had a really strange dream…"

But he's lying on his side, snoring. He farts in his sleep.

It's the evening. Mum and Boyfriend have gone out, a movie somewhere. A few of Brad's mates – yes, he does have some – called round and he's out right now. He'll be blind drunk when the night's over and will likely have chucked up in a bush somewhere. So I'm here on my own, literally holding the baby.

"Okay you, get your umami here," I say as he sucks on the teat of a bottle Mum expressed into.

Jasmine sends me a text. They're crowded tonight and the manager has said more than once he could have done with me there.

"Wanna go outside?" I say. "Or are you just going to lie there and fill your nappy? Big sister Rhonda really appreciates spending the evening cleaning up baby shit. Hope you appreciate it." He gurgles, grins gummily up at me as I take the bottle away. "You fat little pig. How did you get to be my brother? Okay, half-brother. Just because our Mum couldn't keep her undies on, eighteen years apart. We've got the bogan genes, you and me."

Why don't I have one? Brad and me. All I'd have to do…

Hey, wait. What?

What. The. Fuck?

Where did that come from?

No way. Baby factory is not open. Not now, not ever.

Not even Brad has suggested we have a baby. It'd be okay for him if we did. He's not the one who'd have to swell up to enormous size and push out the result nine months later. And it wouldn't be over then. Oh no. It'll only be starting. Bye-bye life, for twenty years at least.

Yes, they do say, Mum and others, of course I'll want one, or more, one day. But they're wrong. No way do I want a baby. Never did. Never will.

So why am I looking at this baby, my baby brother, and suddenly want one?

This is getting weird.

"You know Tilda?" says Jasmine, as we stand outside in the shade of the back entrance, smoking. Tilda is another of the waitresses, a couple of years older than us.

"What about her?"

A truck pulls up about six metres away. Supplies of meat for this evening. Jasmine leans forward, saying in a hurry before the guys get out of the truck. "She's preggo. Don't tell anyone."

"Wow. I didn't know she had a boyfriend."

"She doesn't. Guy she met on the beach and she really fancied him. Now this has happened."

"That's a bit drastic."

"Sure is. She says she suddenly wanted a kid. All of a

sudden."

"What for?"

"It's the continuation of the species, Rhond."

"That's a good thing?"

She shrugs. "I don't know. Can't say I feel that way. A root might be too much to hope for these days."

But Brad, when he's not too drunk, does it with me three times a night. And that's only been the last month or so. It's not just because there are Christmas decorations in the shops.

Something's going on.

And then I turn my head, to where two men, one white and one Aboriginal, both stripped to the waist, are unloading the truck. They're gleaming with sweat. Normally I'd have a good perve.

It's the meat.

I've eaten it and so have heaps of others by now. But Jasmine hasn't because she's veggo and so's her boyfriend.

I grind out my cigarette under my heel, adjust my blouse and skirt and go back to serve our customers. A couple in the corner are eating the kangaroo in orange sauce. Under the table, her foot, a heeled shoe dangling from her toes, is rubbing the calf of the guy's leg.

"You're hungry," he says.

"Well, I am eating for two…"

Professional smile on my face, I approach their table. "Hi, I'm Rhonda…"

I dream the space dream again and wake just as the roo is licking my face. It is drinking something? What am I, looking up at it?

Am I a virus or something? Maybe you spread me by having sex and making lots of baby roos. Continuation of the series and all that.

240

Where did I come from? Outer space?

I landed right in the middle of the Great Southern Land, in a waterhole.

And the first thing I see? The prominent life form on this planet?

Take me to your leader, Skippy.

After my shift, I go off to Circular Quay. Plenty of tourists around, many of them clearly unused to spending Christmas in the thirty-degree humid Sydney heat. They're taking selfies with the Harbour Bridge and the Opera House. Soon they'll be flying off home – fifteen, twenty hours, more, for God's sake – and spreading whatever it is inside them, inside me, all over the world.

How long will it last? How long can this alien life form and us humans live in the same bodies?

It sounds really dumb. Or scary.

Unless I can do something.

Thank you for your information so far, Rhonda. We'll wrap up soon. This will all be very useful in the current situation. We'd like to thank you for all your cooperation.

This'll probably be the last thing I ever do at this restaurant, as when the manager finds out I'll be sacked. I borrow the key from his belt without his knowing, get it copied, put it back before he notices it's gone.

First thing in the morning, I unlock the door, go into the kitchen and take all the roo meat from the freezers, stuff a carrier bag full, hide it in my backpack. I buy a ticket to Oceanworld, walk around with the tourists.

I stop outside the croc enclosure. The saltie's a big bastard, six or seven metres long, would snap you in two if you met it in the wild. He glares up at me, obviously wishing I'll be his lunch.

Finally, the tourists have moved on, and for a moment I'm alone. Quickly, I take the meat out of my backpack and tip it out into the enclosure.

Take me to your leader.

The croc moves surprisingly quickly, scoffs the lot.

I haven't stopped the alien invasion but I've done my bit.

The Lots of Us

Phillip Irving

I went into the kitchen, where I was making soup. "What the *fuck?*" the other me, on the far side of the kitchen island said.

"What the *fuck?*" I said.

He stared at me. I stared at him. Behind him, the soup bubbled. On the counter in front of him, my chopping board. Shreds of basil, the inevitable stain left by the tomatoes. An empty tin of peeled plum tomatoes on the drainer. I was starving, and I'd Zapped home to make soup.

"You're… me," I said.

"And you're… me," he said.

We stared at each other some more. We both remained perfectly still. The smell of tomatoes and basil and garlic filled the space between us.

"Is that nearly done?" I said, eventually.

"What do you mean, is that *nearly done?*" He was frowning furiously. Beside him, on the counter, a vase of purple flowers.

I looked down at the bouquet of lilacs I held in one hand, the crystal vase in the other. Men don't buy themselves flowers, I'd read, so I'd made a point of buying them. Helped by the fact that the mall's Zapper meant I didn't need to walk home carrying them. And I'd bought a vase, to put them in. "I need some water for these," I said. "And I need some soup. And then… Then we can work out what the fuck has happened."

"I think it's pretty clear what the fuck has happened," the other me said. "Fuck's *sake.*"

"Is it?" I said. I held up the vase. "Water."

He glared at me, his eyes flicking to the hall behind me but always coming back. Then he shook his head, took the vase and filled it. "This isn't supposed to happen," he said.

"What has actually happened?" I said, checking the soup and putting my knife in the sink. "I was on my way back from the mall, to make some soup. I'd bought flowers. And the vase." Suddenly the other empty shopping bag underneath the coat rack made sense. "You bought a vase, too," I said.

"*I* didn't buy *a* vase," he said. "*We* bought *the* vase. *We* bought flowers. Zapped home. That was…" he looked at his watch. "Twenty minutes ago. And now here *you* are."

"Here I am," I said. I frowned. "But I was just…"

"No, you weren't," he said, sounding exasperated. "Twenty minutes ago, *we* were."

"Oh, *fuck,*" I said, realisation dawning. "This isn't supposed to happen!"

"That's what I said!" he said. "*Fuck.*"

My stomach gurgled. "Seriously, though, the soup…"

"For fuck's sake," he said. "Go for it. I've lost my appetite."

I took a bowl and ladled a serving. Fresh tomato and basil soup.

The other me went out into the hall. I heard several solid-sounding thumps, and some swearing.

Bowl in hand, I followed. "Any luck?" I said.

"Says it's still receiving," he said. He pressed some buttons, hit it again, but it was just a metal disc on the floor with a waist-high control console on one side like a lectern. There wasn't much to hit.

"Has that helped?" I said.

He scowled. "Very funny," he said.

I looked at my watch. "Might be in twenty minutes."

"*Fuck*," he said, and stomped upstairs.

I stared at the Zapper, eating the soup slowly, savouring it as though it were a balm to the implications. I was a double, then. I wasn't sure how I felt about that. It should have been chilling to the core, should have had me questioning the validity of my existence, the very nature of existence itself, but all I could think was if another one of us came along then I wouldn't be a double but a triple. And then…

I went into the kitchen, rinsed the bowl, and left the water running, staring at it blankly in the hope that some thoughts might form. They didn't. Other than a growing awareness that I was probably in some sort of shock. I didn't know if there was a name for the sort of shock that seeing a double of yourself brought on. I was aware of some sort of folklore concerning doppelgangers but I couldn't remember what it was, so I looked it up on my phone, in case it was meant to be lucky.

It wasn't supposed to be lucky at all. It was supposed to be the exact opposite of lucky. Not least since a legal ruling a couple of years ago, when the Zappers first came out, that was quite specific about the legal implications for anyone trying to make any duplicates of themselves. There was a lot of information about the implications, and they all sounded very *final*.

"Well, that can't be good," I said to nobody at all.

There was a *Zap* from the hallway, the sound of someone placing a bag on the floor, the sound of someone looking in some bags, and then the kitchen door opened and I walked in holding a bouquet of lilacs and a vase.

"What the *fuck*?" the other me said.

"Oh, fuck," I said.

"You're… me," he said.

"Yep," I said.

He paused, eyes uncertain, then sniffed. "Is that… soup?" he said.

"It's just done," I said. "It'll need heating up." I looked out at the hallway behind him. "Actually, you might want to make some more. Just in case."

"In case…" he said, getting a bowl from a cupboard.

"In case there's any more," I said. I nodded at his flowers. "I'll get you some water for those."

I filled the vase while he heated the soup, then I went into the hallway. Sure enough, the word "Receiving" was still flashing on the control console's little digital display. "Fuck," I said, and patted it, gently, on the side.

"Did that help?" the third me said, behind me, taking a mouthful of soup.

"Very funny," I said. "I need to call the company."

"What's happened?" Three said.

"Well, we stepped into the Zapper at the mall and Zapped back here at…" I checked my watch. "About one. Original us Zapped straight here. I came out twenty minutes later. And twenty minutes after that, along came you."

"Oh," Three said. "*Oh. Fuck.*"

"Yep. I'm not sure what we do about this, but if they can't stop this soon…"

"We're going to run out of tomatoes," he said.

I laughed, bitterly. "And basil."

"So there's three of us?"

"You're number three," I said.

"And you're number two."

"Ouch. I don't like that," I said.

"I don't like Number Three," he said.

"Fair point. Let me call the company."

"Where's Original Us?"

"Upstairs, I think. He… I don't know. For some reason, he seems to have taken it worse."

"Because he's the original?" Three said.

"Maybe," I said. "You'd have thought that would be better than…"

"Being a duplicate," Three said.

"Yeah," I said. "Just, don't Google it."

"Noted."

I went into the lounge and called the company. Muzak chimed in, a repeated chorus of the Zap jingle: *You'll never walk alone*, but the last word changed to *again*. I waited, noticing for the first time that between my sofa and my armchair, there was only seating for three people in here.

"Welcome to Zap. How may we direct your call?" a human-sounding voice enthused, abruptly cutting through the muzak.

"Customer service," I said.

"This is customer care," an identical voice said. "What is the nature of your call today?"

"A fault," I said. "The Zapper is…" I paused, uncertain how much to say. There were three of me when there should only be one, and I wasn't sure how they'd seek to

247

remedy that. "It's developed a fault," I said.

"Please specify the nature of the fault," the voice said, tone unchanged.

The door opened. "I'm going to make that soup," a me said. "In case… Four comes along." He shut the door.

I brought the phone back to my face. "It's… replicating people," I said, wincing as I said the verb, aware that it matched the legalese I'd read about.

"Please give us your full name," the voice said.

"Anton Kobek," I said, sudden outrage sweeping through me as I said the words. That was my name. *Me.* Who I was. Not *Number Two.* None of this should have been happening.

"Mr Kobek, we have sent an update to your Zapper. We will send an engineer in three to ten days to check the appliance's hardware. If you see any unusual behaviour from your Zapper in the meantime, please consider an alternative mode of transport, such as walking."

"Three to ten *days?*" I said.

"If you would like to answer a few short questions about your experience with our customer service today, please hold the line."

I ended the call, then said, "Fuck."

Back in the hallway, the console still blinked "Receiving."

I hit it quite firmly on the side, said, "*Fuck*," again and went back into the kitchen, where I was making soup.

"Two?" he said, stirring.

"Yep," I said. "No luck. They said three to ten days."

"Three to ten *days?*"

"Yep."

"Fuck."

"Yep," I said. I looked at the counter on the far side of the kitchen. There were three vases of lilacs, and another bunch and a vase sitting unattended on the side. "How many of us are there now?" I asked.

"Four," he said. "Original, you, me, and… Number Four. He came in while you were on the phone." He looked at the bubbling pan in front of him. "He said he wanted soup."

I looked at the ornate clock on the chrome wall. It was a little after two. "We're all going to want soup," I said, miserably. "That's what we were coming back for."

Three nodded. "Seen OA?"

"OA?"

"Original Anton."

"Oh," I said. "No. Not since he went upstairs. Have you?"

"No. Do you think he's freaking out?"

"Probably," I said. "I would be."

"And yet, you're not," Three said.

"Not *yet*."

"We haven't done it on purpose, Two," Three said, tasting the soup. "It's not like we've committed a crime."

"If they charge us with a crime we'll get a trial," I said. "I'm worried they'll look on us not as criminals but… Well, I don't know what they'll treat us as."

"They can't… they can't just…" Three swallowed. "Can they?"

"I don't know," I said, trying to keep my voice kind despite still bristling slightly at being called *Two*. "We're not supposed to be here. The Zapper is still *receiving*. I've got a funny feeling the more of us there are, the less likely any of us are to be treated… well." There'd been a debate when the Zappers were first created about the legal status of any individuals who Zapped; it had been resolved quickly enough, but the discussion had never broadened to include plurals, other than to thoroughly proscribe the act of trying to make any.

"Possibly," Three said, unperturbed. "Come, try this."

"I'm sure it's fine," I said, raising an eyebrow sardonically. "We all make the same soup."

"Ah, but you haven't tried *this* one."

I looked from the soup to the man making it. "I'm pretty sure it'll be the same."

At that moment another me came in from the internal door to the garage and looked at both of us. "*Fuck*," he said.

"Yup," I said, looking at the two other of me.

"Soup's done," Three said to him. "Any luck?"

"We've got enough fuel to get to the coast," Four said. "From there... I don't know what we do from there."

"Get to the coast?" I said.

"In case things turn... bad," Three said.

"Things are already bad," I said.

"In case things turn worse."

"There are four of us now, right?" Four said.

Three and I nodded.

"Well, I think the more there are of us, the less likely we are to be treated... well," Four said. "I was doing some Googling down there, and –"

"I told you not to Google," Three said, exchanging a knowing look with me.

"Yeah, well, I did, and none of the stuff I found was in any way *good*."

"Maybe that's what Anton's doing," Three said. "Googling. Freaking out."

"Where is he?" Four said.

"Upstairs," I said. "He went up just after I arrived, and he's not come back down."

"He seems to have taken it harder than us," Three said.

"Because he's the original?" Four said.

I nodded.

"Sort of makes sense," Four said, grabbing a bowl and the ladle. "Better than being a double, though."

None of us really knew what to say to that, and a sort of awkward silence fell. I filled Four's vase with some water and set the flowers in it. Then there was a *Zap* from the hallway, the sound of shopping bags, and the kitchen door opened.

"What the *fuck?*" Five said, holding a vase and some flowers.

"Oh, fuck," Four said.

"You're… me," Five said.

"Yep," I said.

"Yep," Three said.

"*Fuck*," Four said.

"Five," I said. "This is Three and Four. I'm Two. The Zapper's fucked. Keeps creating more us-es." I looked at the wall clock. "In another twenty minutes, there'll be six of us." I looked at his flowers and held out a hand for the vase. "Let me get you some water."

"*Six* of us?" Five said, looking at the three of us in turn. "*Six?*"

"Yes," I said. "Thing keeps Zapping one of us out every twenty minutes. Something's wrong with it."

"*Fuck*," Five said. "Has someone called the company?"

"Yes," I said. "They say they'll be with us in three to ten days."

"Three to ten *days?*" he said, then, "Oh, is that soup?

"It's good," Three said.

"It's *very* good," Four said, his mouth half-full.

"Have some," Three said. "I'll make some more."

Five took a bowl from the cupboard, a spoon, and ladled some of the soup from the pot into the bowl. "Where's the vase gone?" he said.

"Here," I said, and set the vase alongside the other four.

"If this keeps up," Three said, "we're going to run out of room on the counter. And tomatoes."

"And bowls," Four said, rinsing his in the sink.

"We've got much bigger problems than soup bowls," I said.

"An army marches on its stomach," Three said.

"Oh, fuck, that's what they'll call us," Four said miserably. "An *army*."

"This is fucking weird," Five said.

"*Really* fucking weird," I said.

"Where's…" Five did a head count, lips moving as he went. "One?"

"OA," Three said.

"Original Anton," I said. "He's upstairs."

"We think he's freaking out," Four said.

"Why aren't *you* freaking out?" Five said.

Four shrugged. "I was hungry. And… I don't know. There was one of me in here when I came in, and another in the lounge… Is there a word for the sort of shock you feel when there's more than one of you?"

"There was only one of me when I came in," Three said. "But then you said OA was upstairs and… seemed like things were already in motion, I guess. Went into autopilot a bit. I think *I* might be in shock, come to think of it."

"Have you called the company?" Five said. He was staring at the flower vases. I'd thought their purple delicate when I'd picked them up in the store but, seeing them all together, the colour was becoming overpowering.

"Yeah," I said. "Whatever they tried, it didn't work." I looked again in the direction of the hallway. "They're saying three to ten days…" I held out my hands, helpless.

"That's… seven hundred and twenty Antons," Four

said. "Seven hundred and twenty *uses*."

We shivered, collectively.

"That's a lot of flowers," Five said.

Three said, "That's a lot of soup."

"It's a lot of everything," I said. "They won't let that..." I searched for the word. "Lie."

"*Live*, you mean," Four said.

"*Fuck*," Five said.

"*I've* had an idea," another me said, from the doorway to the hall. His eyes were wild, hair unkempt, as though he'd just got out of bed.

"OA!" Three said, then, when the new arrival just frowned, added, "Number One!"

"Just Anton, please," he said. "You... things might need to give yourselves numbers, or... whatever. I'm just me."

"We're all just you, Anton," I said. "We all stepped into the Zapper at the mall. It's just that we've come out here at different times."

"No," Anton said. "*I'm me*. You... lot... are all just duplicates. When Zap get on top of this, and they *will* get on top of this, they'll fix the Zapper, and you'll all just..." he tailed off, presumably as uncertain about the specifics as the rest of us.

"They said it's going to take three to ten days," I said.

Anton's eyes flared. "*What?*"

"That's what I said," I said.

"We have to work *together*," Four said. "We're all in this mess *together*."

"*I'm* not," Anton said. "I'm *me*. I'm *real!* You guys are just... malfunctions."

"I'm not a malfunction!" Five said. "A few minutes ago I was walking to the Zapper so I could come home and have some lunch! And now you're telling me I'm not fucking *real?"*

Anton's eyes flicked to the wooden knife block, then to Five, standing right beside it.

"What was your idea, Anton?" I said.

Four, maybe having the same thought, also looked at the knife block and then to Original Anton. "Yeah, *OA*, what was your idea?"

"Well," he said, but I could see him weighing up the odds and finding them against him. "We could… I mean we could *all…"*

"All *what?"* Three, presumably reaching the same conclusion as the rest of us, said.

"Well, you know, next time one of us… comes through… We just…" he looked from unflinching gaze to unflinching gaze but pressed on. "Kill… it?"

"Fuck off," Five said. *"I* just came through. Telling me if I'd been twenty minutes later, you'd have done me in?"

"We're *here,"* Anton said, pleading. *"We* know what's happened, and we're conscious of it, and we've diverged. We're no longer the same as the original that went into the Zapper. But anything coming through from now, at the moment it comes through… It's just a duplicate. Of me. Of *us.* It's an echo. A ghost. Not real."

We exchanged glances that varied from appalled to bemused. "It keeps the numbers down," Four said, his tone unreadable.

"It's fucking barbaric!" Five said.

"What the fuck did you read on that Google search?" I said.

"I read about what they do to those who make duplicates," Four said, indignant.

"Did you also read about the penalty for murder?" I said.

"It's not murder," Four said. "Not… technically.

254

Because they're not… *We're* not…"

"Is it not better we do it than… whoever they send out for this sort of… thing?" Three said, wretchedly. "You said yourself, the more of us there are, the less likely it is we'll be treated… well."

"In which case we don't want to set a precedent for murdering ourselves!" I said. "How can we expect *them* to treat us as human if *we* don't?"

"No, he's right," Anton said. "It's the only way. We keep the number of duplicates to a minimum and when they do come to sort everything out, we…"

I saw the moment he connected the dots from the flicker in his eyes and the sag in his shoulders. "We get done for murder," I said. "And you still get done for duplication. And we get… whatever Four's read they do to duplicates."

"Actually, it's conspicuously vague about the duplicates," Four said. "I think that's worse. You know, I really don't *like* being Four," Four said.

"Wait, am I Five?" said Five. "*Fuck.*"

"There's going to be a Six in a minute," I said.

"Oh, fuck," Original Anton said.

"We can't just murder him, Anton," I said.

"Really?" he said. "It's not… a grey area?"

"Have you been Googling the same stuff as Four?" I said.

"What's on Google?" Three said. "You told me not to look so I didn't look."

"Oh, *fuck*," Five said, looking at his phone, then, "Wait, how can they have just not decided…"

"What if we just told the company that it had stopped?" Four suggested.

"Then we'd be stuck murdering ourselves for… ever," I said.

"Well, no," Four said. "I mean, they're still sending

someone to check the fault, aren't they? Just ask them to do a factory reset, or whatever it is they do."

"And in the meantime?" Three said.

"Well…" Four said, and drew a finger across his throat, with a mock grimace.

"Is it me," I said, "or are we getting a *little* callous? This is *us* we're talking about. That Zapper is churning out *uses*."

"He's right," Five said. "We have to remember they're still *us*, even if they've not come out the Zapper yet."

"Unless we take care of the problems as they *do* come out the Zapper," Anton said.

"They're not *problems*; they're *us*," Five insisted.

Original Anton looked up at the clock, then at the rest of us. "Not much time to decide," he said.

"We're not deciding," I said. "We're not doing it."

"That is a decision," Original Anton said.

"Then that's the decision," I said.

"Fine," he said. "Stay here, then."

He marched past the knife block and took the oversized chef's knife from where I'd left it in the sink and went out to the hall. The rest of us stood, silent and watchful, nobody wanting to be the first to move.

"Fuck this," I said, and went through the door to the hall.

He was standing by the Zapper, just inside the front door. His breathing was quick and heavy, his eyes unblinking. "Stay away," he said, not turning around. "If you think I won't do you, too… well, you know I will."

"Actually, I don't," I said, walking past the staircase, towards him. "Whatever this is, it's not something *I* would do."

Behind me I heard the kitchen door, the other us-es filing into the hall.

Anton did turn, then. "I'll get at least one of you,

before you can take me," he said, eyes unsettlingly calm. "Think on that." He was just the other side of the hall rug from me, now. "You want to be first?"

There was a flash of light from the pad and another me appeared, holding a bouquet of lilacs and a shopping bag with a vase in it, and said, "What the *fuck*?"

Original Anton turned, drew back the knife, and I jumped forward and grabbed his wrist. He turned, snarled, tried to drive the blade at my face, and I kneed him in the crotch.

"Didn't see that coming, did you," I said.

He grunted, fell back against the front door.

"You're... me," said Six.

"Yep," I said, grimly.

"You're... all... me."

Anton groaned and sank to his knees, but then lunged low at Six with the knife. Six yelped, dropped the bag and the bouquet, and crouched to catch Original Anton's wrists, and the two of them struggled to and fro, the blade an ever-deadly presence between them.

"What the *fuck*?!" shouted Six.

"I'm... *sorry*," said Original Anton.

The knife pressed against Six's throat. He pushed it clear, then OA half-stood pushing it back, the blade wavering centimetres from finality.

I picked up the shopping bag, swung it around in an arc and into the back of Original Anton's head. I think I'd expected something cinematic, a shattering of glass, shards flying, Anton spinning dramatically away, blood trailing from his lip. There was none of that. A very heavy thud that sounded, in no way I could fully comprehend, *wrong*. And Original Anton crumpled like a shirt.

"*Jesus*," said Five.

"What the *fuck*?" said Six. "Why did he...? What did

you…?"

"Wow," said Four. "Those things are really heavy."

"What now?" said Three, looking at where Original Anton appeared to not be breathing.

"*What the fuck is going on?*" said Six.

"The Zapper's fucked," I said. "We all went into the Zapper at the mall at one o'clock; one of us has come out of *this* one every twenty minutes since."

"You mean we're all duplicates?" said Six.

"He's not," said Four, pointing at Original Anton.

"I think I'm going to be sick," said Five.

"Do you want some soup?" Three said.

"*Soup?*" Six said, mouth hanging open. He looked down at Original Anton, looked at us each in turn, then said, somewhat guiltily, "Actually, I'd love some soup."

"Go through," I said. "I'll… take care of this." I checked Original Anton's pulse, which was, of course, not there. I turned him over so his sightless eyes met mine. It was the very worst feeling I'd ever had, the thing that settled in my chest, then. And yet, somehow, not quite real. I was responsible for Anton being dead. Switched off. Released into oblivion. And yet, being able to look from the dead Anton to all the not-dead Antons made it false, somehow. Even while part of my brain wouldn't let go of the fact that I'd killed the *original* Anton, another part was asking why his reality should somehow have been more significant than mine, or Six's. "Fuck," I said, looking at his unmoving chest. "What the fuck now?"

There was a knock at the door. I swallowed, looked around, my own eyes so wide I could feel the lids strain.

"Come on," Four said, quietly. "The garage." He crossed the rug and picked up one of Anton's feet. Five took the other. "Quickly," Four said. Six took his right arm and Three took the left, and together they bore him away from me.

"Take a breath," Three said, and nodded at the door. "And deal with that."

I looked down. The vase had killed Original Anton, but it hadn't drawn blood.

There was another knock at the door, and someone shouted, "Mr Kobek, we're here about the Zapper."

I took the vase into the kitchen and filled it with water, trying to stop the picture of Original Anton's face from floating in front of my own, identical, one.

There was another knock. "It's important you let us in, Mr Kobek."

I put the flowers in the vase, checked there was no sign of any of the others of me, and went to the door.

"Hi, Mr Kobek," a man who looked to be in his late twenties said. "My name is John. We got your call, about the duplicates. I got here as quickly as I could. We're quite busy, I'm sorry to say."

I tried not to wince. I'd mentioned replication on the phone to the company in the lounge. I wondered if Original Anton had done the same while he was upstairs; how much detail he'd gone into. "Are there lots of… situations like this?" I asked, ushering him inside. I couldn't stop looking at the floor, as if for evidence of this crime I'd committed that hadn't technically been invented yet.

"Oh, no," John said smoothly. "This is the first time it's happened." He smiled in a way that looked utterly unconvincing and set down his toolbox. I looked through the open kitchen door at the clock, and calculated how long we'd have before Seven joined us.

"So how do we fix it?" I said.

"Well, we tried a remote patch. I assume you switched it off and on again, so…"

"Wait," I said. "What?"

"Turned it off and on again. You know? At the mains?"

I swallowed. Looked down at the waist-high console by the wall. "I didn't know it was connected that way. I thought… I don't know what I thought."

The man shrugged. "Oh! Well, let's give that a go." He knelt by the machine and reached behind it.

"Wait!" I said, and he paused, and frowned up at me.

"I mean… Should we do that?" I said. "What if… what if someone's coming through?"

His frown deepened. "Well, you already came through, didn't you?" he said.

"Yes, but I mean…"

"Can't let it keep running if it's creating duplicates," he said. He chuckled. "We're in enough trouble as it is."

"Are we?" I said and glanced anxiously in the direction of the clock again. Ten minutes' time. If we did nothing, a seventh me would appear in ten minutes. If we switched the power off at the mains, then he wouldn't. There was something awfully final about that. Flicking a switch to prevent a being coming to life. Even if that being would be a duplicate. But then, we were all duplicates, now. I didn't feel any less alive for that. But then, Seven wasn't alive *yet*. But in ten minutes he *would* be.

It was complicated and circular. I had no way to rationalise it, much less articulate it. But it wouldn't stop turning around in my head while John watched me, his eyes narrowing.

"Where are the… duplicates?" he said.

"What?" I said.

"You said there was one coming through every twenty minutes. So there must be… what? Four or five by now? Six?"

"Oh…" I tried to think of a cover, something that wouldn't arouse suspicion or encourage any further questions. "They went away."

John sighed. "Mr Kobek, the penalty for self-duplication is *very* severe."

"I haven't duplicated myself!" I said. "*Your* machine malfunctioned!" I was still looking at the clock. What would Seven make of it, I wondered, if he emerged to see himself talking with a Zap technician about unplugging the machine that was making duplicates, of which Seven *was* one, in order to prevent any more duplicates being made? Come to think of it, what did *I* make of it, as a duplicate still having the conversation?

"Right," John said, and pulled out the plug.

The light, and any hope of there being a seventh Anton Kobek, died. "Well that's that, then," I said. He hadn't killed anyone. Nobody was gone that had been there before. But the next moment still felt heavy as it passed.

"That's that," the technician said, standing. "Where are the duplicates, Mr Kobek?"

"I don't know," I said, half-truthfully. "I don't... I don't know where they went."

"Mr Kobek, there are strange behaviour fluctuations when people get... duplicated. It... does things. To the mind. Hence, it's a very serious matter. There's a *reason* the penalty is severe."

"I thought you said this had never happened before."

"Oh, yes." He nodded, slowly. "That's... right."

"So you're talking, what? Hypothetically?"

"Yes," he said. "That's right. Hypothetically."

"So, hypothetically, what's the reason the penalty is so severe? What, *hypothetically*, does it do... to the mind?"

"Well, hypothetically, you create a zero-sum game," he said. "You can't have more than one of a person. So, hypothetically, there would be increasing hostility until..." He shrugged. "You can guess the rest."

I glanced involuntarily in the direction of the others of me, already carrying one of our bodies. "So, hypothetically," I said, uncertainly, "what would *cause* the duplicates to get aggressive?"

"What?" he said.

"I mean, if there's a situation where there's been hostility…"

"Hypothetically."

"Hypothetically. Why would they… I mean, how would you even know who's the duplicate and who's not?"

He frowned, and for the first time he really looked at me in a way that made me wish I hadn't asked. "Well, technically, there's no difference. Physically, they'd be the same."

I tried not to look relieved. I was the most original of all the Antons, now, but I was not the original Anton. But then, I wondered, was Anton still original, if he'd Zapped in the first place? Or was the anti-Zap propaganda true: if you Zapped then the original you was left a pile of molecules in the Zapper's receptacle, and the one that arrived at their destination just a replica, regardless? "So there's no way to tell?" I said.

"Well, *you* must know?" John said, laughing awkwardly.

"Of course, I know!" I laughed, too, just as awkwardly. "I just… Wonder how a duplicate would know. If nobody was there to tell them."

"Well, that's… never happened before," he said.

"Of course it hasn't," I said.

"No, I mean…" He frowned again, looked on the verge of continuing, but turned instead to the Zapper, which he plugged back in. It whirred, and it buzzed, and it flashed the message 'Ready', and then went into standby. "Well, the machine's fixed."

"Looks sorted," I said. "Kept saying receiving, before."

262

"When it was making duplicates," he said.

"Well, I *assume* it made duplicates," I said. "But if it did, they'd already gone before I found them. That's why I asked."

"What time did *you* Zap, Mr Kobek?"

I was ready for that one. "About one," I said. "And I came straight through," I added quickly, pointing at myself. "No duplication here. No sirree."

He nodded wearily. "I need to take a look around."

I followed him into the kitchen. "Lots of flowers," he said. "All identical…"

"That's when I realised there was something wrong," I said. "Kept coming back in and finding another vase just… sitting there. It was really weird. And I *like* flowers."

"Bowls on the side?"

"I like soup, too," I said.

He narrowed his eyes, then nodded and went to the door to the garage that held five other versions of me, one of them dead.

I swallowed. "There's nothing in there but my car," I said. "And some boxes."

"I'll look for myself, if you don't mind," he said.

He opened the door onto the cool clutter beyond, turning to watch my reaction. I kept my features as painfully still as I was able as he manoeuvred himself between assorted boxes and my car, looking into the car's windows, peering into some of the boxes. I held my breath, straining to catch any sound that might betray us, but heard nothing. When John had made it to the far end of the car and was peering under the front bumper, I saw another me creeping around a box, his finger to his lips.

"You got the keys to the car?" John said.

I looked at the other me, who shook his head, eyes wide. "Um, not on me," I said.

"Would you mind?" John said.

I looked at the other me and shrugged, before going back into the kitchen. The keys were in my pocket but I let the door close before fished them out and opened it again.

I was two steps back in the garage when a hand went over my mouth and pulled me down behind the car. Two of me were standing near to us, one behind two stacked boxes, one visible beside him. One of them was talking in relaxed tones: "See, I said there wasn't anything in there."

I felt the car move against my back, and then John's voice, from inside. "Fine. But you understand I had to look."

"Of course," said the me behind the box. He was holding the visible me up, moving his hand as he spoke. I looked, aghast, at the me who'd pulled me down behind the car.

He nodded, and mouthed, *"Original Anton."* Then shrugged.

"Check the door," the me holding the dead me up said. "The key's in the kitchen. If it's locked then they didn't get out that way."

I heard the car door close and then I was manhandled up and into view beside the boxes. Beside me, the me carrying Original Anton slipped away out of sight, and the me who'd been crouching behind the car got into the boot and pointed at it meaningfully.

"Locked," John said, and turned.

"Well then," I said, and closed the boot. "Like I said, I didn't see anyone."

He frowned, looked around. "Well, they're not in here. I need to check the rest of the house." He went past me into the kitchen, leaving me to exhale slowly while I looked around, wondering how four live and one dead of us had managed to keep out of sight.

I waited until I heard footfalls on the staircase, and hissed into the seemingly empty space, "Well?"

Nobody spoke. A hand came out from behind two large storage boxes, making the finger sign for OK.

I went back into the hall and waited.

Eventually, John came back down the stairs. "No sign of anyone."

"I don't know what to tell you," I said.

He looked at me, eyes narrowing. "Did you… something with your hair?"

"Absolutely not."

He was still staring. "Mr Kobek, this is serious…"

"I know," I said. "I Googled it."

He nodded, still looking unconvinced, his expression still that of someone trying to remember a face from a long time ago. "If they try to come back…" he said, lamely. "If you hear from any of them…"

"Of course, I'll let you know."

"*Immediately*, Mr Kobek. You'll be monitored, as of now. Duplication is a big deal. The penalty…"

"I know," I repeated. "Google. Only thing it didn't tell me was that you can turn it off and on again."

"Well, you're not supposed to," he said. "In case…" He sighed, gave me a very weary look, and picked up his toolbox. "In case someone's partway through," he said. "Like, they've been Zapped into the scanner at one end, but they've not yet emerged from the receiver at the other. If the receiver's turned off…" He shook his head, sadly, then added, quickly, "it's never happened! Of course. But it's… *hypothetically*… not good."

"Hypothetically," I said. "So, is it, *hypothetically*, a different person that comes out than goes in?"

"No! Of course not. It's just if you go in and you don't come out…"

"How's that different to going in and coming out again, if you're the one who went in?"

He swallowed. "*That* conversation is above my pay grade." He looked past me again, then shook his head, turned, and left.

"Is any of this covered in the warranty?" I called after him, but he didn't so much as look over his shoulder. I stared after him for a little while, trying to make the implications of what he'd said feel real. They didn't, of course. I remembered going into the Zapper and I remembered coming out. No different to a hundred other times. Except…

The others were waiting, when I went back into the kitchen. OA's body was lain across the island, its hands folded across its chest.

"What was with the puppet show in there?" I said.

"He turned just as we'd got him out of the boot," one of us said. "I improvised."

"We need to get rid of it," another said. "We can't risk that happening again."

"Wait, who's who, now?" I said.

"Four," the one who'd spoken said.

"Five," Five said.

"Six," another said, then laughed when one of the others opened his mouth to protest and said, "Only joking. Three."

"Six," Six said.

"And I'm Two," I said.

"Well, there's no One, anymore," Four said.

We looked at each other for a moment, that strange feeling that we should all be thinking the same thing but probably weren't. Different Antons, now. Our synaptic processes diverging the more time we spent in our own company, experiencing all this from slightly different vantages.

"That went pretty well," I said. "You know, if we play this right, we could really turn it to our advantage," I said.

"You think?" Four said, looking thoughtful.

"Five of us," Five said. "All duplicates. Whatever we do, we need to do it together."

"Can't let anyone know about us," I said. "That guy was very clear. The penalty for duplication is severe. I think the penalty for being duplicates would be even worse."

"It's not a crime, is it?" Six said.

"Not technically," Five said. "Not according to Google. But nobody's quite decided what it *is*."

"Are we… perpetrators, or victims?" Six said.

"Neither," I said. "We're *evidence*."

"So what do we do?" Five said.

"Let's get rid of that body. Fortunately, nobody is likely to look for him if everyone thinks he's still here."

"Did you mean to?" Six said. "Kill him?"

"Not really," I said, aware that they'd all paused to look at my response to that. "I think I was trying to, sort of. When I hit him. I knew I was hitting him hard enough. But I didn't think it would… I didn't think it *would*."

"He wasn't right," Three said. "In the head, I mean. OA wasn't right."

"I don't think I had a choice," I said. "He was going to…" I mimed a throat being cut.

"Why?" Six said. "Why me?"

"Not just you," I said. "All of you. Of us. As in, any more who came through. *However* many more." I shuddered, then shook my head. "Anyway, let's go."

"Hang on," said Six. "How come you're in charge?"

"I guess I just… am?" I said. "Now I'm the oldest."

"He's Number Two," Three said. "We've no Number One…"

"Does that mean he's the original, now?" Five said.

"I don't think there is an original, now," Three said.

"I don't think there ever was," I said. "Original went into the Zapper in the mall. We came out. I'm not sure what that means anymore."

"So, is there a difference?" Six said.

"Not according to the technician," I said. "Physically, at least."

"Actually, there is," a different voice said, from the front door. We turned as one. John was holding what looked like a briefcase in one hand, some sort of wand attached to it by a wire with the other. "It's a bit long-winded," he said, "but it's *very* accurate."

Four, nearest to John, exchanged a glance with me, but I shook my head. "What difference does it make," I said. "You already said we're physically the same."

"Almost," he said. "But you've all physically come into being a matter of minutes ago, and this gizmo will tell me how many minutes, given enough time. Now, if you want to speed up the process, you can just tell me who the original is, and we can avoid wasting time."

"What'll happen to the rest of us?" I said.

"The rest of you shouldn't be here," John said, sympathetically. "There's no *space* for more than one of you. I mean could you imagine?"

"That didn't answer the question," Four said, darkly.

John's eyes went down to his hip, perhaps as a warning or perhaps involuntarily. A pistol holstered there. Either way, not a good sign. "The rest of you will… go back in," he said. "Now," he said. "Anyone going to save us all some time?"

Four and I took a step apart, and I gestured to the body on the worktop. "That's the original."

John sagged. "Not *again*," he said.

This time I narrowed my eyes. "It's always the originals that crack, isn't it?" I said.

He nodded miserably, then raised a sardonic eyebrow. "Hypothetically? Every time."

"So," I said. "What now?"

We looked at each other, at John, at the gun at his side, at the kitchen knives, the vases.

"Let's not do anything rash," I said.

"Whatever we're going to do, we need to do it quickly," Four said.

"What's that supposed to mean?" John said.

"Nothing," I said, eyes on Four. "Nothing at all. Okay?"

Four pursed his lips, frowned.

"I need to make a call," John said. We looked at each other, and he added, "For advice! Okay? I promise I'm not the bad guy here. I just need to know what to do."

"We can't go back in," Four said. "There is no *in*. Is there? If you go in and you don't come out…"

"I can't *officially* say," John said. He looked at us in turn, then smiled sympathetically "Let's just say *I* don't use them." He slipped the wand into a holder on the briefcase and took out his phone. "I've got a code 429. Original is code 404. Please advise."

A voice spoke, but too quietly for me to hear.

"What do you mean, not the machine?" he said. His eyes widened, and he reached for his gun. "*All* of them? I thought that couldn't happen!"

Behind him, the front door opened. Another me, lilacs in one hand, shopping bag in the other. He peered in, saw John, frowned, then saw the rest of us and said, "What the *fuck*?"

Behind him, approaching from all directions I could see through the front door, more of us, more lilacs, more shopping bags, vases, uncomprehending expressions.

"I think you need to put the gun down," I said.

John nodded, placed it on the floor beside him, his eyes wide. "It's the network," he said. "The *network*! That *can't* happen!"

"Hypothetically?" I said.

"An *army*," Four said.

"*Fuck*," Six said.

"They'll have to decide what we are now," Five said.

The others of us gathered beyond the door, frowning, clamouring, swearing.

Three sighed. "I'll get the soup on."

The Rampage of Rampant Redwood at the Ginger Girls Gala

Ian Watson

Some famous persons are born on a mountain top in Tennessee and strangle a bear when they're only three. People such as USA folk hero Davy Crockett.

Crockett shares with Big Steve Redwood them both being notorious storytellers as well as themselves being the heroes of many tall tales. However, Redwood isn't homicidal in the usual manner of USA heroes. Redwood is a gentle giant. He's ruggedly handsome like Nathan Fillion in the *Castle* series on TV. Amongst the ladies, Redwood is a bit of a stallion, so the stories go. Colour him romantic and raffish, but not *too* rash—it's vital not to get trapped by matrimony no matter how ravishing is the femme fatale, nor for that matter how ravished she is. Occasionally Mighty Steve needs to flee to another country. That isn't because a furious father or a jealous husband might stab him—but to avoid being pinned down like a moth.

To begin with, he's obliged to escape hot-foot from the county of Devon in the former United (now untied) Kingdom.

Let's back up briefly...

Steve claims that his great-grandfather— "one of the California Redwoods" —immigrated to Devonshire England in the 19th Century due to a hunger for ginger nut biscuits and ginger snaps. Instead of ginger, Great-Great-Papa encountered in Devon scones piled with strawberry jam and clotted cream. These pleased him sufficiently, as did a local redheaded lass called Sincere (or so her name sounded) so he remained in Devon. G-G-P imagined that the lass with such a name would be faithful, but actually 'Sinsir" is the Welsh word for ginger—such a strange coincidence. After a few years Sincere was unfaithful. But never mind that. G-G-P's semen had already become flesh locally.

Fast forward to 20th Century grand-grand-sonny Steve growing into a lusty lad. In 1968 he flees from Blighty ahead of a would-be bride with a scone in the oven. Blighty is what Brits who are away from England call their nation. *The Blighted Land.* (Like *The Waste Land* by T.S. Eliot.) Never mind what dictionaries say about 'Blighty', the nickname is caused by *collective precognition* of the doom of Brexit sinking England the same way Atlantis sank.

Redwood hides in Turkey, famous for its Golden Horn. The Beyoglu district of Istanbul houses bordellos full of Turkish Delights. This is before the Natashas come from Russia. Redwood teaches Turkish ladies his native language, an easy job if ill-paid. He's also therapeutic, like a Victorian vibrator. He itches to write, and he also itches but there are doctors for that.

After a few years, his interest in Istanbul and his luck runs out. Wife-beating Effendis pursue him. Desperate deserted daughters likewise, Fatimas with foetuses.

He hides in Arabia, famous for its harems of dusky languishing maidens all needing to learn English in anticipation of future mufti-approved Disney Channels and chic consumer Chanel Channels.

Several more countries ensue during the Mighty Redwood's mythopoeic "Mystery Tour" years. Shall we reveal romantic Romania? In Romania all young women are gorgeous; consequently, none of those women realise that they're anything out of the ordinary—not until they have a Steve to explain their charms.

Need we name Malta and neighbouring island of pleasure Gozo (at least in Spanish)?

Presently the Mighty Redwood washes up in Madrid, and so begin his Mad Years

(which last until the start of his Moribund Years). During this best of times a few love affairs—in his mind or in reality—accompany teaching, translating, penning and polishing prose, and gathering loyal Spanish friends, who may not always know one another.

Alas, slowly Big Steve becomes decrepit and dysfunctional, or at least he says so. His only compatriot of yesteryear from Blighty is Old Ted in Luarca, El Moribundo in the North. Presently Steve becomes El Moribundo of Madrid.

What can pep up Steve sufficiently? What can serve as Monkey Glands for Redwood? Direct injections of ginger into his brain? His ingenious lady doctor thinks *maybe*.

She's well aware of Steve's supposed genetic craving for ginger things. She admires how bravely he rations out ginger bikkies through times of scarcity. How he relies upon pals to procure those bikkies while determined not to exploit those pals.

El Corte Inglés department store in Madrid stocks posh ginger bikkies in its Club de Gourmets section. Boasting a royal warrant, there are bikkies from posh Fortnum & Mason with 300 years of pedigree in London's Piccadilly.

For slightly less prosperous customers El Corte Inglés's giant supermarket offers Walkers Stem Ginger bikkies. However, Walkers are Scottish. Let there be no tartans in this tale. Steve is a Son of Heaven sorry we mean Son of Devon.

Proudly—sensibly—Steve refrains from assigning his pension in whole or in part to El Corte Inglés to pay for imported ginger bikkies. Such an action would signify absolute addiction requiring a clinic.

He is stuck on the gingery horns of a dilemma. How can he feed his craving without impoverishing his chums?

Steve's devoted Doctor really deserves a personal name. She plays such an essential role in the end—literally in the *un-do* part—of El Moribundo. (*"Translate that!"* giggles the fiend.) But we cannot blab her real name. Let's call her Zingi, eh? Ginger has lots of zing in it.

It does concern Zingi that mainlining ginger directly into El Moribundo's brain by hypodermic syringe might cause a Dr Jekyll & Mr Hyde situation. By night Steve with heightened senses and strength may roam the alleys of Madrid sniffing out stronger gingers. What a rampage if he breaks into El Corte Inglés. The wreckage. The terrified security guard who claims his hair went white at the sight of El HydeMoribundo hunting, drooling, amber light beaming from his eyes. [Guard's name is for sale; contact author. See your own name in this space.] That's without even mentioning the thousands of ordinary grocers all over who blithely sell umpteen toes of raw root ginger often near bars of chocolate.

Steve-Hyde may cause scandalous headlines. His Doctor might be defrocked or whatever you do to a médica who misbehaves.

Doc Zingi muses much like a medieval alchemist about molecules of ginger mixed with molecules of cocoa beans. But also in modern terms is there some gingery equivalent to methadone to maintain Steve without causing dizziness, sweating, and vomiting? El Moribundo needs to be full of beans as well as gingered up. Doc Zingi knows that excessive espresso estimulus might be fatal to Redwood's heart. And too many beans can cause explosive flatulence. She hesitates.

But now a miracle occurs!

Every year in the Low Countries a Ginger Girls Gala happens. More than twenty thousand Redheads travel from all around the globe to play ginger-themed games. For younger Gingers there's Ring-a-Ring-a-Redhead and Catch a Ginger by The Toe. For adolescent Redheads there's Glow-Up the Freckles on Your Ginger using Dots of Radium Make-Up, cookie workshops with picnics, and dancing. For more mature Redheads there's dressmaking using ginger gingham, painting, photography, and classic Ginger Rogers movies. Boys with red curls and bald guys with ginger beards—neat Vandykes and bushy Vikings—join in the fun. Red Ale is drunk and Rum'n'Raspberry Cocktails.

Rejoice, for this year Madrid is to host a Ginger Gals Gala! A Fiesta of Pelirrojas will happen in El Retiro, the big central park! Doc Zingi only needs to position El Moribundo suitably in El Retiro for her patient to experience jubilation in the positive sense. A bit like sliding him into a superscience superscanner. A bit like Lourdes. Surrounded by Gingerbread Girls, he'll reboot for sure.

For the sake of surprise Steve is kept in the dark about this. A nerdy geek person friendly with Doc Zingi jams Steve's radio remotely with static and hacks his Facebook feed. This'll isolate Steve for a few days harmlessly like sensory deprivation. Meanwhile, Doc Zingi borrows a vintage invalid carriage from the Madrid Museo de Medicina.

In such a carriage, a moribundo can sprawl almost full length. The plushly upholstered antique is well-cushioned for the comfort of bodies with bed sores. What's more, it's big enough to carry the anaesthetics delivery system which will keep El Moribundo in oblivion during the kidnap from his flat until awareness suddenly resumes amidst a host of Gingers.

Zingi's cousin Primo is a vet and very muscular. That's because his speciality is the euthanasia of big dogs such as mastiffs and Great Danes and wolfhounds, easily equal in weight to a Redwood.

Primo is also a master of animal anaesthesia during surgery. Not that Doc Zingi is out of her depth in that regard, she just doesn't have an Anastasia we mean anaesthesia certificate. Primo also has access to a Green Cross ambulance perfect for conveying an antique invalid carriage with recumbent passenger. The deluxe invalid carriage of upholstered wicker can either be pushed from behind or propelled by the passenger turning a handle, like the original first invalid carriage made by Farffler the paraplegic watchmaker of Nuremburg as everyone knows.

Having an ambulance will allow entry to the Retiro Park. This plan cannot fail.

Stage One: While Steve is snoozing, Zingi enters his

bedchamber gently grasping a pad soaked with traditional ether capable of mercy-killing half a dozen chihuahuas. Steve is wearing pale blue pyjamas appropriate to the moribundity ward of a public hospital.

Stage Two: This is a bit like *Games of Thrones* where hefty Hodor carries crippled Bran Stark. With a heave and a ho, Primo loads limp Steve over his shoulder in a fireman's lift. He takes Steve down to the street. Gently he deposits him supine upon the carriage parked on the pavement, then connects up the feed of propofol. Four Pals of Steve are guarding that piece of paving near to a corner café called Loony Moon—not its true name. We're close to the Central Mosque; not saying which direction. Nonetheless feel free to admire the realism of this story, no expenses spared.

Stage Three: This done, two Pals push the wheelchair up the ramp into the ambulance. Primo sits next to Steve in case of excessive bumps while squeezing propofol into a vein during the 4 km journey from the Street Without a Name building number withheld.

Clad in a green vet's coat, Doc Zingi drives the van. A Pal in the passenger seat navigates. The other three Pals follow on slim city rental scooters in case of tight traffic.

Today, the great day, is sunny as usual. The forecast is for 10,000 Pelirrojas to be around or near to the statue of Satan in the park by noon. (Caution: the belligerent bird with the bright red chest is a *Petirrojo* not a Pelirroja.)

Why, in the very heart—more exactly, the lung—of Redwood's Madrid is there a statue celebrating Satan? Why is that statue at exactly 666 metres above sea level, this being the Number of the Beast?

Do not ask these questions! But should Doc Zingi have taken this into account? No, for she is a rational science-based person.

Nor has it occurred to the Doc nor to the Pals of

Steve that the black invalid carriage closely resembles a lidless coffin and the motionless haggard occupant looks like a corpse. This 'uncanny valley' aspect does ease passage through the milling crowd of Redheads who squeeze the 'package' onward in case it may be something wet blanket or aguafiestas. Thus the invalid carriage achieves momentum. Primo pushes faster through the Gingers enjoying their mass joys. Zingi hurries alongside, monitoring the Anastasia. The four Chums of the Moribundo in casual anoraks surely can't be bodyguards. What *does* betray the whole party as out of place is that *none of them have red hair.*

"¡Coño!" exclaims Zingi. "¡We should all have worn red wigs!"

"¡Mierda!"

"¡Me cago en dios!"

"¡Me cago en la leche!"

That would certainly have changed the complexion of things. However, not a single Sherlock Pelirroja pays attention. Red joy is infectious. All around the invalid carriage is gingery jubilation. Like an anticyclone or a tornado—one of those meteorological things that has nothing to do with meteors—the streams of happy femhumans with bright gingery red hair are picking up speed towards their central focus, the statue of startled Satan being dragged down by a big snake into a pool where goblins spout.

Like orange suns sucked around a black hole, celebrating Gingers now carry along Redwood's carriage amongst themselves. Doc Zingi no longer administers Anastasia.

Eyes opening. Ecstasy of ginger light everywhere. Is the Sun going nova? Is the sky full of Day-Glo Van Gogh sunflowers? There's so much ginger light that sight spills over into taste. Oh Crumbs, Oh Caramba, can Steve be in a heaven special to himself?

How the lips and freckles and contours of the Redheads dance. Can Steve be having a blissful fit—rather than an apocalyptic fit?

In his feebly striped pyjamas, he arises manfully from his carriage. Miraculously he strides—we repeat miraculously; you saw how wrecked he was lying upon his bed previously!—marvellously crossing the cordon of gold and ginger marigolds also known as maravillas.

Resurrected in the Retiro, Redwood plunges barefoot into the fountain itself. Rampant he rears, kneeing the gaping frilly-winged goblins, bashing up against Satan's pedestal.

"Oh Ginger My God!" he howls. "Great is Ginger! Ginger is great grated!"

"Ginger Gingers! Redhead Redheads! Ginger Rogers!" chant the girls and the gingery guys in unison here and far.

Satan vibrates. The Serpent *recoils* in a sense of this word *never used until now*—mark this moment well, imagine a boa constrictor tightening around its lunch. Satan reverberates. Identifying today as She

Satanica falls upon Steve Redwood
crushing his freckled bald cranium
from which spill his brains to feed
fish in the fountain
Oh Mighty Steve
Our Moribundo
Amen.

Statement From the Prime Minister Regarding the Time Travellers

Andrew Wallace

As Prime Minister, one expects to make unexpected statements. But even after I heard the rumours that led to this one, I didn't think I'd be standing here having to actually talk about it.

Like most rational people, I do not frequent the kind of outlets that parrot conspiratorial nonsense. However, one particular 'conspiracy' has resurfaced with sufficient regularity to have affected at least two Home Office policies.

This interference must stop. We face an unprecedented

global security situation, and fake problems simply take resources from real ones.

I have therefore reluctantly agreed to this press conference to make clear that my government has listened to these concerns and can categorically state the following:

No one from the year 2345 walks among us.

However, a simple and quite reasonable denial has not worked thus far, so I will refute the claims underpinning the conspiracy one by one, and then take questions.

First, there is no 'time ship'. There was an experimental facility in Stevenage that developed engine parts for the new Dragon jet fighter, and which has become the focus of attention for those seeking to 'commune' with humans from the future. Development of the Dragon components was of necessity secret, but now the fighter is in use I can safely confirm its existence.

Secondly, a man *did* accost two joggers on the outskirts of Maidstone having seemingly "appeared from nowhere." The man then said, "Don't worry, I'm not a Terminator."

Admittedly, that is exactly what you'd expect a Terminator to say, but the man in question is not a cyborg sent back in time but instead is 42-year-old Gideon Smurfit, a local unemployed man. He is *not* a time traveller. He was in all likelihood hiding behind a hedge, although local CCTV footage has been inadvertently wiped. We are looking into why. Most CCTV is recorded over in a week or so. That is probably what happened here.

Thirdly, the government is not using tomorrow's quantum technology to create today's weapons. The Dragon jet fighter has been in development for over a decade. It was not completed ahead of schedule by 'cheating'— indeed, the leader of the Opposition has made much of the project's delays and overspends. He cannot have it both ways, and I for one am sick of people talking Britain down.

282

And finally, the sunny outlook for the economy is due to diligence on the part of my government. It is certainly not thanks to information gained from people from the future, who know how 'things are going to turn out'. If the country cannot have faith in its own abilities, then we are in a sorry place indeed.

I will now take questions.

Mr Smurfit cannot make a statement because he is unfortunately deceased. He was tortured to death for the winning lottery numbers, which of course he did not know. Two local women have been arrested. Mr Smurfit did not have a family, but our thoughts and prayers at this difficult time are with, err, anyone who might have known him.

No, absolutely not—no. No! The Dragon jet does not fire lasers, masers, phasers, muon rays, puon rays, gamma rays, or charged particles along any of the aforementioned. It does not have a rail gun—nobody does, not even the Chinese. It does not fire photon torpedoes and neither does it have a tractor beam.

There is room for a single pilot, and I can categorically confirm that it is plane-shaped, not saucer-shaped, and has not abducted anyone.

Oh, for God's sake. It does not have the ability to destroy a planet. It is not a death star, not even a small one.

I cannot give its exact technical specifications for security reasons, although I can confirm that some of its weaponry is laser-guided.

Well, I'm sorry that's going to disappoint your readers,

Laughs in Space

Gregory. But I can confirm that the Dragon fighter has seen action in Europe and the Middle East, and due to its world-beating British technology and the skill of our heroic pilots two long-standing conflicts look close to resolution.

The Dragon jet does not fly in outer space! It has not been to any other planets.

It cannot traverse wormholes. It cannot dematerialise, or achieve faster-than-light travel or warp speed. It cannot miniaturize and be injected into anyone.

The Dragon jet is an extraordinary accomplishment. It is a world-class scientific and military breakthrough that showcases the very best that Britain has to offer!

It's got a higher altitude capacity than equivalent combat aircraft.

Of course, I'm not disappointed it doesn't go invisible. It's a genuine scientific and military breakthrough that showcases Britain's… Well, you know.

Aha! Hahahahah! Oh dear me. Oh! Hohoho. I have—that's a good one—not been possessed by my great-great-great-great grandson via neural quantum entanglement.

I shouldn't have to prove it!

There is no such thing as neural quantum entanglement.

No there isn't.

No. There. Isn't.

284

Because I say so. And science. Science says so.

As a politician, one tries to become used to that sort of personal attack. Also, as this press conference demonstrates, I am willing to answer the tough questions. So, to summarise my humble achievements in public service: I became Prime Minister after a long political career that has given me invaluable oversight across a wide number of government departments. I was not 'overlooked for decades.' I got this job through ability and loyalty to my party and my country, and I refute in the strongest possible terms the absurd notion that one of my special advisors is a Man from Tomorrow.

There is no need to 'distract' from government failings by creating a psychological operation about people from the future. For example, GDP is at record levels.

Well no, obviously not since record began, but certainly the last [mumbles] years.

I admit it depends how you count it, but 2020 was much worse.

We have a plan, a very good plan, to tackle the unemployment brought about by machine learning and so-called AI.

Soon. The plan will be revealed soon.

I see. So, either people from the future have given the government information that has allowed it to create new weapons, or the people from the future are a distraction from government failings that are as fake as men from Mars. Which is it?

My apologies. 'People' from Mars.

We are not concerned about immigrants from the future. But I tell you this—if there were a sudden influx of unwanted chronological asylum seekers then—unlike the opposition—this government will take a jolly firm line with them!

A points-based system, yes.

No, I don't know how we'd send them back—they're not even here! No one is here! I mean—obviously, some people are here, but we were all born here, as it were.

There is no top-secret government policy to 'Stop the Beams'.

There are no beams! For God's sake! One minute you're saying there's a time ship, a-a-a-and now, *now* you're saying people are arriving here in *beams?* Which is it—ships or beams? And how would time beams even work?

We are not going to be 'replaced' by our own future offspring.

Or rather, yes, we are—but-but they will be our own children, the ones given birth to in our own time. They will not be a genetically perfect, super-advanced race of ultra-humans from the distant future.

In theory, yes, a super-advanced race might see us as we see our less-evolved ancestors, but since there are no time travellers the problem will not arise.

If I could—

I didn't expect that level of… ah… detail.

Well, yes, I have been briefed about the idea of future wavelengths in a quantum state agitating particles in our own time. I have also heard the theory that this process could accrue matter. But if you're really suggesting that these inconceivably tiny processes could form a human being then you want your bloody head examined—
Or rather, ermm, I would have to disagree. With that proposition.

Can we move on…? Fine. Errrr, I imagine a being formed by chronologically agitated quanta would probably look like… Morph. Does anyone else remember Morph–?

I doubt that even in the year 2345—numbers conveniently placed next to each other on a computer keyboard—there exists the ability to influence matter in the distant past.

No, it was not the government that suggested the time trav– hypothetical time travellers came from that year.

The conspiracy seems to have originated, as they all do, on an obscure chat forum used by malcontents, fascists, and men who can't get girlfriends. It certainly did not come from His Majesty's Government.

They are not the same thing, how dare you! I'm thinking of wrapping this up. People are being very silly and frankly rude—

I have just spent the last ten minutes telling you all that *there*

Laughs in Space

are no time travellers.

I'm sorry that you don't believe me, but I can assure you I am not being, to use your phrase, 'half-arsed' about this.

I am not 'unconvincingly' pretending there are no time travellers in the hope that you believe there are!

I assure you that Mr Gideon Smurfit does—or rather did—exist.

I have no comment to make on whether he was 'uncannily beautiful'. I didn't see him, dead or alive.

No, you can't see his body. It has been cremated.

It did not glow with an unearthly light.

Because it's common sense! Anyone who witnessed that would have been burned to a crisp alongside Mr… the poor Mr Smurfit.

Mr Smurfit was unemployed. Perhaps he couldn't afford a computer on which to have a social media account. Not everyone has a social media account. I don't.

No, not having a social media account doesn't mean I'm from the future.

I'm afraid I can't explain why there are no photographs of Mr Smurfit. As I say, it was a tragic case and our thoughts and prayers –

I certainly can't comment on the two suspects in his murder.
288

The case is ongoing.

As it is in the public realm, I can confirm that one of the suspects may have been a leaflet deliverer for the opposition party. But that is neither here nor there.

This government certainly did not frame two innocent women as a cover-up! The case will go to trial, and you will learn the outcome at the same time as me.

They are not 'crisis actors'. That is a loathsome phrase, and this government will have no truck with such gibberish.

No one from the future has been tortured to death so that we can learn the secrets of tomorrow.

Granted, if someone from the future had arrived in our time and, say, had an accident, a permanent or fatal accident, then, ah, that would be one way of ensuring that when I said, 'No one from the year 2345 walks among us' it was true. In that, they wouldn't be walking anywhere. But that's not what happened. Nothing happened, other than a terrible mistake and the horrible crime that resulted.

Likewise, if these hypothetical time travellers arrived from further in the future than 2345 then that too would be a way of ensuring the truth of my statement. But there are no time travellers. From anywhere. Or, rather, any-*when*.

In none of the online conspiracy forums has anyone mentioned an invasion. I mean, there have been rumours about a 'rising tide, and a 'swarm'. But no invasion, goodness me. No.

Laughs in Space

Again, speaking hypothetically, I would have to say that people with the technology to travel in time, whether in some kind of temporal vehicle or by transmitting a signal that became, so to speak, flesh, then even the Dragon jet would have a hard time fighting them off.

But let's look at this logically, as—again—a, ummm, theoretical problem. We may not have the ability to win a war against people from the future, but we would certainly give them a bloody nose! So why bother fighting us at all? Why not go further back, before the time of nuclear weapons. Indeed, before the time of technology. It would be easier, wouldn't it? With a much smaller human population in the past, our hypothetical time warriors wouldn't need to fight at all. They could just settle, with technology that would be miraculous to the locals of the period. And yet there is no evidence of this ever happening. An event that seismic would have left evidence, surely?

No, I don't think Jesus was a time traveller.

I have no comment about Elvis.

As far as I am aware, none of the particle accelerators anywhere in the world have found any new particles that could become 'anchors' in our time for travellers from the future.

Yes, in theory, that could explain why there is no evidence of time travellers appearing before now. But, as I say, the world's particle accelerators are proving expensive to maintain, and do not contribute to the GDP of any country. That is why two of the larger ones have been mothballed and future projects are indefinitely on hold. You see? Even if there were the possibility of creating a chronological 'anchor' particle that could be agitated sufficiently to stick to other particles and thus form a sentient molecule—it's not going to happen. The boffins have blown it. Again. Instead of this airy-fairy unicorn stuff about bits of the universe that may not even exist, let's have a common-sense approach to the problems we face now. Climate change is upon us, inequality is worse than ever, and war has left parts of Europe uninhabitable.

I will not sanction public funds being used for defences against a made-up enemy. There are no time travellers, I've said so numerous times. Although… I can understand the desire to believe that there are. Because if there are people in the future powerful and successful enough to reach us, then that tells us there is a future to look forward to, does it not? Perhaps the glorious future my generation dreamed of, when the year 2000 was a distant, fabulous dream rather than… Well, this.

I consider us as a nation to be sufficiently surveilled. Granted, there may be a need to enhance surveillance of the population if there was, say, the threat of an invasion from the future. But there isn't.

There are no time travellers! We are coming to the end of a devastating war in Europe, and we need to concentrate on rebuilding, not preparing to start another war that will, I can assure you, never occur.

Look at it this way, if people from the future invade and kill us, then how do they get born? Answer me that. Anyone?

Oh, you are going to answer—

Well, I suppose people in the future would see who is going to be useful and who isn't. And they might have pretty firm views about who isn't useful. Or they might be able to tell whose descendants are going to cause trouble, or war. Maybe they don't kill all of us, just the ones they don't want messing things up, or that they don't need. And we can't possibly know who that might be, so we would have to protect everyone. But we haven't got the budget for that.

No, I'm not for a moment suggesting we should prepare a budget for that eventuality, even a hypothetical one.

No, I'm definitely not saying that.

Not at all.

No further questions.

Failed Experiments in Eugenics

Fiona Moore

1. Breeding the most brilliant scientists on Earth with the most beautiful supermodels.

This was the first successful funding bid of the Practical Eugenics Project, and, though we suspected that the scientists on the funding committee had motives for supporting it other than the pure advancement of knowledge, we decided not to question our good fortune. The true academic challenge of the project (aside from that of getting the supermodels to breed with the scientists, which was easily solved through the use of artificial insemination, shortly before we received notice of our first funding cut) was the difficulty of simultaneously retaining the beauty of the supermodels *and* the intelligence of the scientists, as the efforts of our predecessor organization, the Institute of Applied Eugenics, had led to unpredictable results (mostly involving various ugly/smart beautiful/dumb combinations, or else a homogenous population of average-looking people of average intelligence).

The experiment was initially deemed a success when the resulting population transpired to be beautiful, at least relative to the general population, and to score highly on IQ tests. However, the flaws in the project were revealed when the population reached the age at which they began to specialize in particular scientific disciplines. We then discovered that their aptitudes were only for disciplines related to beauty, and the enhancement of beauty. The geometry of hairstyling, the physics of shoe construction, the chemistry of seductively clinging miracle fabrics. As our Project Chair pointed out to the funding committee, this was not too surprising; the application of light and dark shades of makeup is just the creation of clever optical illusions, plastic surgery is a form of microengineering, and of course, our sister organization, the Practical Anti-Aging Project, is entirely devoted to the preservation of beauty and vigour in the elderly.

Although the committee were somewhat mollified by the financial dividends resulting from the experiment (in particular, the hair dyes and nail polish shades invented by the experimental subjects have proved unusually successful with the public), the experimental subjects are currently being retained in social isolation out of concern for what their altered genetics might do to the economy were they to be released into the general breeding pool. Meanwhile those of us on the Practical Eugenics Project attempt to figure out what went wrong, and not to confront the possibility which occurs to us all on dark sleepless nights, that there's a message somewhere in all of this that we're failing to comprehend.

2. Creating a slave race.

The idea of creating a species which is completely willing to serve, and exists to please its masters with every fibre of its being, has long been one of the key goals of the Practical Eugenics Project, and, although we had anticipated difficulties getting the research plan past the Ethics Committee, we found that they supported the project wholesale, on the ground that the demand for philosophical debates on whether it is right to make another sentient being serve one if the being in fact gains pleasure from servitude tripled the moment the project was announced, launching a new golden age of employment for philosophers specializing in ethics.

Early experiments were successful in creating a truly servile species but failed in that the slaves would serve anyone unquestioningly, leading to problems when, for instance, a slave was ordered to kill a person by its owner, but was then ordered not to do so by its intended victim, and consequently suffered a breakdown trying to work out which order to obey. Attempts to induce a hierarchical priority system of owners led to confusion amongst the experimental population. And so, after a brief foray into the moral possibilities of applying the Three Laws of Robotics (abandoned after our Project Chair read enough of the works of Doctor Asimov to conclude that this was only of practical use to short fiction writers), the ultimate solution was to design a system of groups who would be loyal to one living being, and one only. While the backers of the experiment, an insurance and shipping company, initially expressed doubts, as their aim was to develop teams of slaves who would be loyal to particular corporations, these were soon resolved by creating the institution of the corporate slavemasters, individuals to whom the corporation's slaves would be bound. Some corporations elected to hire a single slavemaster, while others maintained several specialized teams of masters and slaves, and the project was deemed an initial success.

However, once the institution of corporate slavery was established, the true flaws in the scheme became known. Should a slavemaster choose to leave the company, the company's slaves must either go with their master and serve his or her new employer, or else they would refuse food and pine away to uselessness. Consequently, competitive recruitment of slavemasters escalated, with companies bidding extensively to have access to particular teams of slaves, or simply to hamper their rivals through the removal of a key group. This period is still widely viewed as a golden age among members of Human Resource Management departments.

When the insurance and shipping company supporting the project lost its entire team of dealing-room slaves to a nearby merchant bank, they pulled the plug on the project. This came as something of a relief to us, as we had not told them that the Practical Anti-Aging Project had recruited our slavemaster and her entire team of lab slaves, who are currently making great headway in the area of skin regeneration and anti-wrinkle treatment. Our one regret is that we did not have time to instil the planned biological redundancy and sterility in the experimental population, meaning that they will live out their natural lifespan. And breed, the social and political consequences of which hardly bear thinking about.

3. Creating a master race

A fairly simple one this; take a continent about the size of Europe, people it with groups of different physical, intellectual and emotional strengths and weaknesses, and wait several thousand years for basic Darwinian principles to do their work. Earlier experiments had, however, found that affection and lack of aggression meant that, rather than outcompeting the weaker specimens, the stronger specimens had a tendency to protect and encourage them. In this experiment, consequently, we inhibited affection and encouraged aggression through pharmaceutical and therapeutic treatment, which would, of course, be discontinued once the forces of evolution had been set upon the desired path.

The key problem became evident after only a few decades, when it emerged that, lacking affection, the superior specimens failed to raise offspring to maturity, breed, or, indeed, do anything much other than rip each other to shreds in bids for dominance. We continued to monitor the experiment, predicting that we would have a population failure within a short space of time, and, indeed, it was not long before only a single specimen remained. We prepared for a postmortem analysis, anticipating its death from starvation or natural causes in a short space of time.

Two thousand years later, and the specimen still remains, having neither visibly aged nor died. It roams the continent victorious, occasionally pausing to defeat some new potential competitor-organism. Although this experiment could, therefore, be taken as a success on our part, responsibility for it has now passed to the Practical

Anti-Aging Project, and what they will conclude from the experiment has potentially grim consequences for anyone attempting longevity treatments.

4. Cloned organs for transplant

Our next project was a simple enough idea, barely even worthy of being categorized as "eugenics," but certainly enough to retain our status as a project while we developed more worthwhile experiments. In a sense we considered ourselves lucky, as the experiment might have gone to another institution; however, anti-abortion legislation passed shortly before we put in our proposal, intended to combat the argument that human embryos are simply undifferentiated collections of cells, had enshrined in law the idea that all human tissue should be considered human, and thus, experimentation with cloned organs is officially eugenics, which remains legal in modern society. Delighted at having found such a loophole, we set about perfecting our organ-cloning techniques, certain of being able to make a good deal of money in the private medical care sector.

The problem, inevitably, came when a young scientist in the Practical Anti-Aging Project invented a device capable of communicating with human organs, and conclusively proved, through a series of published dialogues with a cloned liver, that the disembodied parts in fact had independent life and considerable intelligence, as well as understandable moral objections about being transplanted into what, to them, was effectively a total stranger. Having learned, through the scientist and through the inevitable horde of journalists who descended upon the laboratory, about the structure of society, they demanded the right to education, self-expression, and fair trials, which, legally being human, they were entitled to.

At the time of writing, a legal case is still pending over whether it is desirable to transplant a liver, who is being hailed as the foremost composer of our age, into its intended host, a garbage collector who suffers from terminal cirrhosis due to protracted alcoholism and a wantonly-ingested bad diet, and whose I.Q. scores are so far below the acceptable level as to cause some members of the Practical Eugenics Project to suspect his very humanity. At the same time, citing the case of two kidneys who recently collaborated on an artistic bestseller and an ovary who has made a name for herself as a mathematician, certain fringe members of the anti-abortion movement have launched a campaign arguing for the dismemberment of all human beings in order to allow their individual organs to achieve their full potential. A counter-campaign was launched on the grounds that legally, corporations are people, and that therefore one might consider a human being a corporation. The campaign shut itself down when someone raised the challenge of the anti-monopoly laws, although apparently some of the larger mega-corporations are now considering funding the anti-organ-rights movement.

We would get more involved in all of this, but, as our Project Chair recently lost her job to her own spleen, we are afraid of the potential repercussions.

5. Creating two rival eugenics institutions and pitting them against each other in a Darwinian competition for professional survival

In hindsight, we are mainly just surprised that it took us and the Practical Anti-Aging Project as long as we did to figure out what was happening. We are currently setting aside our differences and working collectively on the problems of "why is it happening," "what is it all for," "who is in charge of it," and "how the hell can we end the whole thing and

get them for this?"
        Experiment results are pending.

Everything is Relative

Simon Hall

Everything is relative. When light erupts from the surface of a star it is fired at two hundred and ninety-nine million, seven hundred ninety-two thousand, four hundred and fifty-eight meters per second through the endless vacuum of space. This is known in scientific circles as bloody quick.

It's so bloody quick that the word "fired" probably doesn't do it justice, but for all its wonder human language is yet to conceive a word that truly reflects the speed at which light travels. Our best effort thus far is light speed which is two words and therefore doesn't count. So we shall stick with "fired."

When a particle of light was fired from the surface of Kepler 45831 it hurtled bloody quickly through its solar system. Unimpeded by solid objects, it flew through the endless nothingness of space before smashing its way through the atmosphere of a planet in a nearby solar system, 30 trillion miles away. Depending on the branch of science, this is either referred to as 5 light years or a bloody long way. But in the grand scheme of the universe, 5 light years is really no distance at all. Everything is relative.

Most of the light particle's brothers that reached this distant (or nearby, depending on perspective) planet failed to hit anything of any interest, bouncing off rocks or trees to be observed by nothing more incredible than a rabbit doing traditional rabbit activities like grazing or scratching, while it considered getting back to other traditional rabbit activities that shall only be alluded to here.

This particle of light, however, having slowed to a positively glacial 670,415,504 miles per hour, hammered into the eye of a human. Something travelling at that speed should have, by right, taken the human's head clean off and had the particle had any mass it probably would have done.

For the light, all this had taken no time at all. Not no time at all in a metaphorical sense, literally zero time had elapsed between leaving the star and hitting its target.

From George Hill's perspective, lying on a blanket with his new wife tucked under his arm, the light had taken 5 years to get there. At the risk of labouring the point, everything is relative.

George pointed up at the source of the light, now a tiny, twinkling dot in a sea of similarly tiny, twinkling dots.

"Do you see that star there?"

Katie followed his finger and nodded. She couldn't see exactly which star he was pointing to, there were thousands and a happy night of drinking cocktails had taken its toll on her ability to focus, but she also didn't think it was that important, so she nodded anyway.

"Yes," she said contentedly, "What about it?"

"That is my honeymoon gift to you, my wife." Saying wife caused a jolt of joy to run up his spine. "I have bought you that star and named it Katie, after you, the light of my life."

12 years later…

The phone beeped and Katie's face disappeared from the screen. It was replaced by a message from WhatsApp asking George to rate the quality of the call.

"It wasn't great, WhatsApp, it wasn't great."

He sighed, put the phone down and opened a drawer of his cluttered desk, pulling out a thick, official-looking document. He had been putting off signing it, desperate for some last chance to prove to Katie that they were meant for each other.

He moved his laptop out of the way, put the bundle of papers down with a thwack that had a heavy finality to it and began to search for a pen. Eventually finding one, he signed his name on the dotted line. The pen had no ink in it. It left only an imprint, the ghost of his signature.

George swore and threw the pen into an overflowing bin. His inability to sign away his marriage was possibly a symbol of his reluctance to do so, but it was more likely a metaphor for the disorganised chaos his whole life had become.

He put his head in his hands, his mind filled with the empty silence of the house and the myriad mistakes that had led him here.

Suddenly, an alarm ripped apart the silence. George jerked to attention, causing an avalanche of folders, circuit boards and other detritus from his life as a hapless IT manager to cascade to the floor as he shot out of the room.

The kitchen was filled with smoke. He'd forgotten the food he had been making when Katie called. The sauce of the baked beans had all but boiled away leaving a thick slab of burnt haricot across the bottom of the pan. From the grill, the charred remains of two thick slices of bread pumped noxious smoke into the small, dirty kitchen.

George turned off the grill and hob, tossed the remnants of the toast into the overflowing sink, opened a window and grabbed a broom from the corner with the deft skill of someone who had done this many times before.

He began to frantically wave the brush head under the smoke alarm which failed to silence the screeching animal.

George let out a long, self-pitying moan. "This is an absolute piss take."

He turned the broom around and drove the handle repeatedly into the howling beast until it shattered into pieces that rained down on the floor.

Silence rang out through the smoke.

George's shoulders slumped. He angrily wrenched the dry-erase marker from the magnetic noticeboard on the fridge and, with a violent scrawl, wrote "Buy pen, sign divorce papers, replace smoke alarm." He underlined the message with such force the marker exploded soaking his hand and the fridge in black ink. He stood for a moment, breathing heavily, then stomped out of the house in search of a fish and chip shop.

"Cheer up, mate. It might never happen!" said the barman cheerily.

"It's already happened, that's why I'm drinking," George slurred in response. With a monumental effort, he raised his pint glass off the bar. "Give us another."

"I think you've had enough, pal."

"Who are you to tell me when I've had enough?"

"I'm the owner of this establishment."

George looked into the younger man's eyes. His shoulders sagged. "Great, my life's worse than a prick in a trilby."

"Right. That's definitely enough—"

"I'm going, I'm going."

George lurched out of the pub and down the street, veering wildly. It was very difficult to see straight or effectively get his bearings but eventually, he reached his house. As he staggered to the garden gate, he found his path blocked by four strangely dressed man-shaped blurs. They appeared to be wearing skirts.

As one, the blurs dropped to one knee and said, "My Lord, blessed is He!"

Confusion filled George's alcohol-sodden brain. He looked from one figure to the next for a while, then promptly vomited over his garden wall. Praying this release of toxins would bring his bizarre hallucination to an end, George looked slowly back at the path. They were still there.

In unison, the two men on the left looked at the two men on the right nervously, the two men on the right shrugged in perfect timing at the two men on the left. All four sank to their knees again. "My Lord, blessed is He!"

George nearly fell backwards. He closed one eye and the four fuzzy shapes became two distinct figures, kneeling next to each other. Strange skirts came down to their knees; blue skin stretched over taught and impressive muscles; small tufts of dark black hair were tied up on top of their heads.

"Whothehellareyou?" said George, barely parting his teeth for fear of being sick over these two oddballs. There was something strange about them that he couldn't put his finger on.

"We are your humble subjects, my Lord," said the one on the right, "Your most loyal servants. We come to you for hope in our hour of despair, oh Holy One."

"Collecting for charity, are you?" George tried and failed to look at his watch, it was surely well past midnight. "Isn't it a bit late for that? It'd better be a bloody good cause."

"You are our last hope, my Lord," said the one on the left, his face stricken with concern.

"Well, I haven't got any money to donate to…orphaned rodents or whatever it is. And please, call me—" he paused to swallow down some sick in his throat, "—George."

The two men looked at each other in terror, then bowed their blue heads.

"We cannot do that, it is blasphemy, Oh Holy One."

There's definitely something weird about these two, thought George. He fished his keys out of his pocket and staggered up the garden path.

"Come on, let's go and have a drink and you can tell me all about these poor gerbils. And enough with all the 'my lord' stuff. We're mates now." At the third attempt, he got the key into the keyhole and pushed the door open. He turned to face the two blue men.

"Yes…er…yes…George," they said, flinching and closing their eyes, their blue faces screwed up as if expecting some terrible punishment.

"You know wha', I like you guys…you're rubbish at fancy dress, though…I've no idea who you're supposed to be." George turned back to face the two men, framed by his doorway, his face screwed up in concentration. Something
306

that had been trying desperately hard to register finally clicked into place in his head. "You're both fucking blue."

Ramrod straight, George passed out and fell backwards, crashing heavily into his hallway.

"My Lord, his Holiness…er, George?"

George's world slowly came back into focus. Well, the small bit immediately in front of him did. Unfortunately for a man who does not deal with surprises well at the best of times, the small bit of world immediately in front of him contained the two blue, athletic and slightly intimidating figures that he had hoped were a mad invention from the night before.

He flinched and tried to back away from them but found that the back of the sofa was very solid and refusing to play ball.

"Who are you and what do you want?" he said.

"We are your humble subjects, my Lord. We are in danger and desperately need your help."

"What do you need my help for? I can't do anything."

The two blue men laughed. "Of course you can. You have almighty power across all of the universe, oh Great Sender of the Message. You can write truth into the sky for all to hear."

"I have no idea what you're talking about," said George, "The only messages I send are work emails. Is this an HR thing? Has Carol complained about me again?"

"You are testing our faith. I can see that, Lord. Come with us and we will show you."

George struggled to his feet and pushed past the strange men. Spotting his phone on the table, George snatched it up and saw he had a missed call from Katie. She had left a message! He pressed play and put the phone to his ear.

"George, do you think this is funny? Sending two men dressed as fucking Smurfs to break into my house! How dare you!? I know you're angry but—" with a scream the message ended. George spun around.

"What the hell have you done with Katie?" he demanded.

"The enemy have the heathen Goddess. We must go now, my Lord, or it will be too late!"

The two fucking Smurfs were stood on a metal platform, its edge gilded with a bright, white light that hurt George's eyes. They darted forward, grabbed him by an arm each and pulled him onto the plate. George struggled to free himself but their strength was impressive. He wanted to fight but a strange tingling had begun to vibrate in his feet, as if thousands of joules of energy were being pushed upwards through his body. It had reached his navel. The cluttered, cramped coffin of a living room around him began to shake and shimmer in front of his eyes. The vibrating had filled his head and suddenly he felt his whole body stretch up into the air.

And as soon as it had all started, it finished with a juddering in his knees. George's whole body shook as the energy dissipated; his teeth chattered as he looked around. His room had disappeared. His house had disappeared. His whole planet had disappeared.

As has previously been stated, everything is relative, time especially so. We may think of the relentless march of time as a constant but in reality, it is inextricably related to space. For example, if Tom, Dick and Harry were sat perfectly still having breakfast in London then, because the earth is spinning on its axis, they would still be moving at around one thousand miles per hour. It is this speed that creates our experience of time in the first place.

If, having polished off their croissants, Tom were

to stay in London while Dick hopped on a train to travel through, let's say, Hampshire, then relative to Tom, Dick's experience of time would slow down as he travelled faster, meaning he would arrive in Brighton for a spot of lunch having experienced a slightly shorter morning than Tom. Admittedly, the state of the British rail network may cause this hypothesis some trouble.

Now, if Harry were to finish having breakfast and then travel at the speed of light to the moon and then on to Brighton he would arrive at lunchtime, ready for fish and chips on the seafront with Dick, but time would have slowed down so much that he had still not digested his pain au chocolat. This is called time dilation. It essentially means time is relative to the individual.

For George, this was his experience of travelling 30 trillion miles from his house in Kettering to a little planet that, until recently (in the lifetime of the universe), had been named Kepler 45831-C, it took absolutely no time at all. Everyone else had to go the long way round.

On Earth, five years passed. Five years in which George and Katie Hill became strange anomalies in police reports. Five years in which their families mourned and tried to move on. Five years of rumours and wild theories about exactly what happened on that fateful night.

Five light-years from Earth, in a tall, marble chamber in a grand temple, five hundred blue people chanted as one. They sat on benches, lining the walls in a semi-circle, facing a stone dial at their centre.

"He is coming. He is coming."

Their chanting grew faster and faster and louder and louder. The looks on the faces grew more intense. The moment was coming, the moment they had been waiting for all their lives.

"He is coming! He is coming! HE IS COMING!"

A beam of brilliant, white light shone down from the ceiling. The room seemed to vibrate with power, energy shook the very walls of the temple. The marble floor reverberated with a resounding thud. And as suddenly as it had started, it finished.

Standing in the centre of the room, a heavily hungover and bemused-looking George stared around him at the hundreds of excited faces staring back. As one they rose to their feet.

"He is here!" shouted an exultant voice from behind him. George turned to see two people facing him: one tall, blue and imperious, the other white and excited. For a moment George thought he was staring into a mirror. The white face had his eyes and hair, it was more or less the spitting image of him.

"Toto, I have a feeling we're not in Kettering anymore," said George to himself.

"Toto? No, this is Trilby," said the blue woman patting a hand on the other George's shoulder. She was tall and languid and wore a long, white robe with a set of shoulder pads from which a large oval protruded vertically, creating a sort of halo behind her head.

"Welcome, Oh Holy One."

"Welcome!" chorused the watching mass.

The woman turned to address the crowd, "Our Lord and Saviour is here. He has come to deliver us from the evil heathen horde and into a new time! A time of peace and freedom from our evil oppressors!"

She turned back to George. She seemed to be expecting him to say something. The crowd watched with bated breath, awaiting the first words of their god.

Overwhelmed by the strange turn of events, George decided to latch on to a mystery that felt more within his
310

grasp. Pointing at his doppelgänger, he said, "Sorry, did you say his name was Trilby?"

"This is the history of our people. Every generation was blessed with two oracles who were given the wisdom to receive your holy messages."

The blue woman, whose name, it had taken her taken her quite a long time to convince George, was Pisstake, led George and Trilby through a grand hall with high ceilings and beautiful marble statues of…him.

Enormous tapestries adorned the walls of the hall and Pisstake pointed at one.

"In the beginning, the gods created the almighty star Katie, and the planet George in her orbit. The people worshipped Katie, the Goddess of Light, and George, the God of the Earth, for two hundred years in peace. Their messages of love were interpreted by the oracles. One male and one female.

"But the peace was ripped in two when came the Disagreement of the Porcelain Throne. The wise oracle Playstation interpreted your wish to have the throne seat up, whilst the blaspheming oracle Spinclass claimed Katie wanted the throne seat to be down.

"It caused a rift between our peoples. The Katienites began worshipping the Closed Throne, while we Georgians, the true peoples of George, praised the Open Chalice! The ensuing war decimated a generation.

"But things didn't stop there." Pisstake pointed from a tapestry showing people worshipping what looked, to George, like a toilet with the seat up to one of the people bowed in front of a vase of flowers. "Over the next hundred years, the fighting worsened. The Battle of You Never Buy Me Flowers, the Skirmish of Who's Janice and Why is She

Texting You and the Assault of But Your Friend Sharon is a Total Nightmare raged between us and the Katienites.

"Eventually, after the War of You Always Say You Have a Headache, the differences became too much and thus came The Great Divorce. The Katienites declared all-out war on the Georgians and swore to destroy us. They were immensely powerful and we humble followers of the true leader retreated to our safe haven, here in the Temple of Ket'tring."

Pisstake gestured around her at the great hall. George's mind sagged under the weight of what he'd heard. It was madness, and yet, somehow, it all fitted together. He and Katie *had* argued about all those things. They *had* driven a wedge into their marriage.

"That was when our ancestors attempted to find you, to bring you back here to save us from our evil persecutors. They harnessed an old magic and sent men to the Planet of the gods. We thought the mission had failed.

"For the last 4 generations no word has reached us, no new messages could be divined by our oracles, until Trilby here. He received a new message that foretold your coming."

"And his name is actually Trilby?" George asked.

"His name was derived from the last oracle to receive your blessing two-hundred years ago," said Pisstake, "Your final message to us, 'a prick in a trilby.'"

"So what am I supposed to do now?"

Pisstake and Trilby exchanged an unsure look.

"But you are here to save us, oh Mighty One, to lead the Georgians to safety and free us from the tyranny of the Katienites," said Trilby, an almost pleading note in his voice.

"And how am I going to do that? I don't know how to free anyone from anything. Especially tyranny. That sounds

312

like a really difficult thing to free people from," said George.

"You are a powerful god, my Lord, you can write truth into the stars," said Trilby, "I'm sure you'll find a way."

George didn't feel like a powerful god, he felt like a swimming pool lifeguard being asked to mount a rescue at the bottom of the Mariana Trench: out of his depth.

"Can we *please* give it a rest with all the 'my lord' stuff," said George. "Just call me George."

"But it's blasphemy to call you by your name, oh Supreme—"

"Well, I say it's not. Don't I get to decide? I am a god... apparently."

A figure strode out of a door at the far end of the hall. He was a heavy-set, powerful-looking man who was nearly as broad as he was tall. He wore an army uniform, with a gun slung over his shoulder. He completely ignored George which made George feel a lot more comfortable, he was used to being paid no respect whatsoever. It was like a touch of home.

"Pisstake, we need to talk. I have new intelligence that I'm sure you and our *new guest,* will find very worrying." He laced the words "new guest" with as much venom as he could and shot George a dirty look.

"My lord, this the leader of our army. He's called—"

"Don't tell me, it'll be something mad, like Moron or Bollocks."

"No," said the man, in a tone that suggested he thought George was a moron who was talking bollocks, "I'm Replacesmokealarm. My name was—"

"Derived from one of my last messages. Of course it was," said George wearily.

"Look," said Replacesmokealarm. "The latest intelligence suggests the Katienites have found a weapon so powerful it will end the war and wipe us out completely.

We must act."

"A challenge from our mortal enemy," said Pisstake, seriously. "But we have the power of a god on our side, Our Lord Almighty will strike them down!"

"I'm not a God! I'm an IT manager! What do you want me to do, update an operating system at them? Reorganise their files?" Pisstake was nodding vigorously as if these sounded like excellent angles of attack. Resigned, he turned to Replacesmokealarm instead, "What's this weapon I'll be facing then?"

"We don't know. But it is supposed to be able to destroy our claim to George."

"But I'm George…" said George.

"No, not you, *my Lord*," said Replacesmokealarm with contempt. "George the planet. Our planet is called George."

"Hang on, it's blasphemy to call me by my name but it's not blasphemy to call the planet George? Doesn't that get confusing?"

Before Replacesmokealarm could retort another soldier hurried over, looking panicked.

"What on George do you want, Whatsapp?" snapped Replacesmokealarm.

"It's the Katienites, sir. They've sent us a message; they want to talk."

George, Pisstake, Replacesmokealarm and WhatsApp were sat in the main war room. Maps of the planet, dotted with pins, hung on the walls. On the desk in front of them, a screen showed the leader of the Katienite army. She was a mean-looking, bulky figure with a stare that made George very glad that he wasn't within arm's reach of her.

"We demand your surrender!" she demanded, "You

will give up your claim to this planet and be fired into space!"

"And why would we do that?" retorted Replacesmokealarm, "You'll be the ones to surrender and you'll be fired into Katie to burn for a thousand years!"

"I don't think this is an especially constructive discussion," muttered George.

"We know you have captured the heathen goddess," said Replacesmokealarm, "for this treachery against George—"

"Katie! Katie!" shouted George, trying to lean into shot.

"No, we have the tactical advantage, you fool," hissed Replacesmokealarm, trying to push George back into his seat, "They don't know we have you."

"Oh, shut up. I am your god, do as I say." George pushed Replacesmokealarm out of the way and positioned himself in front of the camera.

There was the sound of a commotion on the other end of the video call and the shot on screen dipped as the camera was retrained on Katie's worried face.

"George, what the hell is going on?"

"Katie, they're all mad. We need to sort this out. Can we find a place to meet?"

There was a brusque voice off camera, "No, Goddess of Light, we must keep you safe."

"Oh enough of the goddess rubbish," snapped Katie, "If he gets to be a god then so do I! It's blatant sexism!"

"Katie, these people are still killing each other for being heathens, I think they're probably still quite a way off feminism," said George, "We need to get them together for some...peace talks."

"Peace talks? You think they're capable of peace talks? They want to fire each other into the sun, or Katie or whatever the hell they call it."

"OK, so what are we going to do?"

"Well, my lot reckon they've found some temple. It's our best lead to working out what the hell going on, can we meet there?"

"And this is where they've found the weapon?"

"I don't know if weapon's the right word," said Katie. "They reckon there's an ancient text there. Apparently, it has evidence of the one true god. It'll tell them who created their world, you or me, I guess."

"Right, well get them to send us the location and we'll meet you there."

"And let's not bring too many people with us, I'd like to avoid being caught in the middle of a full-scale war."

The image of Katie disappeared and was replaced by a message asking George to rate the quality of the call.

"That was pretty good actually, WhatsApp, it was pretty good."

"Were you talking to me, sir?" asked the junior soldier.

George, like many of us, had often imagined what life might be like out in the universe. He'd had many happy daydreams about walking on the surface of another planet. These daydreams usually involved brave interplanetary expeditions, Star Trek style, boldly going where no man had been before. They rarely started with alien abductions and had certainly never involved becoming a deity in a religious conflict.

But whatever the circumstances of his arrival, here he was with the chance to see vistas hitherto unseen by human eyes, and yet the views of George, the planet, were almost entirely ignored by George, the man. He barely registered the strange, spindly trees with their bright yellow leaves and rich red moss. He didn't even see the 6-legged, purple lizards that scuttled across the forest floor, or the birds, with wings more akin to helicopter blades than those of a plane, that buzzed around the canopies.

For even after a morning of light-speed travel, doppelgängers and tapestries of his failed marriage, the strangest thing that George, the man, had experienced on George, the planet, was discovering that the vehicle for his first trip across an extraterrestrial plane would be an exact replica of his father's battered, old Land Rover. It was identical, from the dented rear bumper, when he had misjudged where the garden wall was, to the burn holes in the dashboard, when he had misjudged where the ashtray was, it was the same car.

George sat in the passenger seat staring at perfectly mundane things, like the old tape cassette player, rather than the extraordinary world outside. He opened the glove box in front of him and found an old log book, a tin of fish hooks and a half-eaten packet of pear drops. So uncanny was the imitation that George was convinced it was the same car. Pisstake had explained that the design had come from a previous oracle called Athousandpoundsornearestoffer.

The forest around them disappeared and was replaced by sweeping desert, the sand a crimson red, the large sky a deep purple.

"We're approaching the location now," said Replacesmokealarm from the driver's seat, "I assume you have some kind of plan?"

"Look," said George, "I need to know what's going on, if this place holds answers, then we need to explore."

"This has all the hallmarks of a cunningly conceived trap to me. We should have a strike team ready to—"

"No," George interrupted, "Katie promised me. She's coming with a small team; so are we. We're not here for a fight, this is a…joint mission."

"And you're sure we can trust her," asked Pisstake leaning between the seats, "It wouldn't be the first time she has been dishonest. She is, after all, an evil, heathen, false Goddess."

"Do me a favour, Pisstake, when we get there, let me do the talking."

10 minutes later, the Land Rover pulled to a halt. The temple was not what George had expected. It resembled an enormous satellite dish because that, in fact, is exactly what it was.

Parked a little way away, Katie and two other figures watched as George climbed out of the car. Relieved to see someone who wasn't blue or completely barking mad, George rushed forward and embraced Katie. She hugged him tightly back.

"I thought they hated each other…" said Replacesmokealarm, as he got slowly out of the car.

"There are more things in Katie and George, Replacesmokealarm, than are dreamt of in your philosophy," said Pisstake sagely.

"So, who are your two?" George asked, indicating the two figures over Katie's shoulder. "Wait, is that your mum's Saab 9-3?"

"Oh, don't ask. This is Pilates, the leader of my army, and Bottomlessbrunch, my High Priest. I'm slightly worried about what their names say about my life."

"You think they're bad, mine are called Pisstake and Replacesmokealarm," George laughed, then indicated the building, "What's the plan with this then?"

"Pilates, how do we get in?" said Katie turning to the enormous, intense leader of the Katienite army who was currently eyeing Replacesmokealarm with the kind of ferocity a lion might eye a limping gazelle doing a strip tease with. Katie waved at her to get her attention. "Pilates! Get us in there!"

"Follow me." Pilates grudgingly took her eyes from her opposite number and walked towards the building. They followed her around the ancient structure until she found a door. It was rusted on its hinges and refused to budge when Pilates tried to kick it in.

"Replacesmokealarm, give her a hand," said George. Replacesmokealarm stared at George as if he had just been asked to slit his own throat without making a mess of his uniform. George glared intently back.

Replacesmokealarm reluctantly trudged over to join Pilates at the door. They stood shoulder to shoulder.

"Ready. 3, 2, 1, go!"

As one they kicked hard. There was a screech of metal on metal as it gave way, showing darkness beyond.

"Follow me," said Pilates, lighting a torch and shining it inside the room.

"You should all follow me," said Replacesmokealarm, barring Pilates' way as he produced his own torch.

"We found it, I'll lead the way," retorted Pilates.

"The pair of you pack it in," said Katie, marching over to them. She took the torch off Pilates and stepped over the threshold. The rest of the group followed, lighting their own torches.

Inside the soft beams illuminated what looked like a canteen. Rows of dusty tables stood down the centre of the room, rotting remnants of ancient meals were congealed on some, others had been overturned.

The group moved slowly into the room. George spotted a strange shape ahead of him, a misshapen lump lying on the floor. He approached it slowly and knelt down. It was a yellowing skeleton, sprawled face down, a knife stuck between two ribs in its back. The sight made the hair on the back of his neck prickle.

"Looks like there was some kind of fight here," he said to the others.

A click made everyone jump and look for the source of the noise. Katie had reached the far wall and was flicking the light switch on and off.

"No power," she said, "we need to see if we can get this place back up and running. Come on."

They followed Katie through the doorway and into the corridor beyond. A stench of rust and decay and something more biological rose to meet them.

"Hey, look at this," said Pisstake, shining her torch on the wall. "It's a map, but it doesn't look much like a temple. Where's the chapel? Where's the vestry? Is this how you heathen Katienites worship in your heathen churches?" Pisstake turned to the Katienite High Priest.

Bottomlessbrunch wore a robe similar to Pisstake's. The only noticeable difference was the ring that circled Pisstake's head vertically was laid horizontally across his shoulders, jutting out like an elongated ruff.

"It's nothing like our temples either," he said calmly, ignoring, to George's intense relief, Pisstake's accusations about his heathen ways of worshipping.

"It looks more like a research station," said Katie, looking closely at the labels. "There's laboratories and maintenance rooms and, look, a generator. That'll be where we need to go."

As the group began to search the building, looking for the generator, George couldn't help but notice that this building represented the most advanced technology he had yet seen. In one room, they discovered disks much like the one he had travelled here on, only larger. Presumably some form of prototype. In another was a series of chambers that sent chills down his spine. He wasn't sure what it was about this room but he felt as if something terrible had happened here. The chambers seemed about the right size for a person. He pushed the thoughts of what horrible experiments they could be for out of his mind.

For a people that could whisk him and Katie to another solar system in the blink of an eye, he had expected spaceships and robots and laser pistols. For the first time, the technology he saw around him finally seemed to tally with what he had envisaged…but it was all so old. Something didn't add up. How had they lost all this knowledge?

"Here it is! The generator!" shouted Pilates, pushing open a door.

Inside was a massive, ancient machine, all pumps and pistons, clearly capable of producing mammoth amounts of power.

"Anyone know how to get this going?" asked Katie.

"I do," said Pilates and Replacesmokealarm as one.

"Well get to it then," said George. The pair moved off into the room, leaving George and Katie with the two High Priests.

"So what is this place?" Katie asked, "I thought it was supposed to be some sort of temple."

"We believe this is where our world was created nearly 500 years ago. It holds the secret of our place in the universe," said Bottomlessbrunch, "Where your benevolent words were first received, oh Perfect O—" Katie shot him a threatening look, "Oh…Katie," he corrected lamely.

"You've been having trouble with that too, have you?" said George, smiling. He watched the two soldiers working on the generator thoughtfully. "Hang on, did you say 500 years ago? Your race is only 500 years old? How is that possible?"

"That is what our religious scholars have derived from the sacred texts too," said Pisstake, "500 years since the first great message and the creation of our people. We believe that is here somewhere. A powerful weapon that will reveal all."

"So the weapon isn't a big gun?" George asked. "I thought it would be a big gun."

"Knowledge is power," said Bottomlessbrunch, "Having final proof of which of you is the most powerful and the one true god will give us ultimate righteousness in this life and the next."

George was about to tell them they were going to be sorely disappointed if they did find anything when he was interrupted by a shout from Replacesmokealarm, "Ready?"

"Ready!" came Pilates reply, "3, 2, 1!"

Stood at either end of the generator they each pulled a leaver and, with a gut-wrenching rumble, the ancient machine slowly pulled itself back to life. Pistons started to pump, firing out steam with an awful, spitting hiss. Far above them the rows of lights started to brighten; their hum drowned by the furore below.

"Piece of cake," said Pilates returning to them.

"Good job, Pilates," said Katie. Pilates mumbled something only Katie could hear. "Sorry, what was that?"

"I couldn't have done it without Replacesmokealarm!" Pilates shouted louder than she intended before going bright red. Katie turned away to hide her laughter.

Now with power, the group returned to the corridor outside, the heavy door swinging shut behind them, deadening the noise. As they walked back the way they had come the noise of the generator was replaced with a soft humming.

"I'd know that sound anywhere," said George happily, pushing a door open, "Servers!"

The server room was covered in dust but the newly powered up towers hummed and whirred, their lights flickering as if delighted to be back up and running. For the first time in his life, George was happy he worked in IT.

"Let's see what we can find in here!" A solitary terminal sat at the far end of the room, George reached it and flicked the power switch. The screen blared into life. George had never had trouble with computers, it was people he could never understand. In a few minutes, he was into the mainframe.

He opened a file and started to look through it. There were hundreds of documents and he didn't know where to start. He reordered them by date and looked at the oldest one. It was about the setup of the research facility, there was no mention of him or Katie or gods of any kind.

He closed the document and then looked at the most recent ones. The first was a security report about a fight that had broken out between two groups of scientists, there had been deaths. He opened the next document. Although most of it made no sense to him, he managed to understand the gist of it: it was research into light-speed travel and now their names were everywhere. The document before that was something to do with DNA infusion, again he noticed both his and Katie's names several times.

He continued to scroll back, opening documents at random. Suddenly, he gasped and his jaw dropped.

"What is it?" asked Katie.

"It's…it's the form I filled in," said George, "When I bought you that star."

"What? When we got married? How have they got that?"

George scrolled through the document, he remembered filling it in, entering Katie's name to be the new name for the star, sure it would be something they would treasure forever.

"That's where they got your name from," said George,

"They must have received this from the website."

"But then how are you involved?" Katie asked.

George scrolled to the bottom of the document to a section marked "billing."

"Here, it's got my name, here and…my credit card details. They sent my fucking credit card details into space!"

The other documents he'd seen began to make sense, and from the dates, things fell into place. George turned to the aliens gathered behind him.

"Your race isn't hundreds of years old, it's thousands. You had scientists here with amazing technology. They began to search the skies with this satellite dish and intercepted this," he indicated the document on the screen, "They thought it was a message from us, they thought we were gods.

"They altered their DNA in an attempt to talk to us, two people on a planet trillions of miles away. That's why you have the oracles that can hear us. That room with the weird chambers—that was for changing DNA.

"When that failed, they created a technology to try to travel to us but a fight broke out about who they would travel to meet. It wasn't magic or gods…it was just incredible science."

"So you're not gods?" asked Pisstake. It was hard to read her face, she seemed to understand what she was hearing whilst also desperately wanting to avoid admitting she was wrong.

"No," said Katie, "just like we've been trying to tell you."

"But how did your name end up on here?" said Bottomlessbrunch, pointing at the screen. "Surely that's an act of an incredibly powerful god."

"Because on our planet you can buy a star and have it named after you. Or someone you love," said George, looking at Katie, "I bought Katie a star, your sun, as a wedding present. That information was somehow beamed into space and your scientists managed to find it. But they misunderstood what it meant."

"You bought a star? Who did you buy it from? It must be a pretty awesome deity if they can just sell star systems to other people," said Bottomlessbrunch, "Who are they?"

"No, it's just a silly website—"

"So whoever you bought the star from is the one true god," Pisstake interrupted, elbowing George aside and scrolling up to the top of the document. "Our creator, the one true God is...Buyastar.com!"

"No," said Katie imploringly, "Don't you understand, that isn't a god either! It's just a company! You've been worshipping gods and where has it got you? You've nearly wiped yourselves out over silly differences! Over some stupid argument we had! It's ridiculous!" She looked at the two priests in their robes and bizarre headgear. "I mean, you two have got bloody toilet seats on your heads!"

"That's just the kind of attitude we'd expect from evil, heathen, false gods like you!" retorted Pisstake.

Katie screamed in anger. "Look where you can get when you work together, look at what you can achieve." She indicated the building around her. "Life isn't easy, it's not simple. You have to listen to each other and actually hear what people around you are saying."

"Buyastar.com was clearly tricked by you two and your mad ramblings," said Bottomlessbrunch.

"Yeah," Pisstake agreed, "but we won't be drawn in by your lies!"

Katie looked ready to blow a fuse, but George took her hand. "Let's just leave them to it, shall we? At least they won't be bothering us anymore."

"As false gods, you are hereby banished back to your land! Be gone! Your blasphemy in the name Buyastar. com shall continue no longer!" cried Pisstake theatrically, pointing a dramatic finger to the sky.

The metal disc Katie and George were standing on shook and vibrated. A bright light engulfed them as power worked its way up their legs and their bodies stretched up into the air.

For the people of George life continued peacefully under the light of Katie, well more peacefully than it had been. In the instant it took the two false gods to return to Earth, two hundred years had passed on George. Two hundred years of generations living and dying, two hundred years of rebuilding their society, two hundred years of happily worshipping their new god Buyastar.com.

On earth, 10 years had passed since George and Katie had disappeared. And while their families were happy to have them back, they couldn't understand how two people, on the verge of divorce, had one night decided to go on an impromptu inter-railing trip together, forgetting to mention to anyone where they were going, or how, in all that time, they hadn't aged a single day.

Katie walked into the little kitchen in Kettering and put the kettle on. George had left a dirty teaspoon in the sink again and she felt an old frustration begin to boil inside her, but she let out a long, deep breath. At least he remembered to put the toilet seat down these days.

Everything is relative.

Killing Time

Ida Keogh

"N ext!"

The hard plastic of Humphrey's chair pressed against his spine. He shifted uncomfortably as he waited for the next applicant. A shrunken pensioner peeled from the front of the queue and began an impossibly slow march to his desk. Just his luck. In one hand the woman clutched a paper form and in the other a cane which struck the floor with a violent arrhythmia, setting his teeth on edge. Slumping further, he cast his eyes to the infomercial screen on the far wall. That garish poster appeared again:

Has your dream life or the existence of a loved one
been wiped out by the Timeline Redistribution?

You could be entitled to compensation!

The estimated waiting time flashed up as fluctuating between thirty-seven and thirty-nine hours, and drone footage showed the crush of pedestrians camping in the re-purposed car park and spilling into the streets for miles around. Humphrey shuddered at the sight. For a brief moment, he was grateful his own application was being advanced internally. It shouldn't be long now until he was back to his intended lifestyle: jet-setting around the globe on a bank account with more zeroes than there were people in the queue, and all those people waiting on his every word.

An alternate memory came unbidden. The scent of hot sand and expensive cologne. The gentle murmur of surf and rustle of palm trees. Chilled champagne by his side, tiny droplets of condensation easing down the glass. Men laughing, congratulating him on some business deal.

A spike of pain shot through his skull. Then the woman's cane sounded again, metal against tile aggravating his migraine, and he was brought back to his present reality as a Level Four processing clerk in the Department for the Administration of the Timeline Redistribution Compensation Scheme.

The hall was an elongated parallelogram—a nightmare of architectural design—and his triangular station was wedged into an acute corner. It was directly under an air vent which alternated between Arctic squall and furnace blast. In his view, which he expressed frequently to his supervisor Avika, there ought to be laws against such working conditions.

The old biddy finally made it over to him and arranged her spindly body into the waiting seat with a relieved sigh. She smelled faintly of talcum powder, a slight improvement on the usual unwashed stench Humphrey was faced with.

"Name?" Humprey asked.

"Mrs Antonia Danilenko," she replied, her voice wavering like a gurgling drain.

"Application number?"

She pushed her crumpled sheet of paper across the desk. "Forty-six thousand, seven hundred and fifty."

Humphrey tapped at his keyboard, wincing at the repetitive strain which was developing in his right wrist. "So, what's the nature of your alternate memories Mrs Danilenko?"

She wrung her hands together, blue veins squirming under translucent skin. "I've lost my cat," she said.

"Your cat."

"Yes. I keep seeing him in waking dreams. His long whiskers, his fluffy white and ginger fur, his pink little toes. I've never had a cat in this life. But my husband passed away not long ago and it's all I can think about; that I was meant to have a companion now, a warm little friend to ease my heart. I hear him purring. Sometimes meowing. It gives me a terrible headache not having him here."

Humphrey squeezed the bridge of his nose. "I'm sorry for your loss, Mrs Danilenko. But I don't think you quite understand what we are doing here."

"This is for compensation, yes?"

He reached for a laminated page, its corners curled back from over-use, and slapped it down so that the writing on the shaded concentric circles faced the old woman. "This diagram represents the compensation levels arising from the Timeline Redistribution last year, March 2052. The estimated range is forty-nine years, taking us back to an unknown but fundamental alteration of the Timeline in around 2003."

"Yes, I'm aware. I just…"

He pressed a pink index finger into the sunny target in the middle of the page. "This is the epicentre. The highest level of recompense is for those most affected by the change and its ripple effect through time. Now, I don't like to talk about myself, but just as an example, my own alternate memories suggest that my parents would have been very close to the bull's eye. We'll find out the details when I go to the Quantum Perceptor, but I expect that by rights I should have been rich by now. Very rich. When my application is completed, I expect to see significant compensation." He moved his finger to the outermost pale-yellow ring. "This is the minimum level of compensation. We've moved past the destruction of livelihood or the erasure of entire families and we're into the territory of marrying the wrong person or some such. Sticky mess, that. The divorce rate is up several hundred per cent. Now you and your cat…are somewhere over here." He trailed his fingertip off the page and kept going until it was right at the edge of the desk.

Mrs Danilenko's lip trembled. "All I want is my cat back. But if I can't have him, I could at least give another cat a home and love it just the same. There is a shelter near my flat; they will let me have one. But it's too expensive to keep on my pension. I just need a little help. Please?"

Humphrey picked up his favourite rubber stamp. He pressed it firmly into a pad of dark red ink, then transferred it to the creased application form. "Application denied," he said. "Next!"

Come four in the afternoon, Humprey found himself in the tiny kitchenette in the basement. He had wanted ten minutes to himself, but Avika was already in there chatting to another third-level clerk. He scooped a teaspoon of powdered tea and two sugars into a biodegradable cup and stood back while scalding water turned it all into a dark brown soup.

"What about you, Humphrey?" Avika asked.

"Hmpf?" he replied, trying to judge the right moment to touch the cup without sustaining third-degree burns.

"Nathalie and I were just talking about our alternate names. I quite like Avika. It's strange to think that in the original Timeline, I might have been called something else."

"Perhaps I'm a Nathan," Nathalie said, her eyes drifting off into a happy daydream.

Humphrey's lip quirked into a smile as he thought about what the Quantum Perceptor might reveal for him. "I'll find out soon enough. I imagine I'm supposed to have a much better name than Humphrey. Something catchy, with an 'x' in it, perhaps. I'm not saying that I'm special, Nathalie, but my application has gone to Level Two already, above both of your heads. I won't be crammed behind a desk much longer, I reckon."

"Hey, some of us like this job!" Avika said, prodding his shoulder and making his tea slosh dangerously close to his fingers. "We get to meet all sorts of interesting people. Besides, having a job at all is a miracle these days. Do you remember the cutbacks in 2035, back when we were still the Department of Social Security? Sixty per cent of the clerks gone overnight. You do realise that now the budget has been re-purposed for the compensation scheme there are no benefits for the unemployed either? Just cold streets. You should be grateful they kept you on."

"I've been Level Four for over a decade, Avika. I'm wasted on this place. I'm only a couple of steps above the unpaid interns, for goodness' sake."

"Well, work hard, gather just a few less complaints, and perhaps you could get another promotion by the end of the year. Speaking of hard work, your break's up. Back to it."

The clock ticked forward towards the end of the shift. Humphrey watched the second-hand struggle on, inexorable but sluggish somehow, as though it were deliberately trying to hold him back. He wondered, not for the first time, what he would do if he could alter the Timeline himself. Maybe start with a better-situated desk and work up to world domination. Right now though he wanted more than anything to be able to move time forward, to save himself from another thirty-six minutes of tedium.

One by one the grubby public thrust application forms at him. He eventually granted escalation for a man who said he would have been a great politician but refused to entertain a little girl's dream that she ought to have had a sister. Children were notoriously unreliable, after all. A woman claimed that her wife would have been the first person to step foot on Mars. Highly implausible, but he did rather like the idea of space travel. He was just deliberating whether to reach for the red stamp or the green when Avika bustled over to his desk.

"I'll take this one, Humphrey. You're needed upstairs."

"Upstairs?" He felt a tingle up his spine. "I'm going to the Quantum Perceptor?"

Avika's mouth was pressed into a taut line. She was probably jealous. "That's what they said. Something about convergent data. You've been fast-tracked."

Humphrey's chest swelled. He pushed back his chair with a clatter and edged his way round the sharp corner of the desk. "Well, then. Goodbye, Avika. I doubt I'll be seeing you again."

He gave the waiting crowds a jaunty little wave as he made his way to the stairwell, then took the steps two at a time.

A huddle of people waited for him in front of the first-floor reception desk. *Rectangular*, he noticed. A woman in a sharp suit stepped forward. "Application twenty-four thousand, three hundred and two? This way, please." It irked him slightly that there was no introduction, no warm clasp of hands. She strode off down the corridor, past the Level Two offices. Faces peered at him through pulled-back blind slats. He had to hurry to keep up. A quick glance behind confirmed that the rest of the group were trailing him; one slightly less kempt suit with a pile of paperwork, one lab coat and one overly muscled security uniform.

The woman activated a very fancy fingerprint recognition pad and they all piled into a tiny room. In the centre was something which looked like the lovechild of a distressed computer, a dentist's chair, and the sort of ludicrous helmet you might find at an old-fashioned hairdresser. The chap in the lab coat ushered him over and gestured at him to take a seat. Before he could protest, he was being strapped down, while the muscle not so surreptitiously locked the door.

Sweat beaded on his forehead. "What's going on?" he asked.

The woman who had spoken to him first was fiddling with the controls of a viewing screen on the opposite wall. "Do you know what we do at first level, Humphrey?"

"You approve high pay-outs of compensation?" he asked, feeling a cold lump in his throat. "That is what I'm here for, isn't it?"

The woman smirked. "You think the Government is paying out billions just because people have been dealt a different hand in this Timeline? How naive." She strode to a small desk in the corner and picked up a familiar laminated diagram. "This is the ripple effect caused by the alteration of the Timeline in 2003."

"Yes, I'm familiar with the…"

"No, you're not. Please don't interrupt. You believe we have been using this to assess levels of compensation. The higher the disruption to the individual's life, the closer they are to the target, yes? No. The Timeline Redistribution is anything but even. Some people are winners, some are losers. What we are looking for is the source. The Quantum Perceptor ekes out alternate memories. We're not just interested in family trees and missing persons. We're looking for significant dates. News items. What changed in 2003 that someone might have wanted to affect? We have spent the last nine months collating and cross-referencing, waiting for specific factors to pop up in application forms. Clues, Humphrey, and those clues all lead to you."

"Why me? I was just a child in 2003!"

The woman rolled her eyes. "The Timeline Redistribution took place just last year, in 2052. Someone travelled back in time to 2003 and made some tiny change, then came back to 2052 and *BOOM*. The whole Timeline explodes. Time travel doesn't exist here. So we need to see who might have had the education, the financial resources, and the right influences in their life to pull it off. It would have to be someone very, very rich. Like you, for example."

Humphrey's eyes widened. "I've changed my mind. I am withdrawing my application. Let me go immediately."

"I'm afraid not. The application form does have detailed terms and conditions on the reverse. Did you not read those? You've already consented to the extraction of your alternate memories. There's a small chance it might not be you, but I'm feeling pretty confident." She pulled the helmet over his forehead and flicked a large red switch.

The pain was immediate, a shuddering vibration which started at his temples and drilled deep into his brain as alternate memories flooded his hippocampus. *Moving to a house with a swimming pool. Ice cream and endless white sand summers interrupted by extra maths tuition. A better private school. Holidays spent in the corner of a boardroom. His first job as a junior executive. The lavish party when his father made CEO. Inheriting the company, along with his father's coveted platinum watch.* A whole other life jostled for space in his head, a clamour so intense that he couldn't bear it. He blacked out.

"He's coming round, Ma'am," a deep voice said.

Humphrey opened his eyes and winced at the bright light, then at the security guard leaning over him. When he turned his head away a line of drool remained, the goop connecting him to the plastic covering of the chair he was still lying on.

The woman's face swam into view. "Welcome back, Humphrey," she said, all shiny teeth.

"How long was I out?"

"Oh, around nine hours or so. We wanted to make sure we got everything."

"So, was it me?"

"Yes, just as I thought. Though none of us could have predicted the alteration you made."

"Well, what was it?" He tried to sit up but found he was still firmly restrained.

"It will come back to you when your brain catches up. But the short version is that in 2003 a Private Member's Bill was put before Parliament proposing the abolition of trade unions. In the original Timeline, it seems it would never have got off the ground. But in this Timeline, the vote was swayed. You bribed a number of politicians it seems."

"Why would I want to do that?"

"Indeed. We were hoping you would tell us. We can see what you did but not what you were thinking. There were hundreds of Bills enacted around that time. This was one of the least obvious candidates for being tampered with. I think that's why we missed it. So, what were you up to in the other Timeline in 2052?"

Humphrey tried to focus through the excruciating pain in his head. *The time machine.* It was nearly complete, and he was deciding what to do with it. So many possibilities. He sifted the mental list, and one thing stood out. It was genius.

"The ethics department. They kept sending me memos on the implications of time travel and whole essays on compliance with international safety regulations. The constant nagging was driving me mad. I just wanted to get rid of the lot of them. But there were so many rules and regulations in the other Timeline. I couldn't fire them all without union consultation. Then I remembered my father talking about the vote back in 2003; how businesses never had the opportunity again to quash the unions. He always said it held back his vision for the company. So that's what I decided to change. Better for him, and better for the future of the company I would inherit. It was foolproof. I don't understand what went wrong. Why am I here?"

The woman narrowed her eyes. "What didn't go wrong?" She tapped at a keyboard under the viewing screen and an image popped up on the screen. The time machine, in all its glory. Humphrey buckling himself in, while technicians waved their hands at him and pointed at graphs and pleaded for him to stop.

"You rushed the completion of the project. The Redistribution left echoes of the other Timeline. The alternate memories, the headaches. And as for history, the Trade Union Abolition Act 2003 had a cascade effect. Without unions to negotiate there was a wholesale erosion of workers' rights across Britain. Perhaps it took hold sooner than you expected. You may be too young to remember, but in this Timeline your father's contract was terminated in a mass redundancy exercise in 2008. He never went on to become CEO. Here, you never had the fancy education, the inheritance, the connections. So, no time machine."

Humphrey paled. "I… I did this to myself? I've spent most of my life in this awful place."

"You're lucky to have a job at all. There's a terrible unemployment problem in this Timeline, and that's entirely your fault. I've seen your file; I know you've been complaining about everything from your shift patterns to the ambient temperature. Do you know there would have been laws regulating all of that if you hadn't interfered? But you don't need to worry about this *awful place* anymore."

"Why? What's going to happen to me?"

"Now that we have your memories, we also have the blueprint for building our own time machine. It should only take a few years for us to put the Timeline right. I understand the government is quite interested in legal action against you when we do. That does rather present a conflict of interest for your current work in the Department, though."

"What does that mean?"

"It means you're fired."

About the Authors

Robert Bagnall

Robert Bagnall was born in Bedford, England, in 1970 and has written for the BBC, national newspapers, and government ministers. Five of his stories have been selected for the B*est of British Science Fiction* anthologies, and he is also a previous L. Ron Hubbard 'Writers of the Future' competition finalist. His sci-fi thriller 2084 - *The Meschera Bandwidth* is available from Amazon, as are two anthologies each collecting 24 of his eighty-odd published stories. He stood in South Devon for the Green Party in the UK's 2024 General Election, and can be contacted via his blog at meschera.blogspot.com.

Lindsay Comer

Lindsay Comer is based in South Wales and holds an MA in Creative Writing from the Open University. Her fiction, poetry and creative non-fiction has been published internationally in lit mags and journals including: *Gwyllion Magazine, Wishbone Words, The Unwritten, The Daily Drunk, Viridian Door, Litmora Literary Magazine, Scarlet Dragonfly Journal, The Dirigible Balloon* and *The Hooghly Review*. She also has a short story forthcoming in *Grimm Retold* (September 2024.) You can find her on Twitter- Lindsay_Writes3

Gary Couzens

Gary Couzens has had stories published in *F&SF, Interzone, Black Static, Midnight Street* and other magazines and anthologies, with the collections *Second Contact and Other Stories* (Elastic Press, 2003) and *Out Stack and Other Places* (Midnight Street Press, 2015). "The End of All Our Exploring" was reprinted in *Best of British Science Fiction 2021* (Newcon Press, 2022). Film and book reviews have been published in B*lack Static, ParSec, Interzone Digital* and *Cine Outsider*.

Richard Dadd

Richard Dadd is a writer, comedian and voiceover artist. He runs The Late Night Sweet Shop, Birmingham's only dedicated Alternative Comedy gig. His writing includes the critically acclaimed short film *The Last Bookshop,* a satirical fantasy imagining a future where the last books in existence are hoarded by an ancient shopkeeper (available on YouTube). His voiceover credits include the game *Divinity: Original Sin* (Enhanced Edition). And if you fancy some theologically inflected comedy nonsense, check out his podcast *Tea With The Devil*, in which he voices Satan. He'd like to thank The Pag for all the encouragement.

Rick Danforth

Rick Danforth is an author from Yorkshire, England, where he works as a Systems Architect to fund his writing habit. His short fiction can be found in *Hexagon, Translunar Traveller's Lounge*, and many other places. Two of his stories have been shortlisted for BSFA awards. He one day hopes to introduce himself as an author without feeling awkward about it.

Alice Dryden

Alice Dryden's short stories have been published in anthologies themed around sci-fi cats, pirate dogs, animal spies, and sci-fi cats again (sci-fi people sure do love cats), as well as the occasional title not involving animals. She also writes in the furry fandom under the name Huskyteer and edited *The Furry Megapack* for Wildside Press. She has Kind Of A Thing for Troy Tempest.

Paul Eccentric

Paul is a published author, songwriter, poet and playwright who's probably best known as being one-half of the comedic beat poetry combo, The Antipoet. He has played hundreds of festivals including Glastonbury, The Edinburgh Fringe, Camp Bestival etc. After over 40 years of writing and performing, and having several books published, Paul is now thoroughly enjoying writing his series, *The Periwinkle Perspective* published by Caffeine Nights Publishing. Paul lives in Aston Clinton, Bucks, with his wife, Donna, and runs three telephone box libraries whilst looking after cats; a goat; various chickens and Samantha, the very naughty Herman tortoise.

Cait Gordon

Cait Gordon is an autistic, disabled, and queer Canadian writer of speculative fiction that celebrates diversity. She is the author of the award-nominated, disability-hopepunk adventure, *Season One: Iris and the Crew Tear Through Space!* Her short stories featuring disabled and/or neurodivergent heroes appear in *Spring into SciFi 2024, We Shall Be Monsters, Mighty: An Anthology of Disabled Superheroes, There's No Place*, and *Stargazers: Microtales from the Cosmos*. She has had poems published in *Polar Borealis* and *Mollyhouse*. Cait also twice joined Talia C. Johnson to co-edit the (award-nominated) *Nothing Without Us* and (award-winning) *Nothing Without Us Too* disability fiction anthologies.

David Gullen

David Gullen is a two-time winner of the British Fantasy Society Short Story competition. His work has appeared in magazines, anthologies and podcasts including *F&SF, Tales from the Magician's Skull, Parsec*, and reprinted in *The Best of British Science Fiction*. His long-form work comprises the SF novel, *Shopocalypse*, and the modern fantasy, *The Girl from a Thousand Fathoms*. He lives in South London with his wife, fantasy writer Gaie Sebold. Find out more at www.davidgullen.com.

Simon Hall

Simon Hall is a stand-up comedian, poet and aspiring novelist. For the last two years, he has been taking his first stand-up show, *4 Big Cs*, to a variety of comedy and fringe festivals around the country. This year he is performing his debut poetry show *Unhappily Ever After* at Edinburgh Fringe, a darkly funny anthology where Simon reimagines the lives of fairy tale characters. You can find his work on TikTok and Instagram @simonsayscomedy or on Facebook @simonsaysstandup.

Dafydd Rhys Hopcyn-Kitchener

Dafydd is an accountant from Swansea. He is also the author of Westerns, romances, as well as science fiction and horror stories. Dafydd enjoys all kinds of genre fiction, but his greatest inspiration is his beautiful girlfriend, Julie.

L.N. Hunter

L.N. Hunter's comic fantasy novel, *The Feather and the Lamp* (Three Ravens Publishing), sits alongside works in anthologies such as *Best of British Science Fiction 2022* and *Hidden Villains: Arise,* as well as several issues of Short Édition's *Short Circuit* and the *Horrifying Tales of Wonder* podcast. There have also been papers in the IEEE Transactions on Neural Networks, which are probably somewhat less relevant and definitely less entertaining. When not writing, L.N. occasionally masquerades as a software developer or can be found unwinding in a disorganised home in Carlisle, UK, along with two cats and a soulmate.
https://linktr.ee/l.n.hunter

Laughs in Space

https://www.facebook.com/L.N.Hunter.writer

Phillip Irving

Phillip Irving is a writer and editor in Leicester, UK. He's influenced by a lifetime of Pratchett and Gaiman but writes like neither. He's had short fiction published by Flame Tree Press and Space Cat Press, as well as featuring in *The Best of British Science Fiction 2021* and *2022*. He's a member of Leicester Writers' Club and the Leicester Speculators writing group. When not writing or obsessing over grammar he can be found at home with his wife and cat, or in his local pub, which both have also been known to frequent, or dabbling in stand-up comedy.

Ida Keogh

Ida Keogh is a Surrey-based science fiction and fantasy writer. In 2021 she won both the BSFA Award and British Fantasy Award for her short story Infinite Tea in the Demara Café from the *London Centric* anthology (NewCon Press). Her debut novella *Fish!* was published the same year and was longlisted for the BSFA Award. Her publications include work in *Writing the Future* (Kaleidoscope), *Shoreline of Infinity* magazine, the *British Medical Journal*, *Best of British Science Fiction 2020*, *Major Arcana* (Black Shuck Books), *Under the Radar* magazine, *Fudoki* magazine, charity anthology *Fuel* and *Best of British Science Fiction 2022*.

Emma Levin

Emma Levin is a writer of comedy, sci-fi, and comedy sci-fi. Her short stories have appeared in anthologies (e.g. *The Best of British Science Fiction 2019 & 2021*), in magazines (e.g. *Shoreline of Infinity*), online (e.g. *Daily Science Fiction*), and in many recycling bins. She received training in writing for broadcast through the BBC's 'Comedy Room' Writers' Scheme, and some of her jokes have turned up on the radio and in video games. You can find her online at: https://emmalevinwrites.com/

Akis Linardos

In a cove of a Greek island, Akis was born a rather peculiar infant and has only grown stranger every year. By day, he's a researcher of biomedical AI and ethics, hoping there's something less dystopian to come from this technology. His short tales have wormed their way into *Apex Magazine*, *Gamut*, *Apparition Lit*, and *Heartlines Spec*, among others. Visit his website for updates on his dreadful machinations: https://linktr.ee/akislinardos

Lindz McLeod

Lindz McLeod is a queer, working-class, Scottish writer. Her short prose has been published by Apex, Pseudopod, and many more. Her longer work includes the award-winning short story collection *Turducken* (Spaceboy, 2023), as well as her books *Beast* (Hear Us Scream, 2023), *Sunbathers* (Hedone Books, 2024), *The Unlikely Pursuit of Mary Bennet* (Harlequin, 2025), *We, The Drowning* (Android Press, 2026), and the collaborative anthology *An Honour and a Privilege* (Stanchion, 2025). She is a full member of the SFWA, the club president of the Edinburgh Writers' Club, and is currently studying for a PhD in Creative Writing.

Alex McNall

Alex grew up adventuring in the woods of the Pacific Northwest, relying on his imagination to keep himself entertained. He may never have super powers, travel through time, or go to outer space, so instead he writes about it. He lives in the San Francisco Bay Area with his lovely partner and motley pack of three rescue terrier mixes. He's recently met a life goal of ingratiating himself with his backyard squirrels and delights endlessly in feeding them.

Fiona Moore

Fiona Moore is a BSFA Award-winning writer and academic whose work has appeared in *Clarkesworld, Asimov, Interzone*, and six consecutive editions of *The Best of British Science Fiction*. Her most recent fiction is the short story collection *Human Resources* (NewCon Press) and her most recent non-fiction is the book *Management Lessons from Game of Thrones*. Her publications include one novel; five cult TV guidebooks; three stage plays and four audio plays. She lives in Southwest London with a tortoiseshell cat which is bent on world domination. More details, and free content, can be found at www.fiona-moore.com, and she is @ drfionamoore on all social media.

Marisca Pichette

Marisca Pichette is a queer author based in Massachusetts, on Pocumtuck and Abenaki land. Find more of her work in *Strange Horizons, Clarkesworld, Interzone, Nightmare Magazine*, and others. She is the flash winner of the 2022 F(r)iction Spring Literary Contest and has been nominated for the Bram Stoker, Pushcart, Best of the Net, Elgin, Utopia,

Rhysling, and Dwarf Stars awards. Her Bram Stoker and Elgin Award-nominated poetry collection, *Rivers in Your Skin, Sirens in Your Hair*, is out now from Android Press.

Iris Taylor

Originally from New England, I've lived in many different places and have worn many different hats. I'm currently a Head of Operations for an e-commerce website. When not buried in spreadsheets, I read, enjoy plants and music, or make art with my husband. We share a home on the California Central Coast with one very spoiled dog named Libby. More: iristaylor.com

Lavie Tidhar

Lavie Tidhar's work encompasses literary fiction (*Maror, Adama* and *Six Lives*), cross-genre classics such as Jerwood Prize winner *A Man Lies Dreaming* (2014) and World Fantasy Award winner *Osama* (2011) and genre works like Campbell and Neukom winner *Central Station* (2016). He has also written comics (*Adler*, 2020), children's books such as *Candy* (2018) and the *Children's Book of the Future* (2024) and created the animated movie Loontown (2023) and webseries *Mars Machines* (2024). He is a former columnist for the Washington Post and a current honorary Visiting Professor and Writer in Residence at the American International University in London.

Andrew Wallace

Andrew Wallace's novels include *Dread & the Broken Witch* (Luna Press), *Celebrity Werewolf* (NewCon Press), the far-future *Diamond Roads* thriller series, and Hitchhikers-meets-

Bond rocket comedy Space Gravy (AC Experiments). With daughter Lana he wrote the middle-grade fantasy epic Imelda & the Horned Owl, from which an excerpt was selected for a comprehension book with a print run of 75,000 (CGP Books). Andrew's short fiction has featured in Virtual Futures, the BioFutures Festival in Vienna, and LondonCentric. Upcoming projects include Black-Mirror-style anthology *Deviant Database* (NewCon Press) which accompanies a unique, innovative solo stage show. He lives in Kent, England. www.andrewwallace.me @AndrewWallaceDR

Ian Watson

SF veteran Ian Watson began writing in East Africa then Japan in the 1960s. Nowadays Ian Watson lives in the north of Spain where the climate's lovely, not lethal, a bit like Brexitland but less cruel. Recently Ian's been promoting his little book *The Monster, the Mermaid, and Doctor Mengele* all across Spain. Next up is his first full-length novel in 20 years: *New Adventures of a Chinese Time Machine* (from NewCon Press), controversial, crosstime, and comedic.

www.ingramcontent.com/pod-product-compliance
Lightning Source LLC
Chambersburg PA
CBHW021242190726
48289CB00005B/1440